# A Rose That Never Fades

## HYMNS *of* GRACE

Book 1

Brieanna Sturm

WESTBOW
PRESS®
A DIVISION OF THOMAS NELSON
& ZONDERVAN

WestBow Press books may be ordered through booksellers or by contacting:

WestBow Press
A Division of Thomas Nelson & Zondervan
1663 Liberty Drive
Bloomington, IN 47403
www.westbowpress.com
844-714-3454

Scripture taken from the King James Version of the Bible.

ISBN: 978-1-6642-2467-4 (sc)
ISBN: 978-1-6642-2469-8 (hc)
ISBN: 978-1-6642-2468-1 (e)

Library of Congress Control Number: 2021903434

Print information available on the last page.

WestBow Press rev. date: 03/04/2021

For my mom and dad, who brought me up in
the nurture and admonition of the Lord.

For God hath not given us the spirit of fear; but of
power, and of love, and of a sound mind.
—2 Timothy 1:7 (KJV)

# Chapter 1

⁓§⁓

It was 1869. She was on the Oregon Trail.

She despised the sight of roses. She loathed their colors, prickly thorns, and soft petals with a passion that she couldn't even begin to explain without wrinkling her nose. Love often revolved around these beautiful flowers, but she couldn't disagree more with those false testimonials of undying devotion and romantic promises of the future. Her hatred for the flower was not because of the fact that they were called roses—she frankly adored their name. Her father had nicknamed her Rose and used it since she was a young girl. She merely loathed the flower because of the thing that it symbolized.

She twisted the rose stem in her fingertips. She was mesmerized by its rich hue and elegant scent. The vibrant, red petals were closed around the middle bud, which had begun to open and bloom. The fragrance was indeed wondrous. Nevertheless, her instincts told her to crush the wonderful creation in her hands and forget about it. Much to her dismay, she actually wanted to smell it, to gather its sweet aroma, and to fill her thoughts with its promises of love and beauty.

*Such naive feelings*, she thought as she groaned inwardly.

Her anger was not the flower's fault, far from it. She quite enjoyed nature and its refreshing hope, but he had ruined that picture. It was all his fault. He was to blame for her lack of trust and the rising hatred within her bosom. The mere sight of a rose toyed with her imagining of him and placed fear in her heart. For weeks, she had refused his fanciful letters and extravagant gifts, only to gain warnings and threats of every kind in return. He was relentless and forceful.

Two days prior to her running away from home, she had written him a letter of rejection, leaving it tucked beneath a stone outside her parlor window. She was right to suspect that he would be watching her from there, for he had indeed received her note as she had planned. His next actions were not pleasant in the slightest. She had come to greatly regret her actions and pondered the thought of giving in to his vilest wishes instead.

Pride, dread, and renewed ambition arose. She would rather die than be his to have and to hold. A single rose had been left among the ashes of her quaint home just outside Kansas City. He had burned her only home to the ground, leaving her with nothing. Not even her parents had survived the catastrophic event that had taken place. The remembrance of their suffering brought stinging tears to her eyes. She had loved them so dearly, and they had given her everything in the world while sacrificing their own needs and desires for hers. She had been their only child and their baby girl of twenty years. They had wanted her to grow up in a God-fearing home filled with gentle love. Her heart ached so tenderly for them.

The rose she now carried had been the last one that she had received from her admirer, or rather, her destructive shadow. She had regrettably found out that he was truly a force to be reckoned with. She had learned not to trifle with him, which had led to the only solution that she could think of: *Run. Run far away.*

She had climbed aboard the first coach out of town and had ended up in Independence, Missouri. She had stayed for several days in the old false-fronted hotel, using the earnings that she had. But to her disbelief, he had trailed after her. The romantic yet threatening notes and poetry had not ceased. She wondered, *Can I ever be rid of him?*

The sincere words of his last letter had been forever etched into her mind. It was a nightmare of perfect English and elegant penmanship.

*My dearest Rose,*

*Why are you running? My love for you grows daily. Oh! How I admire your lips and the softness of your voice. I wish to kiss your red lips, run my hand through your chocolate curls, and proclaim our love to the heavens. But alas, you run and leave me as dirt in the gardens of our hearts.*

*I will find you again, my Rose, and next time, you will not leave my side. I will clip your thorns, remove your stem, and pluck you from the soil. Do not think that I will not ensure our love, sweet, sweet Rosemary. Your parents had to learn the depths of my capabilities. I do hope that you will not challenge me again. You cannot hope to flee my sight. I will capture you. I will follow you wherever you go, and nothing can keep us apart.*

*Your loving admirer*

She remembered reading over the letter the night that she had left. Her hands were shaking, and her eyes were wet with tears of pain and terror. His handwriting was dark. He must have put hard pressure on the rose-scented paper, which meant that he was furious and desperate. His words were not empty. She would never again disregard them so carelessly—not as before. She had endangered all who had crossed her path with her foolish apathy. Holding on to the lessons that she had learned, she kept to herself upon arriving in the city of Independence.

Alone and afraid, she had remained shy to most and had only trusted herself. With little funds left, her weary mind made a conclusion. She darted for the first thing that ran across her path: a missionary family. They were religious people looking to settle out west and start works for the Lord. Rosemary believed in God, although not as strongly as her father and mother had, and she couldn't hope for a better option.

The missionaries, Jackson Cole and his outspoken daughter, Charity, gladly received her, even though they knew full well that she didn't have the money or the rations for such a journey across the Oregon Trail.

They took her in and gave her a spot on their wagon without asking much in return. Part of her was torn between telling them the truth and keeping silent. Any time she made a motion to blurt out the whole thing, dark memories of her past flooded back into her mind instantly. She had befriended them without telling the whole truth. It killed her inwardly, but how could she put them in harm's way quickly after affirming a welcoming friendship? She pleaded for forgiveness from God for her cowardice and hoped that when the time came, the Cole family would forgive her as well.

She sat still, frozen in thought, as the wagon shook and trembled on the rough terrain. The walking and sitting had taken their toll on her back and legs. She was incredibly sore and drained, but that was no matter. She was safe from her the awful clutches of her admirer at least for the time being.

An enlightened expression moved across her face, and she tossed the mangled rose over the side of the wagon, where it would be trampled and torn beneath the horses' hooves, oxen's feet, and wagons' wheels. It would do her no good to hold onto a relic from him. No good at all!

Her destination was undecided. Her future was undetermined. But she found that relief and safety were welcoming trades.

"A beautiful day, ain't it?" declared the traveling preacher, Jackson Cole. He was a farmer, a preacher, and the kindest elderly man that Rosemary had ever been acquainted with. His wrinkled smiles and soothing tones brought peace among the wagoners.

She returned a slight smile in return. "I agree." She mentally slapped herself for ignoring his side of the conversation and blamed the rose for her distracted mind.

Calls came from farther up the caravan, and everyone halted abruptly. Jackson pulled on the reins to halt his oxen before they had a chance to ram the bumper of the land schooner, which was in front of them.

Rosemary stood so that she could catch a glimpse of the urgent matter. It was at times like this one that she wished she had been born taller than her abnormally short stature. Her eyes scanned the faces of those near the wagons, carts, and riders, who were seated on horses. She estimated that there had to be less than thirty people on the train, fifteen of which were women and children. A total of ten wagons and carts were in line, with the wagon master at the front and his supply man heading up the rear. At that moment, none revealed answers to her questions. Her anxiety soared to abnormal heights. Why had they stopped so early in the afternoon?

A tall rider, who was dressed in black and with a dark-brimmed hat, rode up to their wagon. His closely shaven face was darkly tanned and scarred from years on the trail, but Rosemary could see that he was young—possibly five years her senior—and quite handsome. His stallion was dark gray, topped with a saddle of black leather. The rider's demeanor screamed mysterious and dangerous, but his expression, although made of stone, was not alarming but rather calm and serene.

He had ridden up to every wagon to speak with the families, eventually making his way toward their wagon. He reigned in his horse beside Jackson and tipped his brim politely in their direction.

Likewise, Jackson dipped his head to greet the rider and then asked, "What seems to be the hold up, Mr. Chronicle?"

The dark-clad rider shook his head. "No need for the mister part. Call me Mace." He paused briefly. "We'll have to make camp for the night. It looks as if Mrs. Webb is dealing with a bad case of wagon sickness. We'll rest up before getting an early start tomorrow mornin'."

Jackson sighed with understanding. "Can't be helped, I s'pose."

"Ric's telling everyone to make the camping circle." With that, Mace rode off atop his stallion and told the others.

The preacher wiped his sweaty brow and then sighed. "Poor gal, that Mrs. Webb. Doesn't help that the woman is close to her time with the pregnancy either."

In succession, the wagons lined up to form a tight circle beside a steady flowing stream. A fire was made in the center of them, and many prepared for the early start that would take place the next morning. It was too early for supper, so most of the women sat around the wagons, gossiping and giggling.

Because Rosemary's tight curls were a sporadic mess and her skirts were stained with dirt, she decided to head to the stream instead. She thought that washing her hair and dipping her sore feet in the cool water might bring about a refreshing outlook and give her an excuse to exit the women's circle. She gathered her comb and ribbon from the luggage that she had and then informed Jackson of the place that she could be found.

She skirted around their wagon because she was nervous of meeting new faces. Her heart nearly leapt from her chest when a boy of about thirteen greeted her from behind. She whirled on her heels to face him. Her skin was pale from fright.

"Ma'am," he said and then grinned. His ruddy appearance was lighthearted and cheerful. "You dropped your ribbon." His hand opened to reveal her pink ribbon in his dirtied fingers.

She lowered her head. "Oh, thank you."

"Name's Andrew," he said, introducing himself as she took the ribbon. His other arm held dozens of sticks and twigs for stoking the fire. He appeared harmless enough; however, Rosemary was not one to lower her guard for any man … or boy.

Following Andrew was a small blond-haired girl. Rosemary estimated the little girl, who had pink ribbons and frilly dress, to be about five years of age or younger. She was quite adorable. The girl clutched a ragged, stuffed toy rabbit. She held it as if it were all she had in the world. Her eyes were large, pretty, and innocent, and they matched her girlish appearance. Her irises were unlike anything Rosemary had ever witnessed. They were a dark shade of violet.

"Drew!" the girl exclaimed, tugging on the older boy's sleeve. "I wanna help too."

Andrew frowned down at her and shook his head. "No, Macy, getting firewood is men's work. You're just a lil kid. You oughta go back Ma."

"But I wanna help!" she said, pouting with her bottom lip quivering as if she was about to burst into tears. She held her stuffed rabbit more tightly.

Andrew (Drew) sighed with exasperation. The young child was winning him over. "Fine, Macy, but you can't go into the woods. Only carry twigs back and forth to the fire."

Happy enough to have that chore, she smiled brightly up at him and then bashfully at Rosemary as she noticed the ribbon that Andrew had handed back to her. "Pretty," she said, beaming.

"Guess it is kinda purdy for a girl's trinket," he said, complimenting the hair tie with a wide grin. "Are you traveling with the preacher man?" he asked Rosemary as Macy toyed with his pant leg.

Rosemary nodded. "For the time being."

She had grown uptight around men and boys, for that matter, since her admirer had come calling. Though she regretted the idea of being hostile toward them, every man seemed so untrustworthy or malicious in her eyes. In every look or gesture, she managed to find some form of wicked behavior. Whether great or small, she saw every lustful and possessive thought in their eyes.

She thought, *Women are just objects to them. They're no more than pretty pieces to admire, look at, but never touch.* Those words, she knew, had not always been her own. Her admirer had clouded her judgement. How was she supposed to decipher his rough-edged statements from her own thoughts? He had soiled her mind, ruined her confidence in men, and left her feeling helpless and scared.

She snapped out of her trance when Andrew gave her a baffled glance and then asked, "Are you feeling all right? Need me to get the doctor?"

As he asked a mouthful of questions and Macy mostly repeated them, Rosemary took notice of the many bruises that plagued his scrawny form. There were too many to count. She knew that most boys liked to play rough, but the scattered black-and-blue bruises on his throat, cheeks, and arms seemed somewhat odd nonetheless.

That wasn't all. Behind his gray eyes, she saw more than just simple, naive boyhood. He carried a form of character and respect for others behind them. He might have been young, but there Rosemary didn't believe that he was as carefree and childlike as he appeared to be.

"Oh, no, I'm just dazed is all," she smiled half-heartedly. "It has been a rather long morning of travel."

Her stomach was in knots at his question. A doctor most definitely would not help in this situation with her admirer. Perhaps, a sheriff could but not a doctor. Of course, she had already considered telling a local lawman back where she'd grown up. She had doused the idea quickly, for her admirer had threatened to kill off her friends one by one if she did. All this had led to her predicament now, and she had all but abandoned her friends back east. *It was for their safety,* she reaffirmed inwardly.

"I'm quite fine," she said as she forced another smile to coax the young boy and wonderfully sweet little girl to stop asking. Her statement sounded odd, and she felt like somewhat of a con artist, but they took it without hesitation. They were innocent children after all.

Andrew beamed and pushed his much-to-big hat back above his brow line and then carried onward, saying, "Well, have fun with your daydreamin' then." He steadied the twigs in the crook of his other arm and took Macy's hand. He continued to taunt and tease her about wanting to do men's work and laughed when she complained in a squeaky voice.

Shaking her head with a sigh of amusement, Rosemary continued her march to the riverbank with her ribbon now in hand. The sun reached its highest point in the sky, casting down rays of heat upon the plains. It illuminated everything with warm and hope-filled light. There was barely a breeze, which made the land hot and humid. For late spring, it was so blisteringly warm outside that an early summer appeared to be blooming.

Rosemary cupped her hands and dipped them into the water before splashing some of it onto her arms, neck, and face. The cool river water felt tremendous on her burning skin. Next, she dunked her hair, soaking it completely. It had been a day or two since it had had a good washing, and she was relishing every second of it. As droplets ran down her temples and neck, she pictured a time when her family had played in the bodies of water that were next to their humble home back east. She stopped herself from experiencing too much of the fond memory. Instead, she faced the fact that they were all gone. Dead. She thought, *I'm alone.*

"Hi, Rosie!" came a squeal of joy. Long arms of a darker shade than her own wrapped around her neck from behind. She was pulled into a forced hug and shaken about.

She smiled, exclaiming, "Charity, you gave me such a fright!" Breaking free of the hold, she turned to stare up at her acquired friend from the wagon train. The girl was young. She was not much younger than Rosemary was. She was plumper. Her chest was of considerable size, and her waist not as thin as Rosemary's was, but her bright red hair was an adorned jewel that all envied.

Men seemed to flock to this sweet and flamboyant young woman as sheep to a shepherdess, but she barely paid them any mind, at least when her father was around. She was a wild thing at heart, and Rosemary had come to understand that very well in the previous week.

Charity Cole, with her green-and-brown starburst eyes shining like two jewels, chewed her bottom lip. "Sorry, Rosie. I just thought it was funny that we both had the sense to come to the river at once. My ragged hair could use a good scrub and then some!" She giggled airily.

Sitting down beside Rosemary, she asked, "It's a shame that we have to stop so frequently this early on in the trip, don't you think?" Her fingers undid her hair from its bun and then let loose the fury of curls and tangles to be brushed and washed. The freckles on her dimpled cheeks reflected her mischievous personality in a way that Rosemary thought amusing.

A sigh escaped Rosemary's lips. "Mr. Chronicle informed us that a woman is having wagon sickness farther up in the train. She appears to be so unwell that we've had to stop quite frequently."

"Yes, Pa told me the same thing. I believe the woman is expecting her first child, and that's the reason for it all," Charity stated, struggling to wring the water from her fiery locks. "All sickness aside, it is rather exciting to be expecting such a gift from God. I pray my time is soon for such a blessing."

Rosemary could not agree less. She found it all to be a trap that was set by men. Although she had loved holding little ones when she had helped her mother at the hospital, she would never agree to have one of her own. That joy would not be hers to cherish, for she loathed the idea of marriage and belonging to any man. *Those devils and their tricks,* she thought.

She secured her curls with pins, locking them in place with such ferocity that she wondered if she would have any curls left. She then tied a pink satin ribbon atop her head. Taking a breath, she only nodded at Charity's words, knowing that if she spoke, she would only lie to her friend. She adjusted her skirts and straightened her posture.

"If it continues to get hot like this during the day, I might just melt away to nothing," she said as she fanned herself. She felt warmer than ever without the breeze.

Charity snickered. Her gentle and sweet expression turned several shades of fuchsia. "I fear I've already begun to do exactly that." Her teasing had always been about herself, but she could draw laughs from almost anyone, including Rosemary. The two girls giggled. Charity snorted in her fit of laughter.

Standing, Rosemary dusted off her skirts and fixed the sleeves of her blouse. After saying a goodbye to Charity, she strolled back to the wagon while being careful to avoid most of the bodies that were walking about. Birds sang from the woods that surrounded their makeshift camping circle, and the warmth of the day carried with it a renewed vision of peace and safety. If she trusted and knew Him better, she would have said that God was shining down on her from above, smiling, and blessing the choice that she had made to escape on the wagon train.

She was no more than ten yards from her appointed shelter when she saw the shadow of someone stumbling back from the space between the previous wagon and her destination. A scream erupted from her mouth as she fell backward with fright. Her heels dug into the earth, went into a small hole, and tripped her. She tumbled backward. Her arms flailed as she sank into a large barrel of their water supply, soaking her backside and waist.

She was folded almost in half in the barrel's opening. She was a spectacle of curls, pink gingham skirts, and rage. Red blotches made their way across her pale skin, and her eyes fumed with fire at the perpetrator. At first, she sat there scrunched up, frozen in anger and shock, but then her mind was sent into a tizzy of emotions upon hearing a melodious voice.

"Oh! I beg your pardon, darlin'," the voice said in concern and with apology. It was soothing, smooth, beautiful, strong, and wondrous. It sang its way into her ears. Her eyes, which stared first at the dark and dirtied boots, worked their way up slowly. She saw the most ruggedly handsome man that she had ever set eyes on. He was dressed in dusted trousers, a white shirt, and a dark vest. A neckerchief of checkered red had been tied about his neck. Short blond tufts of hair stuck out from beneath his brown, wide-brimmed hat.

She trembled upon seeing how tall and rather fetching he was. Even under his vest, she could see the definition of his muscular frame. He was fit and trim. His skin was tan from blistering hours in the sun. But his eyes—oh, his eyes—were like two pools of sapphires. They were mesmerizing, deep, and soulful.

She was struck with awe and amazement. Her mouth was agape, and she could only sputter and not speak a lick of sense. Her nails dug into the sides of the barrel when the man extended a calloused hand to her. "Sorry for the scare, lil lady," he said, smiling. "Allow me."

She shut her mouth, clenched her teeth, and panicked. Her chin was raised in defiance. She met his extraordinarily kind gaze. "No, thank you, sir," she refused from behind a tightened jaw and infuriated glare.

Gathering what was left of her pride, she struggled to lift her bottom out of the barrel's mouth. Water that remained in the barrel sloshed and swayed violently beneath her. She grunted and grumbled in an unladylike fashion until the man let out a soft chuckle of amusement. "Well, you certainly won't get out that way, darlin'."

Feeling most embarrassed and infuriated, she stared up at him with tightly knit eyebrows and a wrinkled nose. "Do not call me—" She couldn't finish her words, for in her outburst she had leaned too far to the right, knocking the keg over. Hitting the ground hurt her, and she winced at her left arm, where obvious bruising would likely take place.

Water poured out from around her as she squirmed to get up. Her natural ringlets fell around her face as her hairpins lost their grip. Her ribbon fluttered to the ground and became soaked in a puddle of clay and mud. Strong hands grabbed ahold of her thin waist and lifted her high off the now sodden soil. She tensed up like a wild cat being tamed and her fingers became claws.

"Unhand me!" she protested, clawing at him with her sharp nails.

"Easy now, darlin'," he said, as he set her gently back down on a dry patch of grass. He raised his arms in self-defense. The imprints of her nails were still visible on his forearms.

"Do not call me that!" She fumed. Her nostrils flared, and her chest heaved. Her body tingled all over due to frustration and displeasure. She got to her feet, shivering and hugging herself. The eyes of everyone aboard the wagon train had seen the event, and Rosemary could feel the heat of it on her flushed cheeks. Her face only reddened more as she drew a breath and fired up a storm of words at the man. "How could you! You dirty, no good …" Her words trailed off when she heard his humored tone laced with playfulness.

"Whoa, now," he cooed. "There's no need for name calling."

"How could you sneak up on a woman like that? I have a mind to slap the daylights out of you." Her chest heaved when she heard his snickering, which he didn't seem to want to hide.

"Have you no manners?" she asked. Her rage rekindled after hearing his low breathless chuckles grow into a bellowing howl. "Did your mama teach you to snicker and snort at a lady in distress? You ought to be ashamed of yourself!"

He hid a smirk with his hand, cleared his throat, and then rubbed his neck. "Sorry, darlin'. I meant no harm. Seeing a purdy calico like yourself fall in a water keg, well, it 'bout plumb tuckered me out with laughter is all." He knit his brows together apologetically and said, "I never intended for you to fall. Honest. Can you forgive me?"

She stomped her foot, her shoulders hunched, and her fists were now at her sides. She didn't care about his sympathy or apology. Her temper kept her from accepting another word from him, especially the petty nickname that he'd given not once but thrice. "Do not call me that!" She bristled and gave him no chance at redemption.

The laughter of everyone was not helpful in healing her pride, so she marched off without another word to the scoundrel. Her soggy skirt swished, and her shoes sloshed as she fumbled forward, but she paid it no mind. Her fury was aimed at that much-too-fresh stranger for making her jump. She remembered her ribbon that was on the ground. How could she turn and go the way that she had come from when *he* would be standing there and laughing at her no less? Her pride would not allow her to collect her ribbon. She walked at an even stride back to the confines of her and Charity's wagon.

Suppertime was no different. She ended up finishing her supper within the safety of the wagon with Charity by her side. She hadn't spoken since earlier that day. Her self-pity grew. She wanted nothing more than to cry or scream the night away. Her fingers toyed with the shredded end of her quilt, undoing the stitching in one corner.

"Rosie, it was just an accident," Charity finally said. "I'm sure he didn't mean for you to fall into that barrel." Her sly grin contorted into a snicker as Rosemary flashed her a warning glance.

Rosemary set down her dishes. She drew her knees to her chest, resting her chin on them. "That fool," she mumbled under her breath.

She wished Charity had been there to help her out of the barrel instead of him. At least she wouldn't have laughed about the matter until they were alone. She wouldn't have drawn all that attention. She thought, *It was his fault!*

She flung herself back onto her pillow. Her hair flew all around her face. "I wish never to see that man's face again." Dramatically, she released a moan. At that instant, a knock sounded outside.

Charity answered it while rising to her feet and peeking out the closed flaps. "Yes?"

A man of average height and stocky build stood at the wagon's entrance. He had slicked-back hair and a black, worn hat. His thick mustache was the same shade as his hair. His eyes were a dull gray. When he spoke, his eyes flickered with a fondness welcoming to any woman.

"Ah, good evening, young lady." He greeted her by tipping his hat and gracefully bowing. "I do apologize for interrupting, but may I ask for the dinnerware?"

Her smile growing, Charity quickly opened the other flap of the wagon and then replied, "Why, of course, Mr. Marsh. Allow me to get them for you."

As her curiosity spiked, Rosemary rose from where she had been sitting to see what the commotion was about. After she gave a befuddled glance to the missionary's daughter, Charity said, "It's the supply wagon driver, Victor Marsh. He's just here for the dishes."

Leaning against the side frame of the wagon's entrance, Rosemary peeked at the visitor. His appearance was nothing spectacular. His clothes were rugged and somewhat soiled, but his build was most impressive. It was strong and muscular. Whatever his height was, she knew that he stood a good foot-and-a-half taller than she did. He wasn't as tall as the man who had shoved her into the water keg.

His face was clean, and his mustache was trimmed, although

day-old stubble covered his jawline. His intriguing glances and silken voice were heavenly. The pleasant scent of herbs and spices wafted from him, filling the air with their odor. The corners of his mouth lifted up in a warming smile, and his stance shifted ever so lightly with interest. "Good evening, lovely lady."

She had not anticipated his charming glow; otherwise, she would have realized that she was staring into his big gray irises sooner. She pulled her head inside the wagon out of utter nervousness. She refused to reply, not knowing the man or his character. She didn't want another man teasing her or her ill temper.

The awkward silence didn't last as Charity fumbled her way out of the wagon with her arms full of tin plates and cutlery. "Here ya are, Mr. Marsh."

He held the dinnerware stacked in his muscle-bound arms. He dipped his head in gratitude, saying, "Ya'll have a good night's rest now, ya hear? Should ya need anything, I'm only one wagon down." He whistled happily, as he made his way to the supply wagon with dishes clanking in his grip.

Rosemary watched him take his leave and then closed both flaps of the doorway. Her fingers brushed the wooden frames while she returned to her spot on the far side of the wagon floor in front of boxes of food, farming tools, and carpentry equipment.

Charity lay down next to her with her eyebrows raised in curiosity. "Was he handsome?" she asked, placing her chin on her palms dreamily.

"Who?" Rosemary asked as her back stiffened uncomfortably.

The younger girl laughed in disbelief. "The man that bumped into you!"

She sighed with exasperation. "Are you still on about that?" She hesitated for a second. Then with a roll of her eye and a click of her tongue, she answered, "I suppose, but far too much for his own good."

She fell backward onto her and Charity's bedroll. She put her arm over her face in the hopes that once she removed it, the event would've never happened. "I wish this trip would end," she groaned.

Charity grinned brightly. "If I had been saved by a handsome fella like him, I'd be off to the nearest chapel by now."

If looks could kill, Rosemary would've murdered her friend three times over. She removed her arm from her face and then stared up at the ceiling of their wagon. The shadows of the lantern played with her vision. Shapes and figures formed before her and danced in the light of the flickering flame. The shadows twirled, leapt, ran, and then disappeared above the white-tarp interior.

Oh, if only she could be one of those figures. She wanted to disappear from the sight of her restless admirer and the eyes of all men, especially that *scoundrel* who had pushed her into the barrel.

A yawn erupted from Charity, and she laid her head down. "All will be forgotten tomorrow, Rosie. You'll see." She yawned again, closed her eyes, and slept.

Rosemary watched her for a few seconds as she pondered the words, *I pray so.* She blew out the lantern and then placed the quilt over both her and Charity. She snuggled deep into her realm of dreams where she could be free of her admirer and that man, or at least, that's what she pleaded.

# Chapter 2

*Sweet, sweet Rose, Where have you gone? I miss you so. Do come back to me, Rose. Why have you run away from me? Did you like the note I left you? I will find you my dear. You cannot hide forever. Come back to me!* Rosemary awoke with a start with his words still lingering in her ears and the scent of fresh roses in the air. Every night she had the same nightmare, and every night, she ceased sleeping soundly. Even in her dreams, he would haunt her, so there really was no escape. He followed her no matter where she ran.

She sat up, wiping the weariness from her hazy vision. Hearing voices outside gave her the incentive to get up and ready. With her fingers, she began to tame her curls and tie them back. She had wanted to tie the pink ribbon in her locks, but she quickly recalled its disappearance near the water keg. Tying her hair back with a different fastener, she fashioned it into a ponytail that was low over her right shoulder.

She chose a brown skirt of comfortable cotton material from Charity's luggage, along with Rosemary's own simple white blouse. Having only two outfits of her own, she was granted free reign over the missionary girl's clothing and shoes. Of course, due to their size differences, Rosemary had to adjust much of the length and width of the outfits that she chose. But who was she to complain? She tucked one last part of the blouse in and then began to feel her confidence returning after yesterday's mishap.

To her left, Charity still slept soundly. She gave her friend a gentle nudge, which turned into a fierce shake as Charity refused to awaken.

"No," she slurred. "Please. Five more minutes."

Rosemary shook her head, "You won't get any breakfast if you don't get up." Her warning came through like a charm, and the younger girl finally awoke.

Charity's eyes flew open, and she flung herself from the warmth of the quilt. She threw on a few things that she had grabbed from her luggage. Then she ran her fingers through her tangled locks before messily tying them into a bun. Nothing ever stopped her from food¾not even fashion or beauty. In Rosemary's opinion, however, Charity looked as stunning as the gorgeous city girls back east.

Ready for the trip ahead, the two girls exited the wagon after a quick cleaning. Then they headed out for the morning meal. The sun had yet to fully reveal itself on the horizon, and the breeze was swift and chilly. The scent of coming rain lingered in the air as dark clouds gathered overhead.

"Storm's a brewin'," informed Mace Chronicle, the mysterious second on the wagon train. He tipped the brim of his hat back to gaze up at the ever-darkening sky. Stroking the stubble on his chin, he turned to Jackson. Each of them looked concerned and bothered.

Rosemary held her shawl tight around her shoulders and peered up. Charity did the same thing. The dark rider was indeed correct. A storm was on its way, and it was no small one at that. Without much cover from trees or shrubbery, the long wagon train would find it hard to gain much ground.

Jackson and Mace took long gulps of their coffee before rustling up the rest of the men to help them pack. Several ladies were gathered around the fire, eating the remaining breakfast items and brewing the last of the coffee before heading out. Charity and Rosemary barely had enough time to eat and drink their fill before the wagon train's leader whistled and called for everyone to line up the wagons. Though Rosemary had not met the wagon master, she had heard how dashing he was from many of the women who gossiped around the fire at night. She'd heard some say that his charm, ruggedly tall stature, and knowledge of the terrain were stunning. She doubted it.

"Everyone." A strong powerful shout was heard above the howling wind. "Gather round." As the group huddled together, Rosemary caught a slight glimpse of the brave leader that the women had been raging about. His dark felt hat sat low on his forehead and just above his sapphire eyes. His fists were planted firmly on his hips. Rosemary just about lost her composure. Her head was immensely dizzy, and her heart was pounding like a drum in her chest. She thought, *It can't be the same man.* She clenched her teeth and frowned but listened to his confident voice all the same.

"A storm is coming soon," he began, addressing everyone with a stone-like expression, which was unlike the lighthearted curl of the lips that she'd witnessed on the previous day. "We need to move faster, double our speed and distance. We move out in ten." The group disbanded after he had finished and rushed to complete their tasks and line up.

Rosemary stared at the man who had made a fool of her on the previous day. She felt red splotches on her cheeks returning at a rapid pace. The tips of her ears burned, and her nose scrunched up in disgust. She was utterly mortified by his very existence. He was the wagon master no less. He had taken it upon himself to make a fool out of her! She realized that the trek across the Oregon Trail might not be as easy as she would've liked it to be.

Noticing that the missionary's daughter had vanished during her short trance, Rosemary set her eyes to scouting the disbanding crowd for her. Twirling around on the heels of her boots, she kicked up dirt and rushed to find Charity or her wagon. Grass trembled in her wake as she furiously made her way so that she could dodge the venomous mockery of the wagon master or any other man. Her rampage stopped when a familiar baritone called from behind her, "Howdy, darlin'."

She snapped her head to the left, looking over her shoulder. There he was, running to meet her. Her heart leapt from her chest, and she began to walk briskly away without a word. Her boots dug into the earth, but with his long strides, she was no match for him. She could hear the faint clink of his boot spurs as he picked up speed. He caught up with her in moments. He kept up her pace as he walked by her side.

After removing his hat, he fiddled with the brim. "I hope you ain't frightened of me for scaring you yesterday," he said. "Truly, I meant no harm."

Halting, she raised her face to meet his dashing gaze. She could certainly see the reason for the fuss of the womenfolk over his looks. He was well kempt for a man of the trail and not badly spoken either. He seemed learned. *Though he appears to be no gentleman, he acts respectably decent for a no-good heathen,* Rosemary remarked inwardly.

She spoke not a word but glared with as much malice toward him as she dared to muster. A soft shrill, "Humph," escaped her buttoned lips. Her pointed shoulder knocked against his arm as she went to brush past him. She was met with a large arm in her path, which was blocking escape. The red splotches burned and spread across her cheeks, and outrage threatened to boil over deep within her soul.

"Darlin', it seems you have quite the dislike for me." He stated the obvious.

Rosemary scoffed, "Oh, you think so?" Tilting her eyes skyward, she shoved his arm away so that she could leave, lifting her skirts as she did so. Her ears pricked when he continued to follow her. His tone was like a thorn in her side.

"Well, I'd hate to have hurt such a purdy lil' thing as you. I really didn't mean for you to take a swim in that keg. I'm quite sorry for it. If you're willing, I'd like to ask for your forgiveness."

Her veins burned in her temples. She forced herself not to make a scene, but words that no woman should ever consider voicing pressed sorely against her lips. She bit her tongue, holding back an outburst, no matter how much she wanted to let the man have it. Her mother had always warned her about the deceitful tongue and its sinful nature. The last thing that Rosemary wanted was to disappoint her deceased mother, but the temptation was very strong nonetheless.

For each three stomps she took, it took him one stride to keep up with her rampage. How could she possibly rid herself of him? *Stubborn man!* she thought.

"I was hoping to make it up to you somehow," he stated simply. "I don't want hard feelings the entire ride. It's a mighty long journey to be at odds with each other."

Her teeth sank into her bottom lip, biting and chewing it ferociously.

If she were not a lady, she would surely slug the stranger for following her around. The action crossed her mind several times over, but she couldn't make the decision become reality. After all, she was a Christian young woman. It wouldn't be sensible or Christ-like. Then again, what did she know of Christian behavior? She had doubted for so long that it hurt her to think about it. It was the memory of her mother that made her ponder such things as keeping a good character. Oh, but all the same, she longed to lay one hit on the man's handsome jawline.

"Do you mind leaving me be?" she snapped back, ignoring his plea.

He cocked his head to the right, looking down at her with wondrous and curious eyes. A sideways smirk crossed his perfect lips. "Not until I get a name."

*This man and his inquisitive mind,* she thought. She fisted her hands and stiffened her back as she stopped once again. For what seemed like many agonizing minutes, she pondered the idea. Giving her name was not a bad thing. She had yet to learn his, so it was only natural for strangers to exchange names. In fact, it was customary.

His calm, almost childlike, soulful, and blue-eyed gaze met hers, leaving her breathless. She couldn't look away, and in her heart, she despised the urge to do so. Her eyes remained fixed. "Rosemary," she said at last. "Rosemary Barker."

He smiled, placing the Stetson atop his crown once more. While dipping his head to her, he introduced himself. "Ricochet Chapel. Call me Ric. You must be the young lady traveling with the missionary."

"Well, it appears as if you know all there is to know about me, yet I know nothing of you—apart from you leading this escapade." She paused with sarcasm on the tip of her tongue. "Tell me. Do you always rudely embarrass a woman before introducing yourself, or am I the exception?"

The smile on his lit-up face seemed to cause her cheeks to flare with the wretched, red splotches as before. The dimples deepened in his cheeks, which seemingly added to his already handsome features and characteristics. She found him too irresistible to turn away from.

"Never purposely embarrassed a woman in my life," he declared. His expression entertained a smirk well on its way across his jawline. "On my honor, you are the very first."

Blinking back her interest in his charming behavior, she straightened her blouse. "I suggest you find a new woman to prey on, Mr. Chapel. I find your company rather tiring. Good day." She turned with her chin held a tad high.

The burning of her ears continued upon feeling his stare following her all the way back to her wagon. She forced each step, folded her hands in front of her, and resisted the urge to glance behind her, thus giving him an incentive to speak to her again.

It was not until she boarded her wagon that she found the courage to look back. He still stood there like a hawk that was majestically watching and speculating on her every move before taking flight. He moved to his gelding. Surging flames burst in her chest. If he was searching for a woman companion, he could mosey on to the next wagon because Rosemary wouldn't have it, nor did she long for it. *Move on, Mr. Chapel. Move on your way,* she thought.

# Chapter 3

Ricochet raised an eyebrow and shook his head slowly. Watching the temperamental young woman storm off only sparked his inquiring mind. Twice, he had encountered her beauty, and twice, he had been shunned by her stiff-necked pride. Never had he met a challenge disguised in ringlet curls, pink lips, and rosy cheeks. She was a vision and an angelic flower, but she was also laced with a prejudiced tongue and fiery personality.

His lips curved up in a smile at the recollection of her red cheeks on the day that she had fallen in the barrel. Remembering her damp curls and pursed lips caused laughter to swell in his chest. His fingers reached in his pocket for the satin, pink ribbon that had fallen from her hair. He had a mind to return it to the young lady, but facing her temper now might prove most difficult. No. He would hold off. He would surprise her with it later. It would be an excuse to meet her again.

What was wrong with him? He couldn't meet her again. She'd likely have him running for the hills on their next encounter. The flaming gaze had not only been abhorrent but also panic-stricken. Was it nervousness that he saw in her eyes? Why, she'd been as skittish as a mouse cornered by a tomcat in a barn. No. There was definitely something deeper than just the run-of-the-mill, shy, or agitated act that women seemed to use during their flirtations. Hers was genuine terror. She was afraid. Afraid of him.

Just what had he done to deserve that kind of attitude from her?

Nothing came to mind. Knocking her into the barrel had been an accident. Surely, she didn't hold that against him. He'd apologized, so what more did she want from him? Should he beg for her forgiveness on his hands and knees? Well, he wasn't about to make such a ridiculous performance as that. She'd probably be over the incident in a day or two anyways. Then he would talk to her. For now, he'd wait.

The smirk plastered on his face was questioned by his second when Mace Chronicle strode over from the Webbs' wagon. Mace's brow creased, and it was shrouded in a mask of mystery. "What's with that face?" he asked, lacking emotion as always.

Ricochet shrugged. Playing dumb was a better option than speaking his mind. "What face?" he replied quizzically as he went about the routine of saddling his stallion, Gage. Refusing to look Mace in the eye, he stroked Gage's long mane, giving his ride a good pat on the neck afterward.

"You ain't all that good at lying, Ric," Mace informed him. His face was without expression as he checked the Colt Paterson revolvers, which were in holster that were strapped to his belt.

With his brow furrowed in confusion, Ricochet, only shook his head and asked, "What are you on about?"

Mace's gaze remained fixed on his task. "We should move out quickly, otherwise, we'll be caught in the storm," he explained in an attempt to change the subject.

Ricochet pinched his hat's crown as he peered up at the gathering clouds. Thunder softly rumbled overhead, followed by a breeze that had begun to pick up. Rain was on the horizon, and the scent had spooked the horses and oxen. They needed to move swiftly in order to pass the large body of water ahead. He shuddered at the very thought of crossing that river. Flooding was a possibility that he just couldn't toss aside. The river was treacherous enough already, but with rain flooding it's murky banks, they would have trouble reaching the other side. Were it him riding by himself, he could make it without problem, but with the caravan, it would be no easy task.

He swung up into the saddle and steered his horse toward the front of the wagon train. With a jerk of his head, he signaled the wagons to follow his lead. Moving at double the speed from the day before, he had high hopes that they would reach the river before the storm hit. A look to his left revealed Mace traveling just as urgently by his side. Both men glanced at one another. Determination was in their eyes. Then they rode onward in silence.

Though he hated the quiet, Ricochet preferred to be left to his own thoughts, which were swimming with the fascinating woman known as Rosemary. She was a vision, an angel even. He hid a sly grin and thought, *An angel with the temper of a devil.*

He never pictured himself as the settling down type of man or one who would start a family. But lately, it was as if he was beginning to think that way. He wanted a wife, one that would be sent from God. He had begun to pray for the day when God would give him the right woman or even a glance at one in his life.

Sadly, many had come and gone within the past year. They all appeared beautiful and friendly, but they were just that and nothing more. He was near to giving up the foolish idea and spending the rest of his days being the leader of a wagon train on the Oregon Trail. He would be a lone bachelor. Perhaps, that's what God had decided too.

The first drops of rain hit the brim of his hat, splattering loud enough for him to hear it. His eyes narrowed. The storm was upon them. He straightened and turned in the saddle. "Mace, pick up the slack. The river will be flooded if we don't get a move on."

The buttoned-up man nodded and jerked his black stallion back to go back to the wagons without so much as a second glance. Ricochet gazed at the trail that led into a forested area. They would reach the body of water in a matter of hours, but would that be enough time to get across before the rain flooded its banks? He prayed for it as he brought Gage to a speedy canter.

# Chapter 4

"Rosie, are you feeling all right?" asked the glowing redhead.

Rosemary's hair was tousled and her eyes were dazed, but she did her best to smile reassuringly. "I'm quite fine, Charity. A little tired is all." She wasn't lying. She truly felt dizzy and exhausted, but how could she explain the real reason for her absent mind: the wagon master with the passionate, blue eyes. Her cheeks warmed at the thought. Why was she thinking about him? He was a stranger, a mountain man, and a wild frontiersman.

Her fists clenched and her back stiffened. She thought, *What am I thinking? He's nothing but a womanizer with a winning smile, kind eyes, tall, broad shoulders* ... She bit down hard, setting her jaw tightly as she shook her head in hopes of clearing it. *No! Rosemary, what are you on about? You have a long journey ahead. There is no room for pleasure or mistakes. Safety is your top priority right now.*

Settling down in her seat, she adjusted the bonnet atop her head, which barely kept her curls hidden. Charity sat on her left. The girl was reading a rather lengthy novel, which Rosemary never cared to do. The redhead was practically snickering and giggling aloud, too interested in the book to care about the light drizzling of rain.

On the far left, Charity's father and the traveling preacher, Jackson, sat. His graying hairs stood up straight in some places where he had attempted to comb them down and the wind had misplaced them. He held the reins to the oxen that were pulling the small wagon along in good time with the train. He hummed happily. It was a rather soothing sound compared to the rumbling thunder that was growing louder overhead.

His cheerful tune stopped when Mace rode up beside them. The dark-clad rider dipped his head in greeting before informing them of the caravan leader's intentions. "The river will most likely flood should the storm pick up," Mace voiced.

As his wrinkled brow revealed concern, Jackson replied, "Let's pray that God will hold off the rain until we've crossed over."

The men continued their chatting in hushed tones to keep from spooking everyone and sending them into a panic. Charity raised her nose from her book. Her eyes seized every inch of the lone rider who was riding next to them. She leaned closer to Rosemary, who had found an interesting patch of trees ahead to stare at. "He's like the mysterious rider from my novel," she whispered delightedly. "All dark and handsome."

Rosemary peered up at the sky. "Charity," she quietly remarked, "keep your nose in your book. Men are nothing but trouble."

The pouting face and scrunched nose told her that the redhead was quite displeased with those words. "Don't be so disheartening!" Her words came out as a shout. She received a puzzled expression from her father and an emotionless swivel of the eyes from Mace. Charity's face flushed red, and her eyelashes lowered considerably.

It caused everyone to become dreadfully quiet, until Jackson broke the cold silence of the group by saying, "Well, we will pick up the pace."

Mace nodded in response; however, his eyes rested on the freckled redhead sitting bashfully and twiddling her fingers. He touched the brim of his Stetson with his forefinger and said, "When we reach the river, I'll inform you of further instructions."

For the first time since they had met him, Mace unleashed a smile, even though it was a bit odd and unusual. Rosemary could tell that Charity was relishing every second of it as he passed by. It was true that the rider was as Charity had stated: intriguing and devilishly handsome. Yet a certain air about him caused Rosemary to shiver. *His mannerisms may be intact, but his eyes are that of a gunslinger: cold and heartless,* she thought.

Rosemary felt a harsh pinch on her hand. Charity spoke excitedly in her ear after clasping a shaking hand on Rosemary's hand. "Did you see that smile?" She dramatically placed a hand upon her heaving chest while raising the other to her forehead. "I thought I might faint!"

The older of the two simply shook her head and said, "Charity, a captivating smile doesn't deserve your undying devotion."

It was close to two hours when they reached the river. The storm had settled in for the long haul. The sight of the river ahead was enough to make anyone's heart sink with dread. It was just as Mace had said. The river was flooded with debris. Tree branches, dirt, and moss floated swiftly down it. Tips of rocks and trees jutted out in various places.

Although the rain had held off for most of their journey, it now began to pour, unleashing its wrath from the heavens. The weary caravan came to a halt at the bank. Rosemary could scarcely hear Ricochet's bellowing tone from where she sat, but his words were unmistakable nonetheless.

"Everyone," he called above the wind's mighty roar. "This is the safest place to cross the river. I understand that it has flooded considerably, but if we don't cross now, the water will continue to rise, and we won't get another chance." Thunder crackled overhead, and then Ricochet continued his words of warning. "I want every woman and child inside or sitting atop the wagons. Men, you will steer the oxen. Horses and livestock must be tied to the side or backboards of your wagons. The medical supply wagon will be first, the Jones' second, the Cole's third, Isaac Beckett's fourth, and so on. My supply wagon will be last to cross. Any questions?"

Many men had voiced their concerns about the treacherous path, yet none went against him publicly. Hushed murmurings were heard throughout the caravans, including Edward Jones's. He was a farmer who seemed to be the noisiest of the bunch.

Rosemary closed off her awareness of their frantic worries to focus on the danger that lay ahead. She had heard tales of travelers who had perished after falling into fast-flowing rivers. Although she had never been afraid of water or swimming, the images of drowning in the murky depths ahead tied her stomach in knots.

Following Charity's lead, she crawled into the covered part of the wagon. They made quick work of tying boxes and trunks together before settling themselves onto the front seat beside Jackson.

Rosemary busied herself with smoothing the folds of her skirts as the caravans lurched forward with a jolt. She closed her eyes slightly to calm herself. The sounds of rushing water and pouring rain filled her ears. Her wild imaginings of wagons tipping while crossing the river only grew the fear that was in the pit of her stomach. She fidgeted in her seated position when Jackson spoke while holding the reins. "Hold on, ladies. It might be a bumpy ride."

Charity held onto her father's steady arm while Rosemary sat stiff with worry. The three didn't speak as the front wheels entered the water. Rosemary gazed up at the dark skies.

She wondered if her admirer was still searching for her. Was he now fighting the same storm in his anger to find her? Had he given up his quest and gone after another woman? The possibility, she decided, was ridiculous. He had gone after her family and attacked anyone who got too close to her. *A possessive man like that would never turn tail and run,* she thought as she swallowed hard. *No. He's still out there.*

She yelped softly when the water jostled the wagon and battered its right side with incredible force. It felt almost like being on board a ship on the open sea; however, the current seemed far swifter than what she had imagined the ocean must be like. After all, she had never been to the ocean. What did she know of open water and boats? She had only seen paintings and pictures of them.

The caravan struggled and sloshed in the strong river's current. The oxen, although protesting unhappily, fought with all their might to reach the other side. The wagon in front of them halted quickly, and Jackson reigned in his oxen, pulling back as far as he could with a loud "Whoa, whoa!"

"Everyone, stop! Stop!" It was Ricochet. He shouted loudly and with urgency. All land schooners were at a standstill. The water rushed through the wooden wheels and licked the bottom planks of the seats. The oxen began to low loudly. They were eager to get out of the wet and mud as much as their owners were. Something had happened ahead of them.

Rosemary gripped the seat. Her back was as stiff as a board. "What happened?" She voiced her inquisitive mind.

"Is it the medical wagon?" Charity asked no one in particular. "Has the axel broken again?"

Jackson frowned grimly. "Perhaps. Mr. Chapel said he patched it the best he could without having the necessary spare parts handy. Might be that the waters are too rough on it. Could've knocked something loose."

As if in response to their questions, Edward Jones, whose wagon sat idle in front of them, yelled back, "It's the med cart. Seems the axle's busted. Ric and Mace are hitching it to their buckskins to drag it across."

Jackson nodded and asked, "What do we do?"

Edward shrugged. "Ain't nothing to do besides wait. Ric said he'd help maneuver the other schooners once he got the Webbs' med cart far enough across."

Charity gasped, "This is awful. What happens if the river floods more?" She rubbed her arms and moved closer to her father.

Rosemary only wished that she could comfort her frightened friend, but how could she when her own fears were running rampant? She gripped the seat hard. Her knuckles turned a deadly shade of white, and she leaned over so that she could see behind the Jones' large wagon. She barely caught a glimpse of the men as they worked eagerly to pull the cart to shore. As she leaned farther, a gust of wind swept over her head and whisked away the beautiful white-laced bonnet she had borrowed from Charity.

"My goodness!" She exclaimed and leapt up to grab it. Her boot hit the post of her seat, and she tripped her forward. Within a split second, she was falling headfirst into the murky depths below the wagon. She heard shrill screams and shouts coming from Charity and Jackson as her body hit the water, and she sank under the wagon's axle.

The unrelenting and swift current had her now. It carried her beneath the harness that was tied to the oxen and on down the river. Her small frame hit rocks and debris. She was battered by tree limbs. The river seemed to drag her under the more she struggled, and her body was pulled farther and farther from the caravan. As she kicked repeatedly, she reached for the muddy surface. She needed oxygen so desperately. She burst forth from the water, sucking in deep breaths before being dragged under once more.

Her skirts were heavy, soaking wet, and pulling at her waist. It took so much effort to swim up for air than she thought was possible. Would she be one of the travelers who died in the river as in stories? The thought of her pale body being taken by the depths of the river made her cringe and sick inside.

Bubbles left her lips as she made one last attempt for air. She stroked harder than before. Her feet became entangled in the lacy edges of her petticoat. Her vision was blurry, but she kept swimming in the hope that she would reach the riverbank. Whether it was a rock or tree, she didn't know. It had hit her side with such power and force that her remaining breath, which she clung so dearly to, was stolen away from her aching lungs. She doubled over. She was limp in the water. It hurt. It hurt badly.

Her body convulsed, wanting air but getting only mud and water. She held her side as her hair flowed in front of her face. Her eyes, once a shade of chocolate brown, were turning a dull, gray, and almost lifeless color. She was losing the will to fight.

Something hit the water beside her, causing massive waves and fizzy bubbles. Long, snake-like tentacles swam with immense skill and endurance, gliding through the current and wrapping around her waist. She was drawn close. The arms squeezed her tightly and refused to let her go. Hefty fingers closed around her wounded side, engulfing her in a dizzying spell of agony. Her eyelids closed slowly. She was unable to muster the strength to put up a fight. She fell into darkness; a void of what appeared to be endless but restless sleep.

# Chapter 5

❧§❧

Ricochet's breathing was ragged as he fought his way to the riverbank. The limp beauty in his arms weighed him down, but he didn't dare let her go. The current beat against his face, debris tore at his legs, and swamp weeds tugged on his leather boots, but he moved forward with every ounce of strength he could muster. His strokes ripped through the current with incredible speed, even though the bank seemed to grow farther away rather than closer.

Why had he jumped in? He knew the danger of such an act. Many had fallen in flooded bodies of water and never made it out. He'd seen it with his own eyes many times before. But the moment that he saw her hit the current, his body reacted before he could think clearly. Had it been wrong of him to take the risk? Perhaps he should have waited. *For what?* he thought. *For this woman to drown and be swept farther down river?*

He'd been right to dive in after her. It might have been foolhardy, but it was right. His heart wrenched when he finally found her unconscious and floating several yards from the wagons. Her paler face did little to comfort the fear that had begun to form in his chest. His first deduction was that she had drowned before he had reached her. But the faint heartbeat that he heard in her chest upon reaching her sodden form gave him hope. That was something that he clung to.

Rosemary's head was barely above the water's surface, and he desperately tried to keep her afloat no matter how hard he fought to keep himself from going under. He coughed and sputtered as a rush of muddy water entered his mouth and flew up his nose. The impact was enough to bring stinging tears to his eyes. His grip loosened on the helpless young woman, but he managed to readjust his hold on her upper arms.

Seeing her beautiful, sodden face pressed against his body made him quiver. He wouldn't say that he enjoyed facing the rapids, but it was awfully nice having a woman as pretty as she was so close to him, and boy, she was pretty.

They rounded a bend in the river. Boulders and tree limbs jutted out all over. Surely, he could latch onto one of them and pull them to shore. *God, please get us to the shore.* His prayers were repeated and seemed to grow louder in his head until he thought he was saying them aloud.

A sharpened boulder scraped his back as he turned to shield Rosemary from its rugged edge. His breath caught in his throat. Then he unleashed an odd sound that even he couldn't believe came from his mouth. The pain of the impact had sent his whole body trembling.

They continued to float down the river. Ricochet did his best to keep Rosemary's unconscious body afloat, but he was getting tired. How long could he last before he too gave out? The farther they went, the farther the wagon train would be from them. He knew it would take them quite a while to get back. He needed to get to the shore. With what strength remained in his legs and free arm, he gripped the rock that had winded him and clung to it. He saw the shore. He kicked hard against the rock to launch himself and Rosemary out closer to the shoreline as he prayed harder than ever.

His prayers had been heard, for he came nearer and nearer to the river's edge. Wearily, he kicked against the current until his feet felt the pebbled bank. He dragged himself and Rosemary onto land. He was crawling and spitting water. A cool gust of wind tugged at his soaked clothes, taking his breath away. He shivered. "Thank You, God," he said as he looked skyward and raindrops splattered his already drenched face. "Thank You."

Before he tended to himself, he peered down at the unconscious young woman whom he had desperately attempted to save. His eyes scanned her from head to toe. He was mesmerized.

She was ghastly pale except for her lovely pink lips, which provoked wild imaginings that he hurriedly pushed aside. He refused to allow his flesh or the devil take hold of him. The young woman could be dead or dying, and he was thinking of kissing her awake. He couldn't succumb to that kind of selfishness and definitely not while the woman was in dire straits.

He blinked back every outlandish thought in his head and placed an ear to her chest. He found that the lump in his throat had grown so large that he could barely swallow. There was no heartbeat, no gasping for air¾nothing.

A fire lit in his heart, and a compelling motion took hold of him. He knelt over Rosemary. He'd have to put into practice the things that he'd learned from his many years on the trail. Flattening the palms of his hands over her chest, he arched his back up and then forced both palms down and up in quick successions. He pounded on her heart once and then twice, before parting her plump, wonderful lips and aggressively smashing his atop her own. His breath filled her mouth time after time. He shoved down on her chest again. It was a never-ending loop of hitting her chest, forcing air down her throat, and praying.

Ages went by; however, he refused to stop. He could *not* lose her, not after trying so hard and risking his own life in the process. He continued on for several more minutes, but it all appeared to be hopeless until he battered her rib cage so forcefully that her head lurched and she spat up muddy water. Her eyes, which were barely opened into slits, gazed up at him. The sight brought a warm sensation to his chest. Her teeth chattered, and she remained limp, but she was alive.

He stroked a dark curl from her face, smiled, and said, "Glad to see you alive, darlin'."

He couldn't begin to express how joyful seeing her actually breathing made him feel inside. A swell of happiness enveloped his entire body, more so than he had expected. His efforts had not been in vain. The treacherous river wouldn't take another life this time. Not this time.

Staring into her large brown eyes, he became lost and entranced. No sooner had she opened them, she closed them again. Exhaustion had taken its firm hold. He sighed with fatigue. His aching arms and legs threatened to collapse.

The rain continued, and the thunder ceased to soften its roar. They needed shelter and warmth before pneumonia set in or worse. He forced himself onto his feet. His legs felt like jelly. However, his concern was mostly for Rosemary.

He had noticed that she had a wound on her side. The mere sight sent chills up and down his spine and a tingling response in his neck. She needed medical attention, but without the doctor and his medical expertise, she wouldn't survive long.

Sure, Ricochet had basic medical training. As wagon master on the Oregon Trail, one never knew when healing abilities would be needed. It seemed that he had used the knowledge frequently in the past few years. Whether it had been for himself or a pioneer under his leadership, his wisdom on the matter of medicine was helpful yet limited. He knew she would need Dr. Webb's capable hands for such an operation, not to mention the grotesque shape of her left shoulder. He shivered for the third time.

A fire sounded good right about then, but shelter was first on his agenda. Not knowing how long it would take the others to find them, Ricochet set to work looking for a place to dry out. He spied an overhang of rock just a few paces ahead. It wasn't much, but it would keep them out of the storm until help arrived. Depending on how far the river had taken them, they might have to wait awhile on a rescue party, if the pioneers even thought they'd survived the rapids.

He gently lifted Rosemary into his arms. He was growing terribly fond of having her so close. His stumbling strides made for a difficult time getting past the slick pebbles on the river's brink, but he managed to carry her up the hill and under the overhang. He did it despite the sickening agony in his back.

Upon inspection, Ricochet found that the overhang wasn't as rough as he had first depicted. It had plenty of room for a body to lie down under and stay dry while having a fire, although it wasn't much bigger than the inside of a covered wagon. It would have to do.

He laid Rosemary on the moss-covered ground, being careful of her shoulder and side. After getting a better view of her shoulder, it appeared to be out of joint, which meant that he would have to put it back in place. A harsh shudder ran along his spine at that. At least it wasn't as bad as he had first thought it to be. Putting a bone back in its socket was a normal occurrence for him. He'd even been unfortunate enough to set his own limbs in place many times before. It would ache like nothing else for a few days, but it was the only way for recovery.

Fire¾they needed that first. He set to work gathering any semi-dry twigs and branches he could find near their makeshift campsite. It would be dark soon, and their weakened state was like an open-feast sign to wolves and the like. But a warm fire would send those critters packing for the hills.

After several attempts at starting the fire, Ricochet managed a large spark that caught on the twigs. He surrounded the fire with stones to keep it at bay and then nestled down to warm his hands. Once he had the feeling back in his fingertips, it was time to bring Rosemary over. With all the carefulness in the world, he brought her near the small flame. Now for the part that he dreaded most: putting her shoulder back in place.

He took a breath. Then he gripped her collarbone with one hand while the other held her arm just above the elbow. It wasn't going to be pretty getting it back into the socket nor was it going to be painless, but he hoped that she could forgive him for what he was about to do. She moaned and shifted her head at his touch, but she didn't open her eyes. Maybe the exhaustion would keep her asleep through it. He could only pray that would be the case.

He could not delay it any longer. He lifted her arm slightly and then forced the shoulder back. The breathless gasp that came from Rosemary's mouth made him weak in the knees, but her limb was finally going to heal. He saw her eyes barely open for a split second and her brow crease in unbearable pain. Then she was sleeping again. The poor thing's frown of discomfort about set Ricochet's heart to breaking.

His whole body ached from head to toe, and he wanted nothing more than a hot meal and warm bedroll to curl up in, but seeing how help hadn't arrived yet, he was far from getting that. He brought his one knee up to rest his arm and chin on. The spot on his spine where the rock had hit was definitely bruised and excruciating.

He had to question whether saving the woman had been the best decision. However, she'd likely see him as a hero and thank him tremendously for his courage. Having a woman swoon over him might not be so bad after all. Pride lit up in his chest. He was a hero. A smirk crossed his chapped, thirsty lips. With all the illogical thinking he was doing, he knew that he couldn't go to sleep no matter how much he wanted to. He needed to stay alert for a team of pioneers to arrive for their rescue. Surely, they had seen the smoke coming from his fire.

Several hours passed until he heard the canter of a horse. Mace stumbled upon them. His black stallion whinnied and snorted softly, shaking its head as if to say, "*You fool.*" The dark-clad rider dismounted and hurriedly made his way toward them.

"You both all right?" he asked. His expression never changed from the usual straight glare that he always had.

Ricochet eyes squinted, and his nose scrunched to see through the raindrops that were dripping off the side of the overhang. He nodded and said, "For the most part. She needs the doc. Got a nasty lookin' spot on her right side. Her shoulder's seen better days too."

With his tone never ceasing from its deep mellow vibration, Mace tipped his hat back to allow rainwater to drain from the brim. "I can have her back at the caravan in no time. Jones is bringing Gage." Hearing his stallion's name made Ricochet both wince and grin. He loved the beautiful chocolate-colored mustang dearly, but with the hurt he was in, he didn't think he could sit in the saddle that long.

"You go on ahead," Ric ordered as he lifted the young woman into Mace's arms once the rider was back atop his stallion. "I'll catch up."

It was not long before Jones arrived with Gage in tow. The stallion of dark brown was a welcoming sight, but the man leading him was a true pain in the rump. Ricochet took his time to swing into the damp leather saddle. He eased into position carefully to keep the pain at bay. He patted the good-tempered beast on its neck. "Atta boy, Gage," he said and smiled.

Jones sat back with the reins of his own mare in his grip. "Chapel! You must be some kind of hair-brained cowpoke to pull off such a stunt." His boisterous voice could easily be heard down the riverside and even above the rain and thunder. "Jumping willingly into a river? That's absolutely absurd."

Ricochet raked his fingers through his hair and combed his shortened bangs from his eyes. "Jones, I didn't see any other fella fancying the task."

With those words lingering in the wind, Gage took off into a fast gallop up the riverbank at his master's command. The two riders and steeds made it safely back to the wagons within the hour, and Ricochet couldn't be happier.

The clouds appeared to be clearing, but the rain had yet to cease. Per Doctor Webb's request, Ricochet and Mace agreed that the caravan should stay to make repairs and give the doctor all the time he needed to ensure that Rosemary was well on her way to recovery.

# Chapter 6

All was dark and silent. The void was so thick that Rosemary could feel it surrounding her. This happened every time that she closed her eyes or slept. The eerie darkness returned to haunt her dreams. The silence was deafening, and the shroud of black took her breath away.

*Rosemary.* The same voice that had always taken hold of her nightmares was speaking. *Rosemary. Where are you, my sweet? Where are you?*

He was still searching for her, even after putting a huge distance between them. Was it all for naught? She dared to think of the things that he might do to her, if he found her … *when* he found her, that is. It was only a matter of time before he would catch up to her. Among her nightmares, she knew this was very much the truth.

The voice of her admirer continued to growing louder and louder and closer and closer. She wanted to cry, to scream, but like all her nightmares, no sound escaped her mouth. All that she could hear was *his* voice, and his alone. *Rose! Return to me! Rose!*

She awoke with a start. Perspiration was beading across her brow. She lay flat on her back beneath a heavy, warm quilt. A sheet of white canvas hung overhead, and the pitter-patter of raindrops were splattering on top of it.

Her first instinct was to go back to sleep and dream away the agonizing pain that she felt in her right side. But fear that the nightmare would return made her think otherwise. Carefully and slowly, she sat up and moaned groggily. The throbbing of her abdomen was unbearable, and a headache came in thunderous waves. Curiosity took a firm hold nonetheless.

She peered down at the clothes she was wearing. She recognized them all too well. It was her own nightgown and shawl. Her curly locks had been neatly done up in a braid tied with a silk ribbon. The recollection of the river's disastrous rapids and debris lay on the tip of her memories, but the figure of immense strength and dashing heroics swept it away. Once she had hit the water, she hadn't remembered anything else besides her fight to live. Puzzled and eager to rise, she shifted her left shoulder and received a stab of pain in return. Opening her mouth in a silent cry, she tensed and waited for it to subside, before looking down to see that her arm had been wrapped tightly into a sling that was hooked around the right side of her neck.

She decided on staying put for the moment. Moving hurt worse than anything that she had experienced thus far. Her side hurt most of all. Placing her right palm against the left side of her gown, she felt beneath the soft fabric, a thin bandage that hid a long line of fine stitch work on her skin. She felt maybe seven or eight stitches, although she didn't have the stomach to check and make certain of that number.

She sat for a minute while resting her head on a box to her right. She closed her eyes lazily. She was tired, so tired. But she refused to rest without knowing her whereabouts. The covered fortress where she was staying was not her own. Where was she?

A ruckus of voices and squeals sounded from outside the wagon, and a ragged Charity fumbled inside. "Rosie!" The grin on her freckled complexion grew as she reached to grab hold of the dazed Rosemary. "You're awake! Oh, I've been worried sick about you. How are you feeling?" A thousand questions all at once flew from her plump red-stained lips.

Rosemary could hardly sit right let alone give answers. She tiredly leaned into Charity's arms. "A little exhausted."

Her friend glowed with a bemused smile. "I'll say. That river carried you clear down the rapids, it did. How you made it out alive is truly a miracle of God."

The headache continued its pounding, and Rosemary thought she'd keel over due to the stinging pain from her hurt side. She warred through it while keeping a wearied glow and cheerfulness in her expression for Charity's sake. "What exactly happened? I know I fell over, but how did I—"

Charity cut her off as words sped out. She didn't bother to wait for the full question. As her words reached Rosemary's, they became slurred and slowed, as Rosemary grew dizzy. She couldn't focus on the meaning of Charity's excited speech or the colors surrounding her. Black spots clouded her vision, and a sickness welled up in her belly. Nausea quickly overcame her.

Before Rosemary had a chance to succumb to the blackout, another body entered the wagon. A woman was following him. The man wore a gray suit, which was completed by a bowler hat and tie. His sleeves were rolled up, and his coat was on the woman's arm. He quickly spoke to Charity, telling her in hushed words to leave. Once she hollered her goodbyes and made her exit, the man approached Rosemary.

"Miss Barker," he greeted. "My name is Dr. Jacob Webb. How are you feeling, my dear?" His tone was pleasing, kind, and understanding.

She swallowed, begging her stomach not to toss up what was in it. She shook her head wearily, trying hard not to cry. "It hurts," she managed.

He nodded once with his mouth in a thin line. "Of course, it does. I'm sorry to say that it will be that way for a while longer." He whispered words to his assistant, who was his pregnant wife, Katrina. She began to rummage through the box next to her for something Rosemary couldn't see.

Jacob leaned forward, inspecting her shoulder carefully. Then he placed a palm on her forehead. "It seems she has a fever," he declared to his wife.

With her brows knit, Katrina asked, "Should I gather fresh water?"

"Yes. Plenty of cool water from one of the kegs and a few scraps of cloth."

When Katrina had left, the rather young doctor helped his patient back into her bedroll on the floor. "Just rest, Miss Barker. You'll make a quick recovery if you rest." She didn't protest in the least, but followed his commands with earnestness, despite the emptiness in the pit of her stomach.

The next morning came and went. They flew by for the recovering and extremely weak young woman. She found it hard to sleep and eat.

A few bites of mushed berries and moistened bread were all she had the appetite for. Katrina had encouraged and sometimes forced water down her throat, claiming that dehydration could cause typhoid fever or worse.

Jacob had checked in every hour of the day, consoling her and changing her bandaging as they became soiled. She still had a fever, but by evening, she was fit enough to sit up and have real food. The dizzy spells had stopped by 4:00 p.m., and the fever had broken by 5:00 p.m., leaving her relieved and starving.

After having a light meal of bread, hardtack, and apples, she was finally able to rest that night in the midst of the Webbs' medical wagon. Katrina had sung softly as Rosemary drifted off into a relaxing dreamland. Her thoughts were filled with wondrous things.

The next day, Rosemary awoke later in the afternoon. She was groggy but happy to have at least one peaceful night's sleep for a change. The nightmares that had plagued her every night for the past few weeks had stopped, except for one night. She was grateful, even if it was only for that one night.

After having spent almost five full days in bed, Jacob thought she should get up and stretch her legs. She wanted to object and to lie beneath her covers of safety and warmth, but Katrina's pleading smile and angelic voice persuaded her to get up. One painful step at a time and with Jacob and Katrina at her sides, she walked around the circled wagon train.

The sunshine was beautifully inviting, and the promise of new life had been quite a sight. She gladly welcomed the fresh smells of the outdoors, after having to breathe the musty medicine wagon's odor. Her fellow pioneers grinned, smiled, and expressed relieved sighs as she walked on, one step in front of the other.

Charity had joined her shortly after Rosemary had exited the land schooner. She filled Rosemary in on all the stories that had gone on without her. It wasn't until Katrina led Rosemary back to the wagon that the excited young lady left her alone.

"Rosemary, dear," Katrina began. Her belly and face were swollen, but she was just as pretty as ever. "You must take it easy for a few more days. Jacob says you must push yourself to recover but not to go above and beyond. You still have much healing ahead of you."

Rosemary eyed her with a soft smile on her lips. "I'm ever so grateful to you and your husband's kindness, Katrina. I can't repay you. I have no more funds for the bill I've costed you." She peered down at her arm, which was resting in the sling. She knew that medical attention was no cheap undertaking.

Katrina placed a gentle hand under Rosemary's chin, lifting it to meet her glossy and compassionate green eyes. "No. You mustn't worry over such things. My husband and I were glad to be of some help to you. It is his job to help people, is it not? Don't even think of the bill. I only wish you to know that it is only by the miraculous hand of God that you are alive right now."

*Hand of God?* What had that meant? There was a time before all this when Rosemary had believed in the Almighty more than anything else in the world. She regretted to admit that her faith had been lacking in recent months due to the harsh—and painful—experiences brought on by her admirer.

She had begun to question how a being of immense power and knowledge could have allowed something so wretched and heartbreaking to happen to one of His so-called children. Her prayer life had ended, after diminishing one event after another. The *hand of God* surely gave her no proof that He cared for her or her troubles. It was up to her alone to seek out peace and comfort. No God or man, for that matter, was going to help her, so she would have to rely on herself.

Katrina, sensing Rosemary's restless spirit, placed an encouraging hand on the wounded lady's shoulder. "Do not fret, Rosemary. The expense has been taken care of, and you need not worry over it. Jacob will charge no one for his expertise as long as we are on this train." She wanted to protest, but an argument with an angel would be as useless as a heavy winter coat on a warm summer's day.

The past few days that Rosemary had spent in the confines of the wagon as the train continued west, she had pondered over her questions about the incident at the river. She hesitated to ask the Webbs, although she was eager for answers. If she began asking questions, they would begin to wonder about her background. That was something she never wanted to bring up again.

Katrina, with a knowing glimmer on her tanned face, handed her a bottle of medicinal herbs in warm water as she had every day on the previous six days. "Are you wondering about the day you fell in the river?"

As Rosemary's jaw dropped, she considered what to say. It was as if the woman of wisdom could read her mind as well as concoct medicinal teas and powders. After several minutes of silence, Rosemary answered, "Yes."

Katrina moved the straying golden strands from her oval face. "When you fell, everyone was worried. It was the scariest thing any of us had seen on the trail thus far, and we were sent into a tizzy of emotions. You were in bad shape when Mr. Chronicle brought you back to camp. He carried you on his horse for about a mile before reaching the wagon train."

*Mace? He saved me?* Rosemary thought. She chewed on the information, soaking it in. She had never thought that Mace Chronicle was the caring type, least of all chivalrous. The fact that he had brought her back from the rapids shocked her. Perhaps, she shouldn't have judged him before she got to know him. But how could she ever trust the character of a man after what she had seen in the past. The admirer had all but ruined the image of the knight in shining armor that she had read about in fairytales when she was younger.

Blowing away the steam from her medicinal tea, she took a sip of the bittersweet brew. The warmth ran down her throat and into her full belly. It seemed to heal all the aches and pains on its way down.

Katrina watched with eyes glowing with sympathy. "You were out cold for almost a day, but you awoke that night. The fever took its toll."

Rosemary nodded. "I remember the fever and headaches."

Silence enveloped the small schooner. The only sounds were those of the men leaving on a hunting party on the other side of the camping circle. The baritone voices went quiet, as they left the circle for the surrounding woods for fresh game, which would likely be served that evening for supper. The rest would be dried and saved for traveling.

As her mind still swam with the river incident, Rosemary embraced the thought of Mace saving her from the rapids. No man that she had encountered had ever risked his life for the good of someone else. Somehow, it seemed untrue. She considered showing her gratitude, but pride halted her because he was a man. She'd much rather face a rattler than ever show appreciation to the opposite sex.

It could've been a mistake on his part. He probably hadn't wanted to save her, but he had been pushed into it. Yes, that had to be the case. Men never went out of their way to save women. Women were only playthings in their eyes and nothing more. What did emotions and feelings matter to the stronger gender?

Avoiding Katrina's puzzled look, Rosemary asked, "Do you think God cares about what happens to us down here?"

The wiser woman's tone was gentle and barely above a whisper. "Yes, He cares very much for His children. His Word promises that He will never leave us nor forsake us."

Those words festered in her soul. Rosemary practically tasted her own bitterness. How long had she run from the Creator? *Long enough.* Did He even care about her now? "But what if one ran a longtime from Him, would He even consider forgiving that person of her folly?" Thinking aloud and voicing her concerns, she began to wonder why she had brought the whole thing up. What was it about Katrina that made Rosemary want to spill everything and lay all her cards out on the table?

Katrina stifled a splendid huff of enjoyment at Rosemary's curiosity. "If you have to ask, you must already know the answer, Rosemary."

That night, falling asleep proved most difficult for Rosemary. Katrina's words echoed in Rosemary's head and held onto her consciousness like a spider clinging to its web. She couldn't stop thinking about it. *You must already know the answer, Rosemary.* Did she know the answer?

The horrific throbbing started in her left side, and her breathing slowed in order to keep the pain at bay. Jacob had to remove her sling, no matter much her shoulder still ached, before she could bed down for the night. She had full reign of her arms again. The six days of rest had been needed, but some people had started to complain about reaching the West before late fall.

They would get caught in more storms, if they had to make another stop as long as this one, not to mention the snow on the mountain pass that they had yet to climb. Just the thought of it made Rosemary shiver. She couldn't help but wonder if everyone blamed her for the accident. But it wasn't like she had wanted them to stop their traveling on purpose.

Snuggling deep into her quilt, she accidentally nudged Katrina, who lay asleep next to her. The pregnant woman didn't stir, and her soft snores continued. Rosemary closed her eyes in a final attempt to sleep. It was only after another hour that rest finally came, and she fell into a spiraling nightmare as she had before. This one she couldn't seem to awaken from.

# Chapter 7

He had tried hard to hide the alarming rumble of laughter that had been in his chest, but somehow, it had all come out, as the young acid-tongued woman had spouted at him. He couldn't hear above his own snickers and howls. After all, how could he help himself? Her outrageous way of stomping about and pouting like a child amused him.

Yes, it was not at all ladylike to act in such a manner as Rosemary had, but he quite adored the spectacle: Her curls bounced as she shook her head, and red patches sporadically surfaced on her cheeks. He choked as he considered quieting her rambling by landing a big kiss on her mouth. Oh, that image pleased him ever so much, more so than it should. He quickly batted the foolish idea aside. No Christian man should think that way.

Rosemary's small chest heaved as she gripped the seams of her skirts. "I hate you ever so much, Mr. Chapel!"

Her skirts frilled at the ends as she stumbled on her way. She was a heaping mess of rage, beauty, and insults. Had he just dreamed it, or had he really seen tears beginning to form in her eyes? The gleam of fun faded from his face. He never meant for the teasing to go that far. Perhaps, he had crossed the line somewhat.

The young filly had been up and about when they had finally camped late that evening. The wagons made a corral for the oxen, livestock, and pioneers as usual. Rosemary had just exited the Webb's caravan when he went to check on her. The nervous look that she gave him all but stopped his heart—she was truly stunning.

He offered to get her a drink from the water keg when she stumbled over his foot and fell headfirst into its opening. Her curls fell loose from their pins and down her shoulders to frame her circular face. He couldn't help the way he snickered. It was comical. He only found it so funny because her injuries had mostly healed, it being almost a week and a half after the river incident. Otherwise, he'd be digging his own grave right now.

She half growled, half screamed at him. "Don't you ever come near me again!"

"Darlin'," he pleaded, "it was an honest accident. My boot caught your skirts."

She huffed loudly. Her chin dripped water, and her eyes were waterlogged. "You wicked, wicked man! I shall report you to the minister if you ever touch me again!" She had turned on her heels and left.

He fiddled with Rosemary's ribbon, which he had pulled from his pants' pocket, finding it to be enchantingly soft. He sighed aloud in despair. The last glimpse of her rigid back was all he could catch before she entered the Webbs' wagon. Guilt gripped his heart. Licking his lips, he meditated on the idea of facing her and pleading for forgiveness. But she was angry with him. Of course, she wouldn't forgive him so easily. It was utter foolishness to think that a woman would forget and that she would be reasoned with so quickly after a spat. Why, it was preposterous!

It was beyond his comprehension why he became so clumsy around her. Somehow, she brought out the boy in him. He became childish and giddy.

Stuffing the ribbon back in his pocket, he headed to the supply wagon, eager to clear his head. Victor Marsh was waiting for him at the wagon.

"Hey," Victor greeted with a thin-lipped frown while taking inventory. His expression was grim, as usual. Victor had always treated him, and every other man, with such gloom.

His treatment of the womenfolk, however, was a different story. Ricochet had only just met the man one day before they'd started out west along the Oregon Trail. But the wagon master understood that this seasoned man of forty-three was a seducer of the other gender and a womanizer. Ricochet had never much cared for the man, but he hadn't seen any reason to knock him around.

"Taking stock, Victor?" Ricochet asked, knowing the answer.

Victor spat. He never went anywhere without a wad of chewing tobacco, which Ricochet had notably disagreed with on several occasions. He stood from his crouched position next to the boxes of food and emergency weapons. "Ain't you a smart one, boss." His sarcasm had been riling up Ricochet's nerves the past few weeks, but the wagon master had never been one to turn down a body on his wagon train who wanted a new start in life, no matter how much his patience with the man was wearing thin.

"Well, wise guy," Ricochet put his hands firmly on his hips. "How's the stock?"

Victor shrugged, scratching his head wearily. "Not much jerk left. We'll be needing to catch wild game soon, I reckon'."

"I'll round up some men after supper and decide on the matter." Ricochet nodded and then turned to leave. "We're heading out early tomorrow, so no more of your late night chattering with the womenfolk." His last jab at Victor made the atmosphere tense.

The older man by about eight years straightened his back and stretched his arms above his head. He was the biggest brute on the train, and the wagon master knew that if there was ever a serious spat between them, Ricochet might just lose. Victor smirked cockily, "You jealous of my charm, wagon boy?"

Ricochet had never found a man that he'd come to dislike or that was hard to agree with at least something on, but Victor seemed to rub him the wrong way every time. The man wasn't happy unless Ricochet was upset or agitated, which greatly bothered him. The wagon master wanted peace aboard his train and not strife.

Then again, Victor hadn't been the only one to cause problems. Edward Jones had only increased his complaints since joining up back in Missouri. Now *he* was quite an excruciating pain in Ricochet's side. The man was incorrigible and a devilishly sly player. He had disagreed with all Ricochet's commands. His boisterous cursing and backstabbing comments were vile. Perhaps, Edward's involvement in the Civil War had caused his harsh character and demand of unearned respect. Ricochet felt sorry for the man's wife and son because they had to live with that kind of difficulty every single day.

It seemed that Edward and Victor had formed some kind of alliance. They both murmured and complained behind Ricochet's back. They relentlessly disagreed with his rules and regulations. On the start of their journey, those two had gotten a rude awakening when they'd found out that Ricochet was no pushover, yet that never stopped them from attempting to smother his confidence.

He eyed Victor sternly. "Call me wagon boy again, and you are off this train. Am I clear?" His tone held no sign of mercy.

Victor held his gaze, much to Ricochet's surprise, as he answered back in a snarky voice, "You got it, *boss*." He practically spat out the last word in mockery of the wagon master.

Ricochet clenched his jaw and spoke through his teeth. "Are we good here, Mr. Marsh?"

Victor cocked an eyebrow and crossed his arms tightly over his chest, with muscles flexing. "Are we?" He egged on.

Ricochet knit his brows with frustration and barked out orders to the large man before leaving. Victor Marsh was a pompous and arrogant type of curly wolf. Yep, that was the man's title. Curly Wolf was a rough-and-tough man with a bad attitude. Ricochet breathed deeply and counted to ten in his attempt to calm his anger. Shrugging off the problems and concerns that he had for the men of the train, Ricochet headed to his stallion.

After he had fed Gage and ensured that the reins were securely staked down, Ricochet wound down before supper while the animal grazed. Gage nickered, bobbed his head, and nudged Ricochet's face gently. "Atta boy, Gage," he cooed as he stroked the buckskin's thick neck.

"Quite a spectacle you made earlier," a familiar tone said.

Ricochet turned to see Mace leading his own stallion, Midnight, toward the wagon hitch to tie him up. The tired wagon master unfurled his saddlebags a little ways away from the horses. He unbuckled his weapon holsters and removed his Stetson before giving himself a good washing at the water keg that was beside him.

"What are you on about? I did nothing of the kind," Ricochet said.

Mace took out his revolvers some feet away from Ricochet, readying them should anything go awry. "Oh, no?" His baritone reached Ricochet's ears quizzically as he took out a cloth in for cleaning the guns.

After a quick wash around his neck, face, and ears, Ricochet sat down with an exhausted sigh and contemplated the day. He cleaned his revolver as if it was in its prime, but in reality it was at least three years old.

Holstering his weapon, he looked up at the sky and replaced his Stetson atop his head. He picked at the grass around his crossed legs and tore the blades into shreds. The sun had been excruciatingly hot, and he was beginning to feel its rays from beneath his hat's sturdy brim. The cool water around his neck had dampened his shirt collar and vest, but it was welcoming after facing the heat of the day's end.

Supper came and went, and still, there was no sign of Rosemary coming out of the Webbs' makeshift home. He'd wanted to show his remorse, but that did not happen. He ended up sleeping under the stars and thinking about the way to be granted her forgiveness.

Morning came all too early as it always had for Ricochet. As wagon master, he had to be up before the rest of the wagon train, as well as the men he'd placed as watchdogs in the corral. He stretched, yawned, and stared at a barely visible dawn approaching. No one stirred, no one apart from Mace Chronicle, who'd taken third watch in the night. Victor Marsh had taken the second watch, and Isaac Beckett, a young blacksmith hoping to start up his business out west, had taken the first watch. The wagons were all silent, and the lanterns had been doused in the night. The remains of a campfire sat in the middle of the caravans' circle.

Ricochet headed for the supply wagon and woke up Victor for the morning meal. Although he would've appreciated the mean, middle-aged cook staying asleep, his stomach protested to the point that he gave in. Breakfast would not be started by itself. He knocked lightly on the wagon's entrance. When one knock didn't work, he tried again and again. After pounding the sixth time on the wooden frame, a bellow barked back, "I'm coming. Keep your spurs on."

Victor opened the canvas flaps, scratching his neck in a dazed and none-too-friendly manner. "What do you want?"

Ricochet kept his composure as calmly as he could muster and then ordered, "Start on breakfast. We need to get a move on if we're to reach Fort Kearney by tomorrow afternoon."

He huffed a little too loudly. "I hear ya."

With that, he stumbled back into the confines of his wagon and got ready for the long trek ahead of them. After the supply wagon's driver had been awakened, Ricochet went after the rest of the men.

By 5:00 a.m., the pioneers were eating breakfast. Then they lined up their wagons. When 6:00 a.m. came around, they were on the trail. The sun was rising at a quick rate. Ricochet set Gage at a steady pace head of the train. Mace was at his side.

The line of wagons was arranged as it had been before: Dr. and Mrs. Webb's medical wagon was right behind the wagon master's, the Jones' wagon was second, Jackson's was third, Beckett's caravan was fourth, various others rode after them, and Victor's supply wagon headed up the rear.

All was set, and the dawn brought the clearest skies and warmest breezes for a midsummer's day. If all went well, they would reach Oregon City by late September.

Ricochet relaxed in the saddle with one hand on his thigh, and the other holding the reins. He smiled widely as Gage walked onward at a consistent speed, feeling comfortable on the open terrain. Adjusting his hat brim, Ricochet turned to peer over his shoulder. Some men sat atop the wagons and steered them while many walked alongside them, including Mrs. Webb, who was far into her pregnancy. He admired the woman for her sweet spirit and willing character. She always managed to find good in the bad.

"Mace, keep heading the train," Ricochet ordered. "I'll be back." He steered Gage to the medical wagon behind them. He rode beside Mrs. Webb, keeping a safe distance should his stallion get spooked. Dipping his Stetson to the doctor and his lovely fair-haired wife, he greeted them with, "Mornin'."

Dr. Webb answered, "Ah, good morning, Mr. Chapel." He adjusted his small spectacles before they could slide off the tip of his nose. "What can I do for you?"

"Just thought I'd check in on you and your wife," Ricochet explained. "Is it all right for her be up and walkin' around like that?" He lazily gestured with his forefinger to her.

The doctor nodded at Ricochet's basic knowledge in the medical field. His words were kind, and the matter entertained him. "Katrina is fine, I assure you. The jerks aboard the wagons are much too rough for her and the baby. Studies have proven that pregnant women do better if they exercise rather than rest all day."

Katrina blinked in agreement with her husband and then put a hand on her swollen belly. "Jacob is quite right, Mr. Chapel. I do feel ever so better today. No need to worry about me. I'm keeping up quite nicely with this pace."

"Well then," Ricochet said as his tender smile widened, "I will leave you to your walking." With that, he fell back even farther to check on each wagon individually.

The Jones' wagon proved most difficult to inspect, however. Edward had hassled him after he'd ridden beside him and asked about his wife, Autumn, and his son, Andrew. Finding Edward to be troublesome and despairingly hostile, Ricochet went to the next wagon. This one he was especially been anxious to check on because it was Jackson's wagon.

He pulled the reins back and led Gage to the side wheel. He dipped his head to the old preacher. "Brother Jackson."

Jackson did likewise and welcomed him with a weathered but warm smile. "Ric, what can I do for you?"

"God's sure blessed us with a beautiful sunshine this mornin'. If this kinda weather keeps up, we'll be at Fort Kearney in no time."

"No doubt about it," the man said while he gazed ahead with a vague smile upon his wrinkled expression.

Ricochet continued with the small talk for some time. He talked about the weather, his stallion Gage, and Jackson's devotional from the previous evening around the campfire.

It was not until Ricochet began to mosey on down the line that

Jackson called out, "If you're lookin' for Rosemary, she's out walkin' at the rear of the train with my daughter, Charity."

An awkward chuckle of embarrassment escaped Ricochet's mouth, and he had to stop and take several seconds to compose himself before correcting the preacher over his shoulder. "I wasn't looking—"

"Don't you even try foolin' me, son. I knew you were lookin' for her the moment you rode alongside me," the wise and all-knowing man of God said. He jerked his head back. "Now off you go. You're chasin' a mighty fine but temperamental woman." He laughed as Ricochet tipped his head down in the slight relief of his humor. "Best you keep on your toes."

"You hit the nail on the head," Ricochet replied with a shake of his head. He kicked Gage's sides with his spurs, and then they trotted to the rear of the train.

Feeling a rather strange sensation in his chest, he slowed his hazel stallion to a snail's pace and placed a hand inside his shirt. His bare chest beneath his buttoned down shirt seemed to be as normal as before. But inwardly, it was a festering tizzy of odd emotions, which he'd never known before. This happened every time his mind traveled to the image of the handsome Miss Barker, which had happened more than he would've liked it to.

It could've been the way she stuck out her chin when she unleashed her temper or stomped away after a good teasing, her hair bouncing as she went. He gave a soft snicker at that—her curls bobbing and bouncing whenever she let them down, which was not that often. The ringlet curls were a spiral of golden brown, and the aroma of lemongrass followed her wherever she went. And those eyes were two swirls of chocolate with long stunning eyelashes, which were so shy and alluring that they drug him into a wild heat every time he glanced at them.

*What I wouldn't give to*—he stopped himself short of such a thought. It certainly was not proper to think up so whimsical a thing as kissing a strange woman, especially for a godly man. He was ashamed that he'd mustered it up, could imagine Rosemary wanting him to kiss her, and loved the very *idea* of kissing her.

Drawn from his thoughts, his ears picked out the sweet voice belonging to the one who had taken hold of his every rational way of thinking. Swallowing hard, he drew closer with his stallion at a slow and steady trot.

"The story was quite fascinating, Mr. Marsh," Rosemary voiced. Her head was lowered, and her voice was barely a whisper.

"Mr. Marsh," Charity inquired, "how is it that you know so much about everything for such a young-looking man?" She carried her pink skirts in her fists at both sides, swaying them gently to and fro. Rosemary walked to the right of Charity. Her hands were folded behind her back, and her skirts frilled as she walked.

As soon as Ricochet heard the name Marsh, his expression contorted, and his nose scrunched up as if he had come across a foul stench in the air. Breathing out through clenched teeth, he regained his confidence and moved on. He was now within earshot of the tobacco-reeking cook, Victor Marsh, who sat atop his wagon led by a pair of oxen.

"I'm not as young as you might think," Victor beamed proudly with a small wink to the ladies. "Man like me doesn't get around without learning a thing or two." He leaned forward to place his elbows atop his knees. "You ladies sure are good company. I got plenty a story to tell, should you want to hear them."

Charity swapped a look of pleasure with Rosemary and then nodded to Victor three times quickly. "Oh, do go on. Your storytelling is mighty fun, Mr.—"

"Call me Victor," He said, waving his hand. He waited a moment before going into another tall tale, but Ricochet had already ridden up to them, stopping the charade. Victor huffed loudly for all to hear. "Ric." His gloomy tone revealed nothing but his disappointment for the intrusion.

*That's right, Victor. Quiet that proud trap of yours.* Ricochet smirked inwardly. The wagon master dipped his head. "Victor." His greeting was curt with a hint of tension. As he gazed upon the two ladies treading beside him, Charity glimmered warmly while Rosemary found interest in the spinning wheel of the wagon.

"Morning, ladies," he said and smiled.

The redheaded preacher's daughter returned a grin. "Good morning, Mr. Chapel. What brings you to the back of the train?"

He shrugged, leaning back in the saddle and squaring his shoulders.

"Wanted to see the view." He was surprised to find that his eyes instantaneously flickered to Rosemary at that reply. The brunette raised her head to sneak a glance at him and then looked away. He cleared his throat, shifting his gaze to some other distraction in the hopes that he hadn't been as obvious as he thought he had.

"I, uh," he fumbled, searching for something to say to Rosemary. What should he say? He had thought up hundreds of ways to apologize before riding in search of her, but now that she stood directly to his left, he was speechless. Perhaps he should pay her a compliment beforehand.

That was when he found the ribbon in his pocket¾Rosemary's ribbon. Sorting through his thoughts, he considered giving it to her first and then begging for forgiveness. He reached into his back pocket, took out the satin hair tie, and then leaned down in the saddle to hand it to the beautiful brunette. "Since I'm here, I'd like to deliver this. It's a mighty purdy thing, and I'd hate for it to be lost to its handsome owner." *Atta boy, Ric!* He cheered to himself.

But instead of the batting of eyelashes and the gorgeous, nervous gleam that would come from other women, he got a prideful humph and a retort. "I don't want it back."

Her tone was stern, warning, and ill tempered. Ricochet felt as if he was in a dance with a rattlesnake. He had to sidestep the venomous bite and the swipe of the fangs. He raised a brow ever so slightly. "No? Last evening, you appeared to want it badly enough that you were diving for it."

The pun was as clever as ever, yet it did nothing to improve her attitude. Her chin lifted defiantly. He was in for another spouting match, and somehow, he longed for it. Just the tone of her voice made his heart skip a beat. Her tantrums were like watching a storm roll in. First, she would lift her chin high. Second, her bottom lip would start to protrude. The third thing that happened was what he found most intriguing: The red spots would appear around her collarbone, crawling up her elegant neck and jawline.

"You can just keep the filthy ribbon for all I care. I don't want anything to do with you. I will not be prey to your teasing any longer, so leave me be, or I shall call Brother Jackson on you." That was the second time she had warned him about calling the chaplain on him.

He tipped his head. "Now, now, I was only returning what was yours. If you don't want it, then I guess I'll have to keep it. Though not sure what I'd do with a satin thing like this." He lifted the ribbon high and then shoved it into his pocket once more. Finding his attempt at redemption to be a total failure, he kicked his spurs into his mustang's sides and then rode off without so much as a glance over his shoulder. *Tough one, she is,* he thought.

# Chapter 8

❦

She'd had all she could stand of the man's relentless teasing and awful humorous ways. It had been several hours since he'd tried to return her ribbon. She'd managed to avoid contact with him thus far. There had been no glances or words, but how long could she make it last?

The cover of the Coles' wagon had proven to keep her safe from his view, and she'd warned Charity not to allow him passage to their wagon at any cost. The preacher's daughter had kept her word, which greatly relieved Rosemary. She was glad to be back in Jackson, Charity, and her wagon after Jacob had re-bandaged her side, but she dearly missed Katrina's close company and the conversations that they had had.

As she sat on the floorboards and listened to the chatter of the wagoners and their oxen lowing and moving steadily outside, she recalled that moment when Ric had come on horseback to the rear side of the wagon train. His broad shoulders were held so confidently, and his body flowed with the horse's movements as if he were one with it. His brow had been shaded almost black beneath his brown hat so that she could scarcely tell what emotion was on his mustached face.

When he had ridden off so swiftly, she had lost all sense of purpose and prejudice. Why had she been so angry to see him and then so disoriented when he'd gone? Her body was an irritable bottle of fervor about to implode. She simply couldn't resolve the feelings that she felt.

It was at lunchtime on the next day when they reached a small establishment. Ricochet nominated a guide to take some of them to town while some would mind the wagons. Mace Chronicle and Isaac Beckett had volunteered. Isaac drove the cart while Mace rode his horse, following behind. The shopping group consisted of Autumn Jones, her son Andrew, Lily Garrison, Jacob Webb, Charity, and Rosemary. The eight of them rode to the town, which was a few miles from their camping circle.

Jacob's wife was too sick to do the shopping, so he took off in the direction of the nearest mercantile along the boardwalk. Not too far behind him, Autumn and Andrew Jones and Lily Garrison followed. The frilly Lily Garrison was a young lady who was traveling with her father, mother, and younger sister, Macy, to start a homestead out west. Isaac Beckett, with his feelings not hidden, trailed after the young woman, who was no older than Rosemary, intent on helping her with the shopping.

With her awful sense of excitement in a whirl, Charity exited the wagon and zoomed for the nearest building, which was Miller's Mercantile and Dress Shop. Rosemary shook her head at the strange girl's frenzy and then went to exit the cart. Clumsy as she was, her petticoat caught on a nail, and she tumbled forward. As the ground came closer to her face, she was sure that she would feel the sting of the impact in a second. Time seemed to stop, as she closed her eyes and braced for the compact dirt below.

It never happened. She never felt its terrible blow to her face. Instead, she embraced the strong arms of a tall able-bodied man: Mace Chronicle. His hat's brim was low over his gaze, and his long black coat was dusty from traveling the plains. He was sturdily built and infectiously quiet. She couldn't speak a word to him. He held her for a moment and then freed her petticoat from the rusted nail and set her on her feet.

"Watch your step," he warned softly and with care.

She straightened her dress, smoothing the fabric down. Bashfully, she lowered her head and gaze to the dirt, embarrassed at her own clumsiness. Twice now, he had come to her side and rescued her from danger: the river and now the cart. He had been so uptight and silent, but he had been watching like a hawk. She had pinned him as dangerous and mysterious at first. Was there a chivalrous bone in his body after all?

Mustering up her courage, she spoke in a shy voice, saying, "Thank you, for your assistance."

"Try to be more careful, Miss Barker."

A lump formed in her throat at his curt and deep-bass reply. She felt helpless under his gaze. "Th-that makes twice that you've come to my rescue, Mr. Chronicle." She held her breath when his head tilted as if he were confused by her gratitude. Had he never received a woman's praise?

He lifted the brim of his Stetson just above his brow line, and his nose scrunched in question. "What are you on about? I haven't done anything worthy of praise."

She had planned on her thanks being noted and for him to move on, but that was not the case. He seemed genuinely baffled. Men were so confusing and none too bright. She was learning that more and more. Finding her voice again, she explained, "The day at the river, and now here. You've rescued me twice."

His brows lifted for a moment and then plunged farther into a creased V-shape. He lowered his head to her with his hands firmly planted on his hips. "Miss Barker, what exactly do you think happened at the river?"

"Why, you jumped in to save me, of course."

He shook his head. "No, Miss. That wasn't me."

Her lips curved up as she forced her tone to remain calm but definite. "You carried me back from the river. It was you who saved me."

Standing tall and shaking his head once more, he spoke. "Miss Barker, I did carry you back to the train, but I sure didn't dive in and save you from the rapids." He hesitated as if pondering the right way to continue. "It was Ric who swam after you. He went a good few miles downriver before I found you both."

She felt absolute shock. Rosemary was deaf to all the hustle and bustle of the fort and a stranger to all senses. Her thoughts processed the information, chewing and digesting it. *Ricochet swam after me?*

She found it hard to breath, think clearly, and swallow. The man with a tenacious humor and a slap-worthy smirk had come to her rescue in the river. For days, she'd been led to believe that the strange, silent Mace had done the heroic act, but it was Ricochet. He'd done all the heroics.

"The wagon master?" She questioned, not believing it to be the truth.

"The wagon master," Mace confirmed with a dip of his head.

Her heart felt heavy, heavy with daggers of guilt. She had treated him so terribly, so much so in fact, that she almost regretted her mouthing off to him the day before. Almost.

Chewing her bottom lip—a habit she'd developed when she was a young girl—she reckoned that an apology was in order for Ricochet Chapel. But apologies were not her thing. She'd never been comfortable with them. She had found that they were for weaklings. *Excuses. Those are just excuses. I can't back out this time. He deserves both my thanks and atonement. It would be dishonorable not to.*

She might have been temperamental and untrusting of others, but she was not dishonorable. She had to face the wagon master again with remorse and in great haste. She couldn't possibly keep these censured feelings on her chest any longer than she had to. She'd do it the moment she got back to camp.

Her gaze shifted upward to meet the curious stare of Mace. She realized that he hadn't said a word but had only watched her with a lost expression. Looking rather odd and lost in a trance, she composed and excused herself from his awkward presence. She headed for Miller's Mercantile to find Charity, hoping to rush her along so that they could get back to the wagon train. A tremendous amount of guilt was killing her inwardly.

"Oh, Rosie!" Charity rushed to meet her, upon her entrance into the quaint shop. In her hands, she held two different-colored shawls: one as white as snow and the other rose pink. "Which one do you like?"

Rosemary, who was at a loss, said, "Charity, I know for certain that your papa doesn't have money for those. And shouldn't you be shopping for supplies?"

Charity made an annoyed click with her tongue. "I've already completed that. Mr. Beckett just took my packages to the cart. Now, which one?"

With a roll of her eyes, Rosemary lowered her friend's hands, which were holding the clothing. "We simply cannot afford them."

With her tone like that of a disappointed child, Charity remarked, "Surely, my papa won't mind if we use some of the funds."

Staring at the shawls made of silk and lace, she found them all too tempting. Indeed, the pieces were beautiful, and they outshined any of Rosemary's own clothing, but the price seemed awfully high. The pink one caught her attention the most. It had a rose pattern on the back and finely stitched lace on the front. But she couldn't possibly take advantage of the old preacher by using his money, especially when they had such a long journey ahead of them.

Rosemary sighed in exasperation. "Put the shawls down. Let's go back to the cart." Forcing her friend's hand, the two of them placed the clothing down and exited the mercantile.

"Afternoon, ladies," Victor Marsh said in a smooth tone from the boardwalk. He tilted his hat with one hand while holding a package in the other. "Find everything?"

Charity smiled. "I didn't know you were heading to town too; otherwise, we would have invited you along with our group, Victor." As the preacher's daughter talked, Rosemary noticed the eye of the cook on her. His eyes flickered with a fondness that she couldn't decipher. Insecurity set in.

He chuckled. "I had some work to get done beforehand. May I escort you ladies back to the cart?"

Following him across the dusty streets, Rosemary noticed how confident and charming he appeared, but it was not at all in the manner of Ricochet, who had a sense of humbleness and security. The wagon master performed his duties with discretion and compassion when he wasn't teasing her. Victor was almost the opposite.

When they arrived at the rendezvous, Lily Garrison sat in the front of the cart, eyeing Isaac Beckett with bashful eyes and an elegant blush. She and Isaac were in deep conversation while Autumn and Andrew sat close to each other and kept quietly to themselves. They returned with haste to camp before suppertime. Charity conjured up a storm of stories, as Victor rode his stallion next to her.

Rosemary kept mostly to herself, speaking only when Charity asked her a question. She eyed the stranger to their far left: Mace, who rode with watchful eyes. His words lingered on the edges of her mind. He hadn't rescued her, but Ricochet had. Ricochet was the hero that had taken control of her thoughts. She'd had the nerve to send him on his way, time and time again, and she had done so in a none-too-friendly manner.

It was another half an hour before they reached camp. The women went to make the evening meal. Once dinner was made, Rosemary trekked out on her own for a spell. Although she was starving and at her wit's end trying to keep Charity's flirtations with Mace Chronicle at bay, she set off to find the wagon master. It was about time that she ended this guilt down in her heart. Once it was done, she could be rid of it and move on to ignoring him and other men.

She searched for him where she had seen him hours earlier. He had vanished into thin air. Puzzled, she decided to first eat supper and then take another gander around the camp. Surely, he must be close by.

Supper was a fresh supply of berries found by one of the men, fire potatoes, and venison stew. The venison had come from Edward Jones, who had been hunting only hours beforehand. He sat proudly admiring his handiwork. He had already finished his second plate.

Dinner was cleaned up and put away, but there was still no wagon master. Rosemary was beginning to think that he had up and left or died somewhere. Somehow, she cringed at the thought of him dying. His strong muscular frame lying on the ground didn't seem right. Her heart ached at the imagining. A deep longing and a sighing crept up into her soul.

She drove it aside, wondering what had gotten into her. Men were evil. She shouldn't be craving his undying attention this way. Getting back to her mission, she rolled her shoulders back. Her left one was still achy. Then she marched on to find him. Dusk was on the camp, and there still was no sign of Ricochet Chapel. Angrily, she gave up the chase and stormed her way back to the Coles' wagon.

Many of the pioneers had started to head inside their land schooners for some sleep because they were exhausted from the long day. Two watchmen stood guard over the corral: Isaac and Edward.

For a minute, Rosemary halted, taking in the beautiful view of the moon rising above the mountains. Early stars twinkled overhead, and the sun started its descent below the horizon. She trekked back to her wagon, but before getting too close, she found the desperate need to relieve herself. Why hadn't she noticed it sooner?

Heading over to where the women's relieving sight was located in the wooded area, she scurried behind a tree. It was not too deeply in the dark but was far enough away so that no watchman could see.

She finished and started to head back when someone's hand clamped down on her shoulder and another over her mouth. Her muffled cries went unheard, and she whimpered helplessly. She did the only thing she could think of and clawed at the hand on her lips. Then she dove for freedom once he was stunned. She wasn't quick enough, for the hands had her pinned once again, this time against a tree trunk. She fought harder than ever. Panic seized her when she remembered the note that her admirer had left before she had run away.

I will find you again, my Rose, and next time, you will not leave my side.

Her pulse quickened. He'd found her. It was him! Dread and fear filled the atmosphere surrounding her, and she trembled all over. Her arms might be pinned, but her legs most certainly were not, so she kicked with all her might in the place where no man ever wished to be kicked. The toe of her boot struck hard in his groin, and immediately, his grip loosened. It was a tactic that her pa had warned her to use in times of distress.

He let out a loud moan, collapsing to the dirt in slow motion. When she heard his voice, she realized that she knew him. He had been the one that she had been looking for all this time. She leaned back against the trunk of the tree. "Mr. Chapel?"

After a few seconds, she heard his wavering voice spoke while he hunkered on the ground in a fetal position. "You pack a mighty wallop," he winced and eased back into a sitting position next to a tree root. He held his eyes shut. The moon lit up his sweaty face. His left hand went to his thigh, rubbing it and occasionally slapping it due to the pain. "For all that is holy—" he didn't finish for another agonizing spasm took its hold.

In shock, Rosemary held her tongue. Then a relieved and amused smile curled her lips upward. She placed a hand over her mouth to stifle the growing laughter, but a giggle escaped nonetheless. The whole event had been so frightening until Ricochet, the big strong wagon master, had fallen. She doubled over with howling laughter. Her cheeks reddened, and her lungs were breathless. Her knees hit the ground, and before she knew it, she was in tears. It had been so long since she'd laughed in such a way, so very long.

Ricochet got on his knees, but he was still bent over uncomfortably. Because of his heavy breathing and groaning, he could not speak a word, but she could sense that he was not delighted by her reaction. Rosemary continued to laugh and snicker, but feeling Ricochet's warning glare on her, she stopped.

Even though it had gotten dark, the moon rays glowed around them, and she was able to see clearly. Her eyes adjusted to see his outline. He was standing slightly bent but on his feet nonetheless. He picked up his felt-covered hat, which apparently had fallen during the struggle. He sighed and then said, "I haven't been struck like that by a woman since my ma tanned my backside when I was a boy. Don't you know it ain't right to kick a man?"

Rosemary rose to the defense, now standing up. "Serves you right for sneaking up on a lady. I thought you might be—"she stopped. There was no chance she could mention the admirer, not to him. Her anger kindled against herself for even considering it so recklessly. Carefully, she reconstructed her words, and a smart comeback flew from her lips. "That should make you think twice before snatching a woman the way you did. What were you up to on the women's side of the woods anyway?"

He shrugged his broad shoulders with a hefty laugh. "I suppose I did deserve it. I hadn't meant to scare you, but there was a nice lookin' buck standing over there, and I didn't want you scarin' it off. I've been out hunting."

Rosemary noted the large barrel of a rifle that was lying on the ground by his feet and several corpses of rabbit, pheasant, and other small game tied together with rope. At least, she knew he wasn't lying in the hopes of catching her off guard so that he could have his way with her. He'd really been hunting or trying to do so before she'd disrupted him. Relief washed over her.

He rubbed his neck, "However, this site is for the men. Didn't anyone tell you?"

Her cheeks flushed pink, warming tremendously. "This is the *men's* side?" She gulped and chewed her lip, feeling embarrassed. Her back stiffened as she realized the risky situation that she had walked into. *Any man could've seen ...*

He chuckled as he rubbed his thumb once beneath his nose. Laugh lines formed around his eyes and at the corners of his mouth. "Don't fret, Miss Barker. I didn't see anything apart from you walking toward the camp. But next time, you should pay more attention to which side's yours. Also, that surprise attack," he blew out a breath, "is best saved for a real attacker." He chuckled again.

Silence fell over them. Nothing could be heard besides the chirping of crickets and the occasional howl of a coyote. The breeze was light, not even strong enough to blow the tree limbs. Rosemary swallowed, which sounded like a roaring waterfall in her ears compared to the quiet of the woods. Then she admitted, "I've been looking for you all over camp since before suppertime."

She could see the silvery light of the moon outline his stance as he listened to her words. He shifted closer. "Oh? Why's that?" His curious tone made her heart skip a beat and then two.

She pressed her back close to the trunk. The bark dug into the fabric of her blouse. "I wanted to thank you and also to apologize," she further admitted but tensed as he moved closer.

"Is that so?" he asked as his head tilted with innocent confusion. He was so close now that she could smell him. He had a woodsy and manly scent. He remained respectful of her personal space. "What for?" He prodded her for more of an explanation.

Her eyes grew wide, and she searched for words that were lost to her now. She had no retort or remark to give. It occurred to her that no other pioneers were near the spot where they stood. She and Ricochet were alone¾together.

A dizzy spell hit her, and her legs buckled. She shouldn't be there, especially with the man she so disliked. It wasn't proper, and it sure wasn't something that she wanted. Hadn't she mentioned that his company was tiring and that she hated him? She should've heeded her own words and run back to the wagon by now, but she couldn't seem to move. She didn't want to move. It was a dangerous position for an untrusting woman to be in.

"The river!" she blurted out at last as she recalled her mission. "You saved me from the river. I wanted to thank you personally for that." She felt the sting of the healing cut on her side as she shifted.

"Go ahead," he said, crossing his arms and waiting.

Agitated, she balled her hands into fists. He'd been expecting her gratitude since that day, and he cockily awaited her to show it. Well, no man would force her to say or not to say what she wanted or didn't want. But knowing that the right thing to do was speaking her thankfulness, she grumbled through clenched teeth, "Thank you."

He thought for a moment and then laughed while shaking his head. "Ya know, that seemed kinda harsh for a thank-you. I don't think I want to accept it. I did risk my life for you after all. It doesn't seem right that I get an ungrateful scowl for it." He rocked back and forth on his heels mockingly.

Rosemary, who was at the point of simmering, raised her voice to a shrill scream. "You vile man! I wish you *hadn't* saved me!" She raised her right palm to land a slap on his cheek, but his large hand clasped her wrist quicker than she could maneuver around it. She tugged against his grip, but his strength greatly outmatched her own.

"You are a puzzle, Miss Barker," he teased, as he grinned wider. "You'd actually be quite fetching if you weren't so temperamental. What's got you all up a tree?"

This was the closest that she had ever been in proximity to a man, while being conscious that is, and she thought her heart would leap from her chest cavity. She trembled, and her belly was in tight knots. His head lowered to hers, and it donned on her just how tall he stood— or maybe her height was lacking more than she realized. In panic, her eyes widened.

He narrowed his eyes. "Look, I haven't done a thing to deserve such an attitude, and yet, it seems as though you think I have it out for you."

"Let me go," she half whispered.

"Why is that?" he said, pressuring her. "I'm trying to set things straight here."

She cried aloud, twisting her arm in his grasp. "I said, let me go!"

Flashes and images of roses and letters scattered around in her mind. The gifts laced with threats and empty professions of love were the admirer's way of coaxing and deceiving her to follow him. She'd learned from him that men were users and takers. They didn't care what happened to the weaker sex, as long as they got what they wanted. Her admirer's words surfaced once again: "You cannot hope to flee my eye."

She trembled. Her back was as stiff as a board, and her heart was beating like a drum. Ricochet's power and grip scared her, not that he held her wrist tightly or threateningly, but it brought back a time of terror in her past that still haunted her. A faceless shadow of a man followed her no matter where she ran. Tears burned the back of her eyes, and she wriggled from his grasp. "Stop! Please," she begged. "Just let me go."

He backed off a step as his brow wrinkled in concern. "Miss Barker, is something the matter? I didn't mean to …" He trailed off and let her go as if she were a rattlesnake about to bite him.

She knew that he'd seen the hurt and twisted expression on her face, but she had no strength to hide it. Her eyes were glossy and dazed, and she was frozen in terror. She stared through him as if he were made of glass. "Don't hurt me," she pleaded softly. "Please, don't hurt me."

Kneeling down in front of her now, Ricochet tilted his head quizzically. "Hurt you? Darlin', I promise I ain't gonna hurt you. I was only trying to get some answers. Why would I hurt you?" He didn't touch her again but kept his distance. He searched their surroundings with a careful gaze as if he suspected the thing that had spooked her was present among the trees.

Full droplets of tears dripped from the corners of her eyes. His worried questions were lost on her. She had endured several breakdowns, but none had been as bad as this one. The farther she ran from her admirer, the worse they got. She wanted relief from the nightmare, but it only grew stronger.

Ricochet pressed his interrogations, but she didn't utter a word. Shaking her head slowly, she wondered whether she should blurt the whole mess out to a stranger. Making up her mind, she pushed him back, although he barely moved an inch, and then she dashed toward the campsite.

She didn't heed his calls, but she kept running. She wished that she hadn't gone into the woods. Tears streamed down her cheeks uncontrollably as she entered the caravan's corral and sprinted across the open circle to her and Charity's wagon. She climbed in. She was careful not to step on the sleeping young lady, who lay sprawled out on the floor.

Peeking out through the canvas flaps, she spotted Ricochet running into the circle at a full-on sprint before skidding to a halt. He doubled over out of breath. When he straightened and looked around for her, defeat was evident on his expression. His was gazing at her wagon, and she swiftly ducked back into the canvas to avoid him.

Her pulse thudded in her ears, and her breathing was shallow. Resting her head against the wooden frame behind her, she sat and considered her actions. She hadn't thought that he would be so fresh and blunt. She barely knew him. But every time she closed her eyes, she could see him leaning in close for answers. The image was aggravating, and complex convictions resurfaced. She simply didn't want a man in her life, and most certainly, she didn't Ricochet Chapel. She couldn't give him the answers that he was seeking. It would put him in harm's way. His wooing would have to stop, and she would have to stop the folly that was rampantly taking hold in her heart.

Tiredness set in, and soon, her tears dried as she fell into slumber. Then the nightmares came. This time, it seemed that the admirer had found her, and she couldn't awaken. She'd struggled hard to open her eyes, but exhaustion was too great. She remained in her dreamland with the admirer's words echoing in her ears. *I've found you, my dear. At long last, I've come for you.*

# Chapter 9

❧❧

Early the next morning, Ricochet went for a swim in a nearby creek. Dawn had yet to reveal itself, and he wanted to have a good scrub before the long trek of the trail. He inspected the wide creek for snakes, lathered himself with soap, and then jumped into the creek. He'd never been accepting of the lizard family. He found them too covered in scales and creepy looking for his liking. He didn't skirt around the creatures as a young filly would around a mouse, but he simply knew the dangers that reptiles brought to a fight.

He rinsed off and dried himself. Then he dressed in a clean pair of brown pants and a blue flannel shirt. For the finishing touch, he tied his red neckerchief around his neck and donned his Stetson.

It was now the break of dawn. The sun was rising up over the hillside behind the trees. The sun's rays warmed the treetops, and birds sang happily overhead. The creek's surface rippled as a light breeze blew. Crickets chirped nearby.

Ricochet relaxed, leaning his back against the trunk of a tree. No one would blame him for finding some peace before waking up the pioneers at camp, so he waited for the sun's full rise.

His distracted mind was due to the events of previous evening. Hunting had been his top priority until Rosemary had shown up. It had never been his intention to scare her. A ghost spasm shot down his legs as he remembered it. His gut clenched. The kick to his groin had been unbearable, but nothing compared to the absolute expression of terror he'd witnessed on her face. The woman had sass and a mouthful of spite, but when he'd touched her, it had all vanished, and it had been replaced by fear. Like a storm cloud that is blown away to reveal the sunshine, she'd shone a fraction of her inner self. She was a young, frightened child in the body of a grown woman.

The question still remained. Why was she afraid? She'd flinched when he had grabbed her wrist, and he hadn't meant it to be at all intimidating. He'd thought nothing of the gesture, but now, his conscience was running rampant with guilt. Something about men had Rosemary Barker scared and not lightly.

A sigh escaped him, and he began to pray for guidance. He truly did care for the woman, and he would do most anything to gain her undivided attention. He had wanted to get to know her better, but it was proving to be more difficult the longer they were on the trail.

The way her eyes had dimmed and her expression had contorted during their meeting in the woods told him that there was something deeper that she wasn't willing for anyone to know. The look she'd given him was pure terror. He'd seen her act skittish around people before, but she'd never broken down in front of them the way that she had with him the night before.

He began to suspect that she'd had some trouble in the past with a man, or perhaps, it had been more recent. Just the thought of someone laying a hand on her was enough to boil the blood in his veins. If it were up to him, he'd lock her away from every eye and protect her in a sealed tower for the rest of her life, but that was irrational thinking. She didn't belong to him or anyone else for that matter. He shouldn't be as overprotective as he was, but Rosemary brought something out in him that no woman ever had. He couldn't fathom someone hurting her. *Unless she spouted off something terrible,* he thought as he snickered inwardly.

Whatever the case, something about Rosemary Barker didn't set right in the back of his head, and Ricochet decided, right then and there, he would gain answers before the journey's end.

Standing and stretching, he stuffed the soap and other items that he'd used into the pouch of his saddlebag. He flung it over his shoulder as he made his way back to the wagons. It was time to saddle up and move on. With a little over a thousand miles left of their travel, he was glad to know that they had made good time despite the mishap that had happened at the river crossing. He prayed to God that no other accidents would delay their arrival.

The pioneers awoke and got ready quickly in order to gain an early start on the trail. Breakfast was served without a fire per Ricochet's request. Jerk, hardtack, and dried berries of various kinds were eaten. He ignored the complaints from Edward and Victor for having no freshly brewed coffee, but the wagon master had felt the wind starting to pick up. The last thing that he needed was a fire spreading. They were in for another storm, and it would be a fierce one at that. They would have to get ahead of it.

A plateau of wasteland awaited them, and water would be scarce. Ricochet had already started to sweat just thinking about it. Even in a storm, the plateau would be hot and humid, but at least drinkable water could be gathered from the rain as they traveled.

He made the final call, and the wagons lined up in their usual order. He had Mace ride up and down both sides to make a swift inspection of the land schooners. Then they headed out.

Day in and day out, it had been the same schedule: Eat, hit the trail, have lunch, hit the trail, camp, eat, and so on. The wasteland had been difficult for many pioneers, and water supplies were diminishing faster than Ricochet had anticipated. His only hope for them had been to find a creek along the path, but sadly, nothing had turned up thus far. The storm from days ago seemed like a distant and fond memory. His body ached from sitting in the saddle for hours on end, and he had to shift his weight from one side to the other constantly.

He hadn't spoken to Rosemary since the night in the woods, however, he had seen her frequently rushing around the Webbs' wagon, as she helped Katrina, whose pregnancy was past the due date and made the mother sicker than ever. Although he wanted to approach Rosemary, his courage frankly left him whenever he had the notion to do so. She never even glanced his way, let alone spoke to him. An anxious sensation swept over him.

It wasn't until the seventh day of silence between them that Rosemary rushed to him and Mace. Her face was stricken with worry.

Her voice was hushed but urgent. "It's Katrina." Ricochet held his breath as concern darkened his expression. "She's in labor. We must stop at once."

Ricochet steadied his mustang and stopped. "Then we'll stop." He turned to Mace, who gave him a blank stare. "Inform everyone of the delay. We won't be going anywhere until Mrs. Webb has the baby."

As Mace rode off with great haste, Ricochet caught sight of Rosemary wringing her hands nervously. Her cheeks were flushed pink, her curls were tied messily atop her head, and her backbone was as stiff as a board. He thought she was stunning, regardless of how exhausted she appeared. He slid from the saddle to stand before her. She shied away.

"Katrina will want me by her side," she said, trying to excuse herself.

He took her arm as she was in mid spin. "Miss Barker."

She shook from his grip. Her eyes gazed at anything besides him. The avoidance hurt more than she could ever know. "Please. I must go."

It wasn't a second later that he had his fingers wrapped around her small wrist. She was so fragile and breakable compared to his iron-like grip. He hesitated even placing a hand on her, fearing that she may fall to pieces.

Ricochet awkwardly ran a thumb beneath his nose with his other hand and spoke in a whisper, "Look. If you're avoiding me because of what happened," he quieted all the more, "in the woods or if I hurt you by what I said, I certainly didn't …" He heard a loud strained cry coming from the Webbs' wagon.

Rosemary whirled on her heels again, twisted out of his grasp, and then went wide-eyed with both excitement and distress. That's when Ricochet noticed the frilly Lily Garrison and flamboyant Charity Cole scurrying toward him and Rosemary. They held their dresses high, rushing with all manner of urgency.

"Rosie," Charity began after catching her breath. "Katrina wants to see you."

Her voice like that of an angel's, Lily pressed further. "She's refusing everything we give her until she sees you. You must come quick!" With that, the two ladies half dragged and half pushed Rosemary along.

Ricochet shifted his feet, played with the reins that were in his fist, and watched the women leave his presence. He rested his left hand on his belt. Then he saw Mace, with Jackson in tow, approaching.

Jackson was the first to speak. "Is it true? Is the lady having her baby?"

A nod from the wagon master gave the old minister the incentive to grin. "I'll be praying the labor goes well."

Ricochet half smiled, finding that his mind was distracted, but vowed anyway, "As will I."

The men made quick work of circling the wagons and tending to the cattle and livestock. The women busied themselves outside the Webbs' wagon by knitting blankets, sewing baby clothes, and answering Katrina's every need. The only woman that had stayed inside the wagon with Katrina and her husband, Jacob, was Rosemary.

Ricochet found himself pacing. He'd hardly ever seen a newborn, let alone one on the Oregon Trail. How would the mother and her baby take to life in the Wild West? His curiosity most definitely could have killed a cat, but he tried to busy himself with other matters such as feeding the livestock, attending to the supply wagon's axle, which was in need of a slight repair after the wear and tear that it had taken, and planning a watch for that night. Forcing himself to work on chores, he headed for the supply wagon.

# Chapter 10

"Rosemary," Jacob said, as he looked up from his kneeling position at Katrina's legs, "hand me another cloth."

She did as she was told. She quickly passed the linen to the doctor. She stroked Katrina's forehead, attempting to soothe some of the aching mother's weariness. It had been almost four hours, and there was no baby. Rosemary was starting to feel anxious and somewhat sorry for the young soon-to-be mother. The two women had become so close since the river incident. They appeared to be as similar and like-minded as sisters, but this was one trial that Rosemary simply couldn't accompany her in.

Katrina craned her neck to gaze up at her friend. She had a strained smile on her lips. "Please, Rosemary, hold my hand."

The young woman did as Katrina wished and held her hand as another labor pain took hold. The pains were frequent. She was having one on top of another now, but it had been this way for nearly an hour. The doctor's wife was exhausted. It was then that Rosemary understood how serious childbearing could be, and she never wanted the same thing to happen to her¾not ever.

"Pray with me," Katrina pleaded through clenched teeth.

Rosemary's eyes widened. She hadn't prayed in—come to think of it, she'd ceased praying since her parents' death almost four months ago. She didn't remember how. But for the good of Katrina and the baby, she would try. She opened her mouth and spoke quietly, feeling awkward and strongly convicted inside. She prayed for Katrina's health, the baby to be delivered safely, and Jacob to have wisdom as a new father.

Once she was done, the doctor gave the all clear to push again, and the veins in Katrina's forehead bulged as she gave it her all. After another push, a small heart-melting cry filled the air. Katrina laid her head back into Rosemary's lap. Her breathing was ragged, and her cheeks were severely flushed. Jacob cradled the newborn in his arms, already using his fatherly instincts. He grinned as tears brimmed in his eyes at the miracle before him.

"It's a boy," he announced proudly.

Katrina accepted the beautiful bundle into her bosom, caressing the baby and kissing his head. "Welcome to the world, little one."

Jacob scooted closer to his wife and son and then planted a kiss on his wife's crown. "You did wonderful, my dear."

Katrina smiled and peered up at her husband. "Samuel. We'll name him Samuel."

Jacob wiped his son's face with a damp cloth. "Samuel it is."

Katrina squeezed Rosemary's hand and beamed thankfully in her direction. Rosemary never felt more wonderful in her life.

It was well past suppertime when Rosemary finally emerged from the Webbs' wagon. Food had been left out for her and the Webbs, although now, it was cold. She didn't mind. Her ravishing hunger was greater than her desire for a warm meal. She took a tin cup and poured what was left of the lukewarm coffee in it. Then she took large gulps. The day had been a long one. Another delay in their journey would put them back a few days in their arrival to Oregon City, but the miracle had been worth it.

As the last of the coffee settled in Rosemary's stomach, the wagoners began to gather at the beckoned call of Parson Jackson. The group huddled together and then took their seats around the campfire. Charity found a spot beside Rosemary. Jacob led Katrina, who was holding their newborn, to a seat on a pallet of blankets to Rosemary's left. The new mother was still in a great deal of pain, but no one stopped her from hearing the devotional around the campfire.

Once everyone had taken a seat, the preacher took out a worn leather-bound book from his coat pocket. The cover had been torn, and the pages were a daffodil-yellow color, but Jackson held it as if it was a priceless treasure. He opened the King James Bible to a portion of scripture.

Before reading it, he addressed everyone. "We have seen miracle after miracle aboard this wagon train, and I thought it fitting for us to have a short devotional of thanks to the Almighty. Ricochet and I have been talking about the hand of God being upon us from the start of our journey until to now. It amazes me to see the blessings He has bestowed upon us." He grinned brightly at the Webb family and then nodded to Rosemary.

As she listened to the old-time preacher, Rosemary was drawn in her thoughts to a time when she had enjoyed life and the God who had given her that life. Her father had been a humble barber. Her mother had been a dressmaker. Neither one of them had had enough money. They only had enough to scrape by.

Her mother, Lindsey Barker, had been a woman of servitude and faith. She had never complained about their having the finest fashions or the largest of banquets. They didn't have much in their home, but their small mercantile managed to give them the means to live a peaceful and enjoyable life nonetheless. Rosemary, at one time, had longed to be the spitting image of her mother, but she only physically resembled her mother. Humbleness and character were highly lacking in her.

Her father had been a hard-working shop owner and a deacon in their hometown church of a few members. She had never seen him riled up or angry in her presence. He had respected the Word of God as the final authority. In a way, Rosemary thought that Jackson resembled him, not in appearance but in spirit.

Good memories only lasted a little while before Rosemary before reality sank in. Her parents were dead. They had been burnt to death while she had been off with her young beau in town. She'd taken her sweet time getting home, walking the scenic route. That had been when she saw the horror.

Her house had turned to dust and been burnt to the ground. Her father's body had been nothing but ashes. But her mother¾her beautiful darling mother¾had been soiled of her innocence before she had been tied to a post on the house porch and set fire to. Rosemary could still hear her mother's wailing and fading screams as the fire burnt up her unblemished skin.

Two days later, she had received another note from her admirer, testifying in full detail of what he had done. That had been the beginning of her hatred for the opposite gender, which had grown immensely over the weeks following the incident.

The sting of tears grew as Rosemary recalled the past, and she quickly dabbed at her eyes for fear of anyone noticing, especially Charity. She could never wish the painful burden on her friend.

The devotion concluded after a hymn. Jackson had read from Psalm 23. Then it was testimony time. Near the end, Rosemary saw Ricochet stand to speak. Her heart seized, and her breath caught. He was rather striking in the firelight: a tall shadow donned with a dark hat and eyes of clearest blue that glowed in the twilight. She had not wanted to fall for a man or allow one to hold and kiss her, but she'd begun to have wild dreams regarding such things—a new life with him.

Anger boiled in her veins. She had let her guard down. The delusions taking place caused hate to fester within her breast. *He will never touch me again,* she vowed.

Her ears tuned in as Ricochet gave an account of God's protection in his life. His story was short and vague. It only contained the story of his salvation after his father's untimely death and his journey out west for the first time.

He said, "I haven't been a saved man for very long. In fact, it's been about three years now. A person doesn't quite know what they have until they've lost it. It took God removing everything from my life before I realized that I was a lost and vile soul in need of saving." He hung his head, and Rosemary could taste the bitterness of his words. She, too, knew that feeling. ·

"My old man died before I came to know God. My pa was my hero, my idol. I never got to share my precious gift with him before he passed, and it eats me up every day." His words sang through her ears. It was a flat and mellow note. It shattered the understanding that she carried of the hate inside her. She began to wonder if her malice was necessary. What if she was disobeying the Almighty instead of choosing His way of compassion like Ricochet had? She had never once seen him cuss out another person or dismissed someone out of anger.

He finished his statement of faith with these words. "I've made mistakes in the past, ones that I'm not proud of, but the Lord's sure been gracious to me. If I had the chance, I wouldn't change a single trial He's placed in my life. I know that it's all been for my good and for His glory."

While hearing the end of Ricochet's rather heartbreaking tale of his past, Rosemary couldn't hold back her tears. Something stirred inside her, which had ceased to move since her parents had died and left her alone, heartbroken, and scared: compassion. She yearned to trust in someone bigger than herself, this world, and any admirer.

Her chest throbbed and the dam of kept-back emotions tore somewhat. She excused herself, rising to find a reclusive place to gather her thoughts. She could faintly overhear Jackson concluding the meeting. His voice was the only noise in the night air. She dabbed under her eyes with her fingertips, as she made her way to the water kegs beside the supply wagon.

The majority of her tears had not only been because Ricochet had mentioned his father but also because he maintained so much joy throughout his trials while she retained all the bitterness in the world. He had been betrayed by God and robbed of his father's presence, yet he believed that it was God's will. It didn't seem fair that Ricochet should have such hope while carrying the burden of it all on his shoulders. Yes, he carried great sorrow and pain, but his soul displayed absolute peace. He had a type of happiness that never left him.

Rosemary stopped mid trek. She had never seen him upset, not even once. In the several weeks that she'd come to know him or rather, gotten acquainted him, she had seen no sign of hate¾not like what she bore. His family was gone, and hers was too. It simply wasn't fair! Why did he have that kind of peace and she …

Her hands grasped the sides of the water barrel. Then she leaned over to see her reflection. It was dim but visible nonetheless. The person staring back looked nothing like the girl she had known months ago. She'd changed so much. The stress, loss, and hurt that she'd undergone had taken an immense toll on her physically, even more than she'd realized. Her face was gaunt, her body was thin and frail, and her eyes lacked life. How had it come to this? It had happened by fearing and *hating* everything.

Words could not describe how shameful she felt for the bitterness that had been infused within her soul. Life had been cruel, and her admirer had been even more so. Tragedy had struck unexpectedly, as it had for Ricochet's family, yet her anger had been kindled while his had dwindled. She couldn't comprehend it.

"Miss Barker?" She was fixed on her reflection in the water as another face appeared. Its clear eyes of crystal stared back at her. "Is everything all right? Are you feeling sick?"

She turned to face Ricochet, tilting her chin upward to meet his concerned gaze. Her mouth twisted into a foul half-circle, as she rid herself of the streaming tears. "I'm fine." Her words were hollower than she would've liked, but she prayed he wouldn't take notice.

He did. His voice was kind and compassionate as he said, "Darlin', I'd hate to call you a liar."

Why did he always make her dream up things like him holding her close to his chest, cradling her, or kissing her warmly? That dirty scoundrel played the game too hard for her liking.

He pressed further. His eyes looked for answers, drawing her close to the point where all she wanted to do was throw herself into his strong arms and cry her heart out. She managed to refrain from doing so, but the temptation was there nonetheless.

She lowered her gaze, biting her lip as she did. "Why?" she asked. Then here came the tears that she had so desperately tried to hide and barricade. After several long months, she was near the breaking point. "Why are you not angry?" she said and then half sobbed. "How can you be so joyful for what happened? Your family is gone, same as mine. You said so yourself!" She was practically shouting at him. "My parents were taken away, burnt to ashes! All that stuff you said about God and His grace are nothing but lies. He doesn't care."

He didn't flinch one bit. Instead, he let her continue to rant. "You act as though you haven't a care in the world." Her chest heaved for a breath, and she pointed at her own chest. "I've endured so much." Her voice cracked. "Lost so much. How can you be so trusting of something you can't see?"

His brow furrowed and then softened, as if he fully understood the hurt in her eyes. He placed both hands on her shoulders, gently stroking them with his thumbs. "Rosemary," he said softly, "I know that trust doesn't come easily. It has to be earned. And finding the courage to rely on an invisible being is all the more difficult. But I assure you that I wouldn't be here today without God's merciful hand."

How dare he touch her! She shook his hands away. "Lies! You act so angelic and perfect all the time, but I know that inside, you're as cruel and evil as any man. You're nothing but a fraud, Ricochet Chapel! And I won't succumb to your trickery any longer."

She realized then that this was the first time she had used his actual name—his given name—and no matter how angry she was, she relished it rolling off her tongue. His name was like a stronghold she could hold onto. She felt safe just saying it. Emotions toyed inside her chest, bouncing, fluttering, and tugging back and forth. She didn't know what to do with the pent-up feelings she had, other than let them all out and drown the wagon master in them.

But the instant he had caught wind of her using his first name, she had seen a sparkle in his eyes that she'd never previously witnessed. Besides it filling her with glee, she grew sick in pure hatred. Was he enjoying her temper? Her own question was answered the moment he unleashed a winning smirk. In fact, he was savoring her pain! Oh, that was the last straw.

She stomped her foot, huffing loudly. She desperately wanted to say the no-good words that popped into her head, but her conscience held her back by only a thread. She would have to settle for a slap to his face instead, so pulling back her arm, she catapulted her palm to the right side of his jaw. It wasn't until her hand came within centimeters of its target that Ricochet caught her wrist. It had happened faster than she could have imagined. He pulled her to him with incredible force, jerking her from her planted stance instantly.

"Rosemary." his baritone voice demanded her undivided attention, and she gave it to him, even if it was only for a minute or two. Their eyes locked. His eyes were usually so kind and caring, but now, they were filled with fascinating mystery, which she wanted to dive into and explore. She wanted to know his every thought.

She blinked, and the two minutes were up. Rosemary wriggled in his viselike grip. "Let go of me," she growled through clenched teeth.

As if the last thread of his patience had been severed at long last, a red color lit up his facial features, and Rosemary half-expected steam to billow out of his ears. She'd wanted to urge out some kind of response from him, but perhaps, she'd taken things a little too far. His grip tightened considerably, and she suspected that he was actually furious with her.

"No, I won't," he refused in a none-too-friendly tone. His grip tightened more.

Finally, she would prove that he wasn't the Goody Two-shoes that he pretended to be. But just when a glimpse of his anger surged, it vanished. His calm serenity returned, and his hand loosened around her wrist. He sighed, and her heart skipped a beat. His clear eyes pinned her where she stood.

"You are absolutely the most difficult woman I've ever met, Miss Barker, but don't think for a second that you have me all figured out. Now, I don't know the details 'bout your past, but I imagine some fella hurt you, and that's why you have such a dislike for me and any other man that takes an interest." He paused slightly and then said, "Why, you're downright hateful." He hung his thumbs on the sides of his belt and shifted position. "You think you're hiding behind a mask of pain, but you're not foolin' me. I can see the fear on your face as plain as day. What is it about me that makes you so frightened?"

He wasn't wrong. She had been rather hurtful and mean toward him, but she wouldn't go as far as saying, "Downright hateful." She was merely telling him that she wasn't interested through her harsh comments and fiery glares. Maybe she was being a little dramatic regarding his humorous ways and carefree character. Perhaps telling him that she, "Hated him," was a bit over the top. Bringing all that to mind, Rosemary began to blush and hang her head in shame. A woman never treated a man with such disrespect.

Ricochet continued after not getting a response from her. "There's one thing you oughta know, little filly. Not all men are alike. I happen to care a great deal for you, and I can't ignore the fact that you are all I think and pray about every second of every day. When I think that there might've been another man hurting you, why, I'd do just about anything to keep you safe."

Rosemary's mouth gaped as her tears flowed. She'd never witnessed such amazing devotion and the way that he carried for her in any other man. One minute, he was shouting at her for being so spiteful, and the next minute, he was professing his feelings for her. She didn't understand his way of thinking in the least; however, she was surprised at how hearing his words made her heart ache so much inside.

He was silent for a time to let his words sink into her scarred heart. Then he went on with his confession. "Rosemary, I'm not perfect, and I sure ain't no saint, but I'm trying." He chewed the inside of his cheek for a moment. Most likely, he was stalling to gather up enough courage for his next statement.

"The testimony I gave tonight wasn't everything. My pa did die but before his time. He was shot ... by my brother, Jedediah. We had always been at brotherly odds about everything, but when my pa decided to give the deed to his land as an inheritance to us, it got worse. It got to the point that Jed lured Pa to the barn out back and shot him full of lead. I was out hunting when it happened. I came home to find Pa lying face down in the dirt and Jed holding the rifle. We fought."

His eyes darkened, and Rosemary got the sudden itch to wrap her arms around him and kiss away the painful memory. *Foolish womanly instincts!* she thought.

When he faced her again, his pupils were dilated, and his eyes were cold and sorrowful. "I ended up chasing after him on horseback to a cliff near our property. I aimed to, uh, that is I wanted to kill him. In the end, he fell into the ravine." He ended his tale and then let her go. A strange, empty sensation clouded her mind when he stepped away. She wondered why the blame fool couldn't hold her longer. But then again, she shouldn't want him to.

He swallowed, placed his hands on his hips, and then tilted his head downward, acting very much ashamed. "The sad truth is that he begged for mercy before I chased after him, but I didn't want to hear any of it. I was so full of hatred that I caused the death of my own flesh and blood. I let him fall off the cliff without a second thought. When I had aimed my rifle at Jed's chest, something stopped me from pulling the trigger. I couldn't do it, but sure as the stars, I wanted to.

"Jed called me a coward and said that falling to his death would be a more worthy way to die than for me to grant him any sort of clemency. I caused his death even though I didn't pull the trigger. Maybe you were right in calling me a fraud." His eyes found hers once more. "I'm nothing but a coldhearted killer at heart."

Rosemary cupped her hands over her mouth in shock. She had originally thought that the carefree man was a flirtatious and sly trickster, but she never imagined him to be a deceitful murderer. No, that wasn't quite right. He hadn't killed his brother. He'd certainly intended to, but something had stopped him. He wasn't cold blooded at all, not really.

But a stir of indignation rose up inside her, which said that he deserved whatever punishment came his way for even desiring to kill his own kin. She should've known that behind his calm exterior and beautiful smile, he was no different from her admirer—he was a killer at heart. Of course, she never imagined him as being something so awful, but her gut feeling had warned her that they were similar.

Then again, she never thought any man was kind or compassionate. Perhaps, there were a few that were kind like Preacher Jackson, but it was quite the chore to figure out which ones were honest and which ones were deceitful, so Rosemary made it a point not to bother finding out who was which kind.

Although she now understood Ricochet's dark secret, somehow, she didn't fear him one bit. This was really shocking to her. She had planned to walk away upon learning the skeletons in his closet, but now, her feet seemed permanently glued into place.

What if it had been her in his same predicament? She most certainly would've done the same thing, but that didn't make attempting to kill someone right. If it had been her against her admirer and she was the one armed with a gun, she'd definitely have filled him with lead and gladly watched him fall off the cliff. She'd never admit it aloud, but she wouldn't have done anything different from what Ricochet had tried to do to avenge his father's death. How scary to think that they were so alike and yet so different.

Ricochet cleared his throat awkwardly. "So now you know," he said and then chuckled, not out of amusement but guilt. "I've changed since then," he declared quite convincingly. "God gave me a new chance. I started to travel, and I got saved under Pastor Grant while I was back east. Then I started life out here as a wagon master." He paused and then said, "Hate is a strong thing. Let it fester, and it will destroy you. Let God take control, and I promise that He will never abandon you. He always has a plan and purpose for His children. He is the Rose of Sharon, and He never forgets His promises."

As she dwelt on that, Rosemary was engulfed in a world of questions with few answers. She'd never heard a testament of faith as he had given her right then. He was so sure of his grounding in the Lord. Truthfully, she admired that most about him, and it caused her to swoon uncontrollably. Her knees buckled. The feeling was unfamiliar to her. Yet the two of them suited each other so completely that she might as well chance it all.

Ricochet broke through her thoughts by taking hold of her hand and intertwining his fingers with her own. "May I kiss you, Rosemary?"

Her mouth gaped and her eyes widened. Trying to wrap her head around his question, she noticed his pleading, kind eyes gazing directly at her. He was awaiting her answer patiently.

She'd never kissed a man in her life apart from her father, but that was different. As a young girl, she would kiss her father on the cheek before bedtime. There was nothing romantic or passionate about it. It was an innocent bond between father and daughter. To be entirely frank, she wasn't so sure she even knew how to kiss. What exactly did one do when kissing anyway? Did one just pucker up?

She took a step back, overwhelmed by the odd request. The man was a fool if he thought he'd get a kiss out of her when she barely knew him. She would give him only one answer. He would most certainly be in for a rude awakening when he found that she wasn't giving in to his charm.

She opened her mouth to speak her disagreement, but her tone became squeaky and uncertain. This was not at all how she had planned for her rejection to come out. She attempted to pry her fingers from his. "Mr. Chapel, I can't. We barely know—"

Her reasoning was doused as soon as his lips touched hers. She stiffened as her body grew goose bumps and froze in place. The act sent her into another frenzy of emotion filled with anger, passion, relief, cowardice, and outrage. It was so sudden and abrupt that she had no time to recover. She could only stand as a statue while he took what was left of her breath away. The man was a basket case if he thought she would let him have his way with her. But one small kiss couldn't hurt, just one.

It was like an alternate world in his arms, a faraway place where she wanted to remain. His hands pressed against her back. His biceps flexed as he held her tight. He was so incredibly solid that Rosemary felt that no one could pull her out of his arms, not even the wicked man who'd sent her letter after letter of threats. Ricochet was a fortress of safety with walls that deflected the doubts that arose in her mind.

She smiled as she kissed him at that thought. They broke apart for a spell to catch their breath. When his arms loosened around her, reality set in. They couldn't be together. He was a murderer, for heaven's sake! He was deceitful. He was a robust, vigorous man of faith. She wondered why he was so difficult to figure out.

"Ric," she began, but his lips were already back over her own, cutting off any attempt she would make for ruining the moment.

The brim of his hat shaded both their eyes from the moon's rays shining down and masked their faces in darkness. Her eyes remained open in shock while his stayed closed. That's when she noticed a small but visible scar over his left eyebrow, which ran down to his eyelashes. The mark wasn't at all alarming. In fact, she found it alluring. She wondered what he had seen in his lifetime and the adventures that he had gone on while she had blocked off any hope of travel and excitement. She yearned to go with him and never leave his side.

*Absurd!* she thought. But despite herself, she met his eager kiss with her own. When she kissed him back, a burst of laughter erupted from him, which caused her red splotches to spread like a wildfire up her neck and cheeks. Oh, how she wanted to slap him! She wasn't one who took teasing so lightly. She almost broke away, but he did precisely that before she had even had the chance to push him backward into a heap.

He put some distance between them and searched her face for—she didn't exactly know what he was searching for. All she could do was stand there embarrassed and breathing hard. A twitching of his lips enraged Rosemary to the point of her wanting to scream aloud. He enjoyed embarrassing her. She clenched her fists and raised her chin high in the air, signifying her resolve to defy whatever came next.

"Can't say I expected." He stopped to clear his throat. "That is, I think it best we don't continue this any further tonight."

She bristled. "Continue what? From where I'm standing, you just assaulted me and took advantage of my weakened state of mind!"

He crossed his arms tightly over his chest, which pulled his shirt tautly. "And from where I stand, Miss Barker, I'd say you enjoyed it far too much to call it an assault or taking advantage."

Rolling her shoulders back defiantly, she retorted with a slight snort. "I didn't give you permission."

"Then what do you call this?" He no sooner said those words than his mouth was back over her mouth again. The worst of it was that Rosemary couldn't help but return it. She thought she might be going mad. When they broke off the kiss this time, Rosemary's chin lowered, and she touched her lips with her fingertips. New, salty tears fell down her cheeks and dripped off her jawline. The comfort that came with his touch was something of a miracle, and Rosemary found her eyelids closing in absolute serenity. Her inner walls of solitude shattered like glass and opened to a world of trust in a man. She wanted to run, but her heart betrayed her. She'd found that the thought of kissing him came easier than hitting him.

*Dear Rose, why have you betrayed me?* There he was as always. Her admirer sunk his teeth into her blissful moment. His voice echoed, trounced on her hopes and dreams, and grew as she diminished in spirit. Fear arose once more. She began to build up the defensive walls of her inner kingdom as Ricochet desperately tried to break them down by pulling her into a gentle embrace. The admirer was the true reason that she and the wagon master couldn't be together.

*May I kiss you, Rosemary?* Ricochet's overambitious inquisition echoed in her ears from moments earlier. His question had seemed totally idiotic and ridiculous minutes ago, but if he were to ask that same question now, she'd give her consent a million times over. She couldn't stop being joyful because her admirer wished it.

The wicked man's whereabouts were unknown, and his full intentions were unclear, but the truth that he could kill so easily if she stepped out of line frightened her the most. He could possibly kill Ricochet if she allowed this relationship a chance. The question wasn't if she wanted to trust the wagon master, but if she was ready to fight for his life.

She had made her decision. She deepened her resolve by smiling against Ricochet's chest as he held her close. Their tender but brief hug ended, leaving Ricochet bashfully rubbing his neck and Rosemary blushing harder than ever. She peered up at him. Her heart thumped excitedly, and she wished it would soften its boisterous sound so that he wouldn't know. As he licked his lips, savoring the taste of their previous kisses, Rosemary took two steps away from him.

"I'd say that counts as permission." He smiled with true and honest joy and then said in little more than a hoarse whisper, "You have no idea how long I've wanted to do that. I thought about kissing you the moment I saw you land in that water keg." He chuckled.

Oh, he was downright seducing and frustrating in the same breath. She considered wiping that smug grin off his face with a quick and to-the-point kiss. The alarming thought of her starting the kiss, she knew, would surely shock him out of his socks. The stirred-up fire he'd caused inside her was so aggravating. She pictured herself splitting in two if he continued this charade of his.

"Well then," she huffed, "why didn't you?"

His head was cocked to the side, and his eyebrow were raised tauntingly. "Is that an invitation, Miss Barker?" His hands were now on his hips, and he bent down to look her in the eye.

"Careful now, Chapel," she said and raised her palms, easing him back some. "I did say I hated you, remember? I wouldn't want you to get the wrong idea about me."

Neither teasing nor flirting had ever been her thing. She'd watched Charity do it many times, but now that it was her turn to perform, she hoped that it would intrigue the wagon master and not disarm him. Catching a glimmer of playfulness in his expression gave her all the confidence that she needed to know that her words had very much provoked him.

He eased forward against her hands. "I'll be bellerin' like a cowardly coyote if I let that silly warning scare me off." His face turned suddenly serious when he said, "You're the most beautiful woman I've ever met, and only a fool would think to pass you up."

Lowering her hands and backing up, she didn't speak a word, finding words lost to her. Her mouth felt as dry as a desert. She had intended to slaughter him with her wrath, yet he had clearly changed her demeanor. Her throat seized at every possible word she mustered up, as if God Himself was telling her to be silent for a minute longer.

A sincere and charming grin was plastered on the wagon master's face. "I care deeply for you, Rosemary, and I pray that you'll learn to trust me."

She choked and then gave him an honest and wholehearted smile, which was something that had rarely been seen since the fire that took place months ago. She nodded at once and replied in a faint breath, "I'll try." When she saw that his face was beaming, she made up her mind that fear and hate would no longer be her masters. She had fallen for him hard and so very fast.

Their sweet and heartfelt moment didn't last because Mace urgently ran to meet them. "Ricochet," he bellowed.

Ricochet's arms hung loose at his sides as he turned to face his staff member. "Mace, what is it?"

"It's the doc," he explained between heavy gasps. "His wagon's been ransacked."

Ricochet's brow furrowed deeply as he ordered, "Sit the men down. I want to hear the whole story."

Mace hurried off to carry out his duty, and then Ricochet returned his attention to Rosemary. "Seems one of us always runs away when we get a moment alone." His joking made her blush a deep-red color as she remembered their time in the woods.

"You better go. Can't keep them waiting." She bashfully tucked a curl behind her ear, a gesture telling him that she wanted him to stay.

"I'll be back. Wait for me."

He pulled an object out of his pocket and then stuffed it into her hand, grinning as if they shared some inside joke between them.

Turning on his boot heels, he joined up with Mace and the agitated crowd that had gathered near the campfire. Rosemary opened her hand and discovered the satin ribbon, which he had returned. She sighed longingly after him, watching his broad shoulders and tanned features leave her presence.

*He kept it,* she thought. She touched her lips once again in remembrance of the special, newly discovered bond that they had both shared. She yearned to share many more moments like this one with him in the future, which both excited and alarmed her. What lay ahead of them was unfamiliar ground.

She had had a young suitor before her parents' passing, but nothing serious or devoted ever came of it. The more she thought about the matter, the more intense it grew. Ricochet's actions were not foolish. He actually wanted her, and quite possibly, she wanted him. The feelings that she carried for him outweighed the knowledge she had studied on the subject of a beginning courtship. That terrified her.

She had only taken two steps forward when a scrap of crumbled paper caught her eye. It lay near the spot where Mace had stood only minutes earlier. She thought nothing of it at first, but her curiosity got the best of her, and she opened it. A lightheaded sensation followed soon after she read the words that had been etched on the paper. Her dizziness only worsened and showed no signs of easing. The crumbled note was addressed to her. She wouldn't forget it any time soon, if at all.

*My dearest Rose,*

*I finally found you. Thought you could escape my presence, did you? Rest assured that I will always be watching. Don't forget that you are mine and mine alone.*

*Your loving, Admirer*

"No," she gasped, wildly searching her surroundings for his spying eye. Nothing appeared out of the ordinary, yet she knew that he was out there among the other pioneers. Surely, she would've noticed a new face among her fellow travelers. He'd chased her down after all, and now there was no place to turn. The wagon train wouldn't arrive at its destination for a few months. He had her cornered.

She held the scrap of paper to her nose. She smelled the same scent of rose petals. It was a sweet and innocent smell that brought horrific events. It sickened her, twisting her stomach and tightening her throat.

The lump in her throat formed so suddenly that she couldn't swallow. Suspicions had been aroused in her, rushing along the tracks of her brain at full speed and stirring up strife and fear. Black spots blurred her vision as she attempted to tuck the curls that framed her face behind her ears. Stinging tears welled up. These were not tears of pain and sorrow but of hate. She loathed the feeling, but it had begun to burn so ferociously that she feared it would never leave her. She felt unsteady, teetering back and forth on her heels. She was going to faint.

No sooner had she come to that conclusion, than her legs crumpled from beneath and her skull hit the dirt. The aching in her left side grew. The river's rapids came swiftly to mind, and then all went dark.

# Chapter 11

❧

He tipped his hat as he approached the agitated group of men that stood before him. The arguments of the bunch echoed around the campfire, as fingers were pointed and accusations were tossed to and fro.

Agitated may be too light a term compared with what Ricochet witnessed. He wasn't at all surprised to see that the men had taken sides and threatened to throw punches at one another. Why couldn't a fight break out *after* his meeting with Rosemary? Sometimes he really hated being the leader on this dangerous escapade across the wilderness. Some days, it seemed that his troubles never ended. Still, it was up to him to get to the bottom of this and calm the raging group before something more serious happened.

Upon his arrival, he noticed that Jacob Webb was the center of attention and standing about ten paces across from Edward Jones. Isaac Beckett was close by Edward's side, along with several other men who had gathered to record the event. Jacob shouted accusingly, "I know it was you, Jones!"

Edward growled and spat back, edging closer to the doctor. "I ain't done a thing, Doc!" The man looked like some kind of animal that had been caught dragging a mangled chicken away from a coop. He was frantic and violent.

Jacob sighed, his mouth was a thin line, and his brow was furrowed. "Oh, don't go acting so innocent. I know you did it."

The old farmer wasn't in the listening mood, for he rolled up his shirtsleeves and threatened to knock the man over. "You keep on accusin', and I'll smack the daylights outta ya!"

The threats, accusations, and fisticuffs continued, even after the wagon master had called for them to halt the commotion. Edward was getting more aggressive, several men held his arms back while Jacob rambled on and on. It was getting out of hand.

Ricochet released an ear-piercing whistle, which attracted everyone's attention, including the two agitated party members', Edward and Jacob. Once he had gained their eyes and ears, he tilted his hat back and addressed them with a raised yet orderly tone. "You chuckleheads mind telling me what this caterwauling is about?"

Jacob answered first as he jabbed a finger at Edward's chest. "*He* stole from my wagon!"

"I did no such thing," Edward barked defensively, baring his teeth.

Jacob went on, ignoring the glaring and bellowing from the accused. "I was returning to my wagon when I noticed my supplies had been gone through. I saw him leaving the scene shortly after that."

"I wasn't fleeing the scene!" Edward mocked in a nasally voice. "I heard something and thought it right to check things out. Nothing wrong with bein' curious." He was released by the men who were holding him back. He placed his thumbs in his belt.

Jacob adjusted the spectacles that were on the bridge of his nose and snorted a remark. "Then how do you explain the bottles of ether that were in your hand when I found you? Only a simpleton would believe such obvious tomfoolery."

The farmer's voice rumbled in his throat, and he closed the gap quickly between them. "You callin' me a liar, Doc?" His nose practically touched the doctor's, and Mace held onto Edward's arm so that he could pull him away if anything went awry.

Jacob squared his shoulders and raised his chin defiantly. The doctor had guts. "If the boot fits."

Edward looked as though he would pull away from Mace's mighty grip at any moment. Ricochet had to think of a possible way to fix this mess, or else, a fight of mass proportions would occur, and he'd much prefer not to deal with such a disaster. After all, his mind was on other matters, meaning Rosemary and the fact that he longed to be by her side. The last thing that he wanted to do was keep her waiting by the water kegs. He uncrossed his arms and pinched the bridge of his nose out of frustration. Then he demanded above their bickering, "Show me the wagon."

That seemed to have caught everyone's attention, for they went silent and parted for him to view the crime scene. The land schooner's contents had been tampered with and scattered near the opening. Medical supplies ranging from bandages to needed medications and herbs had been knocked over. But one carton in particular caught his eye—the one containing chloroform and ether. Several glass vials had been spilled and shattered. Little shards littered the floorboards of the wagon.

The way things had been scattered and flung all over the ground made it seem like the culprit wasn't worried about being caught. Maybe he was too cocky or in too much of a hurry to care. Ricochet felt unease settling in his stomach. If he were dealing with a thief among the pioneers, it was another problem that he'd have to deal with and a mess he'd have to clean up.

He thought about the law and moral code that he'd set into place before they'd started this journey: If the thief was caught, he or she would be banished from the caravan permanently and left at the next town, fort, or village that they came across. Even a place by a river or wooded area would suffice. He had never had to deal with that rule before, and he sure didn't want to have to enforce it, but if it came down to it, he knew he would have to punish the thief.

Something struck Ricochet as odd. The Joneses were well off. They had cattle, food, medicines, and necessities at their fingertips. At the very beginning, Edward had vowed that he wouldn't go looking for the Webbs' help, even in dire straits. The man hated doctors and the like. Although he didn't care to inform them of the reason, Ricochet knew that the man would ransack the medicine wagon for spare herbs, bandages, and sedatives.

Then again, what did he know of the man's character besides his bad temper? Absolutely nothing. Perhaps the old badger had destroyed Jacob's wagon to gain revenge for an earlier spat. Maybe he considered it funny. Seeing the way Edward glared, however, made Ricochet guess that Edward might do something this heinous against the middle-aged doctor but not without a real reason.

Ricochet did not turn to face the two angry men, but he inspected the scene further. He asked, "Jacob, did you see him do all this?"

The doctor shifted his feet bashfully. "Well, not with my own eyes. I was headed to my wagon for my medical bag. Macy Garrison has been having the most awful headaches at night. Someone hit me over the head from behind."

The wagon master agreed that it was true. The doctor had a large bump on the back of his head, which had turned a shade of black and blue, yet no blood had seeped or oozed from it. His head hadn't been split, which was a good sign. They needed him out here. He was the *one* and *only* physician between here and Oregon City.

Jacob then took young Andrew Jones, who had been hiding by the wagon's wheel, by the arm and said, "But this boy did! Tell him, son."

The kid looked at his pa, Edward, with a fearful gaze and then rubbed his neck. "I didn't exactly *see* him near the wagon, mister. It was dark. Could've been anyone really."

The young boy was looking rather nervous, as he should be when going against his pa. He hung his head and lowered his eyes. Ricochet had seen Edward, a time or two, treating his son harshly, and he couldn't blame the kid for not coming out with it. But they needed answers. By the sheer terror on Andrew's face, Ricochet guessed it would be mighty hard to coax him into giving up his father's actions, if that was indeed the case.

Edward grinned proudly, reclaiming his boy from the doctor's grip. "There now, ya see. It wasn't me. Could've been any one of us."

Andrew's gazed at his shoes as if they were fascinating. He didn't look up again. The boy was obviously scared of his old man. It didn't take a genius to figure it out. Ricochet reckoned that his statement was true. Edward fit the description of half the men on the caravan. In the dark, it could very well have been any of them.

Still, it wouldn't be right to push the matter aside. The wagon master wouldn't allow a thief to continue his wrongdoing, especially where their only source of medicine was concerned. If there was an accident and surgical expertise was required, they would be in quite a pinch. The culprit needed to be found and dealt with immediately.

Mace came and stood by Ricochet's side, awaiting orders. The wagon master crouched near the broken vials. Only a few of them remained intact. He gestured for Mace to crouch beside him and said, "What do you reckon?" He pointed to the bottles. Then he stood and nodded to the surgical equipment that had been littered across the floor of the wagon.

The darkly clad rider shook her head, "Definitely wasn't an unplanned attack. The suspect clearly grabbed something from that there medical case. Then he took some of the vials. Jacob said some ether was taken, but everything else is accounted for."

Ricochet nodded slowly in thought. "Whoever did it couldn't have gotten away with it before or after supper, which means it must've been while everyone was distracted." It dawned on him quickly like a light turning on inside his skull. "During the devotion, no one would've seen it."

Mace questioned Ricochet's resolve by saying, "But what about the kid? He saw someone. He's sure scared of his pa. Surely, Ed had some part in this."

Ricochet rested his chin in his hand. "Maybe he did see someone, and maybe it was his old man. I say we'd better check the Joneses' wagon to be sure, before we judge him further."

Mace grunted in agreement and took another gander inside the Webbs' wagon. Although he had voiced a question, it appeared that both men were in one accord with the remaining questions that had yet to be answered. They were determined to get the answers one way or another. If it meant searching through every wagon on sight, they'd do just that.

The Joneses' wagon was two wagons down from the Webbs' wagon. They attempted to remove Edward and his wife as they turned over every canister, carton, and crate, but so far, the man and his family were proving to be most difficult.

Autumn Jones was a woman of great taste and little speech, but she made herself known when she wanted to. She'd already smacked Mace's hand when he went to dump out her special belongings, which Ricochet couldn't blame her for. However, the medical supplies needed to be found, so no luggage would be left out of the inspection.

They continued their search while Jackson and Isaac turned away spectators. After tipping over the last box and coming up empty handed, Mace and Ricochet fanned out and began their investigations elsewhere.

The wagon master announced that there would be a bigger investigation and that everyone would have to participate. He made certain to keep his tone calm, and he prayed that everyone would cooperate instead of giving him lip.

Ricochet headed up a search on the far side of the corral while Mace took the other half. The contents of each wagon, cart, and saddlebag were removed, as well as boxes, crates, and barrels. No stone was left unturned. The camp was alive with pioneers pouring out their items of privacy to the wagon master and his assistant, as Ricochet and Mace carried on their widespread examination. They searched wagon after wagon, but they found no evidence of the break-in. They were beginning to lose hope.

Two hours later, a frantic and worried Charity came running to meet Ricochet. *What now?* he thought.

"Mr. Chapel!" His head turned at the mention of his name. He was cautious, but Charity's greeting of urgency caught his attention. Of all the times that the young, wild filly could have chosen to bother him, she chose this very moment when he was at his busiest.

Upon hearing Charity's shrieking, Mace entered the scene. His hat was worn low over his brow, and his stance intrigued.

Ricochet's shoulders sagged, and he sighed. "Yes, Miss Cole?"

She halted in front of him and Mace. A severe flush of red appeared on her cheeks when she noticed the dark-donned rider staring at her. Ricochet peered from one person to the other, with an amused look on his features. The preacher's daughter had never been a puzzle to piece together, but it appeared as though she was now an open book, which anyone for miles around could read freely. It was no secret that she harbored tremendous feelings for Mace Chronicle, however, the man was so silent and wise, Ricochet thought he'd never take poor Charity seriously in a courtship of any kind.

Apparently recalling her mission, Charity regained her speech and gazed directly at the wagon master. "Have you seen Rosemary? I simply cannot find her."

Ricochet sighed once more, finding the reason behind her dramatic entrance rather a letdown. After all, he knew exactly where Rosemary was. "Yes, she's currently by the water kegs next to the supply wagon."

She clapped her hands once with glee. "Oh, good! I was beginning to worry." With that, she hurried off, her skirts swirling and flouncing around her legs.

Ricochet's guilt grew great at the remembrance of leaving the beautiful young woman next to the barrels. He had asked her to wait for him, yet here it was hours later, and he was busy with other matters. As wagon master, he should continue his search for the missing medical equipment and ether, punish the culprit, and then send everyone back to their respectful wagons, but as a man drowning in emotions that he never knew existed, he wanted nothing more than to be by Rosemary's side.

Guilt tugged at his heartstrings until he finally gave way. It wouldn't hurt to check on the lovely lady, would it? He left Mace in charge for the few minutes that he would be gone and then hurried after Charity.

The night had grown cold, and a weary spell cast its shadow over Ricochet. He hadn't realized how exhausted and spent he felt until now. The more steps he took, the shorter his stride was. If the night lasted any longer, he might just collapse where he walked.

At last, he arrived at the water kegs where the romantic moment between him and Rosemary had occurred. His chest was tight, his breathing heavy, and the memory of the wonderful kiss built pride and excitement in his heart. The kiss—kisses rather—had happened so suddenly, and before he had known it, he'd fallen head over heels in love with the angelic yet sassy Miss Barker. He could still imagine his lips on hers. It was a dream that he never wanted to end.

He came to halt beside Charity and looked around for any sign of Rosemary. Her thin frame was nowhere to be found. His brow creased as he said, "Rosemary?"

Charity eyed him carefully after hearing him mention her by her first name. Then she harrumphed quizzically. "You said she was here, right?" The woman was pouting and giving him lip, but he ignored her.

"This is where I last saw her," he stated while puzzled himself. It seemed that she never stayed put, even when she was told to. If he had been in that predicament, he probably wouldn't have stood around lollygagging for hours on end either.

It wasn't until he heard a faint but noticeable moan that he moved forward for a look. After taking two steps, he noted a pair of boots that were sticking out from beside the water kegs. He squinted to clear his vision saw a dark form lying on the dirt. The body was small, and she was sprawled out in a light slumber.

He got down on his knees. "Rosemary! Are you all right?"

Charity edged closer after hearing her friend's name. Soon she too was on her knees beside the sleeping beauty. "Rosie, what're you doing sleeping by the water supply?"

After hearing Rosemary's moaning, Ricochet suspected that she would come to at any moment. The dark bruise on her temple where she had fallen gave Ricochet all the evidence that he required to form a conclusion. "She must have fainted," he uttered quietly, more for his own peace of mind than for Charity's.

As he went to lift her into his arms, he caught sight of her balled up fist, which was holding on to a crumpled piece of paper. Making certain that Charity was distracted, he pried open Rosemary's fingers to take the paper. Whatever it was, Ricochet guessed it had had something to do with her fainting spell.

He stuffed it into his pocket and then lifted Rosemary's limp body. He cradled her in his arms. She weighed hardly anything. She was as light as a feather. She stirred, her eyelids fluttering open and then closed. All he could focus on were her lips, which were pink, still swollen, and so inviting. It took every ounce of his strength to hold back the urge to kiss her, right then and there.

As Charity fiddled with her dress, concern marked her complexion. "Will she be all right?"

Ricochet smiled reassuringly. "I'm sure she'll be just fine. I'll take her to your wagon and have Jacob check in on her to be on the safe side."

The two of them took the still-sleeping Rosemary to the Coles' wagon. Judging by the amount of people that were up and about, Ricochet observed that the search for the missing supplies had continued without much success. He would have to take control of the situation himself, once he dropped the ladies off at Jackson's land schooner.

Arriving at the wagon, Ricochet laid Rosemary in the tarp-covered interior and then left so that no rumors would be spread. He informed the weathered preacher and Jacob of the happenings.

"Sounds like she simply fainted to me, but I'll do a further checkup. It could be that the fall has caused some minor trauma to her wound. I wouldn't be surprised if we encountered more of her passing out in the days to come. Wounds like the one she has aren't at all easy to recover from, let alone having one while traveling this rough terrain. I warned her that walking could be a good thing, but too much of it could cause the stitching to come loose," Jacob said as his chin rested on his hand. "I'll have to perform a full exam tomorrow when she's alert."

Jackson rubbed his neck. "The poor girl has endured a great deal on this wagon train. I hate to see her suffer."

Ricochet nodded his agreement; however, he didn't quite agree with Jacob's theory. Rosemary hadn't fainted before, and she seemed in perfect health prior to him leaving. But had she hidden it so well that he couldn't see it? Thinking back, he could only recall the many kisses that he'd given her and holding her in his arms. He had never seen any traumatic look of pain on her face. Had he shrugged off her being in pain because he'd wanted to kiss her so badly? Guilt played with his rational thinking.

Something nagged him inwardly. The way she had clutched the note in her fist told him that something had her spooked, or perhaps, he was reading too much into it. He couldn't be sure until he talked to her himself. It would likely be a touchy subject, and he would have to tread carefully to get answers. Then again, he always had to tread carefully around her.

Excusing himself, he strode away from prying eyes to view the paper that he'd taken. It had been no gentlemanly act to steal a lady's belonging, but his conscience didn't feel guilty regarding this matter. Kissing her to the point of her fainting made him feel worse. Call him nosy or meddlesome, but he wasn't about to turn a blind eye where Rosemary's safety and welfare were concerned.

He fished for the note in his pocket, found it, and looked it over. What he read aroused more questions than answers, and it certainly riled his temper, even though, he had made efforts and taken lengths to ensure that his anger never kindled again. His older brother had learned that Ricochet's ill temper had been nothing to trifle with.

The words written on the note showed possessiveness. They were etched in an elegant yet violent manner on a scented scrap of paper. It smelled of sweet rose petals like that in cologne. The aroma, as temptingly sweet as it was, reminded him of something that he'd smelled recently or maybe someone. Whatever the case, he knew that he recognized it, and he didn't want it anywhere near his face. The smell was something pleasant yet eerie.

The pressure of the pen that had been used in forging the threat was most intriguing. The pen's tip had obviously torn through the paper in various places. Whoever had written the letter had been furious¾either that, or he was extremely excited. Ricochet knew better than to believe the latter idea.

The darker, harder-pressed writing had been on the last part of the note, which said,

Don't forget that you are mine and mine alone.

The writer was possessive, selfish, and violent. The threat couldn't be clearer. The man (At least that's what Ricochet was led to believe) who had written this was coming for Rosemary Barker. It was a chilling thought to say the least. Just who was this so-called loving Admirer? Was he a jilted fiancé or a former lover? The doubt swimming in Ricochet's head about knocked him out cold. He'd already taken quite a liking to the curly haired, brown-eyed filly. Sure would be a shame for her to run off with someone as low down as the man who was hiding behind the scented paper and frilly penmanship.

He would be sure to interrogate Miss Barker when she awoke, but first, his duty was to locate the stolen medicine and gain control of the frenzy before him. There was no sense in waking her. It had gotten late. Besides, he needed to focus and calm himself lest he should go on a rampage.

Another hour passed, and no evidence of the thief had been found. Mace and Ricochet had come to the same decision: Everyone needed to settle down for the night. A caravan filled with tired and cranky people would make for a longer trip on the following day. Night watchmen were appointed, with Mace and Edward taking first watch and Isaac and Ricochet taking the second. They made certain to have a keen eye on Edward at all times to be sure that he was not stealing from the Webbs or planning to using the ether, which had been collected that night.

Ricochet couldn't sleep when he at last got into his bedroll. The stars were over his head, keeping him company. The world appeared so vast and big before him. The sky was seemingly endless in its dark void above. He thought about how all this had come from the words of the Creator, thousands of years ago.

With that perspective, Ricochet almost felt insignificant compared to Christians who had lived more faithfully and had been more devoted to the Lord than he had. But by the grace of God, the wagon master was there, doing what he could to serve and knowing that the blood of Christ covered the sins that he'd committed and would commit in the future.

With those thoughts taking the place of the previous depressing and somewhat worrisome imaginings, he finally fell asleep, but not without dreaming, which consisted mainly of a married life with a woman. He dreamt of kissing her, claiming her as his own, and settling down in a place that was void of civilization and where it would just be the two of them. Well, maybe they could have a few kids too. Surprisingly, Rosemary's face flooded his dreams, and he gladly accepted them with open arms.

# Chapter 12

It had been a long and wearisome morning thus far. Rosemary was forced to allow Jacob to inspect her side's wound. Then she listened as Charity began her guilt-trip speech because Rosemary had caused such worry.

Everyone seemed to be at odds with one another. Rosemary wondered what had happened after she had fainted the previous night. Nothing about her fellow pioneers seemed as cheerful or team oriented as it had before. The sides had been decided among them. Something had definitely changed in their demeanor.

A few days had gone by, and they still appeared to be their same edgy selves. Rosemary thought for sure that the mistrust would've been cleared up by then, but it had only grown worse. Small spats had occurred here and there, with Ricochet and Mace breaking them up. Everyone had it out for the next person, and it was beginning to remind Rosemary of her own mixed-up, emotional self.

The covered wagons had been packed up, and they moved out in their usual line, but Rosemary found herself walking alone beside the Coles' schooner. Charity was nowhere in sight or earshot. The nosy and flirtatious girl was a wonder. Rosemary guessed that Charity was off with the strangely quiet Mace Chronicle. Rosemary walked alone, in peace, and keeping her thoughts to herself.

She'd noticed that the note from her admirer had been missing since her the previous night. But what scared her most was the possibility that someone had picked it up and read it. Now, it was the last thing that she needed: someone getting into her business and trying to save the day. She'd learned the hard way about letting someone else share her problems. Poor Sheriff Houston back home had met his demise. The fire had burned him, his lovely wife, and daughter to ashes within the confines of their own home. They'd had the same fate as her parents. Rosemary could only imagine the screams of Houston's wife, as the admirer ripped away her decency and innocence as he had done with Rosemary's own mother. It made her shudder.

She shook her head, trying to clear away the painful thoughts. It would do her no good to remain thinking of the things of the past. She had to find that note and tear it up before someone got involved, otherwise, there might just be another massacre on her hands. Next time, it might be Charity or Ricochet who got hurt or worse. She couldn't bring herself to picture their deaths.

"Foolish boy!" The furious snarls of Edward Jones came from the wagon up ahead. Soon after hearing his infuriated expression toward his son, Rosemary spotted his large, sausage-like fingers shoving Andrew's smaller body off the wagon seat and onto the ground. "You'll learn some respect or face walking by yourself the rest of the way."

Rosemary's legs carried her forward before she could stop herself. Since when had she learned to have compassion? *Since Ricochet,* she thought. A giddy sensation enveloped her heart.

She halted in front of the young boy, whom she had been acquainted with on several occasions. Dirt covered Andrew Jones's ruddy face, and massive bruises plagued his scrawny body. His watery, hurt-filled eyes struck Rosemary's heart and rattled her soul. He was but a child, and his father treated him so terribly. She had never actually witnessed the outright abuse until now, but many pioneers could guess what went on behind the scenes.

A frenzied little girl covered in frills and lace scurried to Andrew's side. Her big violet-colored eyes were almost in tears. "Drew!" She cried, grabbing hold of his sleeve and attempting to help the older boy to his feet. He had already been trying to pick himself up when she arrived.

The Jones' wagon moved forward as Edward growled like a rabid dog. "Stubborn, idiotic child!"

Little Macy shriveled behind Andrew, shivering with fear. Andrew acted no better than she had. They both cowered and trembled under the wake of Edward Jones's wrathful outburst.

Rosemary had had enough, and her temper unfurled its fury. "How dare you treat him this way!" She raised her tone as she helped Andrew become steadier on his wobbly legs. Macy clutched his arm. "He's only a boy," Rosemary fumed.

Edward raised his whip threateningly. "Mind your own business, woman. He's my son, and I'll treat as I please."

As the wagon continued onward, Rosemary trailed after it and kept the younger kids behind her. "What kind of father bullies his own son into submission? He isn't some whipping post, Mr. Jones. He's a living, breathing human, same as you." She jabbed a finger at him while her other arm steadied the boy. Macy sniffled, nodding her head at Rosemary's words.

"Why are you so mean?" the five-year-old girl asked, barely above a whisper.

Edward looked outraged and embarrassed by Rosemary's declaration and annoyed by Macy's question. His eyes were like daggers piercing any confidence Rosemary attempted to muster up. His wife and son had a right to be fearful of his wrath.

He said, "Ain't no woman or child gonna tell me how to treat my own. I got rights."

She narrowed her eyes considerably. "For a man as heartless and cruel as you, Mr. Jones, I wouldn't be surprised if those so-called rights landed you in the noose someday."

That did it. Edward raised his whip high as his hardened eyes lusted for blood. His face reddened quickly, Rosemary expected it to explode in a matter of seconds. He halted his wagon. Others stopped behind him. She shielded the boy from his father's view as the older man cracked his whip and eyed her. The leather hurled closer. He was aiming for her face. She turned her head, shut her eyes, and clenched her teeth. She awaited the sting of the blow, but it never came. She never felt the agonizing leather strap on her skin, not even a gust of wind.

Slowly, she opened her eyes to find a man on horseback rearing up on his buckskin before her, Andrew, and Macy. He was the picture of a knight in shining armor, who majestically saved those who couldn't protect themselves, or at least, that is what Rosemary thought. His mustang whinnied and landed back on the ground. His tone reflected belligerence and a hunger for justice. "How dare you raise your whip against a woman on *my* wagon train!"

Ricochet had come to her rescue, and she could almost cry at how heroic he stood before her eyes. His shout had caused the wagons ahead to stop moving. They halted in a straight line. When Rosemary peered closer, she observed the whip wrapped tightly around Ricochet's forearm. He'd taken the hit for Andrew, Macy and her.

"Chapel," Edward began in his defense, "this ain't what it looks like."

Jerking the whip from Edward's fist, Ricochet spat back, "What does it look like, Ed? A man trying to beat a woman? I'll have none of that aboard my wagon train."

Rosemary shivered. His tone was one that she'd never heard before. The ferocity lacing his voice was immense and altogether frightening. She backed up a step or two while clutching the boy tightly to her right side and the little girl to her left side.

Pointing a beefy finger at her, Edward deflected the blame. "She was butting in where she don't belong. I was just teaching her a lesson."

Ricochet closed the gap between his stallion and the wagon and then grabbed Edward's collar with both fists. Their faces were close to the point that their noses were practically touching. "If I ever see you try to harm her or another woman again, I won't hesitate in kicking you off this train and handing you over to the law. Do I make myself clear?"

Edward nodded. His eyes were wild as he trembled with fear. Ricochet shook the man's collar violently before repeating himself for good measure. "Do I make myself clear, Jones?"

"Y-yes!" Edward croaked, and he was released. His chagrined expression lowered to look at the ground.

Straightening in the saddle, Ricochet glared at him for some time before uttering a firm, "Good."

An intense few minutes passed, and then the wagons moved out at Mace's call. The train moved on, but Ricochet fell back in line beside Rosemary, Macy, and Andrew. He slid down from the saddle to walk alongside them. "Are you all right?" His terrifying tone had gone as one of tenderness had taken hold. It amazed Rosemary how fast his temper had subsided.

She nodded once, speaking softly. "Yes, we're fine." Looking down at Andrew and Macy, she was given a shaky smile from both of them, which confirmed that she was correct. The child of no more than twelve or thirteen had hidden his tears. He had a nasty scratch on his cheek from being tossed off the wagon, but no further injuries had been sustained. Rosemary was thankful for that. Macy was only upset because she'd seen Andrew upset.

Andrew hung his head and sniffled. "You shouldn't have stepped in like that. He's mad now." He patted Macy's head as she hugged him.

*And he wasn't before?* Rosemary wanted to ask, but she kept her mouth shut as Ricochet knelt down directly in front of both children. "Son," he said softly, "if we hadn't stepped in, you'd be a goner right now." He placed his hand on the boy's shoulder. "How about you ride up front with me for a while? I'll even let ya lead the wagon train for a bit."

Andrew perked up at that. "You mean it?" His eyes brightened with excitement as his confidence returned.

Ricochet beamed, removing his wide-brimmed hat and placing it atop the boy's head. "Course I do. Now, hop up in the saddle, and I'll take ya to the head of the wagon train."

Macy began her pouting, frowning, and extending her lower lip outward. "I wanna go too!"

There was nothing new about this girl wanting to go wherever Andrew went. They were pretty much inseparable, although Rosemary could tell that Andrew didn't like the thought of sharing his new leadership position with a little girl.

"No, Macy," he said, frowning. "Leading the train is for big strong men. Lil' girls can't be head of the wagons."

When Macy's pouting continued, Ricochet chuckled and clasped the boy's shoulder. "Now, now. A lone wagon master can't lead by himself. He needs an assistant." He then winked at Macy. She was grinning with excitement.

Andrew thought it over quickly before nodding his agreement. "Fine." He went back to beaming widely. "But as my second, you need to listen to what I say."

Macy bobbed her head three times fast and said, "I will!"

Ricochet steadied Gage as Andrew climbed up into the saddle with incredible skill for his age. Then Ricochet turned to Macy. He hoisted the girl up in front of the older boy. Steadying the children and taking the reins, the wagon master then took Rosemary's hand in his and pulled the group along.

Seeing the man that she was beginning to understand interact with the children sent her heart aflutter. He knew exactly how to cheer Andrew up. He even knew the way to settle the small squabble between the boy and Macy. Rosemary dearly admired him for it.

She wasn't very outgoing with children, but after watching the wagon master do it so easily, she wanted to try it too. Perhaps she could get some pointers on the matter from Charity. What was she thinking? She wasn't ready to speak with Charity on the matter of her and Ricochet just yet.

They reached the front of the wagon train quickly with only a little bit of conversation, apart from Andrew's delighted, "Giddyap," and Macy's, "Yeehaw." After the boy had earned Ricochet's trust, Andrew led the train while sitting next to Mace. Charity skipped happily along by his side.

That's when Rosemary noticed that Ricochet's pace had slowed to match hers. They fell back in line from Charity, Mace, and the two young riders. While walking along together, Rosemary couldn't imagine a happier moment. It was funny how her dark mindset had changed since her confrontation with the wagon master. She was getting to know her true self and learning more and more about Ricochet in the process.

"What's on your mind?" he asked after a while.

She blushed and looked away. Apparently, she had been staring at him since they'd fallen behind the others. She had not exactly been staring at him but rather his lips. "Nothing," she replied smugly.

He raised a brow with a cheeky grin plastered across his face. "Why is it that you always attract trouble, Miss Barker?"

Snorting, she asserted her innocence regarding his remark. "I do not *always* attract trouble."

"Oh, really? This makes at least five times I've come to your rescue."

She attempted to pull her hand from his. "You're counting?"

He refused to let go but instead pulled her into a closer stride with him until her shoulder and his bicep touched as they walked. "For you, Rosemary, I'd risk a thousand times."

The tips of her ears burned red, and splotches crept up her neck. She extended the space between them for the sake of other pioneers who might be watching. Words of persuasion came so easily to him while she flopped around like a fish out of water. What did one say to a statement like his?

She could only gaze up at him with her eyes full of wonder. He was simply different from any other man she'd met before in her life. The urge to run her fingers through his blond hair and to kiss him again arose, but the eyes of the other pioneers who were around them drowned it out.

Ricochet chuckled and said, "Your cheeks are as red as a rose."

Her free hand went to her face instantly. She felt the heat in her cheek. *Confound those wretched splotches!* she thought. She sheepishly hunched her shoulders and looked away, hoping that he wouldn't say another word about it. When he laughed, it was all she could do not to slap the teasing look off his face.

"Well, well, if you ain't blushing," he exclaimed, as he pretended to be shocked, gasped, and pointed to her red, glowing face.

She managed a half-hearted slap on his arm. "You are absolutely incorrigible."

He didn't flinch one bit from her playful attack, but instead, he laughed more. "And you're as stubborn as a mule," he remarked. Then he whispered, "Of course, you're much prettier."

They were silent after that. They walked and listened to the nature that was all around them. The birds sang, but few flew overhead. Autumn was well on its way. Crickets were chirping at their feet. A light breeze had picked up. It was chillier than the previous day had been. Soon they would need light coats, heavier socks, and stockings. Rosemary hoped they would make it to Oregon City before the trees were bare of their leaves. That was wishful thinking.

Recalling the amazing event that had taken place a few nights ago, Rosemary had an odd and striking thought. Were they going to continue their preposterous courtship, or whatever it was called? What exactly was a courtship? Was it a path to marriage? What a dizzying picture that was.

She wasn't prepared for a blissful life like that one, let alone one with a man on the trail who had traveled. She had no idea what a wife exactly did. Was she just some wallflower whom a man came home to every night? Was she only a woman who cooked, cleaned, and kept her husband entertained during the cold nights of winter?

Sucking in a breath of air, she could sense her surroundings closing in. Black spots appeared in her vision. She couldn't become a wife. She simply couldn't.

Her mother had surely taught her something on the subject, or at least, Rosemary reckoned she had, but those lessons had since been forgotten. She couldn't recall a single thing. Because she didn't know anything about it, she would just remain single and free to live as she chose. Still, she'd learned that Ricochet could easily persuade her thoughts and put random, foolish, and outrageous ideas in her head.

His hand squeezed her own, reminding her that he was still present. She'd almost forgotten he was there. Putting a hand to her tightening chest, she counted silently to five and breathed out. Her imagination had run rampant once again, causing wild thoughts. She reminded herself that one kiss, two kisses, or even three kisses didn't bring about marriage. That was up to both participants in the relationship, and she most certainly did *not* want that just yet.

But Ricochet's kisses had brought a tremendous happiness to her burdened life. What exactly should she call their relationship?

"Rosemary?" Ricochet questioned for the second time and then squeezed her hand tightly to gain her attention.

She shook her head, cleared away the rabbit trail her brain had chased down, and then gazed up at him. He was so tall that she barely came up above his elbow. The amusing recollection of him lifting her up off the water keg made her giggle from behind her buttoned lips. Since when did she giggle?

"Sorry." She chewed her bottom lip nervously. "What were you saying?"

He tilted his head. His eyebrows were knit as if he were in deep thought. "I was just thinking about the other night."

She held her breath. Had he read her thoughts? The wagon master couldn't really be a prodding tool, winsome, charming, and a mind reader too, could he? She avoided eye contact and gazed ahead. "Yes?"

His back stiffened, and he became serious. There was no smirk, no eye contact, and no lighthearted teasing. Something about him was off. "Someone broke into the Webbs' wagon," he finally said.

She wouldn't say that she felt relieved to change to this subject, but it sure felt good to know that he couldn't read her thoughts. She blew out a breath of relief and then asked, "Was anyone hurt?"

He shook his head. His eyes stared ahead, as if he were in deep concentration. The way that all joking had been set aside in his mannerisms made her wonder if he was as simple and carefree as she'd originally thought he was.

"No, but someone stole a considerable amount of medical supplies, including our remaining bottles of ether. I'd say it was enough to keep someone sedated for a week or more. Some of the bottles had been smashed to pieces. If something happens while we're out here, we'll have no way of performing immediate medical attention. Towns and forts are scarce between here and Oregon."

Her eyes fell to his well-defined biceps, which she could see beneath his shirtsleeve. The way that he'd saved her from the river hadn't been lost on her. His body was built for travel and for weathering dangerous situations on the trail. What was this man capable of should he find the culprit who stole from the medical wagon? Would he kill the thief?

This was the first thing Rosemary had heard about a robbery, but it helped her make sense of the reason why everyone refrained from socializing. It also explained why each wagon had been inspected at the end of every day. Why hadn't she heard of it earlier? She must be oblivious as well as harebrained.

"Have you found out who did it?" she continued, curious as to the reason why someone would do such a thing. The pioneers had to band together out there to survive, otherwise, death was a guarantee. It was utter foolishness to steal from one another and the primary doctor.

"Not yet." His answer was curt and to the point. She saw a flicker of determination within his clear eyes and knew that he would catch whoever the thief was. Hopefully, the supplies would be found as well.

A glimmer of hope sparkled for an instant as she thought, *Maybe he can help me as well.* But that was too unrealistic. Ricochet was notably strong, witty, and handsome, but it was harebrained to think that he would go up against the man who had stolen her parents' lives and her home.

"Rosemary, I have a question to ask you," Ricochet said, once again breaking her train of thought. He peered down at her with his eyes narrowed. "Why did you come out here alone? I know you said that your parents died in a fire, but surely, you had some other relatives back east."

There it was. She had been expecting the interrogation. No preparation in the world could help her form the right explanation to give him. He knew that her parents were dead. They had been killed in a fire. She still hadn't given him all the details. The desire to reveal everything was intense, but her iron will and overprotective nature of him was also. She warred with the idea. She wondered when she had become so protective of him. He was a man for goodness sake!

"Ric," she started and then hesitated until he halted as the wagons rolled by.

When she didn't look up at him, he bent down to look her in the eye. His sincere and handsome features attracted her like a fly to honey. She couldn't avoid his gaze for long.

"Jackson told me how you came to them with little money and asked to travel out west on their wagon. There must be some reason why you would journey all the way out here in this wild unsettled place."

Her heart raced. He'd been gathering information on her. Did he know about the admirer too? The answer was on the tip of her tongue, yet she couldn't bring herself to tell him anything. She might be called a coward, but she wanted to keep the most important thing in her life safe. If that meant keeping the admirer a secret, then that's what she would do. If she were to tell him, his life would be in the hands of the admirer, and she couldn't bring herself to let that happen.

"It's a rather boring and lengthy story really." She shrugged off his sincerity with a wry smile.

"Try me," he said, placed his hands on his hips, and softened his tone. "We've got all the time in the world out here, Darlin'."

Swallowing hard, her eyes went to his firm stare and then to his mouth. He had perfect lips beneath his neat, course, mustache whiskers. She gave an uncertain smile and backed away before she could succumb to his charm and sweet-talking.

Shaking her head slowly, she said, "There was nothing left back home, end of story."

"So you decided to come out to the middle of nowhere? Alone, I might add?" Skepticism was written all over his face, and Rosemary felt pressured to spill everything that she knew. But she didn't.

He shifted his weight to his left leg and furrowed his brow considerably. "I don't buy a lick of that. You ain't exactly a puzzle to figure out, Rosemary. I can tell that something scares you about going back east."

She licked her lips and looked at anything besides his captivating glare. A devilish thought scurried across her mind. Most definitely, a kiss would distract him. He wouldn't press for answers if she went for his mouth. But she couldn't do that with several pioneers watching, so she settled for a harsh remark instead.

"Don't act so smug like you know everything just by looking at me." She crossed her arms. "You might have told me all there is to know about you, but that certainly doesn't mean that I must tell you all about me. It isn't any of your business whether I'm afraid for my life or not."

He chuckled loudly, with his head reared back, bent back down to her level, and said, "Listen, Darlin'. I say it's plumb right my business if you expect any more of my kisses." Then he whispered softer than the fluttering of a butterfly's wing, "Judging by how much you enjoyed them the other night, I'd go further to say that this was a serious courtship, and I already staked my claim."

She fumed as her eyes flashed with fire, which might as well have burnt him alive. "Well, consider this *courtship* off! I don't need you or your kisses." She harrumphed loudly, maybe a little too loudly.

Ricochet smirked as he straightened up. "We'll see about that, Miss Barker." As he turned to leave, he peered over his shoulder and vowed, "I'll find out about your past, lil lady, and whatever you're fearin', I'll end it."

Much to her dismay, Rosemary didn't doubt that he would discover her past before the journey's end. She just hoped that her keeping silent would ensure his safety for the time being. Watching the wagon master stomp off victoriously and so sure of himself made her blood boil, but her stomach was all aflutter. He carried himself with such confidence, as if he had a sense of purpose. His vow wasn't wicked or malicious but was endearing—he only wanted to protect her. But that's what she wanted to do for him: protect him. *If only he weren't so stubborn! Confound him and his iron will!* she thought.

While watching his back, she envisioned him hurt and wounded and the admirer winning. The thought provoked hot tears. She couldn't let that happen. There was no way that she would allow Ricochet Chapel to die on her behalf. The admirer needed to be found. The only problem was how to deal with him once she discovered him. She knew what he was capable of and how vile he was beneath his manly exterior. If it came down to it, she realized that she'd gladly let the admirer have her if it meant keeping Ricochet alive. Her throat constricted. She wondered if it would come down to that.

# Chapter 13

❧❦❧

There Ricochet sat with the barrel of his shotgun aimed at a nearby buck. With the weapon cocked and ready, the innocent life of an animal was at his mercy, but all he could think about was the way his spat with Rosemary had ended earlier that afternoon. He never wanted to anger her or stir up strife between them. He only wanted answers and to find the scoundrel who was responsible for her pain. He wanted to keep her safe.

Her reaction hadn't gone the way that he'd hoped it would. He was beginning to wonder whether she would allow him to court her after the wagon train had disbanded. He hadn't really imagined himself as being heroic, but he desired that the woman he chose would fall head over heels in love with him. Perhaps, she saw him as pushy, possessive, or even overprotective. He had made a blasted fool of himself, yelling and causing a ruckus in front of the pioneers that he was supposed to be leading. Eventually, everyone was bound to know that something had started between him and the lovely Miss Barker but not like this.

Ricochet let his finger pull the trigger, and a loud, "Bang!" sounded. The buck twitched and attempted to run for cover, but it was too late. He'd hit the mark and punctured the buck's lung. Creeping closer, Ricochet let another shot pierce the animal's head. The buck wasn't big, and it wouldn't feed everyone on the wagon train, but it was a good start.

The hunting party was made up of five men: Isaac, Victor, young Andrew, Mace, and Ricochet. Their goal was to gather enough meat for that night's supper and then some. They'd split into three groups, although Ricochet would've preferred only two hunting patrols. Isaac and Victor took the east side of the woods, Mace preferred to be alone on the west side, and Ricochet took Andrew southward.

He originally planned for Andrew to stay back at the wagons, telling him to keep watch, but when the boy begged to go along with him, he couldn't bring himself to refuse. Getting raging glares from Edward, the kid's pa, only encouraged him to bring the boy along just to spite the old man. So far, Ricochet was quite impressed with the young teen's spirit and instincts on the hunt. He'd never seen a boy so well trained in the art. Together they'd caught a few hares and the medium-sized buck.

"Good shot, Ricochet!" Andrew grinned. His ruddy appearance was enlightened and free of worry, unlike when he was back at camp and ruled over by his pa's iron fist.

Ricochet touched the brim of his hat and then hung his single-barreled weapon over his shoulder by its leather strap. "Thanks, kid. Now help me gut him. The others'll be around soon."

He watched Andrew scurry from where they had been crouching downwind and followed him. It almost felt like he was a father and Andrew was his son. Rosemary came back to mind once more. He remembered her sweet aroma filling his nostrils and the taste of her lips on his. The little minx had taken up so much of his practical thinking already, and now he had no common sense to cease the ridiculous imagining of them marrying and having children someday. *Blast it all!* he thought.

Andrew appeared to be puzzled as he furrowed his brow at the wagon master's agitated and yet engaged expression. "Mister Ric?" he asked. "You're making a weird face. Am I doing something wrong?"

Ricochet froze with his knife in hand. He had been about to skin the animal. He peered at the boy and then chuckled to himself at the weird scene that must be playing on his profile. He shook his head. "No, Son, just thinking is all."

His young charge seemed curious but made no motion to press for answers.

*Smart kid,* Ricochet thought. Ricochet decided that since he and the boy were alone, this would be the perfect time to question him about the medical wagon's incident. Carefully, he asked the lad. "Andrew," he began, focusing on the knife in his hands instead of the boy's face, "I was wonderin' 'bout that unfortunate mishap with the medical wagon." Now he turned his gaze to meet Andrew's widening eyes. "Care to tell me what you saw?"

The child tensed his shoulders and focused on his small fists in his lap. "I-I didn't really see anything …" He was obviously scared to recall what had happened, but that didn't sit well with the wagon master. Ricochet needed answers.

Evidence was nowhere to be found, and he was growing impatient. His only witness was this timid boy. "I know you saw someone, Andrew." He pressed further carefully. "It's just you and me. Tell me what you saw."

Andrew gulped loudly as perspiration beaded down the side of his temple. "He said he'd hurt Macy if I told anyone."

*So,* Ricochet thought, *he not only witnessed the robbery but had actual contact with the culprit.*

He wondered how anyone could threaten a child in such a vile way. Names came to mind all too quickly, including Andrew's own father, but Ricochet needed more to go on than a threat. He leaned forward and set his knife down. "Son, I must know who threatened you. I can end it if you give me a name."

A war played on the boy's face as he debated about the wagon master's words.

"Nothing will happen to little Macy. I'll make sure of it," Ricochet added, staking his life on it.

"His face was covered with a cloth," Andrew burst out while his body trembled with enough fear for both himself and Ricochet. "But I knew who he was 'cause I've heard his voice before."

"What is his name?" Ricochet pleaded gently so that the kid would not be spooked.

Andrew's eyes filled with tears of fright, as he parted his lips to voice the name of the culprit. He took a sharp breath, but before he could answer, Mace stepped out from the shrubbery. When the lone hunter had seen their game, he complimented, "Good shootin'."

Ricochet sighed, displeased with his friend's ill timing, and nodded at his partner's game, which was tied up and slung over his shoulder. "Same to you."

At least a dozen hares mixed with two quail hung on Mace's shoulder by a rope. The man was a wonder. He knew tracking and hunting better than anyone that Ricochet had ever met.

"Wow, Mace!" Andrew applauded, as thoughts of the previous topic were forgotten, "That's a lot! How'd you find them all?" He raced to Mace's side.

The normally silent rider set down his loot and urged the boy to come closer with a scarred finger. "Patience. Keen eyes. That's the trick." The two of them went on for several minutes. The boy was awestruck at Mace's expertise and wisdom.

Ricochet could see that Mace could not be behind the robbery, for Andrew was so enlivened by the quiet man's presence. He wondered who could be issuing these threats. He'd interrogated all the men and inspected every wagon at least seven times. There was no evidence to be found. He was beginning to believe that it had all been a hoax.

They gathered the game together. Then they gutted and skinned the animals away from camp to keep bears from getting too close to their wagons' corral campsite. Ricochet had only encountered a wild grizzly thrice before and barely escaped with his life each time. They were not something to play around with, although he'd heard rumors of men who were daring enough, or foolhardy enough, to attempt to kill one for its fur coat.

They made quick work of it and then sat down for a snack of dried fruit and jerky. The snack was followed by canteens of fresh water, which complemented the saltiness of the tough jerky.

"Andrew," Ricochet said after taking a swig of his canteen, "where did you learn to hunt?"

The young boy stiffened at the question and replied with a sour expression on his face, "My pa taught me. Said it wasn't right for a man not to hunt and shoot a gun. He threatened to use me as target practice if I didn't go with him."

Ricochet's heart sunk low in his chest. He hadn't meant to bring up terrible memories but only a conversation with the depressed kid. Afraid that he had made things worse, he patted the boy on the back and grinned, "How about we head back to camp and I'll show ya how to prep these critters for supper."

"Ain't that women's work?" Andrew's features shifted quizzically.

He grinned at the boy's question and then answered, "We can't very well let the women do all the work around here. Why, they'll start thinking us incompetent."

When Mace grinned slightly but smugly and Ricochet asked about it, he only got an all-knowing shrug in return. That led the wagon master to believe that his assistant on the wagon train had already pieced two and two together. He knew about Ricochet and Rosemary, which didn't really surprise Ricochet all that much, seeing how bright and smart the man was. But it made the reality of his small spark with her sink in all the more. At least, he hoped that he and Rosemary still had a spark.

He groaned inwardly at the realization that he would have to apologize to her for his being so persistent and aggressive during their little squabble. Maybe he could get her to see reason, and then she would regret ever not wanting him to hunt down her admirer. Sadly, he knew she wouldn't come to him, so he would have to mend the gap instead.

They packed up their hunting gear, keeping an eye out for the other group to return. Victor and Isaac didn't turn up even when they started their trek back to camp. Ricochet considered going back into the woods to look for them after dropping off Andrew and the game they'd caught. Dragging the heavy buck through the forest on a possible wild-goose chase would be foolish, especially with roaming grizzlies around.

He and Mace lifted the buck over a fallen log. They were careful not to get its rack tangled in the branches. Andrew climbed over the log while carrying the packs and a few hares over his shoulder. The boy wasn't a sissy. That was for sure.

The snapping of a twig nearby stopped Ricochet in his tracks. He halted to listen, and as he did, something zipped with incredible speed by the side of his cheek, making him drop the hind legs of the buck. The sheer force knocked him off balance and took his breath away, but the sound next to his ear scared him the most. His left ear was ringing loud enough to make a bugle seem pathetic. The release of buckshot wasn't a sound that a hunter forgot.

A trickle of warm blood ran down his cheek. He realized that the thing rushing past had also sliced a good-sized mark on his face too. He wiped at his jawline and then regained his stance on the forest floor. It wasn't until he regained his bearings that he noticed that Mace had ducked down and that he was kneeling over something behind them.

Ricochet winced, rubbing his ear to get the infernal ringing to stop. He stumbled closer to see what had spooked his partner just as two men came hurrying out of the woods. He couldn't believe the scene. The still body and the pale and shocked face were all too much. He could feel his snack from earlier creeping its way back up as he fell to his knees. His pupils dilated, and his head shook in disbelief.

Isaac and Victor had arrived. Both were mesmerized by what they saw and holding their weapons, but the wagon master was in too much of a traumatized state to understand their expressions and horrified gasping.

Isaac bent over the small lifeless body of Andrew Jones, caressing the boy's rusty-brown hair.

"Andrew!" Isaac's voice said shakily. He dropped down beside Ricochet and next to the still form of the boy. "I swear it was an accident. M-my gun went off by mistake!"

Mace and Victor dragged Isaac, who was in a hysterical state of mind, away from the scene. Ricochet shook his head and lost all sense of the panic around him. His only focus was on Andrew, who lay in absolute shock. The boy's body convulsed, and his pupils dilated. All the color fled his face. He looked a ghastly and pale sight. Ricochet hesitated to move him but instead held his hands over the kid, pondering what to make of it all.

Shivering and staring up at the wagon master, Andrew whispered in a barely audible voice, "D-don't let him get me."

Ricochet narrowed his eyes in confusion, snapping out of his shock. "What?"

As Andrew choked and started to become unconscious, he reached for the wagon master's shirt. He clutched Ricochet's shirt tight in his trembling fist. "H—he's gonna kill me," he rasped weakly. Then his fist went slack.

Ricochet grabbed the boy's hand and held it tightly in his own. He wondered at Andrew's words. He was baffled by them. "Who?" was all that he could ask. The boy went still, and his eyes closed. Ricochet released his hand and then cupped the boy's face and asked again but louder this time, "Andrew, who?"

# Chapter 14

Rosemary hated herself. Her ears were growing weary of listening to Charity's never-ending babble about men, which had been going on since they had circled the wagons about an hour earlier. She didn't dislike her friend in the least, but sometimes, the younger woman was a mite tiresome.

They had nestled themselves into a spot beside a steady brook and right by the camping circle. Charity, Lily, Katrina with her newborn, Samuel, and she had taken what laundry they had to the stream for a time of washing and mending. With endless travel on the trail, laundry days were a rarity and done whenever possible. It being a Saturday evening and the morrow a Sunday full of devotions and prayer to God, Ricochet had decreed the day to be a time of rest and repairs as usual.

Right now, Rosemary would give anything just to get away from Charity's rampant and all-knowing giggles. "Honestly, Rosemary," she went on with a glimmer of amusement. "Why didn't you tell me that you and the wagon master had been getting along?

Rosemary grumbled while soaking another petticoat in the stream. "Because I hadn't planned anything serious to come of it."

The preacher's daughter held a teasing grin on her freckled face. "I heard that Victor Marsh saw the two of you by the water kegs the other night."

Rosemary felt her throat tighten immensely and she dropped the petticoat she'd been washing. The skin on her face warmed, and her ears turned red. When Katrina joined in, Rosemary thought she'd keel over with embarrassment.

"He's a very fine young man," Katrina said, smiling.

Lily Garrison stifled a snicker as her cherry-colored lips spread into a bashful smile. "And what, pray tell, were the two of you doing without the watchful eye of a chaperone?"

"Doesn't matter," Rosemary huffed, wringing out water from the petticoat in her hands, which she had reclaimed from the stream. "It won't happen again."

"Has he asked for your hand yet?" Charity asked.

Rosemary froze. Her eyes were wide and her back was as stiff as a board. Charity was an absolute wonder, and that was Rosemary being nice. Rosemary couldn't very well spill the events of the other night. It was too delicate of a scene, not to mention the backstory leading up to it. The last thing that she wanted was to tell others of Ricochet's past, which would indeed happen if she told Charity. She would refrain from doing the like and deny everything.

"No, of course not." Rosemary dismissed the idea with a wave of her hand.

As her motherly instincts kicked in, Katrina asked, "How long has this courtship been going on without me noticing?"

Rosemary wondered when the questions would end. She rolled her eyes. "There is no courtship. I told him so myself. The meeting was clumsy on my part, and it will most certainly not happen again." Her own words couldn't convince her that it was just an act done foolishly in the heat of the moment. Her heart beat faster the longer she thought about him, and her ribcage tightened whenever she heard his voice. This was no mistake. She really felt something for him. But what exactly did she feel?

Lily, the shyest of them all, spoke up after several minutes of giggling at Charity's interrogation. "You two do make quite the pair. I'm not at all surprised, seeing how he can't seem to keep his eyes off you. I'd go as far as to say that it was God's leading hand that brought you both together."

*God's leading hand.* Rosemary liked the sound of it. It was almost like a fairytale: the fateful day when a princess was rescued by a knight and then taken to his castle. But stories like that one simply didn't come true, not in real life.

The fight that she had had earlier with him had wounded her spirit.

She wanted to protect him and keep him out of harm's way. The news of her and Ricochet's meeting at the water kegs had obviously spread like wildfire, so the admirer had to have heard of it by now. Her stomach clenched. She prayed that Ricochet would remain safe, but kissing and holding hands would have to stop immediately, otherwise, everyone would be in danger.

Katrina placed a wet but comforting hand on Rosemary's trembling fist. "Are you all right, dear?"

Charity chimed in, "You look pale. Are you feeling faint again?"

Rosemary looked into the sincere eyes of Katrina, the woman who had impacted her life like no other, and forced a cheerful smile. "I'm fine. Just another dizzy spell."

"Why don't you take a break," she suggested, laying Samuel in his wool-coated basket. She returned her gaze to Rosemary. "We'll finish up here. You go lie down for a while."

"But I—" Katrina's index finger came up, and Rosemary was hushed before she had a chance to refuse.

Gaining no leeway with the wise mother, Rosemary caved in and began her trek back to the corral. When she reached the circle of schooners, her head grew dizzier than ever with spinning thoughts and doubts. She knew that what she had told her friends back at the stream was all a big lie. Of course, she didn't think that the kiss Ricochet had stolen had been a mistake. It was quite the contrary. It was purposeful on his part, and her taking pleasure in returning the kiss had been on purpose. Nothing about it was a mistake or an accident. She enjoyed it, and he did too.

She inserted her hand into the pocket of her forest green dress and took out a note. It was of the same material as her previous letters and the same scent too. She read it for the third time that day, and sadly, all the heartache flooded back into mind.

*My dearest Rose,*

*How you have betrayed me! I had thought you to be a smart girl, but now I see that you are as foolish as the rest of your kind—emotional and easily manipulated.*

*Do not fret, my dear, for all will be forgiven. However, in order to gain such mercy and privilege, the wagon master with his charming ways will have to be erased permanently. Unless of course, you make the right decision and pledge yourself to me. I leave it all up to you, my beautiful rose.*

*Your loving admirer.*

She had thought about tearing the note up in case someone got the bright idea to snatch it and read it, but something held her back. Her admirer could be watching her that very minute. She didn't have the courage to challenge him and his art of killing. Deep down, she knew that he was capable of anything, including the destruction of the man that she had shared a single, romantic moment with. The choice to give the wagon master up would be difficult. Then again, his teasing had increased her temper and doubled her emotional strain. But this was to save his life. *I must reject him to save him*, she thought.

"Help!" It was the cry of a man from across the camp. Rosemary, forgetting that she was supposed to be resting under the strict orders of Katrina, crept forward. The man was tall, covered in dirt, and carried a limp body in his arms. She gasped as she saw the awful and horrific scene. Ricochet dragged one foot in front of the other. What had once looked like dirt staining his face and shirt now resembled blood. His hat sat just above his dazed and frightened eyes. In his arms, he held Andrew Jones, who was limp and lifeless.

"He's been shot!" Ricochet shouted. "Get Dr. Webb!"

She went numb from head to toe as many pioneers pushed and crowded to get a better look. Her feet were planted, even though her knees felt wobbly and threatened to collapse. All she could do was watch as Dr. Jacob Webb scurried and broke through the gathering spectators. He uttered some words into the wagon master's ear, which no one else could hear. Then he ushered him in the direction of his own wagon. Following close behind Ricochet were Mace, Victor, and Isaac. Each had sullen expressions on their faces.

A scream erupted from Rosemary's left as a scared mother ran to meet her son's still form. Autumn Jones caressed her boy's cheek and then sobbed into her hands. She moaned, "My baby. Not my beautiful baby."

It about shattered Rosemary's heart when she heard such a cry of grief. Then Andrew's father appeared on the scene, and Mace held him back as he threw angry punches at the hunting party members. After several attempts at trying to land a hit on Mace and Isaac, Edward finally collapsed in a heap of sobs and grief. His wife clutched his shirt. This display of emotion had never been seen on the harsh man's face until now. The event had changed him completely into a true father who cared for his son's life.

The events unfolded before her eyes, and soon, Andrew's parents were sitting outside of Jacob's wagon as the doctor went to work inside. From what Rosemary could tell, the boy was alive but just barely. She wished she had the whole story. So far, it appeared that no one knew it, although many speculated.

Katrina came hurrying by with her newborn. She nearly passed Rosemary up before coming to a swift halt and glancing down at Samuel, who slept soundly in her arms. Turning on her heels, she asked pleadingly, "Would you mind looking after him for a while, Rosemary? I must go help my husband tend to the Joneses' boy."

Not finding much choice in the matter, Rosemary nodded and accepted the newborn into her arms. Samuel was surprisingly lighter than he looked, and he snored softly in a deep sleep. His features resembled his father's more than his mother's, but Katrina's olive complexion was very much present on the newborn's body.

"Sorry to leave Samuel with you, but my husband has asked me to help." She sighed, caressing her baby's cheek tenderly.

Rosemary touched Katrina's hand with a warm and knowing glimmer on her face. "I've got him. We'll be fine."

Katrina's brow furrowed with sadness to leave her baby. Then she forced herself to turn around and rush to aid Jacob in their wagon. Once she was out of sight, Rosemary carried Samuel to the Coles' wagon. She sighed after sliding to the ground and resting her back against the wheel behind her.

Peering down at the precious little miracle sleeping in her tight hold, she smiled. He was so perfect and tiny. The cute way he snorted in his slumber made her stifle a laugh. Maybe Charity had been right about babies being miracles from God. Rosemary never really saw them that way until now. Even when she had helped nurture babies in the hospital as a volunteer with her mother, she hadn't seen them as anything special. Oh, how her mindset had changed since then. It was all thanks to the little guy she held in her lap.

Across the way, she watched as Isaac paced outside the medical wagon while Edward and Autumn, the parents, sat curled up at the wheels. Mace sat by himself several paces away, and Victor crouched low, toying with blades of grass. Ricochet, who had carried Andrew in from the woods, was nowhere in sight. It struck her as odd. She wondered where he was. He knew what had happened to the child, so he should be waiting next to the others for news of Andrew's condition. She shouldn't be worrying over the likes of him, not when her admirer could easily see it. But that didn't mean she should toss her concern for him completely aside.

Samuel stirred, fluttered his eyelashes, and stretched. He was awake. Well, Rosemary could definitely handle a resting baby. What about one who was wide-awake? Her stomach tied itself in knots just thinking about it. What do you do with a baby while it's awake? He started a squirming fit beneath his blanket and then shut his eyelids in an agitated way. His arms stretched out as he let out a soft cry. Then he pulled back and got louder and shriller than anything Rosemary had ever heard.

Rosemary got to her feet, cradling the newborn and bouncing him gently. He still screamed. She put him on her chest and patted his back gently. He screamed more. She panicked.

"You look as if you need some help." The entertained declaration had come from her right. Her head snapped in that direction to see Ricochet leaning against the wooden wheel with a smirk on his face. She hadn't seen him for almost an hour, when he had brought Andrew into camp. Since then, he'd gotten cleaned up and dressed in a fresh pair of britches, a dark buttoned-up shirt, and red necktie.

She harrumphed, turned away, and patted Samuel's back. "And what would a wild man like you know about newborns?"

The question was rhetorical, but he answered nonetheless. "Plenty." He strode to meet her and offered his arms. "May I?"

She made an annoyed click with her tongue against the roof of her mouth and then rolled her eyes. When his eyebrows raised and Samuel's cry worsened to a spluttering choke, Rosemary gave in. She handed the baby over, and Ricochet accepted him into his strong arms. Samuel was small but even smaller in the arms of the wagon master. He displayed amazing meekness at that moment. Rosemary decreed that it was strength under control. Ricochet cooed and hushed the baby's cries until Samuel finally drifted back to sleep.

Her jaw dropped. The man was astounding at calming children—first Andrew and now Samuel. Would he ever stop showing her up?

"There now." He grinned, taunting her temper. "While growing up, Ma always said I had a magic touch."

She lifted her chin, acting as if she were above such digs from the likes of him. "He probably just wore himself out with all that earlier fussing." The excuse she provided seemed lamebrain and weak. She could tell that Ricochet thought this, but he was wise enough to say nothing.

Samuel's began to snore again, but Ricochet gave no notion that he wanted to give the newborn up just yet, so Rosemary allowed the man to hold him a little while longer. Watching him interact twice with children, she was beginning to think that maybe he would make a great father someday. There ran that ridiculous imagination of hers again.

When she thought that the silence had gone on for too long, Rosemary spoke up, saying, "What happened? In the woods, I mean."

Ricochet sighed. His dark gaze didn't leave the newborn, which he held close to his chest. "It was a misfire." His jaw tensed. "Isaac's gun went off as he tried to climb over a fallen tree. It grazed Andrew's head. I'm not sure he'll make it."

Rosemary could sense that there was something else on his mind, but she didn't push for answers. Instead, she let him say it in his own time.

"It was my fault," he choked. She saw the tears slightly filling his eyes. I should never have brought him along. He should've stayed here."

*How the tables have turned,* Rosemary thought. He had been the strong one. He was always smiling and encouraging her to go on. Now it was her turn to do the smiling and encouraging. She watched him slide to a seated, cross-legged position. Samuel still snored away in the crook of his arm. She followed his lead, sitting with her legs straight out and the ends of her dress tucked around her ankles and calves.

She placed a firm hand on his forearm. "It wasn't your fault," she said as her touch gained his undivided attention. "Accidents happen. You couldn't have foreseen it."

"I could've prevented it," he murmured as his wide-brimmed Stetson slide lower on his brow. She wondered how had such a strong heroic figure had gotten to this depressed point. She wouldn't stand for it. The admirer might be watching, but she could care less. Ricochet needed comfort and someone to bear his heavy burden with him and tell him that everything would be fine.

Straightening her spine and crossing her arms tightly over her chest, she stared at the medical wagon. "Weren't you the one that said God had a plan for His children? Why do you doubt Him now? Isn't every life in His hands?" Her cheeks felt hot as she refused to look at him.

As if a light of hope came to life, his eyes seemed to smile and shine with renewed vigor. He chuckled as if finding irony in her speech. "Funny how our roles have swapped." A grin that made Rosemary's heart skip happily appeared on his face. "You're right, darlin'. He does have a plan."

The awkward clearing of a throat halted their encouraging talk, and Rosemary jerked her gaze away from his. Ricochet snorted quietly and peered up from where he sat. Mace was looking off in the distance and floundering in the guilt of ruining the moment.

"I thought you might want to hear about the boy," Mace said as he regained the purpose of his mission. "Jacob's done, and he has an update on Andrew."

Ricochet passed the newborn to Rosemary and then stood to dust off his backside. "Good. I want to hear everything." He gave one last glance over his shoulder at Rosemary, winked, and then followed Mace to the Webbs' wagon.

Watching him leave was like facing the growing emptiness inside her. Once again, she had lost herself to his charm after vowing to stop the whole thing. She wondered how foolish she could be. Her admirer was bound to go after him now, and it would be her undoing. No decision that she ever made had been easy or correct. She wondered why her life couldn't just be simple and why must everything go awry.

She sighed and heard the beginning cries of Samuel as he awoke. When the full-on screaming started, she missed Ricochet's so-called *magic touch*.

# Chapter 15

Ricochet felt embarrassed for losing himself to his emotions, especially in front of the woman he adored. No woman ever found a man's tears striking or attractive, at least, that is what he had been led to believe. He'd ruined the image of his strong, powerful, and charming character by doing so. Frustration was the word for it¾bitter frustration. He wondered what had gotten into him.

Still, recalling her warm, gentle voice of encouragement brought a tug to his lips. If a few tears won him her wholehearted support and care, he would have gladly shed a bucket more to hold her in his arms.

Jacob exited the wagon, wiping sweat from his brow. He greeted them solemnly and informed, "He's stable."

"How bad?" Ricochet asked, hushing his tone in case Autumn, the boy's mother, overheard.

The doctor shook his head. "It's a miracle he's alive. The bullet grazed his skull without shattering it, which is amazing in itself, but he's been in and out of consciousness. As long as we can get him to drink and rest, he should be able to face recovery. It's going to be a long haul for him though, especially if infection sets in."

The wagon master couldn't begin to describe his relief at the good news. Andrew was alive, which meant that he had a chance. A slim chance was better than nothing was.

There was one thing more that had him concerned. Something had been fired during the echo of the first misfire. Not only that, but something had hit the kid while slicing the side of Ricochet's own cheek as well. That had to mean that there were two shots fired and not one.

Earlier, his interrogation of Isaac had been curt, but the troubled man was in deep agony over the incident. The story was that Isaac and Victor had been on their way back to camp when Isaac's gun had misfired and hit Andrew's temple, knocking him unconscious. No one had fired a second shot. But the proof on Ricochet's cheek and the second echo that he had heard proved another theory: Someone had shot at the same time as the first one. Accident or not, someone else's gun had gone off. This was too many mishaps for Ricochet's liking.

"Is Andrew up for visitors?" he asked.

Jacob shrugged. "The boy's out cold. He hasn't woken up." His sigh seemed to go on for several seconds in Ricochet's ears. The pain of the doctor's next words was unbearable. "I don't know if he ever will."

The wagon master stared passed Jacob, watching the medical wagon like a hawk. He had feared that this bullet wound would cripple the young boy. That hadn't stopped him from going to his heavenly Father for a miracle. Even now, his soul cried out to God to show up and do something in Andrew's life.

If Andrew never awoke from this sleep, he would never know another sunrise or walk under the speckled light through the tree branches of the woods. The reality of the situation was heart wrenching, and Ricochet was near his breaking point. With Jacob's permission, the wagon master removed his hat and headed for the place where the young, scrawny Andrew Jones slept.

Upon entering the schooner, he saw the boy's body lying still on the floorboards. Andrew was covered in a thick woolen blanket, and his head was propped up with several cloths and wrapped in a bandage. His pale face looked almost porcelain in the lantern light. Ricochet noticed that with each breath that the injured boy took, his small chest heaved and shuttered. Andrew was alive but just barely.

With a good amount of ether missing from the medical wagon, Ricochet didn't think the doctor would be able to relieve the pain much longer. The poor kid would face a great deal of agony if they ran completely out. He wondered what would happen then. It might be better for someone to ride back to the last town that they had passed and buy some medical supplies. The idea might have to become a reality. He didn't know what other options there were. But that would be a seven-day journey and a hard ride without stopping.

No. He couldn't go with that idea. There was no one crazy enough to send besides him and Mace, and they were both needed to keep Edward and Victor in line. To add to this, Edward had already made threats against Isaac, and Ricochet didn't doubt that the hard Mr. Jones would exact revenge if the wagon master let down his guard. Victor had already showed much disgust for Dr. Webb. If Ricochet or Mace were to leave them unattended, Victor would turn the whole wagon train against the good doctor and his wife. Besides all that, Rosemary would be left unguarded against a raving lunatic. Ricochet reasoned within himself that they would just have to make do with what they had.

He ran a shaky hand through his hair as he breathed out heavily. He had no choice. Something had to be done, or the boy would suffer worse. He kept vigil for a while longer and then made his exit so that the parents could have time alone with their child. He leaped out of the wagon's entrance and then straightened. He saw that Mace was standing there waiting for him.

It was well past suppertime, and the faint smell of roasted deer made his mouth water uncontrollably. He was hungry, and before he could do any solving of mysteries, he needed to eat. The two of them went to the fire and ate the remains of the late meal. Then they handed their dishes to Victor for washing. The supply wagon's driver seemed very quiet. Ricochet guessed that it was due to the horrific event that had happened in the woods.

Victor Marsh was an outspoken, illiterate kind of man that got on the wagon master's nerves often enough to make Ricochet want to strangle the misfit at times. But there were moments when the man surprised him with incredible durability and a well-trained way about him. He could track and hunt. He had keen eyes for trouble, which was why Ricochet had kept him around for as long as he had. Victor wore classy-style clothing, which didn't fit their traveling circumstances. He wasn't a man to be given to comfort and lavish living. He just had good taste.

"How's the boy?" Victor asked, gathering up the soap for washing the tin cups.

Ricochet was careful when he answered because he was uncertain as to whether it was his right to inform everyone of Andrew's welfare. After all, the boy wasn't his. It should be Edward Jones's news to tell. "He's very weak," he said at last.

Victor shook his head as an expression of sorrow clouded his face. "Poor kid. Parents must be heartbroken." He stacked his arms full of dishes and took them to the stream.

*I suppose that'll be the last glimpse of Isaac we'll see when Ed gets wind of what really happened in the woods*, Ricochet thought. A smug grin crossed his face and then disappeared. Victor had always disliked Isaac Beckett. Most of the men knew it. But Isaac never cared for Victor either, so bickering and fighting had broken out between them often, which made Ricochet think that maybe it hadn't been a good idea to leave the two of them alone to hunt. It had been a bad decision on his part.

He had wanted Andrew's story. He had figured that he could get the kid to talk about the medical thief's identity. That decision had ultimately left him with Andrew's near-death experience and none-other-than Isaac Beckett at the trigger.

Isaac's ragged state had everyone worried and on edge. Of course, no one blamed him¾not yet anyway. Edward Jones had yet to hear of it. Isaac wouldn't be up to fighting a grieving father, if it came down to that. The young man had a kind heart toward all, no matter how prideful he could be when it came to sticking up for himself in situations that didn't include him. Ricochet had tried to take the man under his wing and encourage him to be more humble, but it was slow going. Isaac was well spoken, and he had gentlemanlike manners, but when he was angry, he had a mouth on him. He occasionally reminded Ricochet of Victor Marsh.

Ricochet drank the leftover water in his canteen, washing down the taste of deer steak and hard biscuits. Once Victor had left him and Mace alone, the wagon master spoke. "I want you to watch over the boy tonight, Mace."

Mace gave him a baffled look, arching his left eyebrow. "Something got ya spooked?"

Ricochet didn't answer the man's question but informed, "I'm taking a walk. I'll be back before nightfall."

Mace caught him by the arm. He leaned close to his ear and stated, "You heard it too. The second shot going off."

The wagon master hadn't expected Mace to be so keen and attentive to details. He wondered if the silent rider read thoughts *and* had superhuman hearing. Mace astounded him. He thought that the man might have been a hawk or wolf in another life. "Don't let Andrew out of your sight," he warned. "I'm not positive, but I don't believe this to be some tragic misfire."

Ricochet left after Mace had vowed to stay near the medical wagon until he returned. He strode off into the woods, the place where Andrew had been shot. A shudder ran through him. He couldn't think about it, not if he wanted to go through with his investigation.

The sun had begun its descent below the horizon, but there would be at least another hour of daylight. That would be all the time that Ricochet needed to find what he was looking for. He arrived at the scene quickly, considering how much he wanted to turn tail and run back to the wagon circle. His gut clenched at the dried blood that was still staining the earth. It made him sick to think that Andrew could die because of a careless mistake while using a rifle. The dread of going back to the camp and hearing that the boy is dead or would be dead soon scared him. If that kind of news awaited him, he might stay out there for the remainder of his life.

He knelt to inspect the soiled patch of ground. The metallic scent hit him, and he had to back up a ways to keep from losing his meal. He'd been around plenty of blood in his life, but this was an innocent boy's blood. It was a slightly different, bitter scent in his nostrils.

Ten paces ahead was the tree where Ricochet had been standing when the misfire had happened. As if in response to the memory, the scrape on his cheek throbbed and ached. With his jaw clenched, he rose to his feet, walked over to a tree, and felt the bark. The tree was full of life and greenery, and moss and other plants sprouted from its limbs and around its base. But that wasn't what the wagon master was looking for.

He brought his face closer to the tree and spotted a black, powdery substance: bullet residue. A chunk of the tree had been blown away, leaving a gaping hole and the residue of gunpowder. That was what had grazed Ricochet's cheek during the misfire. He was right. The bullet *had* zipped past him.

The rustle of leaves and the snapping of a twig caused him to spin around and whip out his revolver. His eyes narrowed as he examined each tree, bush, and rock formation. Nothing stirred or came at him. He didn't hear a gun go off or feel the impact of lead hitting his chest. All was silent. But he reminded himself that twigs didn't snap themselves. Then again, it was a forest, and forests had animals, birds, and natives in them.

He waited a minute more and then holstered his revolver again. While releasing his breath, which he'd apparently been holding for quite a while, he shook his head. He wondered if he was going mad.

His shoulders slouched. He decided that it was best to head back to camp. The light of the day had gone, and shadows of tree limbs had formed into claws at his feet. He tugged his hat farther down and onto his brow and started the trek back to the wagons.

However, he stopped short. A single scrap of paper tied with a black ribbon hung neatly from the tree that was just above his head. He wondered how he had missed it earlier.

Being six feet, two inches, he had never considered himself a short man, but he actually had to jump to reach the paper. The person who had put it there must have been at least a couple of inches taller than he was or had climbed up the tree to put it there. Unrolling the paper and tossing the ribbon aside, he read the contents carefully. He didn't know what to expect.

It was just a scrap of paper, but after reading what it contained, his every breath seemed to grow harder and harder to take in. A lump the size of a bolder swelled in his throat. He had wanted answers regarding the things that he'd heard and felt during the misfire, but maybe he shouldn't have been so keen on getting them.

The note read,

**Next time I won't miss!**

The scratch on his cheek burned like fire, and he clenched his teeth r in anger. It was evident that someone meant to spook him, but he wondered to what purpose. His gut tightened. His surroundings seemed to mask the barrel of a gun or the murderous actions of a lunatic. The things that had once felt safe and secure now appeared terrifying and dangerous. The note had brought more questions than answers, and it was all Ricochet could do not to storm back into the circle of pioneers and interrogate every one of them individually. He couldn't do that. It would alarm the culprit.

Still, something had to be done. He couldn't stand by and let this madman fix a target to his back. Not only that, but he couldn't think as to why he would be targeted. He had no real enemies, and the culprit didn't seem to have a motive other than to rattle him. Ricochet wondered what game he was playing.

Ricochet scanned the note one last time. The penmanship looked familiar. That was when it hit him and hit him hard. He fumbled around for another note in his pocket: the one that he'd gotten from Rosemary's clenched fist after her fainting spell. He compared them. It was the same handwriting, same scent, and same scrap of paper.

Rosemary's admirer had changed course and settled on taking out Ricochet. That would not stand, not for the wagon master. Something would have to be done. He needed answers, he needed Andrew to testify, and he needed Rosemary to tell him the truth of these happenings.

# Chapter 16

Devotions started early the next morning, and Rosemary thought she might keel over from exhaustion. Yesterday's events had proven most wearisome. Andrew had been very ill the night before, so Katrina and Jacob had tended to him carefully while Rosemary had watched young Samuel. The baby did nothing but cry until Katrina fed and rocked him to sleep before she went back to work with her husband. It was a never-ending loop.

Rosemary was just thankful that Andrew was going to pull through following his head injury, although he wasn't yet fully awake. He felt serious distress because of his head injury and often murmured about being in pain in his sleep. The ether that Dr. Webb had given the boy was almost gone, and it had to be rationed.

Everyone had gathered in the center of the wagon circle to hear Pastor Jackson speak. The service wasn't anything elaborate, but he spoke on true faith and the meaning of being a child of God. To be honest, Rosemary felt convicted. She hadn't been faithful in the least to the Lord since her parents had passed away. Guilt and regret ate her up inside. She wondered she had last prayed to Him. She couldn't recall.

Bowing her head at the ending prayer, she vowed that she would try to have more trust in His power and strength instead of her own. Praying to Him might be a bit more of a challenge since she really couldn't remember how to do it. She would need to practice that, maybe later when she was alone.

The last thing that she wanted was more attention drawn to her odd mannerisms. Charity had done caused enough drama. Now everyone seemed to know about her and the wagon master. Unfortunately for Rosemary, the heat of the conversation was mostly directed at her and not at Ricochet. How miserable it was to hear the women gossiping. It made Rosemary want to scream and pull her curls out. She knew Ricochet had heard some of the ridiculousness floating around, but he hadn't batted an eyelash at any of it. The man was a wonder.

"Amen," Jackson said, raised his head, and beamed. "That will conclude our morning devotions. You are dismissed."

The crowd broke up to eat some refreshments and then do chores. Repair work still needed to be done on the wagons before the next day's long day of traveling. Laundry and mending had piled up considerably due to the ladies being distracted by the previous day's hunting incident. The cattle needed to be fed, and freshwater must be boiled. The list went on and on.

Rosemary yawned while trying to keep it hidden behind her hand. As she rose, Charity linked an arm with her. The flirtatious woman giggled and said, "So what's the story on the wagon master today?"

If only Rosemary could strangle her ... if only. She wondered what kind of friend she would be if she did. A widespread grin appeared on her pale face in such a mischievous way that she had a hard time concealing it. She laughed under her breath and then said, "I'd much rather hear about you and that cool-eyed man, Mace Chronicle."

Charity went plumb red and swallowed hard. She was never the kind to become bashful, but recently, the girl had grown secretive concerning her feelings on the dark-clad rider. It didn't suit her to be so buttoned up.

She fumbled and said, "H-he's a fine man, although he may be cold and somewhat intimidating." Her vision clouded with hopelessness. She knew that he hadn't shared a single interest in the likes of her, no matter how hard she tried to gain his attention.

The sparkle in her green eyes returned as she said, "At any rate, quit dodging the question."

*Great.* Rosemary's attempt at changing the subject had gone out the window. She wouldn't give any details but would give Charity the truth.

"I haven't spoken to him nor seen him since yesterday. He's too busy, and frankly, I'm not sure I want him around anymore."

Well that was a white lie. She actually didn't mind his teasing all that much. She'd grown fond of his humor. A plea for forgiveness tugged at her heartstrings. She would have to pray to God later to ask for His pardon on her lying lips. Sadly, she knew better than to deny her own feelings for the wagon master, but to allow further gossip to continue would be agonizing. In another few weeks, they would be arriving at their destination, and she would be free of it all.

She wondered what she would be free of. She didn't know. Fear had gotten her to this point, and she guessed that her fear would keep her going. But when she thought of fleeing in terror, Ricochet's trustworthy eyes of the clearest blue and his arms built for safety kept the notion at bay. What she felt inside wasn't a silly crush or passing attraction. Something much deeper had taken root, and she would be a fool to think otherwise.

"Rosie?" Charity unlinked her arm with Rosemary's and then showed concern. "You're going red. Is something the matter?"

Rosemary jerked her head to look the redhead in the eye and then smiled numbly, "No. I'm fine. I guess I was daydreaming a little."

Charity backed up a step behind Rosemary. She placed her palms atop Rosemary's shoulder and then whispered with glee, "Don't look now, but Mr. Wagon Master is on his way over here."

It took every ounce of Rosemary's strength not to catch Charity's bolting body by the arm and run off with her. Charity had already fled the scene when the confident Ricochet Chapel arrived to stand in front of Rosemary. He adjusted his Stetson and nodded in greeting. "If you have a minute, I'd like to speak with you about something."

A chill ran up her neck and made her shiver, for Ricochet didn't show his regular humor or senseless teasing. His tone was stern and forceful—the wagon master's tone. She wondered what he would do if she said no. Something told her that she'd better not refuse his request. She flushed pale pink and nodded her head. "I suppose I don't have a choice."

He escorted her away from the other pioneers and around the back of the supply wagon for privacy. Once the coast was clear of spying eyes and ears, Ricochet crossed his arms and glared at her. She wondered what he was up to.

Rosemary played with the frayed hem on her skirt and refused to look at him. Whatever was on his mind was serious, and it included her. She only wished she knew what was to come of this *talk*. She drew in a shaky breath before she asked, "What is it that you wanted to speak to me about?"

He thrust his hand into his pocket and brought out a wrinkled piece of paper. He fiddled with it for a moment with his eyes lowered. The wagon master's expression had Rosemary worried. She wondered what he was trying to say. If he was talking about their courtship and wanting to break it off, she'd gladly accept that. It wasn't her plan to court him anyway. The kiss had been a foolish act on her part, and she was ready to move on. Or maybe these thoughts of rejection were a means of keeping him from breaking her heart. Whatever the case, she was ready. Let him just try to shatter her spirit. She'd been wrong to let him into her life.

But that was not what Ricochet had in mind. The next thing out of his mouth sent her knees buckling. He sighed curtly and then fixed his gaze on hers. Stuffing the paper back into his pocket, he forced a smile and said, "I was wondering if you would like to have supper with me tonight."

She flushed pink. She wondered if a dinner invitation was all that he wanted to ask her about. She grew giddy at the formality of his offer. She couldn't quite remember feeling this gleeful and feminine. Wringing her hands nervously, she replied with a question of her own. "Why should I want to eat with you?"

He cocked an eyebrow and then went silent for a moment before responding. "You know, I keep asking myself that same question, but then, I remember your kiss by the water kegs."

"*My* kiss?" She guffawed. "That most certainly was *your* kiss."

He laughed and placed a hand over his heart in jest. "It was *our* kiss. I wasn't the only one enjoying myself, Miss Barker. So how about it?"

A smile tugged at her lips. She wondered how she could refuse an answer like that. Batting her lashes as she had seen Charity doing around Mace, she unleashed every ounce of femininity she could muster: chest out, back stiff and straight, eyes lowered bashfully, and lips slightly pursed. She'd capture his every attention all right.

*No! Stop! You don't want his attention!* she thought. Her body simply didn't listen to her head. She needed to regain her self-control before Ricochet stole her heart right out of her chest. Her mouth, being the foolish thing it was, wouldn't listen. "I will see you tonight." She chewed her bottom lip anxiously.

He smiled and said, "All right then."

She wondered what was wrong with her. She should've said no. All logic told her to say no. Screaming at herself for accepting the invitation did little good in the matter because she couldn't very well back out now. Even as she watched the wagon master leave, she unleashed a long sigh. Never had she met a man like him. He might not be the perfect gentleman as portrayed in fairy tales, but he came pretty close. That scared Rosemary because she knew that she'd have to dash his hopes of gaining her affection. Her admirer wouldn't spare his life. She was sure of it.

Ricochet couldn't believe his ears. He knelt down beside the injured little boy, whose head had been wrapped securely with strips of cloth that had turned slightly pink in color. After hours and hours of waiting for Andrew to awaken from his shocked state, the doctor had finally permitted visitors to venture into the wagon besides the boy's parents—or rather, mother. Edward Jones refused to visit his own son for unknown reasons, but Ricochet suspected the man was grieving despite the fact that the hard farmer had been an abusive father to the boy.

Dr. Webb had informed the wagon master of Andrew's condition upon Ricochet's arrival. Apparently, the Joneses' boy would recover, although he would have serious scarring. Without the much-needed ether and medical supplies, he would have to face quite a bit of pain and little-to-no relief.

Dr. Webb had said that Andrew would most likely not wake up, but God had already proven that theory wrong. Andrew was awake. Ricochet would get his answers now or never. Of course, he would take it gently so as not to cause the poor kid more pain.

But as Ricochet listened to the boy's answer to his first question, the wagon master was left dumbfounded. He'd expected more to go on than, "I don't remember." Surely, Andrew had just been frightened into silence.

Ricochet pressed further, growing anxious. "Kid, I need a name. I understand you're in pain. Believe me. I don't want to interrogate you right now either, but I need answers. Just one name."

Andrew's brow furrowed, and he winced. "I-I really can't remember." He teared up. "I'm sorry, sir."

Ricochet sighed and glanced back at Dr. Webb. The doctor jerked his head for the wagon master to meet him outside. Ricochet followed the weary, middle-aged man out through the opening in the canvas flaps and a few steps away. They talked in hushed tones to keep from spreading rumors among the other travelers.

The wagon master crossed his arms and frowned hard. "What was that in there? He doesn't remember anything more than his parents and his name!" *Frustrated* was the term that Ricochet would use for the fiery tongue that he was using at that moment. He had to calm himself as the doctor spoke up to reason with him.

"Things like this do happen, Ric. The child was dealt a terrible blow to the head. He suffered major blood loss. What did you expect?"

"Something more to go on." Ricochet sighed while massaging his temples. "Is there anything that can be done?"

Dr. Webb shrugged and answered gravely, "There's nothing we can do but wait for his memory to return. Could be a matter of hours or days. Some instances as these can even take months before the victim regains anything."

"Just let me know if he remembers anything," Ricochet ordered and then started to leave.

"You will be the first to know," Dr. Webb declared and turned back to the wagon.

Panic overwhelmed Rosemary as she got ready for her fast-approaching dinner with Ricochet Chapel. She rummaged through her things and then Charity's, as she tried to decide what to wear. Several dresses lay on the wagon's floor, yet she didn't like any of them. Surely, there had to be something nice for her wear.

*Wait. Why am I so bent on impressing him with what I'll wear?* she thought. She should be pushing him away and not drawing him in. She folded her hands and brought them up to her lips. *I can't do this,* she told herself.

Frustrated, she folded all the dresses and placed them back in their cases and boxes. She'd just have to wear the mangy traveling dress that she had on. She was turning to leave when a bit of lace and pink cotton caught her eye. Curious, she reached for it and pulled out the most beautiful pink gown that she had ever seen. It had white lace around the collar and at the waistline and pink gingham for the skirt and bodice of the dress. Just imagining Ricochet seeing her in that piece of clothing was enough to send her into a tizzy of excitement.

She shook her head. *Stop this. What would your admirer say? Who cares?* She laughed inwardly. *Who cares, indeed?*

Wadding up the gown, she leaped out of the wagon. A small river lay to the left of the wagon circle. Boundaries had been set up for the women to bathe there. Feeling as sticky and as hot as ever, she made her way to the body of water to wash up and dress.

She undid her hair from its messy updo and then hung up the gown that she'd chosen to wear for the evening meal. As she was about to undress, she reached for the buttons on her bodice. A twig snapped, and she froze. "Hello?" she said. Nothing stirred, and no one replied. An uneasy feeling crawled its way into her belly. "Is someone there?" she called again. Still there was no answer.

Goosebumps surfaced on her arms and legs. She wondered if she had imagined it. Surely, her mind wasn't playing cruel tricks on her. The snapping of the twig had been deafening to her ears compared to the soft noises of the small body of water behind her. She felt like she was being watched¾spied on from every side. Every tree had eyes, and every rustle of leaves was a whisper of threatening words.

It didn't take her long to decide that she wasn't going to undress but was going to take a dip with her clothes on. When it was time for her to come out of the water, she simply got out, scooped up her dress, and headed back to the wagon soaking wet to switch outfits. No eye would see her vulnerable and indecent.

Dinnertime rolled around much too quickly, and she had to force herself out of the confines of the Coles' wagon to meet the charming Ricochet Chapel. Every step was agonizing and painful for her to take. She walked on.

Every pioneer had gathered around the campfire for dinner, each grabbing his or her share. Rosemary scurried past them to avoid bumping into Charity, who would most likely tease her for looking so stylish and prim. She couldn't let the girl think that she had fallen for a man. Rosemary had warned her not to fall for Mace. That would make her a hypocrite.

Not looking where she was going, she smacked face-first into a wall of something that was really hard and sturdy. She fell backward. Her skirts were caught underfoot. Her thoughts were of hitting the ground and the pain that she would feel, but a powerful hand gripped her arm and steadied her.

"You're in an awfully big hurry to meet me."

# Chapter 17

Rosemary blushed redder than ever. "I certainly was not rushing to," she stopped and then shook her head. "Why didn't you just move aside?"

Ricochet smiled, hiding a chuckle. He thought, *Yep. That's Rosemary Barker. Always pinning the blame on someone else. The woman is a wonder.* He waited for her to straighten her skirt and pull it out from under her foot before he let go of her arm. He studied her for a moment. She was a pretty little thing dressed in pink and lace. Her lips matched the color of her bodice, and her curls had been done up under a white bonnet; however, one curl had managed to come loose, and it was dangling near her ear. If it were up to him, he'd let loose every single curl from the bonnet, just to see them fall over her shoulders.

The dress was extremely flattering on her. He had to pry his eyes away just to regain his thoughts. She was short and small in stature, but she had definitely been blessed with all the right curves in all the right places. She looked the part of an angelic figure. If only she had the mouth of one.

He dodged her question from a minute ago and took her arm in his. "We'll actually be dining outside the corral tonight." She fixed her gaze on him and looked confused and embarrassed. He reassured her with a grin and said, "Don't worry. I talked with Minister Jackson first. We'll be next to the supply wagon. Everything will be proper."

He could feel the tension in her leave, and he relaxed himself.

Tonight wasn't just a dinner that they would have together. Tonight, he would gain some answers about the note that he had found in her hand a few days ago.

They sat on a blanket beside the supply wagon, where a setup for two had been spread. Once Rosemary was seated, Ricochet sat across from her. He kept his distance, knowing that the old minister would be by to check on them within the hour.

Rosemary piped up after a minute of silence between them. "I didn't want to come," she admitted.

Curious, he asked, "Why did you?"

She went quiet again. Her eyes did not meet his gaze. He set a plate of food before her, but she only pushed the food around with her fork. The wagon master didn't feel very hungry either, but he forced himself to eat a few mouthfuls before setting the dishes aside.

She looked very fetching and young as she sat there. He wondered how old she was: twenty or maybe a year older than that. To be so beautiful at this young age, an angel must have given birth to her.

Ricochet's chest swelled, and his palms grew sweaty. *Since when do I get nervous? Since Rosemary.* Although he wanted to continue the small talk and getting to know her better, he knew that he had some business to attend to before he could indulge in pleasure.

"Rosemary?" he began, not quite certain if he should proceed.

She perked up. "Yes."

He wet his lips and went on. "I have something to tell you, but I'm not sure you'll like what I have to say."

He couldn't read her expression. He wondered if he saw confusion. He took a breath, prepared for the worst, and then removed the crumpled note from his pocket. "I found this the day we … kissed. You fainted by the water kegs, and the medical wagon was robbed."

She squirmed in her seat and eyed him suspiciously. She knew it was coming. He handed her the threatening letter and confessed, "I know about your admirer." She froze as her features tensed and darkened. He wondered if she was going to cry or even faint. He couldn't tell.

She swallowed, read the letter's contents, and shakily asked, "How did you get this?"

"It was in your hand when you fainted."

With aggression, she said, "So you took and *read* it?"

He knew she wouldn't be happy about it, but he needed to get some answers. "I did." She stood there with her cheeks becoming inflamed with red splotches of anger. He wanted to laugh at how adorable she appeared but didn't dare.

"That was none of your business," she declared. "You had no right to read it."

He edged closer to her. "It was wrong of me, yes, but that doesn't change the fact that someone very dangerous is threatening you. I can't stand by and do nothing. Haven't you noticed the accidents and goings-on of the past few weeks? Someone has tampered with wagons, made threats, fired a gun at my head, knocked Jacob out cold, and robbed most of our medical supplies."

She shrunk back from him and hugged herself. "Tampered with the wagons?" she repeated quizzically.

He nodded. "The day you fell in the river. Mace confirmed that one of the wagons had been messed with. Someone had fixed it to fall to pieces when we entered the water. Things keep happening, Rosemary, and I believe it has something to do with you and this *admirer*."

"He shot at you?" she asked as if she didn't want to believe it was true. She stared at his cheek as she reached for the side of his face and then shied away.

The scrape on Ricochet's cheek throbbed. He realized that he didn't want to believe it either. He gestured to the scab that had scarred his face. "At first, I thought it was debris from the misfire, but then I received this." He handed her another scrap of paper. "Whoever this is, he's not only a danger to you but to others who are close to you." He watched her expression change from defensive to broken. Her whole body quaked and trembled violently until he thought she would fall to pieces right before his very eyes.

"I must leave," she said.

He frowned and grabbed her hand as she turned away from him. "No wagon is safe, Rosemary."

"I'll leave the wagons and run back east." Her thinking came from terror. It was irrational and foolish. Running wouldn't solve a thing. If anything, it would only worsen the current situation.

He shook his head and said, "That's just what he wants. Can't you see that he's trying to single you out?"

She pulled away from him, but he refused to let her go. "Then let him! I'm sick of hiding and fearing every shadow," her voice choked. "I can't do this anymore."

At that moment, Ricochet saw her for who she was: a scared, innocent, young woman who longed for peace and safety. He almost choked up himself. Yanking her to his chest, he wrapped his arms around her. She protested at first, but then, the tears came¾so many tears. Her hands clutched his shirt tightly, and her fingernails dug into his skin, but he held her even tighter. She fit so well in his arms.

It amazed him how a woman could make a man feel so powerful with a simple show of tears and sobs. She was confiding in him, and he wanted to protect her from every danger. He'd go against the world, if it meant he could hold her longer.

As he stroked her head, the fabric of her bonnet caught on his calloused fingers. Everything she wore was dainty and pretty. He'd been out fixing wagons and watering horses all day. He felt filthy, even after all the washing he'd undergone. Fear of sullying her bonnet and dress aroused his nerves. He should pull back. He tried. She held on tighter and sniffled into his shirt. She was a mess of water and salt. He wondered how a woman held so many tears.

"Just cry your heart out," he whispered at last, giving up trying to push her away. "I won't leave you." Of course, how couldn't. She was practically attached to his torso. He might as well let her get it all out before he asked any other questions.

Her muffled sobs eventually quieted, and she peered up at him. Her eyes were damp, puffy, and beautiful. "I'm sorry," she murmured, sniffling occasionally. "I don't know who he is or why he's doing this. It's all my fault. I led him here."

He stepped back and lowered himself to her eye level. Cupping her face with his hands, he shook his head. "No, don't blame yourself." He wiped away a tear that had started to run down her cheek. "Whatever happens, you can't blame yourself. Now that I know he's out there, I can put an end to it."

She closed her eyes as if in pain. "He'll kill you. He always finds a way to." Her breath caught, and she began to cry some more.

Ricochet talked over her spasms of chokes and whimpers. "No, he won't. I'll search him out."

"He killed them," she said and then sucked in a sharp breath. "He killed my parents. Singled me out. He'll stop at nothing to hurt me. I have to get out of here. If I stay, who knows what he'll do to …" she trailed off to look into his blue eyes. He thought she might become hysterical. She looked down and continued, "Ric, if he sees me with you, he'll kill you. He said so himself."

The wagon master grew tired with all her talk of him dying. *Can't she see the fact that I want to rescue her from this madness and that I'm trying everything in my power to see her through this?* he thought. He'd have to show her that he was serious, even if he got a slap to the face for it.

He furrowed his brow, tore off the bonnet that was atop her head to see her brown curls sweeping over her shoulders, and then kissed the fear right out of her.

She was so tense and in shock, he thought she'd surely awaken out of the trance and hit him. She didn't. Instead, she melted right into his arms, deepening the kiss further. She tasted sweet and somewhat salty¾probably from all the tears that she had unleashed.

He broke away before he could succumb to temptation. Then he wet his lips nervously. Had that done the trick and snapped her out of her fear-filled state? He sure hoped it had.

Rosemary looked unsteady and dazed. Her lips were red and swollen. If Ricochet didn't control himself, he'd lean in for another kiss right then. The kiss, he reminded himself, had only been to inform her that he was dead set on finding the admirer on her behalf. He couldn't bring himself to kiss her again. That would be taking advantage of her weakened state of mind. He simply couldn't do that.

He reached down to gather up her bonnet and then handed it to her apologetically. "Trust me, Rosemary. I'll take care of it."

She blinked twice, accepted the bonnet, and smiled. All the assurance that he needed was to know that she believed in him.

Jackson Cole chose that exact moment to check on them, and it was not a moment too soon. Ricochet couldn't seem to keep himself from staring at Rosemary's lips. He knew that if Jackson hadn't shown up, he might've just gone on kissing and holding Rosemary without a care in the world. He didn't want to disgrace her.

He asked Jackson if the old preacher would mind escorting Rosemary back to the wagon on his behalf. He watched as the two of them took their leave while he cleaned up the dinner-for-two setup.

Ricochet's head was whirling with emotions he never knew existed, as he made quick work of the cleanup. After he put the clean dishes into the supply wagon, he made his way to his sleep sack. He was tuckered out and needed some rest, although he knew he'd most likely get none due to hearing Rosemary's confession early that evening. It was going to make for a long hard night. It would be a night of thinking more than sleeping.

# Chapter 18

A scream erupted from her mouth that was so blood curdling that the hair on her own neck stood up. She held her hands over her mouth, horrified by the scene playing out before her eyes. She couldn't breathe or move. She could only watch as Ricochet was filled with lead. His body jerked and twitched at every bullet that entered his chest.

He reached out a trembling hand to her, begging her to run and never look back. The fear in his clear eyes made her shiver. He had always been so strong, confident, and solid. Now he was a shadow of that man. He was nothing more than a weak, trembling fraction of his former self.

The admirer stood over him with a blade in his right hand and a smoking, recently used firearm in his left. He was hunkered low over Ricochet's breathless, broken body. The he stood to face her. In two long strides, he was able reach her and point the knife at her throat. He dropped the gun and turned his back to the wagon master, who was no longer a threat.

Rosemary caught a glimpse of Ricochet's hand reaching out to her and then going still. He was gone, leaving her to be the prey of the monster in front of her. He'd broken his promise. He'd abandoned her like everyone else.

The admirer's bony hand caught hold of her head of curls, pulling her close to his face. His breath wreaked havoc on her nostrils, and she scrunched her nose in disgust. His voice whispered in her ear and drove away all remaining hope. She cried aloud and tried to push herself away from him, but he gripped her so tight that she couldn't breathe. Another scream escaped her, and she grew dizzy. A black void consumed her.

"Rosemary, wake up!" Rosemary saw Charity hovering over her when she opened her eyes. The redhead had been shaking Rosemary's shoulders. A wild and frightened look was on her face. "You were having a nightmare."

Rosemary sat up, dazed and disoriented. Dampness ran down her cheeks from recent tears, and her eyes were puffy and swollen. Her throat felt sore, as if she'd really been screaming all night long. She sniffled and hugged herself. "A nightmare?" Her relieved tone came out like a question.

It had been so vivid: the death of Ricochet, the admirer's bloodied knife and smoking revolver, the horror, and the dread. It all made her quiver uncontrollably. She thought about running out of the covered wagon and going to see that the wagon master was safely asleep in his bedroll under the stars, all for her own reassurance. She wanted to cry but in his arms and against his chest. She wanted to feel his breath on her head as he held her tight. To be sure that he was alive and well, she wanted to hold his face in her hands and kiss him for all he was worth. She drew up her knees and wept into them. She rocked in a fast, panicked motion.

Her shoulders tensed when she felt the warmth of Charity's arms around her. "There now," she said, hushing her. "It was all a bad dream. None of it's real."

*But what if it is? What if my admirer has killed Ricochet while I have sat here and sobbed?* she thought. New tears fell. She threw her arms around Charity, crying into the younger woman's shoulder. "He killed him," she said. "He killed Ric."

Charity murmured back, "Ricochet's fine. You're fine. None of it was real." She didn't understand. She couldn't. Rosemary had never told Charity the reason that she'd decided to run out west with the preacher and his daughter.

The contrition that tugged at Rosemary's conscience was great. Her quivering lips parted and she sucked in a sharp breath. "No," she uttered softly. "He'll kill Ric. I know he will. It's my fault."

Charity pried Rosemary away from her own shoulder to look her in the eye. She stroked away the tear-dampened curls around Rosemary's cheeks. "Who will kill him, Rosie?"

Rosemary hesitated. She couldn't tell Charity all this. It would only burden her, yet she must warn her friend of the rising trouble that was practically at their door, so to speak. While she dabbed at her eyes, she practiced in her head how she would tell the preacher's daughter of the past events. It was time to put trust in her closest friend. Ricochet had told her to confide in him, so maybe it was time that she confided in Charity too. Charity was bound to find out at some point. It should come from Rosemary's own lips.

Slowly through tears and choking sobs, she told Charity everything, from the first love letter, to the murder of her parents, and finally, to the misfire incident in the woods. It came out easier than Rosemary had imagined, and the hurt that she felt inside seemed to ease once the tale had been told.

Her expression one of sorrow and sympathy, Charity pulled Rosemary into a tight squeeze. "Why didn't you come to me sooner? The pain you've endured, and still are enduring, why didn't you say anything?"

Although Rosemary couldn't see her friend's face, she knew that Charity was crying right along with her. All this time, Rosemary had thought that her friend would shun her or throw her out for her lies and secrecy. She'd been so wrong in thinking such nonsense.

Charity grieved along with her and consoled her by stroking her head. Closing her eyes tight, Rosemary admitted, "I was scared. I didn't want you to be hurt or burdened. This mess is my cross to bear."

A sniffle escaped Charity, and she remarked, "A cross is a heavy burden. It's best to share the weight and lighten the load by having others help." She smiled comfortingly and pulled away again. "I wish you would've told me sooner. If someone is out to hurt you, I want to help you in any way I can. Surely, you know by now that I am always here for you. I've known for a while that something has been bothering you, but I never imagined it to be like this."

She cupped Rosemary's face as her own green eyes glistened with tears. "From now on, I won't leave your side, not for a single moment and not until this fiend's been caught and dealt with."

The relief of having Charity vow with such courage and thoughtfulness made Rosemary truly thankful. It had been wrong of her to decide on Charity's behalf to go through the trial alone without a friend's comfort. She knew better now. God had placed her on this wagon train for a good reason, and Rosemary was finding that out for herself.

Charity's brow suddenly furrowed as she removed her hands from the grieving Rosemary's face. She harrumphed softly before asking, "Have you any idea who the man is? He must have left some kind of clue."

Rosemary shook her head, hunching her shoulders. "I don't know who he is. All I know is that he's been on my tail since I ran from what remained of my home. He's made no motion to attack me physically thus far, but his words and threats have proven extremely violent. He's even sent a warning to Ricochet." Her throat constricted. "I fear he very well may kill Ric if I don't go along with his plans."

"What should we do?" Charity asked, thinking the matter over. Then she answered her own question. "We should narrow down the suspects. He must be someone on this train."

Rosemary shook her head again. "I haven't the faintest idea who it could be. Everyone has been so friendly to me."

"Then we'll investigate it together," Charity said and then grinned excitedly, eager for the challenge. She gripped Rosemary's hand hard. "He won't be harming one hair on Ricochet's head because we'll find him out long before that. Don't you worry, Rosie. We'll catch him."

Rosemary hoped that would be the case, otherwise, she might just have to face her own nightmares. After another few minutes of talking, planning, and questioning, Rosemary finally fell asleep. Charity kept watch, just in case her admirer came calling or the nightmare returned. Rosemary couldn't have chosen a better friend. She fell soundly asleep while listening to the preacher's daughter hum hymns, which were soothing to her ears.

The following morning, Rosemary awoke with a grogginess that didn't seem to want to leave. Charity, who never wanted to get out of bed in the mornings, had already been up for an hour before Rosemary had awakened. The memory of the previous night hung over Rosemary's head, weighing down her thoughts.

She dressed and readied herself for the long day of travel. Charity had excused herself to go grab some breakfast for them. She was bent on keeping Rosemary inside the wagon when she was not present to guard her. The loyalty of the preacher's daughter was admirable.

Rosemary snuck a peek outside and saw that everyone had gathered around the center of the makeshift camp for the morning meal. Normally, she would've been too shy to participate in the social event, but now that she was cooped up inside the wagon by herself and not permitted to venture out alone, she longed to be out there.

She sighed and went to close the canvas flap, but a bundle of brown paper caused her to stop. On the step of the wagon, she eyed the package with curiosity. Not knowing what it was, she pulled it into the confines of her prison and took a closer look. She thought that she shouldn't be messing with something that wasn't hers, but every guilty feeling left when she read her name across the side of the small package.

Shrugging, she opened it up. Her brown eyes sparkled when she saw what lay within the paper covering. A shawl of pink and white with finely stitched roses made her gasp and gawk. The shawl had been the same one she'd seen in the town weeks ago. Its beauty and fine craftsmanship were all the more wondrous knowing that the shawl was hers. Holding it to her chest, she smiled up at the canvas overhead and then slid over to the canvas flaps. Peeking outside once more, she eyed the wagon master, who was busy packing up the camp. His voice sang in her ears, even though he was only giving orders to the men. She smiled and threw the shawl over her shoulders.

Ignoring the strict warning of Charity, she exited the wagon and ran to meet Ricochet. He was speaking with Mace and Isaac when she arrived. When she called his name, he wheeled around to meet her. A smile broke out on his face, and she realized that he had shaved off his mustache. She halted. "You shaved," she stated.

He rubbed his upper lip and nodded. "Figured it was about time. The thing was a hassle."

Rosemary's shoulders slumped slightly. She'd quite enjoyed the tickle of his facial hair on her lips the night before. A frown gripped her expression, and she had a hard time removing it. When the wagon master eyed her suspiciously, she commented, "That's unfortunate."

Isaac snorted from behind Ricochet and then went silent when Ricochet glared him down. Mace and Isaac made their excuses to leave, each smirking with knowing stares. Rosemary couldn't keep her eyes off the man's upper lip. He appeared so young and less bossy without it. It would take some getting used to.

Ricochet cleared his throat and chuckled. "My eyes are up here."

She blushed and shook her head. "Sometimes I think you do things like this on purpose to distract me."

"What? A man can't look good for his woman?" he teased.

She huffed and then straightened up in the hopes that he would notice something different about her. "I'm not your woman, Mr. Chapel."

He crossed his arms tightly over his chest. "Not yet."

*What is that supposed to mean? Not yet?* she thought. If that implied what she thought it did, and it most definitely did, then she might be facing more than just a whimsical romance on the horizon. A bubbly sensation grew in the pit of her stomach. She tried not to think about it; otherwise, she just might try to kiss him in front of every prying eye. Gathering her composure, she flicked her eyes to her left shoulder and played with the lacy shawl. "Aren't you going to compliment me?" He shifted on his feet and looked confused.

*Doesn't he notice that I am wearing his gift atop my shoulders? The man must be joking around as usual,* she thought. She clicked her tongue against the roof of her mouth. "Why must you keep on toying with me?"

"What are you talking about?" He seemed genuinely baffled by her question.

She would have to spell it out for him yet again. "The shawl. Don't you like that I'm wearing it? After all, you're the one who gave it to me."

He jerked his head back and frowned. "I did?"

An exasperated sigh escaped her pursed lips. "Ricochet Chapel, I'm in no mood for your games. I know this shawl must have come from you."

Ricochet scratched his temple and shrugged. "It sure suits ya fine, Miss Barker, but I've never seen it before today. Maybe it …" he stopped short when the shawl dropped from her shoulders onto the ground.

It dawned on Rosemary that she had been utterly foolish. Of course, the beautiful piece of workmanship wasn't from Ricochet. He could not have known that she and Charity had admired it several weeks ago in town. He hadn't been there. *Foolish,* Rosemary scolded herself. *Utterly foolish.*

Leaving the shawl on the ground, Rosemary turned and ran back to the wagon. She knew who had given it to her, and it certainly wasn't the wagon master. In all her excitement and thoughts of the wagon master, she'd forgotten to inspect the shawl's packaging for a note—a note from the admirer. Her mind swirled with the threats that might be scrawled on the paper. The paper was undoubtedly with the wrapper inside the wagon. Tears stung her eyes, readying her for the violent yet elegant stranger's terrible words. He was the man who had trapped her in darkness and sorrow.

She reached the wagon and flung herself inside to search for the thing that she dreaded most. On the floorboards and crumpled up beneath brown wads of wrapper, there was a scrap of rose-scented paper. Drawing a shaky breath and trembling with fear, she picked up the wadded note and read it.

*Like the gift, Rose? I bought it specially for you. Do give Chapel my regards.*

*Your loving Admirer.*

She wanted to scream aloud, vomit up the bile that was rising in the back of her throat, and run to the wagon master and hide in the safety of his arms. As if on cue, Ricochet Chapel rapped on the canvas flap and asked, "Rosemary, is something wrong?"

Wiping away her stray tears and doing her best to look civil, she mustered up the courage to step out from the wagon and meet his dazzling blue-eyed gaze. She hid the note in her fist and smiled numbly. "Everything is fine. It was just a misunderstanding," she lied.

He didn't buy it. The look on his face said it all, and Rosemary flushed pink. He could read her like an open book. She knew this. Crossing his strong arms tightly over his chest, the wagon master frowned sternly and said, "It's him, isn't it?"

He was referring to her admirer, and Rosemary did not argue with his words. She nodded solemnly and then handed him the note. She'd lied for so long about the man behind the scented paper and harsh threats that she quite often felt alone in the world. But now, Ricochet was there. She was beginning to feel hope again. He cared for her, and the matter of the admirer now concerned him. The admirer had bet on scaring him away. Since that hadn't worked, Rosemary dreaded to think what might happen to the wagon master.

Ricochet read the note carefully, his expression was stern, and it didn't change from its deep scowl. Rosemary almost retreated into the wagon, but he crumpled the paper and said, "What a coward."

Rosemary backed up a step on the hitching rail of the schooner behind her and swallowed. "Ric?" she asked upon seeing his fury awaken.

The wagon master threw the paper at the wagon before running a hand over his jawline. "I've had enough of this. He's not going to keep threatening you." He turned his back to her.

Rosemary grew frantic and touched his forearm. "What will you do?"

She was surprised when Ricochet peered down over his shoulder at her with a smile. She wondered what he was thinking. Something in his mannerism told her that he had changed because Rosemary saw a wild gleam in his eye, which had replaced the anger.

He smirked and replied, "I'm gonna write him a letter."

# *Chapter 19*

❦

*Just one more week.* Ricochet yawned. *One more week of hard traveling and endurance. Then I'm home.*

The bags under his eyes were dark, meaning he hadn't slept well if at all. The admirer business had been getting to him. The identity of Rosemary's attacker had been nagging at him and eating up his ability to sleep and think clearly. He was frustrated, tired, and aching from the previous night's hard bedroll. Sleep hadn't come to him due to the rambling of his thoughts regarding the letter that he had left for the admirer. Even now, a smirk tugged at his lips. The letter wasn't forceful, but it had a demand for Rosemary's freedom from further heartache.

Ricochet had started the letter,

Dear Admirer,

From there, it had exploded. The wagon master had never done anything so brash. He had explained that he disapproved of the admirer's abusive slandering and threats. But Rosemary was most upset by the thing that he'd written in bold letters toward the end.

I intend to marry Miss Barker, and you cannot turn me away.

Rosemary had pleaded for him not to write that. They had never talked of getting married or had even properly established their courtship. Ricochet then told Rosemary that it was a means to get the admirer riled up enough to mess up, therefore, catching him in the act. Ricochet never mentioned the fact that he indeed planned to marry

Miss Barker after all this, but he'd keep that part to himself for the time being, until it was safe to say such things.

After setting the letter outside Rosemary's wagon along with the shawl in the hopes that the admirer would receive them, they awaited a response. It was sometime during the night that the admirer had taken both the returned gift and Ricochet's letter because by morning it was all gone. The plan was going smoothly. If Ricochet didn't hear from the admirer by the end of the week, he would be very surprised. All he had to do was keep his eyes and ears open for attack and pray that he could catch the stranger before the stranger caught him.

What kept him going was seeing to Rosemary's safety, and if all went well, her hand in marriage. He'd have to make sure that Rosemary stayed clear of trouble for the time being. The letter had been written to stir up trouble between him and the admirer and hopefully steer the admirer away from Rosemary. Ricochet had talked with Charity, which had straightened out the chaperone ordeal; Rosemary would never be alone long enough for the admirer to threaten her, should he take his focus off the wagon master and on her.

That straightened Ricochet's wearied posture. Yes, he just had to make it to the end of the trail, take care of this admirer business, and then ask for Rosemary's hand. He sighed. There would be a lot of work ahead. *A lot of looking over my own shoulder,* he thought.

The previous day had been somewhat restful. There had been services and many chores that needed to be accomplished. The early morning had started as all the previous ones had. The days of traveling seemed to go on and on, with hours of walking, riding, herding cattle, and yawning, so much yawning, mainly from Ricochet. He wasn't one to complain, but he'd considered starting to. The coffee from earlier that day was a distant, fond memory. What he wouldn't give for a large pot full of the stuff.

He adjusted his position in the saddle as Gage moseyed along leading the train. He patted the mustang's muscular neck and smiled. "One more week of this, Gage, and then we'll head for home in Wyoming."

He turned in the saddle to peer behind him as he gave the onward call to the train. "Wagons, ho!" The train moved out at his command. He would be very happy when he got home. Home sounded mighty fine about now.

He hadn't been to his cabin in Wyoming for about a year. He'd been hired by some pioneers to lead them across the Oregon Trail. It was a dangerous trek for new settlers. He knew the journey well, having traveled it four times before that. His reputation was known everywhere. It was growing bigger and better. It didn't get any easier, however. The days were long, the chores hard, and the meals were mostly repeated with little variety. No one ever looked forward to the trip, but land out west was something that many longed for.

Ricochet yearned for his own land and his humble cabin, which was a basic square with one room. It was surrounded by acres of land, woods, and a single water source from a river. It was beautiful, and he'd built it up all by himself. He'd made plans to build a barn, break wild stallions, gather cattle, and maybe hire some hands.

What his home severely lacked was a woman. But it seemed that God had provided him with Rosemary Barker, and he was determined to take her back with him, that is, if she'd have him. He wouldn't force it, but he'd make it plain as day that he intended to marry her once the journey was over.

*One more week,* he thought as he clenched his jaw. *Seven more days, eight if we meet bad weather.*

The weather had chilled considerably due to the changing of the seasons. It was now early autumn, and leaves had begun to fall to prepare for freezing temperatures. Ricochet had always preferred the gentleness of spring to any other season, but the coolness of autumn was better than the steaming heat of summer. He couldn't stand the heat during the hot months.

He groaned as he switched the reins to his other hand. He flexed his now free hand to loosen the stiffness. He turned to face Mace, who tilted the brim of his hat lower over his eyes. "I checked in with Jacob yesterday. Andrew's making a quick recovery, although he's still can't walk without a crutch."

Mace nodded, listening, as Ricochet went on. "I wasn't able to figure out who took the second shot or stole from the Webbs, but I can guarantee that they are the same man."

The serene rider rested his left hand on his thigh. "You think someone aimed to kill or to scare you?" He motioned to the scab on Ricochet's cheek. It was a distant reminder that he too could've been killed in the so-called misfire.

Ricochet shuddered even to think of the incident. Whether the true intent had been to scare him or kill him, someone had been out for blood. The wagon master would not stand for this unforgivable act, especially since he was the wagon train's judge and he had to set the law for each person. Although, he reckoned that they would need an actual lawman or the like once they reached a town, if there happened to be one. Law was scarce out here, and it became even worse the farther west they traveled.

"I'm not so sure," Ricochet thought aloud. He meant to carry on the conversation, but a shrill cry rang so loud that he reined his stallion and his own thoughts to a halt. The wagons followed his lead and halted directly behind him and Mace. The scream had followed a loud ruckus of snapping wood and crashing of crates. The cry was definitely one of distress and that of a woman. Ricochet's blood ran cold upon recognizing the helpless squeal. Without a doubt, it was Charity.

He steered his buckskin toward the sound and then spurred it into a fast gallop. His heart was pounding. The horrific sight ahead made his head spin and his stomach clench. He dared to tread farther, practically leaping off his mustang and landing with his knees bent on the ground. He half slid as he ran the gap between him and the fallen wagon. He had heard correctly, when he had suspected that the incident involved Charity. She lay before him on the ground. Her body was limp and unconscious, and her red curls were draped over her freckled complexion, as Rosemary sobbed over her.

"Charity!" Rosemary screamed repeatedly as tears, which were bigger than raindrops, dripped down her cheeks and off her chin. Ricochet wanted to scoop her up in his arms, hold her close, and wipe away every tear that fell from her chocolate-brown eyes. He restrained himself as he neared, and his eyes of clearest blue figured out the whole ordeal quickly.

The Coles' right, front wagon wheel had snapped off the axle, and the wagon had collapsed in the dirt. The wooden wheel had rolled several feet before falling over. The cover of the schooner had come undone. It had been somewhat torn from the sharp corners of crates and luggage that lay within. Some boxes and packed heirlooms had fallen out of the hole and now lay scattered around the accident.

The thing that caught Ricochet's attention the most was Charity. Her head had a rather nasty cut along her temple, but her legs—oh her legs—had been caught beneath the axle of the fallen wagon. Her skirts covered the horrific sight that undoubtedly hid beneath them.

Gathering the calm nerve that remained—if there was any—he pulled Rosemary up to her feet, prying her from her still friend. She put up quite a fight. She screamed and caused a scene until her eyes met his. Then she went limp in his arms. He managed to hold her at arms' length despite the strong pull to hug her tightly. He wondered what the other pioneers would say if he gave into his instincts. It was better to keep her at a distance than to give the crowd any leverage for gossip. Still, seeing Rosemary's worry and frightful gaze shattered his heart.

"Darlin', you need to listen to me," he ordered in his wagon master's tone. "I need you to stay back."

Her lips quivered. She peered down at Charity and then back to him. "Help her," she sobbed helplessly.

He nodded. "I will, but I need you to step back."

With some hesitation, she breathed a heavy sigh and allowed herself to be passed to Katrina and Lily for comfort. Ricochet had to fight his inner emotions to let go of Rosemary's upper arms. In the end, his resolve to keep order and control of the situation took over, and he grew collectively calm. He couldn't delve into his emotions. It was not the time for such nonsense. A young woman needed his help, and a group of pioneers needed guidance.

He steadied his shaking hands as Mace and Dr. Webb approached at amazing speeds. Their eyes were trained on the woman who was trapped under the wagon. Dr. Webb quickly accessed the situation. He leaned over Charity's legs, and checked her as decently as possible with bystanders around.

His eyes never leaving Charity's pale face, Mace asked, "What happened?" His tone was hoarse, and Ricochet suspected that the normally silent rider was more emotionally inclined toward the wild preacher's daughter than he had first let on. Ricochet knelt beside the wagon next to Dr. Webb.

Mace followed his lead. "Looks like the wagon collapsed due to damage around the front of the axle," he stated in shock.

Ricochet's ears were pricked at the sound of the old pastor, who had been previously entranced by the sight, letting out a moan and falling to his knees. The man caressed his daughter's fiery locks as tears welled up in his eyes. "Charity," he cried louder and louder between praying to God in Heaven.

The wagon master clenched his jaw before he too fell into ruin with tears. He straightened and rolled his shoulders back. Charity would die if they wasted any more precious minutes. He ordered several men to go on either side of the wagon. In one hefty heave, they had the front of the wagon off the ground high enough to ensure that the doc could pull the young maiden's legs out. Ricochet noticed that a large rock had been jammed slightly beneath the wagon's axle. Once Charity was free, they released their hold on the heavy land schooner.

Charity lay still as Dr. Webb shifted her booted feet slightly. A sigh of relief washed over his expression. He looked up to meet Ricochet's curious and fretful gaze after first staring at the wedged rock under the wagon. "If this isn't a miracle, I don't know what is," he said as his grin widened. The wagon master knelt beside him and next to the sleeping chatterbox of a woman.

"What do you mean?" he asked.

Jacob Webb shook his head, chuckling. "That rock just saved this dear one's legs a lot of harm. Course, I'll have to make a full checkup to be on the safe side, but there's hardly any swelling on the lower half of her calves. I'd say that stone just took the brunt of the fall."

Ricochet's chuckle of relief sounded hoarse, but he didn't care. The small rock being jammed beneath the wagon was a miracle of God. He couldn't begin to explain the relief that took place in his heart. He knew that everyone had calmed down due to Dr. Webb's words. Even Rosemary, who had crumpled to the ground at one point, lifted her chin in hope.

"Mace, help lift the young lady into the doc's wagon," Ricochet ordered, wasting no further time on rejoicing until they had fully taken care of the situation.

Men and women picked up the scattered crates and boxes and neatly stacked them in a pile beside the schooner. Then it was time to inspect the wagon's axle. Ricochet prayed silently that all was well, otherwise, the Cole family would be walking the rest of the way, and its goods would be left behind. He definitely didn't want to have to force the weathered preacher, his daughter, and of course Rosemary to walk for miles on end with no cover.

Young Charity was situated in the Webb's wagon with her father close by her side and the Webbs making fully certain to tend to any major injuries. Once Ricochet had finished tending to the poor girl and her father, the wagon master made a goal to have the Cole's wagon up and running before dinnertime. He sent only Mace to help inspect the schooner and the other men to help carry the heavy crates and luggage away from the wreckage.

Minutes later, Mace gave a suspicious frown, his brow creased with confusion. Ricochet noticed and immediately asked the cause of his scowl. The normally silent man remained on his knees examining the broken axle before him. "This break here," he gestured to the snapped wood as Ricochet knelt beside him, "something doesn't seem right about it."

Ricochet fingered the piece, and then his own brow furrowed. "You're thinking it wasn't an accident?" he questioned, knowing very well that Mace's speculations were usually correct.

The older rider sighed heavily and rested his right arm on his knee. "It was sound and sturdy when I left it, and there wasn't any sign of it snapping. That ain't no break in the axle," he said, lowering his voice to keep others from overhearing. "It's been tampered with, but I was the only one near this wagon making the repairs."

The wagon master then asked about Victor Marsh because the man had been present when Mace had done the repairs. Mace confirmed that Victor had been with him making repairs but shook his head as he stated, "I didn't let him outta my sight. I was the only one touching this axle."

Ricochet's brow creased with concern, and his interest was piqued. If word got out that Mace had been the one to repair the wagon and that the axle had been sawed in two, the silent rider just might have an angry mob on his hands. Someone was attempting to frame Mr. Chronicle for this unfortunate *accident*.

However, the wagon master knew better than to believe such nonsense, for Andrew had already thrown that possibility out the window when he had fondly taken to the quiet man on the day of the hunting party. But since young Andrew was still unable to provide answers and Mace had been the only one to touch the sabotaged wagon, keeping things quiet would be a tough task indeed.

Ricochet then pardoned himself, knowing that he must speak with a certain someone who would know all about this madness on the wagon train. Perhaps the admirer had responded to his letter.

Rosemary held her friend's hand, stroking it gently. She'd refused to leave Charity's side since earlier that morning when the wagon had collapsed. Nothing on earth could make her move from where she sat within the Webbs' wagon. Charity needed her.

Several times, Ricochet had come to speak with her, but Rosemary only sent him away. He was the last person that she wanted to see right now. This had been his doing. He had angered her admirer with the letter, and Charity had paid the price. The wagon master's haste to catch her admirer had nearly killed her precious friend. Her anger had been kindled against Ricochet. She knew that if he were to force her out of this wagon to speak with him, she'd only speak hurtful words. She stayed where she sat.

"Rosemary?" Katrina's soft tone drew her attention. "You must be hungry. Please eat something. You haven't moved for hours." The pleading in the woman's voice about knocked Rosemary's anger out of the wagon. Mrs. Webb was amazing when it came to the art of persuasion.

Rosemary sighed, but her gaze remained on Charity's sleeping form. "I'm not hungry."

Jacob Webb opened the canvas flap just then and spotted the two women next to his patient. "Katrina, my dear, would you mind changing Miss Cole's bandaging while I prep the medicinal tea? She must stay hydrated."

Katrina scooted to the other side of the wagon and did as she was asked. Rosemary felt as if she was intruding upon their work, but she didn't want to leave¾not yet.

Dr. Webb spoke up. "Miss Barker, I hate to ask this of you, but would you mind giving us room to work? I appreciate all that you have done in helping Miss Cole, but it is for the best that you leave us now." He didn't enter the cramped wagon just yet, but Rosemary could tell that he was itching to get inside. With her in the way, the doctor couldn't move around as easily as it would be without her.

"You must stretch your legs and go eat," he ordered in a caring tone. "It will do her little good if you fall ill from lack of nutrition."

Rosemary was at a disadvantage with both Webbs wanting her to leave, so she obeyed, much to her own disappointment. She exited the wagon, and the doctor leaped inside medicinal leaves and dishes. Her heart ached to return her attention to Charity, but she forced herself to walk away.

She wandered numbly to the clearing, where food had been left out for her by some of the women. She grabbed what remained and sat down on the ground to eat, but no matter how much she forced herself to take a bite, she just couldn't. She wasn't hungry. The thought that her friend had nearly died made her stomach lurch and squeeze. In the end, Rosemary set her plate aside and stared at the withering grass beneath her.

Bad things always followed her wherever she went. Her life was getting tiresome, and she began to think that maybe God had made a mistake in bringing her to life. She thought, *No. How can I think that? God never makes mistakes. He's always right and good in what He does. He has a plan; otherwise, she wouldn't be here now.*

Rosemary folded her hands in her lap and bowed her head to plead with God to forgive her unbelief. Ricochet and Pastor Jackson had taught her better than this. It was her own flesh taking advantage of her weary spirit and giving her these thoughts. She asked the Lord to take away these concerns and give her renewed vigor and strength. After she lifted her head, she felt somewhat stronger than before. Hope returned, and her eyes were opened to the ways that God had blessed her, regardless of the wickedness that had followed her every step.

A hand cupped her shoulder, and she jerked sideways out of alarm. She turned and gazed up to see Isaac staring down at her. "Miss Barker," he addressed. "Sorry, I didn't mean to startle you."

She said, "No. I'm sorry. I'm a bit jumpy at the moment." She shivered slightly when he didn't instantly remove his hand from her shoulder. Isaac seemed to understand this and removed his hand.

He cleared his throat, and she rose to meet him. "I thought I'd make sure you were well. It was terrible what happened to Miss Cole. Will she be all right?"

Rosemary dusted off her skirts and replied hopefully, "Thank you for your concern, but I wasn't the one that was crushed beneath a wagon. I do believe that Charity will be all right, Lord willing."

The young man nodded in response. His expression was unreadable. He shifted awkwardly on his feet and stared at her until she felt anxious. She wondered what he wanted from her. His gaze captured hers in a way that was most intriguing. She had never really talked to the man, who couldn't have been more than four years older than she was. He had never paid her any attention and had always taken to Lily, Mr. Garrison's daughter.

Rosemary noticed many things about Isaac that made her wonder what kind of life he had experienced. His face was boyish, but his dark eyes revealed that of a man who had faced trials and hardships. A mark ran along his left ear. His uncombed hair nearly covered it up. He had said once that he was searching for a new life out west and was thinking of homesteading and opening a shop of some kind. Rosemary couldn't remember what his trade was, but she was sure that whatever this man decided to pursue, he would succeed in.

"I was wondering if you might take a walk with me," he said.

Rosemary blinked and thought it was a funny thing for him to ask, but she complied. They began to walk across the clearing. It was silent for a while before Isaac spoke. "I had heard that you volunteered in hospitals back east with your mother."

At first, Rosemary thought it odd that he knew about her charity work back in her hometown, but perhaps, he had found out from Pastor Jackson or Ricochet. She hadn't meant for any of it to be a secret, so she nodded and said, "Yes. I would go every Monday and Wednesday to help with the ailing and those that needed assistance."

"I see," he said as he stared ahead. His hands were folded behind his back as they walked side by side. "And is it true that you helped with those who were wounded during the war?" His question was quite explicit although friendly. She wondered why he had suddenly taken an interest in her. He'd never attempted to talk with her before.

Not wanting to be rude, she nodded again and answered, "Yes. I have some experience in that area but not much. I only assisted in minor procedures and illnesses with the Union men, but I was never in charge. I was too young. The doctors were always there to ensure their orders. I simply replaced bandages and performed odd jobs here and there."

Isaac didn't say anything for several minutes. Then he stopped walking. Rosemary stopped after taking another step. She turned to look at him, puzzled by his solemn behavior. She wanted to know what he was thinking.

He stared at the ground, at her, and then at the wagon ahead of them. Finally, his eyes settled on her. "Did you ever come to care for a patient or doctor back home? Perhaps an admirer or two?" He laughed at the apparent jest.

The questions put her off. She cocked her head. *Why is he asking this? Is he simply curious, or is there another reason behind it?* she thought. Surely, the man hadn't heard that her admirer was the cause of all these accidents. At least, she hoped he hadn't.

When she didn't answer his first two questions, Isaac said in a more serious manner, "I hope you don't mind my asking about your past, Miss Barker."

In fact, Rosemary did mind. She didn't like the way he asked such impertinent questions. The Civil War had been a bloodbath¾one that she wanted to forget as much as any person would. She had witnessed many people in awful health situations when she had volunteered at the hospital during the war between the North and the South. Some men had been older and heading toward the end of their lives, but others had gotten sick with fevers. Some had even died during the amputation of their limbs.

In truth, she had seen many die from fatal wounds, and they were all tragedies that she hadn't dared to speak of afterward. It had been too hard to speak of such things. One man in particular had been torn to shreds by bullets and died soon after he had been brought to the hospital. Another young man had bandages around his head, and he had become mentally ill after a blow to his skull. She'd witnessed so many families grieving over the men. So many men had lost their lives.

The grief from her parents' deaths flooded back in an instant, and she was reminded of their tragic demise. Darkness had clouded her thoughts. She had crawled her way into fear and terror, as she had so many times before. Tears had brimmed in her eyes, but she hadn't dared to let them fall. Of course, she had cared deeply for each of the patients and doctors back home, but she hadn't dared to step into another clinic again. She hadn't been able to stand the fear of watching another patient lose his life, limbs, or hope.

After sucking in a sharp breath and holding back a choking sob, she asked, "Is there a reason for all these questions?"

Isaac didn't reply immediately, but instead, he stared at her with dazed eyes, as if he wasn't present. His lips formed a thin straight line. She noticed a faint scar above his upper lip.

He faltered for words and then countered by smiling and stating, "I was simply curious."

*Only curious? Was I too devoted to my own state of mind to see that he only wanted to know me better? But why does he want to know me better?* she thought. She'd never encouraged him to want to seek her out. To be completely honest, everyone had thought that he was as good as engaged and soon to be married to Lily Garrison. The two had been inseparable since they had left Independence, Missouri.

Isaac smiled brighter, as if to cover something deeper. "Forgive me if I asked something wrong. I suppose I was a little forward in asking silly questions. I had hoped to get to know you better."

Confused, Rosemary knit her brow and stood straighter. "Why?" flew from her mouth before she could stop it.

He chuckled. It was a strange sound, which didn't seem to match the coldness in his eyes. "Miss Barker, I can't hide it any longer. I've been attracted to you for several weeks, and I was wonderin' if you would consider a possible courtship with me. I know it's sudden, and you don't have to give me an answer right away, but I believe I've fallen for you."

*What? Did I hear him right? Did he just declare that he has feelings for me?* Rosemary thought. He was right to say that it had been sudden. Rosemary didn't know how to react. Instead of saying anything, she remained in silent shock. She couldn't think of one word to say.

Isaac's smile faded slightly, and then he said, "Don't worry. I will give you time to think about it. Please promise that you will think about it. I have longed to tell you for a while, but I didn't quite know how to go about it. I'll leave you now." With those words, he left her in a stupor.

She blinked twice and gawked after him. She should be flattered. After all, Isaac Beckett was not bad in the looks department. He was quite handsome, although not as handsome as Ricochet Chapel. Isaac did have a foul mouth on him at times, but he stayed quiet unless spoken against. He could be shy as well.

He and Ricochet were different from each other. Ricochet was established in his trade and faith in God while Isaac was quickly riled up and easily manipulated by others. They were far apart.

*Hasn't Isaac Beckett already been distracted by Lily Garrison? Maybe I read too much into their relationship, but how did I miss this? Am I blind? Maybe I am just naive to any other man's feelings toward me besides Ricochet.* Her head spun as she thought.

Her pounding head only worsened when she heard Ricochet call to her. "Rosemary," he beckoned and ran across the clearing to meet her. If

She wondered what he would say if she told him of Isaac's confession. He would most likely be upset, or maybe he would laugh it off as something humorous. She vowed, then and there, not to speak of it to him. It was nonsense to stir things up, especially since she didn't know how to tell him what her feelings were on the subject.

"Are you feeling well? Your face looks flushed." Ricochet cocked his head and then bent to inspect her further.

Rosemary backed up a step and lifted her hands to her cheeks. She felt warm. Swallowing back the lump in her throat, she said curtly, "I'm fine."

The wagon master didn't seem convinced and persisted to nag her about resting or lying down for a spell. She rolled her eyes and scolded him for being so overprotective and demanding.

Ricochet put up his hands defensively and said, "I was only concerned for your well-being, Rosemary."

She huffed and crossed her arms tightly over her chest. "I assure you that I am fine. What do you want?" Her tone came out a little more spiteful than she wished, and she saw the hurt in Ricochet's gaze.

Ricochet faltered and said, "I thought you might want to hear my findings on the Cole's wagon, but obviously, you're not in the mood to hear it."

"What findings?" she demanded. "What are you talking about?"

He answered, looking away from her. "The wagon collapsing wasn't an accident. Someone deliberately broke the axle."

"What?" she fumed. "It was sabotaged?"

Looking at her this time, he nodded and then continued, "And I believe I know who did it."

"My admirer," she breathed and put her hands over her mouth to stifle a sob. Charity had been hurt by that monster. Rosemary wanted to cry.

Ricochet touched her arms and caressed them gently. "Listen to me, Rosemary. This means that we are one step closer to catching him. He feels threatened. He's going to mess up, and when he does, I'll—"

"I told you that letter was a bad idea! I told you he would be furious!" Rosemary's fear and anger had surfaced quicker than she could stop it. She had smacked Ricochet's hands away and then proceeded to step away from him. She had shaken her head and pointed an accusing finger at him.

This time, he stepped back, and Rosemary clenched her fists tight at her sides in anguish. "Charity almost died because of you," she exclaimed.

If Ricochet tried to defend himself, Rosemary wouldn't listen. She gave him no time to counter. "I warned you not to get involved. I begged you not to write to him. Ric, why would you do that? Why couldn't you just listen to me?" She hung her head and hugged herself. "I shouldn't have told you anything. I never should've come on this wagon train. And now, Charity—"

"Charity will be all right. Dr. Webb has assured me of her swift recovery," Ricochet said as he reached for her again.

She pushed him so hard that he actually stumbled back in shock. "Don't touch me!" She raised her head to glare at him. What she saw on his face made her almost wince and regret her outburst¾almost.

"This is your fault, Ric! I can't believe I trusted you when you said that everything would be all right."

Bravely, Ricochet stepped forward and softly uttered, "Rosemary, please. I never meant for this to happen. I meant to draw him out into the open. I was hoping he'd come after me and leave you alone."

"Your letter almost cost me my friend," Rosemary countered. "You're no different from him. You always seek to control my every move. Why can't you men leave me be? First my admirer, then you, and now Isaac Beckett—"

"Wait," he interrupted quizzically, "Isaac Beckett?"

Rosemary grumbled at her own ignorance. In her rage, she'd forgotten that she wouldn't mention the young pioneer's profession of love to her. Her head hurt as she attempted to shrug it off as something minor. "He says he's had feelings for me for a long time. That is beside the point. You betrayed my trust."

Ricochet stretched his arms wide in exasperation. "Isaac confessed his love for you? How is that beside the point? When did this happen?" A series of questions flew from his mouth, and his face grew redder than an overripe tomato.

"This isn't about him, Ric," she said. Her tone was shrill.

The wagon master's tone grew suddenly dark and cold, as he said, "I see. So it's about you *and* him."

"What?" She frowned. "No! That's not what I meant."

"Then what did you mean?" He moved his face closer to hers until they were nose to nose. Rosemary could plainly see why the men on the wagon train took his commands so seriously. He was very intimidating when he was angry. If she weren't so stubborn, she'd just about obey anything he said. But she was stubborn and she wasn't going to obey him.

"How long?" he asked forcefully through a stiff jaw.

Rosemary blinked and then asked him, "What do you mean *how long*?"

"How long have you and Isaac been talking?"

Was it just her imagination and wistful thinking, or had she actually seen a glimmer of jealousy in his eyes? "It's none of your business," she huffed, meeting his gaze. "And stop changing the subject. You did a great injustice by writing that letter." Ricochet narrowed his eyes at her, and the same look showed up again.

*So he is jealous after all.* Rosemary could hardly breathe. He was envious that another man liked her, and Rosemary wasn't a bit sorry about it. *Is it wrong to enjoy it?* Somehow, she couldn't hold back the crooked smile that tugged at her lips.

The wagon master didn't back away. "You had better make it my business, or I'll drag the answer outta you." He'd completely ignored her earlier comment. *Typical man!* she thought. She stood on her tiptoes as her chest heaved for a breath. "Your threats don't scare me," she snarled back while glaring intently at him. "And I don't need your protection."

For several moments, the two of them didn't move. They remained in place, toe-to-toe and nose-to-nose.

Ricochet's hot breath brushed against her face as his chest heaved for air. He didn't speak, probably because he was too angry. He had a right to be. She'd practically flung his generous protective nature back in his face and called him a raving lunatic like her admirer.

Rosemary warred with the guilt and regret that were inside her heart, but she was far too angry to be apologetic. Instead, she said, "I don't need your help, and I don't want it."

Ricochet acted as if he would grab her, but then, he moved away and turned his back to her. "Well, Miss Barker," he said coldly, "if that is what you want, I will steer clear. I'm sorry for interfering. It was not my intention to make matters worse. It won't happen again."

Hearing him say that he would stay far away from her made her stomach churn inside and stung more than she thought it would. *Is this really what I want? Of course not*, she thought. She wanted him to hold and protect her, but her words and temper had once again surfaced. The human tongue was a wicked and unbridled thing.

He didn't glance back at her as he made his way across the clearing. He said, "I pray all the best for you, Miss Barker."

She wished he would come back as soon as he had left. None of what she said was true. She did want him. She did need him. He needed to protect her. Tears stung her eyes as she admitted to herself that she was afraid and that she wanted him near. The fact that he didn't even look back hurt more than anything. *Do I really mean nothing to him?* she wondered. After all those heartfelt words and kisses, she was nothing more than a toy for him to play with. Her shoulders slumped, and her head hung low. *What have I done, God?*

Ricochet Chapel might not care enough to gaze back over his shoulder, but Rosemary happened to care a great deal about him. It wasn't until he had left the clearing that she realized that she had made a mistake in pushing him away. She had ruined her one chance at earthly happiness, which she might never get back. The realization was heartbreaking.

Ricochet was a kind and gentle man, and he never made her feel scared or in danger. He might have stolen a few kisses from her—or at least the first—but he had asked her first. At times, he could be a little controlling and overprotective, but he would never hurt her. She was certain of that.

The wagon master had only wanted to help, but Rosemary's own fear had told her that she needed to blame someone, and that person had to be Ricochet Chapel. Every time, she thought about his pledge to her admirer (He would marry her) made her stomach flip and her heart pound.

*This sensation has to be anger. There is no other explanation for it, or is there? I can't be in love, can I? Surely not*, she thought.

# Chapter 20

❧❧❧

Dawn had come and gone, and the wagon master was already beginning to feel a tiring pull at his eyelids. He had not slept the night before, due to the possibility of a psychotic monster being aboard his wagon train and the fact that Rosemary hated his guts. He hadn't dared to close his eyes or to drift off to sleep. His eyes had filled with tears, and his head had filled with thoughts.

Rosemary was fearful and in danger, and two of his charges had nearly lost their lives in what could have been fatal *accidents*. It was bad enough that he had to deal with the horrible thought of losing young Andrew Jones because of a head injury. Now he had to cope with Miss Cole almost losing her legs beneath a wagon axle.

The argument—or rather, the breakup—with Rosemary hadn't helped either. In fact, that had sent him over the edge and into a raging temper. She'd practically called him a monster by comparing him to her admirer, who was a sly and vicious polecat, looking to ensnare her. If that wasn't insulting enough, she'd gone and said that she didn't need or even want him.

His heart sank in his chest. *If she didn't want a relationship with me, why did she allow me the liberty of kissing her?* he wondered as he shook his head. He'd stolen the first or second kiss from her, but she had willingly complied with the others. She'd even kissed him back. He wondered what kind of mind game she was playing.

*And that Isaac Beckett. What is the deal there?* he thought. The man was butting in where he was not welcome. Ricochet had thought to confront him about Rosemary, but he had held off due to his soaring anger. He couldn't go and speak calmly in order to find out what had really happened¾not when he was too angry to listen, and he wanted to slug the guy for creeping his way in between him and Rosemary. That confrontation would have to wait until he had cooled off, which might be a while. He wanted to cry out, "What next?" but refrained from doing because he didn't want to tempt fate.

Several days passed. He and Mace had busied themselves with making repairs on the Cole family's wagon, which had set them behind on their final leg of the journey west. At last, they were able to travel the mountainside trail.

Ricochet was in a foul mood about the mishaps, but that was not what was setting him off. If he thought that he had been agitated when he had received the threat from Rosemary's so-called admirer in the woods and had had a heated conversation with Rosemary earlier that week, he was livid now.

When he had rolled out of his bedroll that morning gone to put on his pair of boots, he had found a small rattler curled deep within the toe of his left boot! He thanked the Lord that the rattler had cautiously warned him of its close proximity; otherwise, he would be having convulsions and problems with his left foot by now. He'd seen what those things could do, and he wanted no part in there venomous bites.

At first, he had shrugged it off as an accident. A serpent had simply slithered its way into his boot and not Mace's boot, even though he had slept across from him. But the note that had been left beside his bedroll had confirmed a gnawing suspicion in the pit of his stomach: The admirer had been behind it.

Even now as he reread the letter, the scent of rose petals tore into his belly, sickening him. He cringed and clenched his teeth.

*My charming friend, Wagon Master,*

*How did you like my little surprise? I certainly hope that my small companion hasn't frightened you too much. Perhaps, I could grant you mercy should you repent of your interest in my Rose,*

As Ricochet crumpled the scrap of paper in his viselike grip, he growled inwardly, *You will be begging for mercy.* He opened the note again and read on.

*By now, I trust that you know how serious I am about stealing Rose away. She is mine and mine alone! You cannot take her from me! Next time, it will be more than just a snake in your boot, Wagon Master. Better watch your back.*

That's exactly what Ricochet had been doing all morning: watching his back. He had never felt so vulnerable to attack. His hand rested on the handle of his gun at all times, and he remained ever vigilant.

With the cold days approaching swiftly, Ricochet reminded the pioneers to bundle up and keep their feet as mud free as possible. Illnesses could set in within the span of a few hours if one didn't take the necessary precautions. Sickness was the last thing Ricochet wanted to deal with. The chill of the brisk morning air made him shiver to the core, but that was nothing compared to the ice-cold fear for Rosemary, which surrounded his heart. He'd betrayed her by writing a foolish letter to her admirer. He'd made things worse.

As he rode onward and led the train through the mountainous terrain, he reminded himself to check on her. With young Andrew still unconscious, Mrs. Jones remained by his side every second that they spent traveling, so Ricochet wasn't concerned about a robber coming after the kid. Edward Jones watched everyone who came near his wagon like a hawk stalking its prey.

Charity stayed tucked away in the medical wagon with Katrina Webb and her newborn. Ricochet noticed that Rosemary walking alongside the wagon and keeping to herself. She appeared to be standoffish toward him, cold even. They hadn't spoken a word to each other since their argument, days earlier. Ricochet had wanted to talk to her and apologize for his assumptions about her and Isaac Beckett and his bad temper, but he couldn't bring himself to approach her yet. Keeping the vow that he had made about staying away had been difficult, but he would manage it with the Lord's help, even if it shattered his heart.

He felt the strong pull of sleep and decided that it was best to stop for the day, even though it was only four o'clock. His back ached, and his head spun. He needed to rest, yet he wondered how he could cope with the thought of someone sabotaging him during his sleep, hurting Rosemary, or trying to finish off the sole witness of the medical robbery, Andrew Jones.

Ricochet swung down from the saddle, led his stallion over to the stock wagon, and tied it up for the night. After tending to his steed, he then went to get a refreshing drink of water from one of the barrels. Although it was quite cold outside, the breeze had begun to pick up, and it was growing darker overhead with little to know sunshine, Ricochet couldn't help but feel as if he were boiling beneath all the layered shirts and the thick coat he wore. Even his scalp was sweaty beneath his hat. He wondered if he was coming down with something.

Doing the chores for the evening proved most difficult in his worn-out state. His boots seemed as if they were nailed to the ground beneath him. Every step took much effort. By six o'clock, he was ready for a hearty meal of beans and fresh game, followed by coffee and dried berries.

It was time for evening devotions led by Charity's father, Missionary Jackson Cole, but Ricochet could hardly concentrate on what was being read from the Bible and the songs. When it was all said and done, the wagon master prayed for forgiveness and his weary mind.

He pinched the bridge of his nose and closed his eyes in a frustrated manner as he began his prayer. *Oh, God,* he started and then stopped. His thoughts were scattered, and he couldn't find reprieve from the chaos that consumed his emotions. *What do I want to ask God? Do I want God to force Rosemary to be my bride? Or am I asking for forgiveness because of the way I treated her the last time we met and maybe for the harsh things I thought about Isaac Beckett?* After he gave up on prayer, he sighed long and hard. The he opened his eyes and looked skyward for an answer regarding what he should pray for.

Parson Jackson approached him. "Ric, you appear to be having some trouble."

Ricochet removed his Stetson and fiddled with its brim. "I'm not the one throwing temper tantrums left and right." He blew out a breath and mentally berated himself for his outburst. The trouble between him and Rosemary Barker had nothing to do with the old preacher. Therefore, he should not take it out on him either. Ricochet looked away and mumbled, "I'm sorry, Brother Jackson. That was uncalled for. I'm just aggravated at the moment."

Jackson smiled and said, "Hmm, lovers' quarrel?"

"It's just that she," Ricochet stopped short. It would be wrong to talk badly about the woman he so-called adored enough to be his bride. His shoulders tensed, and he rubbed the back of his neck awkwardly. "Lovers' quarrel?"

"Son, give her time," Jackson said while placing a firm and comforting hand on Ricochet's left shoulder. "I don't know much about the young lady, but it doesn't take a genius to figure out that she's going through a hard patch, as Christians often do. I've seen the two of you together quite frequently, Ric. This will pass. Don't give up on her."

Ricochet's brow furrowed considerably. "I wouldn't say we're," he said, pausing at the word that wanted to fly out of his mouth: lovers. They weren't necessarily lovers. Come to think of it, Ricochet didn't quite know what they were. *Are we two people who enjoy kissing? No, not just that. Two people in search of God's leading hand in their futures? That's more likely it. But lovers?* Ricochet blew out another heavy breath of air.

Jackson beamed as if he'd just placed a bet and won, which would be wrong because the man was a preacher not a gambler. Still, it made Ricochet want to keel over. "You're lookin' mighty faint, Ric," he teased. "You all right?"

Ricochet opened and closed his mouth like a fish. He was more than happy for the interruption, as Jacob Webb ran to meet him with a frenzied expression from behind his spectacles.

"Mr. Chapel!" Jacob exclaimed, doubled over to catch his breath.

Turning away from the all-knowing preacher, Ricochet cleared his throat and went to meet Jacob. He patted the doctor's shoulder and asked, "What seems to be the trouble?" He awaited an answer from Jacob, who took several large gulps of air. His eyes were wide with excitement. "Andrew is awake at long last!"

All at once, the wagon master shook off the tiredness in his body and stiffened. "Andrew's awake?" He couldn't believe it at first. The boy who almost died of a bullet wound was awake and very much alive! But Ricochet wondered if he would be able to tell him who the culprit of the theft was. That one name could seal the admirer's fate and stop the whole charade of unfortunate happenings on the wagon train. Everything relied on that young boy's words, and Ricochet intended to be present when those words were spoken. The doctor and the wagon master hurried to the Joneses' schooner, ready for anything that came next ... or so they thought.

Rosemary kept as far from the medical wagon as she could. Since they had stopped for the day, she had grown nervous to be around Charity because of the admirer's warnings. Even now, she paced back and forth, as she tried to decide whether she should approach her friend or not. Both options seemed hopeless. The admirer could hurt Charity again. Rosemary didn't want to meddle with the friendship that she had come to enjoy with the preacher's daughter.

Frustrated, she decided to stay clear of the medical wagon and Charity. Her friend's safety was very important to her. She could never live with herself if the bright and boisterous young woman met a terrible end.

"You all right, Miss Barker?" Victor Marsh said with concern, as he carried a large sack over his shoulder. "Something troubling you?"

Startled at first, Rosemary jumped and then whirled on her heels to face him. He was closer to her than she had expected. She nearly ran into his abdomen. She backed up quickly, fumbling for the right apology.

He chuckled and hefted the sack higher over his shoulder. "No need to apologize. It was my fault for startling you." He was silent for a moment, and then he furrowed his brow. "Were you waiting for someone?"

Squinting slightly at the oddly shaped sack over his shoulder, Rosemary shook her head to clear the questioning thoughts that were arising. Then she answered, "No, not really. I was thinking about something."

Victor Marsh apparently seemed quite keen on hearing the reason for her worried expression and proceeded to badger her for answers. When she refused to give any insight, he smirked ever so slightly and more than she felt comfortable with.

"I know just what you need, Miss Barker," he said, hefting the sack toward his own wagon. "I'll be right back."

Although Rosemary appreciated his thoughtfulness and attempting to cheer her, Rosemary wished to be alone with her own anxious thoughts. Five minutes later, Victor arrived without the large brown sack. He extended his hand and gave her a tin cup, which was filled to the brim with a warm, dark liquid. Rosemary could smell a pleasant and almost sweet aroma. She took the cup and stared down at it for a moment, wondering what it was and knowing full well that it was not coffee. She glanced back at him and noticed that he too had a cup filled with the same-looking liquid.

She raised one eyebrow. "What exactly is it?"

Victor shrugged, rubbing his neck as if he was nervous for her to taste it. "Well, it's a little something I've been concocting. It's a kind of coffee, but it's more to help with relaxing than with waking up. Try it!"

His eagerness set her mind to wondering, but nonetheless, she lifted it to her lips for a small taste. The liquid tasted like coffee, but it had more of a thin and silky texture than what she was used to. It was sweet on her taste buds, and it smelled delightful. She would have guessed that there was a lot of sugar in the mixture, but Victor assured her that there was none.

Enjoying the taste, Rosemary drank the entire cupful, following Victor's lead. With her belly warm and her mind now clear, she oddly felt at ease. Victor had been right about the drink.

She handed him her empty cup and thanked him. As she did, she felt a tingling sensation in her fingertips, but she paid it no mind.

Victor smiled and nodded. "See, I knew what you needed." He winked and excused himself to finish what he had been doing before. "Good luck with your pacing."

Rosemary hugged herself because of the slight chill in the breeze but also because of something more. Something deep in her gut could not like the all-too-friendly Victor Marsh. Then again, she had the same feeling toward Edward Jones.

Once Victor Marsh had left her Rosemary, she turned her attention on other matters. She felt strongly about not going to see Charity for the time being. She could not endanger her friend so carelessly. Turning on her heels, she decided to head for the Coles' wagon, but when she did, she was met with the familiar face of Lily Garrison.

Lily, who was on the verge of tears, ran to Rosemary. "Rose!" she cried, nearly falling into the Rosemary's arms.

"Lily?" Rosemary began, steadying the poor young woman. "Whatever is the matter?"

The blond-headed woman sucked in a breath and breathed out through clenched teeth. Her body was trembling. She seemed afraid. "Macy," she explained between heaving gasps. "She's missing! I've searched everywhere!"

Isaac arrived. He ruffled his hair and clenched his hat brim. "Any sign of her, Lily?"

The exasperated woman shook her head and choked back a sob. "No. I simply cannot find her. Ma and Pa have been looking for over an hour already."

His own expression frightened and sick with worry, Isaac placed his hat back on his head and then declared, "We'll find her. She can't have gone far."

Her cheeks stained with tears, Lily nodded and half stumbled over to Isaac. His hand welcomed her hand. She peered back at Rosemary and begged, "Please, help us find her. She's never been gone this long before."

Her words tugged at Rosemary's heartstrings. She couldn't turn away a friend in need. Following the newly courting couple, she joined the widespread search for the little girl. She could only hope against hope that nothing had happened to sweet little Macy.

Ricochet entered the crowded wagon, removing his hat as he did. He quietly approached the resting young boy. At first, he thought the lad was sleeping. He wondered if he should return later when Andrew was awake, but upon further examination of the boy's face, he saw that

Andrew was awake. The lad's eyes were swollen, and there were dark circles under his eyes.

It was as if Andrew had been on death row for several days. No one had thought that he would pull through, but God's miracles knew no boundaries. Ricochet had prayed every day for such a wonderful miracle.

Ricochet nestled himself down beside the boy. His heart thundered in his chest, and his mind asked a million questions all at once. Only Andrew knew the identity of the culprit who had caused the series of unfortunate events. The wagon master needed answers before other lives were put in danger.

"Andrew," Ricochet whispered softly. "It's Ric, the wagon master. Do you remember me?"

The boy tilted his head slightly to peer at the man who had entered his quiet abode. "Ric?" he croaked.

The wagon master cringed at the thought of Andrew not remembering him or the place that they were headed. Possibly, the boy had lost his memories of the misfire, which was Ricochet's worst fear. His stomach twisted in knots. Andrew *had* to remember, for it was Ricochet's only hope in capturing Rosemary's admirer and putting an end to all of it.

Andrew's small round face lit up with some realization, but he barely smiled. "Mr. Chapel," he said wearily. "Were you able to get the deer back to camp?"

Ricochet chuckled slightly at the boy's worrying over the game that they had caught rather than for his own life. Andrew had been unconscious for many days, so of course, he wouldn't know what day it was or how long he had been asleep.

The wagon master toyed with his hat brim and stared downward. "Yeah, we carried it all back to camp."

"Good." Andrew grinned wearily. His pale face caused Ricochet to be sympathetic.

After several more minutes of small talk, the wagon master got to the reason that he had come there. He adjusted his seated position and set his hat in his lap. He leaned close and spoke in a calm yet stern tone. "Andrew, do you remember what I asked you before you got shot?"

The young child looked away and into the distance, as if he was trying to recall every second of that awful day. He swallowed hard and then replied in a whisper, "Yes."

Ricochet placed a gentle hand on the boy's arm and felt just how fragile Andrew had become in few days of rest. Ricochet's brow furrowed with unease, but the wagon master could not hold back his questions any longer. "Who told you to stay quiet about the medical wagon being robbed?" He paused, searching for answers on Andrew's face. "I need to know who threatened you. He may be the one who caused this. Who is it, son?"

Andrew's lower lip quivered as he gulped and breathed out shakily. His chest heaved, needing a steady breath. He was on the verge of tears as he reached for Ricochet's hand and squeezed it tightly, drawing the wagon master closer to him. His voice was barely audible, but Ricochet would never forget the name that he heard.

The wagon master's blood boiled inside him, and his veins throbbed with anger. He arose and let the boy rest once more. Then he instructed Jacob Webb and Edward Jones to stand guard over the schooner until he returned.

Ricochet wanted justice. He would carry it out, even if he had to risk his own life to make it happen. No one who tampered with wagons, destroyed young lives, and attempted to assassinate a pioneer aboard his wagon train would get away¾no one.

His put his hat back on his head and strode toward the wagon on the far side of the circle. His blue eyes were piercing, and his face was red with outrage. *There is no escape for him*, he thought.

Rosemary, Isaac, and Lily had all been searching for what seemed like an eternity. Macy had vanished. Nothing led them to believe that she had been attacked or taken by an animal. They started their search deeper into the surrounding mountain woods. They were cautiously aware of the steep drop-offs.

At one point, Rosemary got a little too close to the edge, and Isaac grabbed her arm before she took a horrific fall into a ravine. Her stomach nearly emptied its contents when she peered below. It was a long way down.

Seeing no sign of anyone having gone over the edge, they continued their search elsewhere. They closely looked for footprints or any broken twigs showing that a young girl had wandered off. There was nothing.

It was late. The sun had not yet set, but it was on the verge of it. The day was coming to a close. Still, they had found no evidence of a little girl running about the mountainside alone. Mr. and Mrs. Garrison eventually rejoined their group and voiced their fears over the matter. Isaac did his best to reassure them; however, Lily second-guessed their chances of finding Macy.

Even though Rosemary had grown weary from the full evening of looking for the missing child, she refused to give up. However, it appeared that there was no hope of finding Macy.

For the first time in a long while, Rosemary prayed. In her heart, she begged the Lord for answers to Macy's whereabouts. She pleaded that they would find her before something terrible happened. Her fears died down, as if someone had offered to carry them with her. The sensation was uplifting. A renewed spirit kindled inside Rosemary, and now she gave hope that they would find the missing girl. The search party continued on.

Half an hour later, hope had come. A small stuffed rabbit—Macy's rabbit—was found near some underbrush. Rosemary picked it up and handed it to Lily, who in turn, handed it to her parents. Mrs. Garrison cried out and clutched the stuffed animal tightly, as she turned for comfort from her husband.

Isaac knelt down in the place that they had found the toy and searched for more clues or tracks. He immediately picked up her trail and suggested that they follow it farther, but they would need more sets of eyes if they were to find the young girl. Mr. Garrison had Isaac lead the womenfolk back to camp while he waited by the last known place where Macy was sited. They all agreed to meet back at that same spot after gathering help. Isaac turned to lead the way back, marking the trees as they went. Lily and her mother followed suit.

Rosemary was the last person in line. Her gut tightened, as if it knew that something was wrong with the whole chase-through-the-woods scenario. Surely, a little girl couldn't develop those types of skills to hide her own tracks. Rosemary wondered if they had all been played.

Rosemary stood for a moment, closely scanning her surroundings while listening for her friends as they moved forward. She looked to her right. She saw nothing. She gazed to her left. She saw nothing. Yet something was out of place. She had learned to trust her gut in many instances, and it had gotten her far. She wondered what was so out of place that it had tied her into knots.

When she could barely hear Lily, Isaac, and the Garrisons, Rosemary gave up on listening to her gut and walked quickly to catch up to them. She had scarcely taken three steps when her head began to spin. Her vision became blurry, and black spots appeared. She could hardly move a muscle, as she fell on her knees in cold mud.

A tingling sensation moved through her fingers and toes, until it had gripped every joint and muscle. She tumbled to her side. Her breathing grew loud. She willed her fingers to move, but they simply refused. Her head felt too heavy for her neck to lift it.

As she lay there helpless and vulnerable, a dark shadow stepped into her line of sight. It had come from a thick band of trees. It loomed over her victoriously. Then it proceeded to heft her high into the air until she begged for the ground. Her mouth was dry and unable to produce words. Only moans and grunts escaped her lips. She fought to look at the person's face, praying that it was Ricochet's and that he had found her helpless and weary in the woods.

As she fought against the tiredness that had swept over her body, she heard the raspy whisper of a voice that chilled her to the bone. "I've found you at last, my dear Rose."

# Chapter 21

❧❦❧

"Where is he?" Ricochet asked Mace for the second time.

The silent rider shook his head. "I've told ya, Ric. I don't know. He up and left everything in his wagon."

Ricochet huffed loudly as his nostrils flared. He whirled around and headed for the wagon, which was directly behind his second in command. He inspected the ransacked schooner thoroughly and found an empty vial of medicinal ether lying on the floorboards. He carefully picked it up and smelled it. The ether's sweet scent was enough to send Ricochet into a tizzy of questions and rage. He gripped the small vial and exited the supply wagon.

Tossing the vial to Mace, who managed to catch it with one hand, Ricochet explained, "Ether. Victor robbed the doc's wagon." He spotted two tin cups next to the wagon's wheel beside his foot. He knelt to get a better look. He sniffed one of the cups. It was ether.

Mace examined the vial and then sniffed it. "That's ether all right. But why steal this? Think he's addicted?"

Ricochet rested his right hand over the gun at his hip. "He's up to something, and I don't think it's 'cause he's an addict." He was about to search the wagon again when a revelation about the empty vial and the two empty cups slapped him across the face. He stood to his full height. His blue eyes widened. "Where's Rosemary?"

Mace put a hand beneath his chin as he thought. He then shrugged. "I haven't seen her or the Garrisons for quite some time now." His dark eyes narrowed. "You think Victor—"

Ricochet cut him off and rushed to find the Garrisons in the hope that Rosemary was safe with them, instead of with the malicious Victor Marsh.

Asking around the camp proved to be fruitless, and Ricochet was at his wit's end. He had asked everyone except for Charity, but he had already made a decision to check with her to be on the safe side.

He approached the wagon as Charity made her way out. She was walking! Of course, Ricochet had to remind himself that Charity's legs had not been broken during the accident, but he worried for her nonetheless. She had been badly bruised, and surely, it hurt her to be up and about.

Charity's feet had shakily hit the ground when he crossed his arms and cleared his throat. "Just what are you doing, Miss Cole?"

Charity had obviously not seen him around the other side of the wagon wheel, and she stifled a shriek behind her hand. She calmed upon seeing him but lowered her gaze significantly. "Rosemary hasn't come to visit me like she promised, so I was heading out to find her."

Ricochet shook his head. "You should be resting. Where is Mrs. Webb?"

The young redhead huffed and steadied herself by gripping the wagon's side. "I am capable of standing and walking by myself, and Katrina went for some food."

Ricochet pinched the bridge of his nose out of annoyance and then proceeded to pester Charity into getting back into the wagon. "Miss Cole, you could have broken both legs. You suffered major bruising, and you should not be up. Get back in the wagon, and I will find Rosemary." He tried to assure her, but he couldn't even assure himself.

Charity narrowed her eyes and then sighed loud and long. "Fine, but you let her know that I'm waiting for her. I cannot believe she didn't keep her promise."

She appeared hurt by Rosemary's actions, and Ricochet hurt knowing that he had not told the young lady the truth. Guilt warred against his better judgement. He opened his mouth to tell Charity everything that he knew, not matter how much he wished to keep silent, but when he did this, a ruckus of shouts, women sobbing, and agitated cattle shut him up.

His eyes snapped to the scene directly behind him as he turned. Isaac and the Garrison women marched in. Their faces showed fear and worry. When he made eye contact with Isaac, it was all that Ricochet could do to hold fast, as he felt the growing dread in the pit of his stomach.

"Isaac," he greeted, "what seems to be the problem?"

Followed closely by Lily and Mrs. Garrison, Isaac shook his head and held out his hands. "We've searched and searched," he began in a muddle of words as the women behind him added to the confusion. "We can't find her, and now Rosemary—"

"What about Rosemary?" Ricochet gripped Isaac's shoulders roughly. He needed to know. He begged to know.

After everyone had gone silent, and Isaac had ceased his frantic half sentences, Lily spoke in a shaky voice. "We went to look for Macy," she stated. "Rosemary volunteered to help us, but when we went into the woods, we couldn't find any trace of her."

Ricochet let go of his tight hold on Isaac and then faced Lily for more answers. "Hold a minute. You said Macy is missing? Why didn't you inform me of this? This mountainside is full of bears and wolves and who knows what else."

If Ricochet wasn't agitated enough already, his rage was now lit. It was his job to guide and protect these people, but he couldn't do that without them informing him of missing persons or the like. He forced himself to bite his tongue before his mouth said something it shouldn't. Somehow, he had to find out about the missing little girl. He knew that Rosemary was tied to it in some way.

He took a step closer to Lily. "Tell me everything."

Lily nodded and began the tale of their trek into the woods while the men gathered their firearms and formed a search party.

Rosemary was in and out of consciousness. She had tried hard to open her eyes, yet each time she managed to open them into slits, the red, flickering light made her dizzy enough to fall into a deep sleep once more. The harder she attempted to wake up, the dizzier she became.

As her senses became more alert, flooding pain spiked in her wrists. Her brain urged her fingers to move, flinch, or even twitch, but they simply refused. Her fingertips were numb, but her wrists ached and stung like fire.

Finally, Rosemary's eyes opened wide. She stirred and heard moaning in her pounding ears. It took her several minutes to realize that the moaning was coming from her own mouth. It took her even longer to stop the sound. A migraine had settled deep into her temples, making her cringe and squint. She closed her eyelids again. The sensation passed, as she grew accustomed to the rays of red and orange light before her. A musty, wet smell filled her nostrils. She scrunched her nose in response to the scent.

She shifted and willed her arms to move and loosen up. They wouldn't budge. Finding herself at a loss to know what to do, she lay still. She was confused by her surroundings. From what she could see in the fading light, dark fangs seemed to tower above her. They came down from the roof of a blackened mouth. Ahead of her, she saw the only doorway out of the monster. Beams of orange light barely pierced the dark from behind the trees outside. Rosemary then knew that she was in a cave. It was cold, and a breeze began to a howl through the cave.

Her back was against a large rock that went all the way to the ceiling. She adjusted her position and found that her wrists had been tied behind her. She was bound to the enormous pillar of rock. The rope on her wrists was extremely tight, and it had deeply cut into her skin. It was loose enough for her to move to a more comfortable position. Wearily, she sat up to give her aching side a break. She licked her lips. They were chapped and slightly split from a lack of moisture. The back of her neck ached horribly. She had no idea how long she had been unconscious in the cave, but judging by the fading light in the entrance, night was approaching.

Her brow furrowed as she recalled the incident in the woods. She had grown so very tired. Then she had fallen over. Then … She swallowed hard as chills ran up her spine. She had seen the admirer. He had found her!

She stiffened as she eyed her surroundings with more caution than she previously had. There was no sign of him or anyone else. She was alone. But a voice in her head told her that he would return soon. She set to work on the rope, praying to God that it would come loose.

Her wrists barely budged when she attempted to slip out of her bonds. The searing pain brought hot tears to her eyes, and it was all she could do not to cry out. She pulled. She tugged. She rubbed. Nothing was working. Fear began to settle in, and Rosemary had to force herself to remain calm and breathe steadily. Having a breakdown would only worsen her situation.

"God," she whispered, her voice so raspy that she barely knew it was hers, "help me." She paused to look down at the floor as her tears surfaced again. "Please, help me. I don't want to die at this monster's hands."

She parted her lips to plead once more when she heard footsteps echoing at the entrance of the cave. At first, Rosemary didn't dare look up, but as the footsteps slowly drew closer and closer, she lifted her gaze skyward. Her jaw tensed as she recognized the face immediately. Then she choked back a sob. "Victor?"

His piercing gaze was nothing like the gentlemanly character that he had portrayed on the wagon train. He smirked, lifted an eyebrow slightly, and then lowered himself to rest on his heels. "Surprised, Rose?" He tilted his hat back with his left thumb.

She gawked in response. This man was nothing like the way that she had imagined the admirer to look like. Rose scents, frilly gifts, and elegant handwriting didn't suit his character in the slightest. In fact, he appeared to be quite the opposite! He was a simple man with nice clothes but

One might have called him a man who liked to flirt with the ladies, but it was never to one in particular and least of all, to her. Rosemary thought she'd been quite the fool. She'd fallen hard for his performance. He'd played quite a farce. Truly, she was astonished and in awe of such skill from the flamboyant Mr. Marsh. She hadn't even once considered him to be this vile and cruel.

She tried to regain her composure, but she could not. After several moments of shock and thought, she could only ask, "Why?"

He seemed to be chuckling at her question. He leaned closer. His eyes were horribly dark and wild. Now she saw the potential murderer and lunatic in him.

"All those churchgoing gals are too prideful. Always volunteering at hospitals, planning gatherings, baking for church get-togethers." He sighed. "Nothing but a bunch of vipers, the lot of them! They act kind, innocent even, but behind all that smiling and sweet-talking, there's nothing but deceit. Their words and vows are like venom poisoning the weak and defenseless!"

She shrank back as if she expected him to violently strike her down. His next words caused her to shudder uncontrollably. He smiled as if the psychotic behavior of only moments earlier had been nothing but another act of his.

"But not you," he said as he shook his head. "You're not like them at all, are you, Rosemary?" His voice hushed to that of a raspy whisper. His tone was a scraping sound in Rosemary's ears. "No, you're different." He brushed her cheek with the side of his forefinger.

Rosemary, who was stunned and confused, sat utterly still. Victor Marsh had acted as if he had known her for a long time, but she had no clue of who he was. She wondered if she had seen him in her town back home. She searched her memories to see if she had ever seen his face before, but nothing came to mind. She recalled every person that she had helped at the hospital when she had volunteered with her mother. She could think of no one. After all the times she had helped in her local church, she couldn't pin his face to anyone else's face. She wondered who he was and what his attachment to her was.

As if reading her confused mind, Victor snickered under his breath. Then he stood to his full height. He had towered over her when she had been standing, but now that she was tied low to the ground, she realized that he was a monstrous man. He was well built, athletic, and gruff. Without a doubt, she knew that getting out of his grasp wouldn't be easy; however, that wouldn't stop her from trying.

Victor rested his hands on his hips and shifted his weight to the right foot. "You've never seen my face before this wagon train," he assured her. "But I've seen you, heard you, and watched you for months. He said I couldn't lay a finger on you yet, but I waited and bided my time. Now he's gone, and it's just the two of us."

Nothing he said made any sense to her. She didn't know who the *he* was, and she definitely didn't want to stay to find out. She tried to swallow but found that her mouth was dry. "What do you want with me? Why have you done all this?" She teared up, and her breathing became strained. "The threats. The killing of innocent lives. The accidents. Why?"

He whipped out a blade from his belt and then knelt next to her once more. The tip of the knife was razor sharp and pointed at her throat. His malicious smile made Rosemary's stomach churn. The fierce glint in his eyes was all she needed to see to know that his plans for her would not be pleasant. Her eyes peered upward as he pressed the side of the blade under her chin. The coldness of the weapon on her skin gave her chills. The way he spoke in a rasped whisper caused a tremor inside her.

"Everything we've done has been for you."

Rosemary's brow creased. She wondered if she had heard him right. At first, she thought that he might have lost his senses, but now, she thought that he was stark raving mad. He referred to himself as *we*. She couldn't help but question him. "We?"

Victor faltered for a fraction of a minute and then adjusted his words. "I have followed you hundreds of miles out here just to get you back. Of course, we," he grumbled and corrected himself, "I had planned on whisking you away after the hunting incident and after your wagon collapsing, but on both occasions, it backfired." Then he spoke of *we* again. Something unsettling grasped at her insides about that, but perhaps, it was because Victor Marsh might be insane or possessed by the devil.

At any rate, she wanted to be as far from him as possible. She wondered if it was possible. No one knew of her whereabouts. She wasn't even certain of her whereabouts. The straits were dire in her current predicament, and no heroics of another would grant her the pleasure of freedom. Escape rested in her own hands. She had to keep him talking for as long as she could or as long as it took to think of some way to get out of her restraints and flee from his clutches. She had to stall.

"You shot at an innocent boy and then hurt my friend." She wasn't guessing about his handiwork, but she was simply stating the facts. "You were even behind that robbery from the medical wagon."

He snickered and flicked the knife to her left cheek. "The boy saw me rob the medical wagon, and he had to be dealt with. I missed the shot, but luckily, his memory of the accident had been wiped clean. As for the wagon, I meant to kidnap you before that; however, that pesky wagon master and preacher's daughter got in my way. I sawed the wagon axle in two in order to take out the Cole girl. I had hoped to get rid of Chapel with the rattler that I placed in his boot, but he caught onto it. Blast him!"

He suddenly became sincere and angry. The atmosphere went from fearful to dangerous, and Rosemary shrank back against the rock that was behind her. "That wagon master," he snapped, "he's foiled one too many of my plans. Several times, we—*I* warned him off, yet he didn't stay away."

Rosemary took careful notice that Victor had said *we* again. Surely, there couldn't be two demented men out there. She pondered the thought of asking him what he meant by *we* but stopped herself short. She guessed that he was merely talking out of his head.

Victor had mentioned warning Ricochet to stay away more than once. Did that mean there was more than one note given to Ricochet? Rosemary had only heard that the wagon master had received one note. She wondered how she had missed the other threats. Ricochet hadn't said a word about them to her. Once again, he had saved her from the turmoil of worrying about him.

She swallowed her sobs of awe and the pleasure of knowing that he had taken so much care to prevent further injury to her already-wounded heart. She didn't deserve his great kindness or affection. She prayed that he would forgive her for causing him such grief and the trials that her admirer had brought him.

Victor finished his rampage about the wagon master by declaring, "Chapel's measly world is coming to an end. Soon that man won't be foiling my plans any longer!" He stood once more.

Rosemary pulled on the rope around her wrists, lurching forward. "No! Don't hurt him! Please," she begged as tears filled her eyes. "You have me. I'm all yours. Just please don't hurt him!"

He bent down to grab her chin. His fingers were rough, and they scraped against her smooth skin. He pulled her closer to his face and grinned wickedly. "As long as he's alive, you'll never be mine."

Rosemary shuddered, and her expression twisted into one of great sorrow. She couldn't let him kill Ricochet. She *wouldn't* let him kill Ricochet. The wagon master had shown her how to live, feel, and trust again. She would sooner let Victor have his way with her than let him take Ricochet out of this world. If she could run away from her captor, only for a moment, she'd warn the wagon master of Victor's coming. All she needed was one distraction. *Keep stalling,* she told herself.

"Victor," she said in the silence, "if you hurt him, I'll never be yours." Her threat seemed to spark a look of excitement in his dark eyes. She'd meant the words as a warning and a caution, but they had turned out to be the opposite. Victor appeared happy and full of laughter.

"There it is," he scorned after a chuckle. "The panic-stricken fear. For a while, I saw little of it. I almost debated on changing my sights to another." He stopped and searched her eyes as if he was hungering for more of the same feeling. Then he continued, "But I'm not one to give up the chase on my victims. Ricochet Chapel will die today."

"You won't win that easily," she vowed. "He's too careful. He will see you coming and then—" she stopped short and saw Victor's other hand whip out his knife again. She flinched and shut her eyes tight. She expected to feel the sting of the blade on her skin. When no painful blow came, she opened her eyes. Victor used the knife to cut her ropes. He released her with as little care as possible, jerking her head to the side. Then he turned away from her and said, "Remove your shoes."

She furrowed her brow, thinking she had heard him wrong. He repeated himself in a growl, whirling around. "Either you remove your shoes or I'll remove them for you. Your choice."

The last thing that she wanted was for him to touch her again, so she did what he had asked or rather demanded. She removed her shoes, taking her time in hopes of delaying his plans. Then she slid them over to him on the rocky floor.

Still holding the knife, he stalked over to her and pushed her to the side. She gave somewhat of a struggle until his knife poked her spine. Then she gave in to his wishes. Confused by this, she peered up as he straightened and faced her.

"Get up," he ordered.

Before she could stop herself, she asked, "Why?"

He gave no answer, but instead, he pulled her to her wobbly feet. He jerked her forward before she was ready, and Rosemary nearly stumbled into his side. She cautiously regained her balance and managed to stop herself. His grip on her arm tightened, and he whispered into her ear with breath that was warm and moist on the side of her face. "Keep spouting questions, and I'll gut him open in front of you."

Rosemary shut her eyes tight, praying that this nightmare was only a nightmare. Victor urged her forward on her bare feet while his blade dug into her back. "Move."

The bottoms of her feet slid and atop the cold slick cave floor. Then she felt the prickly surface of the forest as they exited her dark prison. Rosemary trod lightly after she managed to stub her toe on a sharp stone. She didn't dare ask any more questions as she removed her shoes. Quietly, she prayed that Ricochet would stay away, no matter how much her heart wished for him to rescue her. The sunset lingered as they trekked farther into the mountains.

"There's no sign of her." Mace frowned. He had just met Ricochet at the rendezvous point, with four men in tow. Isaac and Jacob were two of them. The wagon master had thoroughly searched the camp and come up empty-handed. Their search for both Rosemary and Macy had grown cold. Both had vanished as if into thin air. He was beginning to think all was lost. Then they found something.

Isaac called from farther ahead. His eyes were wide and glittering. He signaled with a loud whistle for all to gather around him. Ricochet made haste, hopping over a fallen tree branch and then stepping over a large stone. He halted beside the younger man to find out what the ruckus was about.

Nestled gently between two logs and some brush lay little Macy Garrison. Her eyelids were closed, and her dress was caked with mud. Her soft snores reassured everyone that she was alive and well but simply sleeping. Ricochet put his ear closer to her mouth as if he thought that her breathing might just be a dream. Her exhale tickled his ear, and he praised God for the little girl's safe return. Something on her breath, however, caused him to wonder. He recognized the scent. A few seconds later, his eyebrows rose as he realized that it was ether. She had been drugged.

Isaac lifted the girl into his arms as the terrified parents circled round him and thanked him and the Lord for Macy's safe return.

Mace came and stood next to Ricochet. The wagon master had turned so that he could search the area. The silent rider grabbed his shoulder. "Something about this got me wonderin'," he said, his eyes focusing on the sleeping girl, who was now in her father's arms. "How'd she get all the way out here?"

Ricochet clenched his fists and stiffened his jaw. "Ether."

Mace narrowed his gaze and focused his attention on Ricochet's face. "Ether? She was drugged?" He paused as the direness of the situation dawned on him. "This was all a means of distracting us."

Ricochet nodded slowly. His exhales grew rapid and uneven as his temper soared. "When I get my hands on him …" He balled his hands into tight fists and then whirled around to face the search party. He told one of his men to escort the parents, Dr. Webb, and young Macy back to camp while he, Mace, and Isaac continued the search for Rosemary. After plans were settled, Ricochet's small group left.

Isaac asked, "Think she's still alive?"

Ricochet's hot temper could be heard in his answer. "She has better be."

"And if she isn't?" The younger man questioned curiously.

Ricochet's eyes lit with rage, his expression flushed a deep red, and he replied, "Justice will be done, but I pray that it is not by my hands."

Although Ricochet would like nothing more than to strike down the man who had taken Rosemary, he knew that he couldn't go near him for fear of killing another man. No matter how much he wished to take justice into his own hands, he prayed that he wouldn't get the chance. Blood was already on his hands, and he certainly didn't need any more of it. However, his flesh was weaker in its resolve. Every time he thought of Rosemary being hurt or worse by that monster of a man, he wished to kill him.

Willing himself to keep calm as much as possible, Ricochet sighed heavily. "We'll find her if it takes us weeks." He then added quietly, "I can't leave without her." He became quiet after that and started to track again. He stayed close to the ground and searched for clues. Isaac and Mace followed him.

*God, please help me find her before it's too late!* He begged the Master in the heavens for guidance, wisdom, and strength. He couldn't bear to lose her, not now and not ever.

The sun was low over the horizon. Soon the shadows of night would cover the mountainside. Time put him in a hard predicament. He couldn't leave her out there with that monster, but tracking would be impossible in the dark. He had to hurry. Time was running out!

Her feet were either numb from the cold or the wet, prickly forest floor. Rosemary couldn't tell which one it was. She kept walking, even though her legs begged for rest, her eyes pleaded for sleep, and her belly was hungry for nourishment. Victor's grip on her upper arm and his knife at her back pushed her onward.

She had no idea where he was taking her or why he was taking her anywhere. In her mind, the cave would have been better cover for them than out there amid the trees, where a tracker like Ricochet or Mace could find them.

Rosemary's mind was busy with thoughts of Macy. She wondered what Victor had done with the sweet little girl. *If he killed her, where did he dump her body?* Rosemary thought.

Rosemary shook the image of Macy's lifeless body left somewhere deep in the mountainside out of her head. Tears stung her eyes, and she gingerly blinked them back before Victor caught on. She dared not ask him anything, for he had already made threats. She knew that he would carry them out without hesitation.

They trekked farther into the woods until they met a large river that dove as a waterfall did, before running down into a ravine. They moved near it, and Rosemary got a sinking feeling in her gut that this would be her grave.

She turned to face Victor. "Why have you brought me here?" she asked, puzzled and terrified. She had already witnessed the horrifying power of water when she had fallen into the river during their first few weeks on the wagon train. She shivered at the thought of being thrown into a large body of raging rapids again.

Victor smirked, seemingly laughing at her petrified expression. "What? Are you more afraid of some rapids than of me?" He grabbed her chin and jerked her up on her toes to meet his face. His nose was mere centimeters from hers, and she cringed at the smell of his breath, which reeked of alcohol and smoke. "You'd be better off facing the rapids, sweet, sweet Rose." He chuckled and pushed her to the side as he set to work creating a scene of shuffled footprints around the river's edge.

Rosemary watched in puzzlement and then straightened. She took in her surroundings and slowly backed up a step to see if he'd notice. He didn't. When Victor pulled out her shoes and set one of them down next to the water, Rosemary took a chance and sprinted forward. She had only taken three steps when an arm wrapped around her waist and jerked her backward. She fell into the sturdy frame of Victor Marsh, his vicelike grip winding her momentarily.

"And just where do you think you're going? I ain't that crackbrained, Rose. You think I wouldn't notice you slipping into the woods behind my back?" His voice rose to a rumble in her ears, as he tightened his grip around her waist. His other hand held the knife to her face. "I'd hate to have to scar up that perfect little face of yours, sweetheart."

Rosemary inhaled shakily, raised her foot, and stomped her heel down into the middle of his boot. She proceeded to slam her head back into his chest, winding him. As he stumbled back in surprise, she fumbled forward and grabbed the first thing on the ground.

A minute later, he had her in his arms once again. He lowered his face to hers, and she jammed a sharp stone into the corner of his eye. He howled in pain, and she ran for the trees. She never looked back to see if he was following her. She didn't need to. She knew he would be.

"Rose!" he called time and again, but she pressed onward.

She stopped behind a boulder to take a quick breather. It didn't last long, for she heard him hurrying to find her. She bolted a different direction to throw him off her trail. A tree branch caught the bottom of her dress, and she wrestled with it for several agonizing seconds to free it. During these seconds, she should have spent running. At last, her patience wore thin, and she ripped the side of her dress away from the branch. A good amount of the seam was torn off, but she paid it no mind. Safety was her top priority for now and not style or clothing.

The sun had sunk low behind the horizon, and shadows began to dance and play before Rosemary's vision. Every flickering movement made her jump, and every sound unsettled her stomach. He could be anywhere.

She trod onward with extreme caution and prayed that she could slip between boulders and trees without his keen eyes catching her. She rested her back against a scrawny tree trunk for a moment to catch her breath. The adrenaline that had once coursed through her veins now left her drained of energy to carry on. *How long have I been running? An hour? Two hours?* She wondered, but she couldn't tell.

Darkness had swept over the mountainside like a covering of clouds. The chilly breeze of the night tugged at Rosemary's curls and tore at her clothes. She huddled next to the trunk. Her feet were sore and throbbing. When will this nightmare end? she wondered.

She froze as a voice, faint and distant, caught her attention. It brought tears of relief and comfort to her weary eyes. She sniffled and wiped away a stray droplet that ran down the side of her cheek. "Ric," she whispered hoarsely at first.

"Rosemary!" the strong wagon master's voice called again. He was searching for her. He was on his way!

Her heart ached and she stumbled forward. Her lips parted to unleash a cry for help and a plea for his safe arms. But the cry never made it out of her mouth. A hand of immense strength clamped over her mouth, trapping the scream inside her. Another arm coiled around her waist, squeezing her so tight that she thought she'd pass out from lack of oxygen.

"Sh," Victor whispered, his warm breath tickling her ear. Another teardrop escaped Rosemary's eye, ran down the side of her face, and dripped onto Victor's dirty hand.

Ricochet called out once more. "Rosemary!" This time he was so close. He couldn't have been more than ten yards away, but the dark had swallowed up his image, and Victor had halted her attempt of escape. After Ricochet's voice had long since left that part of the woods, Victor whisked Rosemary farther away from the wagon master's reach.

# Chapter 22

He was at his wit's end regarding this frantic search across the mountainside. The sun had long ago disappeared to allow the moon to take to the sky. A chill took a firm hold over the woods while the night creatures reigned over the land. Coyotes, owls, and mountain lions were now on the prowl.

Ricochet had taken his search party on through the woods. Isaac and Mace agreed to stay with him, regardless of how foolish it was to remain in the dark. They hadn't made it much farther before darkness had covered any sign of a human trail. Hope diminished in the wagon master's heart. God only knew what Rosemary was going through at that very moment. Ricochet tried not to dwell on the horrid thoughts that plagued his imagination. If he did, he'd die of a broken heart.

Ricochet, Mace, and Isaac decided on making camp for the night. They sat near the fire to warm themselves and rest before starting to search again in the early morning hours. Mace leaned back against a rock formation behind him and rested his head for a few minutes. "Do you think there's a chance we'll find her?" he asked.

Ricochet didn't look up from his trance on the flames. He had to admit that his hope had increased when they had discovered young Macy, earlier that day, but now, that hope had disappeared almost altogether. "We'll find her," he forced himself to say.

Isaac sighed. "We lost the trail, Ric. There's hundreds of miles of mountainous terrain to cover. I don't want to give up, but ..." he trailed off.

Ricochet's eyes snapped up to look at his friend, and a fire rose in his chest, which could never be quenched. "I refuse to give up. She's out there." He paused, scowling. "We'll find her."

They talked no more that night. The men fell asleep with their guns at the ready, if anything should happen within the few hours of darkness that were left.

Dawn came all too soon for Ricochet; however, he wanted to get a move on. On the previous day, Mace had left a trail to their location so they could follow it back to the wagons. Ricochet knew that it would only be a matter of hours before the other search party, consisting of Edward, Jacob, and Jackson, would arrive at the wagon circle to await his further instructions. He hated to leave the woods, but he didn't know what else to do.

As he got ready for the long day that would most certainly be ahead, he noticed that Mace was still snoozing rather soundly across from him. He knitted his brow and looked around for Isaac. "Isaac?" He called out, still quiet because Mace was sleeping. After all, it was early.

Although the wagon master thought that it was strange for the man to sleep so soundly, perhaps, exhaustion had finally claimed Mr. Chronicle. Mace had never slept deeply, even when men on the wagon train had agreed to stand guard all night. The silent rider always rose earlier than Ricochet did and went to bed later than any other pioneer did. Ricochet thought that he should let him sleep a few extra minutes, regardless of how anxious he was to get on with the search.

"Isaac?" Ricochet called again. There was still no answer. He wondered where he had run off to. Ricochet was just about to arouse Mace, when a panting Isaac, who was coming across their makeshift campsite, answered him.

Looking confused, Ricochet asked, "Where have you been, and why—?"

"Just come with me. I found a trail!" Isaac cut him off sharply. His thin eyebrows rose in urgency; however, his voice was soft and breathless.

The wagon master's eyes grew wide with excitement. He swallowed and clenched his fists. *God, let me find her. Oh, please, God, let me find her alive!*

He turned to awaken Mace, whose soft snores filled his ears, but Isaac touched him on the shoulder to stop him. "No," he said in a harsh whisper. "We have to go. Now!" Ricochet wanted to question his tone of command, but Isaac drew in a shaky breath and answered his outburst. "We have to hurry. I spotted Rosemary just up ahead." He hesitated then said, "With Victor."

Ricochet didn't waste another second or breath. He followed the young man. This was what he had feared. Victor had been the one writing Rosemary the absurd and forward letters, causing trouble on the wagon train, and kidnapping Rosemary. *He won't get away with it*, Ricochet vowed inwardly. Somehow, someway, Ricochet would get her back, and Victor would be taken to the next town and tried for his crimes.

Isaac led him several paces to the west and stopped so short that the wagon master would've fallen right into him if he had not grabbed hold of a tree branch. His boots skidded, and he looked around frantically for the trail.

As his chest heaved, Isaac pointed ahead of them. "I couldn't sleep, so I decided to scout out the area. I found this, only moments ago, and then I saw Victor dragging Rosemary up ahead."

Ricochet's eyes locked onto something that had snagged on a branch, just a few paces in front of their path. As he crept closer, his eyes narrowed to inspect a piece of material that had been torn off by a rather sharp twig close to the ground. He knelt, touching the fabric. It was pink in color and soft. He untangled it carefully from the twig and recognized the material in an instant. "Rosemary," he said and looked around for more signs of her passing through.

He tilted his hat brim up to get a good view of his whereabouts. He felt the ground and moved brush and fallen leaves. Then he noticed a boot print. It was much too big for Rosemary's foot and most certainly a man's. "Go wake Mace," he ordered. "Tell him of this trail and that I've already left. Then I want you to have him catch up to me as soon as possible. I also want you to wait at our campsite for the others to show up. Victor can't have gotten too far from here."

Isaac nodded curtly and sped back to the camp as fast as a young mountain lion. Ricochet lightly traced his finger around the large boot print. Victor was a big man, and he could hold his own. Ricochet knew that if a scuffle happened between them, Victor just might be victorious. The wagon master would need Mace's help.

A trail formed before Ricochet's very eyes, and he followed it with extreme caution and urgency. His fingers rested on the hilt of his handgun while his other hand stuffed the fabric into his pocket. The trail led him down a windy slope toward a ravine, where a waterfall leapt over the side. The roar of rushing rapids filled his ears as he neared.

Carefully, he stepped out from the tree line and eyed the ground. Boot prints covered the muddy surface and seemed to spin in a circle as if there had been a struggle. Ricochet lowered himself to his knees and felt the boot print. He was looking for any sign of smaller prints, Rosemary's prints.

An object on the bank was out of place. He scurried to look, and when he had spotted it, he immediately sunk to his knees in the mud. His shaky hands lifted the object up to his disbelieving face. *Am I too late?* he wondered. The boot belonged to Rosemary. It was small, covered in leaves, and caked with muck from the forest. The lace-up design on the front was unmistakably hers.

"No," he whispered and looked at the rapids. His mouth gaped open as he spied the terrifying flow of debris and sharp boulders jutting out from the water's surface. Surely the admirer—Victor—hadn't already disposed of her body.

He clutched the boot in his hands and stood. He called out her name over and over, staring at the rapids and hoping that he would catch a sight of her clutching a rock or swimming for her life. "Rosemary!" He cried out, nearing the waters' edge.

His breath caught as he spied another boot lodged between two rocks on the riverbank. The boot resembled the first one. He could almost hear her screaming his name as Victor threw her to her death. In agony, Ricochet fell on all fours, pounding the ground and crying aloud, "No! Rosemary!"

He turned over to rest his back against a boulder. Rocking violently to and fro, he stared at the boot in his hands and shook his head in disbelief. She couldn't be gone. She just couldn't. He looked skyward and prayed in earnest, *God, she can't be gone. Oh, Lord, please say she's not.* He choked on a sob and clutched the boot to his chest. "Rosemary," he cried.

Victor raised the rifle up, steadying it on a boulder in front of him. He had hidden above Ricochet and behind a rock formation that overlooked the rapids. His line of sight was matched to the wagon master, and soon, the man would be dead on the ground.

With her wrists tied tight behind her back and a gag securing her mouth, Rosemary sat anxiously watching the scene play out before her. Her muffled cries of warning for Ricochet would do little good against the raging rapids' boisterous roar. She tried nonetheless, even if it gained a harsh glare from Victor in return.

The admirer straightened his back and lined up his sights, awaiting the perfect moment to strike. He got ready to pull the trigger. A smile of malice darkened his expression. He went to pull the trigger with his index finger, but as he did, Rosemary kicked his right side with every ounce of strength she could muster.

The bullet flew from the rifle and whistled during its flight. Rosemary managed to peek over the top of the rock formation to see the bullet hit its target, much to her disappointment and dread. She sunk. Her eyes welled up with tears as the man below dropped and rolled into the cold rapids. If she could scream, she would have. Instead, muffled cries came from her mouth once more, and she shook her head in disbelief. She attempted to wrestle her wrists free of the ropes when Victor laughed aloud victoriously.

"He's dead!" he shouted and lifted his rifle in the air with utter joy. "The wagon master is no more!"

Rosemary hunched her left shoulder and managed to get free of her gag. The first word out of her mouth was a shrill wail of grief. "Ricochet!" She sank back against the rocks and sobbed, as tears streamed freely down her cheeks. "You killed him!"

Victor lowered his rifle, chuckling. "I always keep my promises, Rose." He said, with a gleam of wicked intentions in his gaze. "And now, you're mine."

Rosemary had had enough. She stood with her back straight and her shoulders firm. "No, Victor," she declared. "I am not yours, and I never will be!" She took one step forward, showing hardly any fear and replacing with pure and righteous anger. "I'm not scared of you anymore. My God will see to it that I am never yours. He will avenge Ricochet's death, and you will be sorry."

With his expression contorting into a mask of mockery, Victor replied, "What god? He hasn't avenged your parents' deaths, the attempted murder of a foolish boy, or the kidnapping of an innocent girl. Your god doesn't exist, Rose. Face it. You're out of time and luck."

"He does exist, and He's more powerful than you could ever hope to be," she argued and took another step. Her mind went back to when Ricochet had confronted her about her fear of men. She had originally thought the way that Victor had. She had believed that there was no God to save her from evil. The precious, few months she'd spent with the wagon master had taught her many things, including faith in the face of great fear.

"You're the one who is out of luck." She raised her chin defiantly. She twisted her wrists in the ropes behind her back, and they loosened. She only needed a little more time, and her hands would be free. "My God will not turn a blind eye to the shedding of innocent blood, Victor. Your wicked acts will not go unpunished."

Her chest cavity ached and throbbed as she began to grieve. She could hardly suck in a breath of fresh air without choking back a sob. Ricochet's words, from a night long ago when the air was warm and winter was a distance off, echoed in her ears. *I happen to care a great deal for you, and I can't ignore the fact that you are all I think about every second of every day.*

His words were so caring and gentle, and they tore at her heart like claws on stone. She missed him greatly, more than she ever thought was possible. But Ricochet Chapel, wagon master of the train heading out west, was gone for good, and nothing would bring him back from the rapids.

Swallowing her guilt at leading Ricochet to his death, she glowered at her captor. Another chance at life had been stolen by the monster who sneered viciously at her. She pulled on her bonds once more. The ropes frayed and loosened their tight hold. She was almost there.

"Do with me what you wish, but you'll never steal away my hope. No matter what, I will defy you to the end. You've already lost." Her words gave her a sense of peace within her soul, which only the Almighty Himself could bestow. Her courage was not her own. It was from God. Beyond a shadow of a doubt, she was certain that He was watching over her at that very moment.

With his veins bulging on his forehead, his nostrils flaring, and hot flames in his black eyes, Victor stomped forward and glared down at her. "I'll make you suffer for those words. What I had in mind before is nothing compared to what's in store for you now." He gripped her face, jerking her upward onto her toes.

"The pain will be so unbearable, you'll wish for death!" Spit flew from his mouth as he growled that promise. He then released her, letting her collapse to the ground. He went to retrieve his rifle, which he had set aside before assaulting her.

Rosemary, coughed, shivered, and rested on her bruised knees. She eyed Victor carefully and then twisted and tugged her wrists until they were free of their bonds, tearing the last of the frayed ends to pieces. She rose to her feet and ran to meet the one who had killed the man whom she had grown to love more than her own self.

Victor didn't see it coming until it was too late. He turned at the sound of bare feet on rock. He met by a violent blow to the face. He remained stunned and baffled for several seconds while Rosemary moved away to ready herself for the next attack. She picked up a good-sized stick and held it defensively, itching for Victor to try something so that she would have the chance to strike again.

Rosemary didn't count on his immense strength and recovery time. Victor was ready to go before she could even attempt another hit. She had speed, but he had vigor.

He towered over her. His cheek had been scratched, and it was bleeding, after her measly swipe while trying to wound him. Rosemary went to hit him with her makeshift weapon, but he simply took hold of the stick and yanked it from her hands. His power and overall stamina was frightening. He grabbed the front of her blouse and slammed her into the rock formation so hard that she thought she saw stars.

Dizzy and winded, Rosemary desperately tried to shield her face from what inevitably came next. She was too disoriented to stop his retaliation. His fist came fast. Her knees buckled, and she blacked out after the blow.

Rosemary awoke to the sound of metal on rock. It rang in her ears and rattled her teeth. One of her eyes opened slowly while the other remained swollen shut, throbbing and nauseating her. She tried to move her head toward the sound of metal, which was in her left, but the slight motion made her queasy. She remained still in order to calm the sensation of vertigo.

Her fingers felt cold and numb, and her shoulders ached. She gathered her bearings. She was able to shift her head and see that her arms had been stretched above her. Her body lay on a rocky surface, and she had been tied to a stone pillar. The ground beneath her was hard and uneven, which made it uncomfortable to lie in that position.

There was enough light so that she could see her every surroundings, but the sun was not visible above her. There were no trees, plants, grasses, or pine needles but only rock. She was back in the cave again. But the atmosphere was far more eerie and frightening than it had been before. Something about the cave made her quake, both inside and out.

The metallic screeching sound stopped suddenly, and a voice spoke up. "You put up quite the resistance." Victor applauded, and Rosemary lifted her head slightly off the stone. She saw that he was testing the sharpness of his knife on his thumb.

"I suppose I misjudged you at first. You're a brave one to stand up to me like that." The knife blade split open the padding on his thumb. "Or maybe you're just a foolhardy person. Either way, you face punishment." He smiled, as her breathing grew ragged. He approached and knelt down to her right, lowering his knife to her throat. "Afraid of me, Rose?" When she didn't answer, he smirked and said, "You should be."

Her defiant gaze gained her an annoyed click of his tongue as he pressed the knife onto her cheek and made a small cut. It stung, but it was nothing compared to the hurt in Rosemary's heart over her beloved Ricochet's death and the inevitable evil that would take place. Her chest ached. The grief and agony of losing him was too great a suffering for her to bear. She'd rather die a thousand deaths than to witness his downfall.

Conjuring up what was left of her dignity, which wasn't much, she scowled up at the murderous man who mocked her grief. It hurt to look at his face.

"That look is very unbecoming, my dear." He removed the knife and watched her closely. "Where is that scared little woman inside of you hiding, huh? Go on," he urged in anticipation. "Scream. Cry. Beg! Just like all the others did."

Rosemary did nothing of the sort, but she remained solemn and quiet. She was in mourning, and there was no room for fear. She accepted that she was a hollow shell of her former self. Ricochet was gone. His laughter would never annoy her again, and his comforting arms would never embrace her as they once had. She decided that her old self had died alongside the wagon master. She refused to allow Victor to stand victorious over her any longer.

Victor muttered a curse under his breath when she gave no hint of distress or despair. He spread his legs and stood over her, keeping her legs pinned down. "You'll beg soon enough," he guaranteed with a sly grin. "I have longed for this moment, sweet Rose. For months, I was told to wait for this moment. Well, he can't tell me to wait any longer."

Rosemary's eyes narrowed. She couldn't understand what he was talking about. Who told him to wait, and why?

Victor's breathing increased, and his eyes were filled with lust. "No one will hear you. No one will find you. It's just you and me," he jeered and pressed the tip of his blade against her top button's stitching on her blouse, just above her neckline.

As he did this, Rosemary swung her right leg upward at lightning speed and kneed him with painful blow that managed to pry a scream of agony from him. He fell beside her and curled into a ball while pounding the ground with his fists.

Rosemary used that precise moment of her incapacitated enemy's writhing state to tug on her bound wrists above her head. She pulled herself up and scooted closer to the rock pillar. Then she vigorously attacked the ropes.

Her attempt was cut short when a hand firmly grabbed her curls and yanked her head back. Victor was up and biting mad. He slapped her so hard that she thought she saw stars before her eyes again.

In a voice not quite recovered from her earlier attack, Victor rasped out, "You are trying my patience, missy. No more surprises from you, otherwise—" He whipped out the knife he'd dropped in the struggle and then aimed it at her throat again. He turned her to face him and growled out, "I won't be so nice."

Rosemary's lips formed a thin line, and she scowled up at him in silence. She wouldn't beg for his mercy. When the first button had flown from her blouse, he slowly aimed for the next, seemingly taking his time to enjoy himself.

Rosemary parted her quivering lips and uttered in hoarse murmur, "You will regret your actions."

Victor, expecting her to plead for his mercy, choked in confused humor. He hadn't thought that she was rebellious until now. She had always struck him as a frightened young thing but not a headstrong wench. He shook his head, stifling a laugh. "You are a peculiar one, Rose. Most peculiar. The others were not like you."

Rosemary could hardly fathom the number of victims that he had under his belt. *How long has he been stalking, killing, and destroying innocent lives? Why hasn't anyone noticed his wicked intentions and put a stop to them?* she wondered.

Rosemary bit her bottom lip to stop the tremors that had started. Her throat constricted and threatened to close up completely. Her thoughts swirled as Victor continued his threats and mockery. She was under his oppression of fear once more. Pleading for her life was on the tip of her tongue, but something halted her words and covered her mouth from doing so.

*You are never alone,* a voice so strongly inside her soul that it rang in her ears and chilled her to the bone. She shut out Victor's ramblings to listen. A verse that she knew well, Matthew 28:20, was being repeated to her frightened soul. *And, lo, I am with you alway, even unto the end of the world.*

She could feel Victor's knife back at work with the second button. Closing her eyes and flattening herself as close to the rocky floor as she could, she began praying in earnest.

Soon it would be over. She would no longer have to run for her life. She wouldn't have to be trapped in a cold cave in the mountains. Soon she would be in the presence of her Savior and held in His arms. She kept her eyes shut tight, imagined what heaven must look like, and hoped that the day would end as quickly as it had begun. Teardrops trickled down her temples as she quit her struggle to escape. Perhaps this was her time to leave the world. Perhaps Ricochet was waiting for her right now in God's kingdom with open arms and that charming smile of his.

Her lips moved to form words, but no sound came out. *God, save me! Please, God, save me!* She held her breath when nothing further happened. She felt no cold blade or calloused hands caressing her face¾nothing.

Her eyes were closed when the cocking of a gun sounded from above her. A commotion broke the raspy whispers of her captor and echoed in the cave. Warm fingers wrapped around her frozen hands and tore off the ropes that bound her to the rock. Her arms fell free. She gathered up her limbs and curled into a fetal position.

"It's all right now. You're safe," a voice cooed as a gentle hand stroked her shoulder. At first, she flinched and whimpered beneath the touch of yet another man, but then she heard the voice once more. "I'm getting you out of here, Rosemary."

She froze. Her brown eyes fluttered open in confusion. *Where have I heard this voice before?* she wondered.

Peering down at her were two dazzling blue irises she had encountered many of times before . They brought a gentle calm to her heart and washed away every hint of grief and fear in an instant. Her brow knit, and her mouth curved up in a relieved glimmer of a smile. She gasped and choked a sob out, reached up, and wrapping her arms around her rescuer's neck.

"Ric!" she exclaimed, "It's you! It's really you!"

In one hand, he held a gun, and in his other, he held her, clutching her close. He breathed a sigh, and then nestled his nose into the crook of her neck. "I pray I'm not too late," he pleaded in a half whisper.

She gripped his shirt tightly in her fists, daring not to release him for fear of this being a hallucination or a pleasant dream. "You came," she sobbed over his shoulder as he bent lower to cradle her.

He moved back from her so that he could clear her face of curls and streaks of tears. His thumb stroked away tear droplets, which had begun to run down her cheeks. He smiled brightly until he saw the horrific sight of her black eye. He frowned and shook his head. "He hurt you," he stated matter-of-factly.

Rosemary kissed the hand that held the side of her face and smiled reassuringly. She wished to talk about something else. "I thought you were dead," she said in hopes of changing the subject instead of embracing the memories of the past few hours. "I saw the rapids take you." Her eyes trailed down his arm, and she noticed a patch of red beneath Ricochet left armpit. Her heart broke as she realized that was where the bullet had hit its mark. Surely, the man had been in pain from such a wound, yet he had fought against deadly rapids to rescue her.

Ricochet lowered his arm and saw that Rosemary was staring at the awful amount of red that was seeping through his shirt. He backed away and stood. "Let's get you out of here." He put out a hand to help her up and smiled.

She was raising her hand to take his when a dark shadow rose up and covered them in its wake. Rosemary screamed and pointed behind the wagon master. "Ric, look out!" she warned. It was too late.

While the wagon master's head was turned for a split second, Victor took that opportunity to strike. He swept Ricochet's legs out from under him and then attempted to wrestle the gun out of his hands. The weapon skidded across the floor and came to rest at Rosemary's feet. The two struggled and tumbled head over heels in a tangle of dust, grunts, and limbs. Ricochet managed to hit Victor's jaw, but Victor landed a blow in Ricochet's left armpit. Yowls, groans, and warring shouts filled the cave.

Ricochet had Victor in a headlock on the ground. He was breathing hard, and sweat dripped down his face and neck. His bottom lip was swollen, and a long cut opened above his eyebrow. "You'll pay for touching her!" he threatened.

Victor laughed through clenched teeth. "And just who's gonna make me, wagon master? You?"

In a matter of seconds, the tables were turned. Victor sat atop

Ricochet and choked him with a viselike grip. "It seems you have trouble staying dead, Chapel. Maybe I should kill you with my bare hands this time."

Ricochet anxiously looked around for his gun, which had slid off to the side during the struggle. His eyes were bulging. He couldn't breathe. Desperately he kicked out with his legs and clawed at Victor's biceps. The man was truly strong, maybe stronger than Ricochet was in hand-to-hand combat. Ricochet's wound put him at quite a disadvantage. His vision became hazy and blurred. He needed a weapon, but he couldn't find his gun.

"Victor," Rosemary screamed and then fired the gun upward. She had shot off a round at the cave's ceiling. Pieces of rock and debris fell around them, and the very mountain seemed to moan and shift in pain. It gained both men's attention. They halted their fight, but Victor refused to give any leeway.

"Your business is with me," she said. "Let him go."

The barrel of the handgun was now pointed at Victor. Although, Ricochet felt uneasy that a woman was handling a weapon and aiming it in the same direction as himself, Rosemary constantly surprised him and exceeded his expectations. He couldn't help the smirk that was on his face.

Victor slowly eased up and then laughed at her tenacity. "What a sight this is! You think I'm afraid of a woman holding a gun?" He paused. "You wouldn't shoot me. You're too good of a woman to do that."

Ricochet wanted to knock the man's lights out for good. He watched as Rosemary's hands trembled, shaking the gun's barrel precariously. Victor was playing with Rosemary's conscience.

"I said to let him go, Victor," she ordered. "I will shoot."

Victor teased, "Have you ever held a gun before, my dear? You seem quite shaken." He was up on his feet in a flash. He pulled Ricochet to his feet and then placed him in a headlock. "Drop the gun, Rose." Victor had Ricochet positioned just right so that Rosemary couldn't possibly fire without harming the wagon master first.

Rosemary gasped, and her spirit of courage began to waiver. "No, don't hurt him!"

Victor tightened his arm around Ricochet's throat, cutting off his airflow. "Drop the gun, and I'll let him live. You choose." His expression darkened.

Ricochet pulled on the man's arm around his neck and uttered an urgent warning, "Don't do it! He'll kill us both—"

Victor increased his grip on the wagon master, shutting him up. "Hand over the gun and come with me, or I'll squeeze him till his pretty little eyes pop out of his head. You choose, Rose!".

Her heart torn, Rosemary considered her options. Victor could and would carry out his threats if she kept the gun, but she knew what awaited her if she let him have the gun. He could still kill Ricochet if she handed him the gun. There remained the slight chance that Victor would honor his vow if she gave into his wishes, but that chance was little to none. Still, that chance was better than watching Ricochet die for a second time. She lowered the weapon and then dropped it to the floor. "Do with me what you wish, but please, don't hurt him," she pleaded.

Clutching Ricochet closely, Victor grinned widely. "Good girl. Now slide it over."

Rosemary did as she was told and watched in earnest as Ricochet was released. His legs gave out beneath him. He coughed, massaged his bruised neck, and gasped for oxygen. She ran to catch him, but Victor was faster. He grabbed a handful of her curls and hauled her backward.

Then he called back to the weak wagon master, who was recovering on the stone flooring. "Follow us, and I'll make you watch her suffer," he advised as he walked backward toward the cave's entrance.

Rosemary screamed as he pulled her hair taut. Victor dragged her out of the cave and into the forest.

"Ricochet!" she squealed as she fumbled to keep up with her captor. Her bare feet stumbled and tripped in her attempts to walk upright.

Rising to his feet with his fists clenched and his temper kindled greatly, Ricochet bolted after them. He wasn't about to give up the chase after coming this far. He sprinted around trees, leaped over fallen logs, and ran across rocks. Every now and then, he could hear Rosemary's shrill cries for help and the stern commands and cursing of Victor.

It wasn't long until he slid on a muddied surface where the ravine lay. He stopped and saw that Victor was aiming the weapon's barrel at Rosemary's temple. His finger was on the trigger.

"I warned you, wagon master," he snarled. "And now you'll watch as I kill her right here, right now."

Rosemary's face was wet with tears, and her lips formed an upside-down U shape. She trembled and gasped as Victor tugged at her hair. The sight made the wagon master cringe, inside and out. The poor woman was battered and beaten almost to death. Seeing her swollen, black-and-blue eye added wrath to Ricochet's heart. Nonetheless, he had to play it safe for Rosemary's sake. He raised his hands in a defensive position. "We can talk this out, Victor. You don't have to do this."

Victor jerked her to the right where the edge of the rapids was. Ricochet took two quick steps and then froze. "No! Stop!"

Victor cackled and waved the gun around without a care for anyone's safety, even his own. *He really is a lunatic*, Ricochet thought.

"If you survived the rapids, she can," Victor provoked, his pupils dilating in keen interest. "What'd ya say? Shall we find out?"

Ricochet shook his head in protest. "Victor, don't do this. You spent months hunting her down. Why throw that all away now? You said you loved her in all those letters, right? Why would you proceed to toss her away without proving your love?"

Victor froze in deep thought as he pondered those words. He didn't even seem to notice that Ricochet was taking a few steps closer.

Ricochet continued, "How could so great of an admirer leave his love so easily? Surely you must want her still?"

The man gazed lustfully at Rosemary, who clutched his hand, which gripped her hair. He appeared mesmerized and seemed to sincerely admire her beauty and desperation. He blinked slowly and then faced the wagon master once more. His lips formed a thin line, and he spoke in a monotone voice. "If I can't have her, no one can."

Time seemed to stand still as Ricochet ran forward and shouted for Victor to stop, but it was too late. "No!"

Her face covered by a mess of curl, and her skirts fluttering in the cold wind, Rosemary fell into the rapids. The splash of her body hitting the rushing waters and the roar of the waterfall covered up the sound of a gunshot ringing through the air and Victor Marsh's lifeless body hitting the dirt.

Ricochet dove into the river without hesitation and swam beneath the water's surface to save the love of his life. His muscles rippled as he tore through the water, searching for her. His eyes squinted as they adjusted to the dark waters of the rugged mountain river. He reached out his hand, caught Rosemary's wrist, and pulled her to him, as the vast flowing current tugged at their bodies. Once she was in his grasp, he kicked to get them to the surface. Debris and rocks battered them from all sides, even more than their first fight in rough rapids after their unusual meeting at the water barrel.

Their heads broke the surface, and they gasped for air. The deafening sound of the waterfall drew ever nearer, but Ricochet wouldn't let Rosemary go. He held her for all that he was worth and kept them afloat as much as he could. A rock, which was just barely visible above the rapids, caught Ricochet's eye. He grabbed it as they were about to sweep past it. Its smooth top was slick. He wouldn't be able to hold onto it for long.

He squeezed Rosemary and peered down into her petrified, bruised, and beautiful face, as foamy waves lapped at her right side. "No matter what happens," he shouted above the howl of the rapids, "I love you, Rosemary. From the very moment I met you, I knew you were the one for me."

Rosemary choked and then clutched his shirt, which was stained and soiled. She kissed him and whispered in his ear, "I love you too."

Ricochet couldn't hear her words. He could scarcely make them out by reading her lips. He struggled to keep his hand clamped on their small anchorage. His eyes found Rosemary's, and he watched her lips once more. He teared up, as he understood.

"It will be all right," she said. "Let go."

He nodded and held her tighter as he let go of the rock's tip. The rapids carried them to the waterfall, as they anticipated the harsh end that awaited them.

# Chapter 23

❦

*I love you, Rosemary.* Those words replayed in her dreams, even amid the nightmares of gunshots and the wagon master's corpse falling lifeless to the ground of a cave. The words gave her warmth and comfort in the dark slumber that gripped her subconsciousness.

Her eyelids opened to make slits, but it took several more minutes to gather the strength to open them halfway and even longer still to open them fully. Her eyes were glazed over in a haze, as she stared up at a wooden ceiling. Quilts made of soft, warm cotton and animal skins lay on top of her stiff body. The bed was cozy, seemingly safe from all harm, and a haven of warmth and peace. She could lie in this haven for days and perhaps months without moving, if she dared to do so. Sleep tugged at her eyelids once more, and she warred with her body to stay awake.

A door opened from the far side of the quaint little bedroom. A hum played and sang its way into Rosemary's ear. She wanted it to continue, but then, a gasp sounded followed by a crash of dishware.

"Rosemary!" Charity exclaimed in disbelief. Rosemary turned her head slowly as a migraine took hold of her temples. She furrowed her brow and saw that her younger friend was laughing in tears of joy and running to meet her on the bed.

"You're awake!" Charity embraced Rosemary. "You're awake at last! I thought you would never wake up again!"

Charity raised Rosemary up into a sitting position and rocked her violently. A glimmer of amusement passed over her face and then faded as she gently broke from Charity's rage of hugs and squeals. Once she had steadied herself, she quizzed the redhead for answers.

"What? Where am I?" She began. Her voice was barely above a hoarse croak, and her throat was as dry as a desert. "What happened?"

She put a hand to her forehead and groaned from the throbbing pain. Her fingers brushed the swollen place on her eye, and she winced. It wasn't the pain that made her cringe but the remembrance of the time that she had spent in the cave alone with the monster known as Victor Marsh. The very memory of his touch and vicious tone sent chills down her spine and put goosebumps on her arms and legs. She could still recall every time he touched with her. The thought made her want throw up anything that remained in her growling stomach.

Charity smiled. Relief was evident on her freckled face. "You were pushed into the rapids," she explained.

Rosemary nodded, understanding that much. She could hear, smell, and see every second of that awful event. She shuddered as Charity continued. "Mace pulled you both from the rapids. Dr. Webb said that you received minimal damage. Ricochet took most of the beating."

Feeling urgent for details, Rosemary stopped her by jumping to her feet. She shook the younger woman's shoulders and cried out, "What about Ric? Where is he? Charity, please, tell me he is all right!"

The redhead's eyes went wide with fear as she made a motion to pull the frantic woman back onto the bed. "Rosie, listen, the doctor said you should take it easy—"

"Ricochet!" Rosemary called and on wobbly feet, sped for the door. She yanked it open and ignored Charity's pleas for her to return to bed.

She steadied herself for a moment in the doorway, gathering the strength to search further in her new surroundings. Her room opened to a bigger room with various wooden chairs and tables. A stove with a pot of steaming water warmed the interior and kept a cozy feeling of home about it. To her left, there were two doors. She fumbled for the first one that was within reach. Turning the handle, she pushed it open. The room was small and bore only a cot and bedside table made of oak. It was a quaint little room, but it didn't have what she was looking for.

"Rosie, wait! You shouldn't be up until Dr. Webb returns!" Charity warned and scurried after her.

Desperate for any sign of the daring man who had saved her life, Rosemary hurried along the cabin's wall to the last door. Her fingers wrapped around the handle, and she held her breath as it opened. The inside of the room was decorated similarly to the first room and the room she had woken up in. There was a cot, a bedside table, and ...

"Ricochet," Rosemary whispered, stumbling into the room. Her weak legs gave out, and she collapsed by the cot where the wagon master slept soundly. A piece of cloth was over his forehead. She pulled herself up onto her knees to see his face. Her fingers stroked his blisteringly hot cheek. He was burning up and sweating as if he'd just been running up a mountain.

Although he appeared to be hot to the touch, his complexion was paler than usual. His breathing was shallow and uneven, as if he were struggling with every breath that he took. His face was battered and bruised. His bottom lip was split open, and his right eye looked swollen. His forehead was furrowed, and his lips were pursed, as if he were in a great deal of pain.

Rosemary gently removed a strand of hair from his forehead and tucked it up into his hairline. "Ric," she whispered, her tone barely audible.

To her disappointment, he didn't stir but continued to sleep soundly. He couldn't hear her. She tried not to cry when she reached for his limp hand and saw the stained bandage around his forearm. "Oh, Ric," she choked. "It's all my fault."

He was so fragile. The big, muscular, and fearless wagon master had been broken. It didn't seem fair that he was lying there helpless in that way. It should've been her. *How could I have dragged him into this mess? What if he never fully recovers?* she thought. Guilt warred with her.

Charity quietly stood in the doorway and hung her head. "Dr. Webb didn't want you seeing him like this until he had explained it all to you."

Rosemary lifted her chin. She was determined to get the rundown of Ricochet's current dilemma. Her eyes blazed. She managed to steady her voice as she asked, "Will he make it?"

Her friend was opening her mouth to speak when a commotion came from the bigger room. Rosemary lifted her head to see who had entered their abode. As Dr. Webb came in, his eyes widened with surprise when he saw Rosemary kneeling down next to the cot that bore Ricochet's sleeping form.

"Miss Barker," he said as he rubbed his head in shock, "you're awake, I see."

Rosemary got to her feet as Charity helped her. "Please tell me he'll make it." She jumped straight to the point, not wasting any time. "Is Ric going to live?" She could feel her bottom lip beginning to quiver.

The middle-aged doctor's greying hairs were tousled, and his eyes were dark from lack of sleep. He sighed and set down his medical bag on the bedside table. "I don't know. I've done everything I can do for him. The bullet wound beneath his left arm is healing quickly with only minor damage, but it's the other one in his back I'm concerned about," he explained, gesturing to his sleeping patient.

Rosemary clutched Charity's arm as she asked, "What other bullet wound? Ric was only shot once. I watched it happen."

Dr. Webb hesitated and then explained, "No, he was shot twice. Mr. Chronicle informed me that another round went off just before he went down. The bullet hit Mr. Chapel near his spine with no exit point. It was quite the mess to dig out."

Rosemary's shoulders slumped, and her eyes welled up with tears. Dr. Webb carefully continued, "Besides that, he sustained a decent amount of bruising around his ribs, a severely sprained ankle, and several deep marks along his back. He also has a fever and the beginning of an infection. If he pulls through, it will be a long road to recovery, to say the very least."

Rosemary nearly fainted with worry and exhaustion. She wobbled, and Charity led her to a chair where she could sit, which was to their left beside the cot.

A man walked in after a few minutes of awkward silence. Rosemary stared off into the distance. His tone was deep and informative. "I got what you asked," Mace Chronicle said while handing over a brown bag to the doctor. As Dr. Webb excused himself and left the room to open the bag and take an inventory of the contents within, Mace approached the cot where Ricochet slept.

Charity steadied Rosemary in the chair before rushing to gather more wet cloths so that she could change out the ones on Ricochet's forehead, neck, and chest. Mace and Rosemary were left alone in silence for a time, a time in which Rosemary wished she could be alone. Mace spoke first. He stood next to her chair. His gaze stayed on his wounded friend in the cot. "He did everything he could to protect you, you know."

"What?" Rosemary uttered, drawn back from her blank stare on the cot.

Mace turned to face her. "I watched him shield you from the debris in the rapids. That's what caused the marks on his back."

The man of few words and little emotion informed her that Ricochet had been shot in the back as Mace arrived on the scene. Mace had taken down Victor with one clean shot through the skull. Then he had been the one to pull them from the rapids after Ricochet had wedged himself and Rosemary between a tree and a large rock near the waterfall.

"You took on too much water and lost consciousness, but Ricochet continued to fight the current till you both were close enough for me to pull ashore," Mace said, nearing the end of his tale. "Shortly after the men on the wagon train found us, we had the doc patch you both up, and we descended the mountains, finding this town at the base. A parson took you both in to stay in his church's mission house. You've been here for five days already."

"What of Macy?" Rosemary asked. "Is she—"

"No, she's just fine," Mace said as he shook his head. "We found her in the woods. She had been affected by the ether Victor stole. She was only a means to get you out of Ricochet's protection."

Rosemary uttered a small breath of relief at those words. She had forgotten about her reason for being in the woods after the horrific events that had played out in the cave. Now she thanked the Lord for the little girl's safe return.

At that point, Charity returned with a tray of wet cloths for Ricochet and three cups of coffee. She handed one cup to Rosemary first and then extended the tray to Mace, blushing all the while. "I thought you might want to stay and rest after all the work you've done in fixing my pa's wagon."

Mace barely smiled as he took a hot cup of black coffee and then said, "Much obliged."

With her hands shaking and her cheeks flushed, Charity scurried to change the cloths on Ricochet. She chatted with Rosemary for a while, even after Mace had gone to bed. She informed Rosemary of everything that had happened over the past few days.

Isaac had found work in the town and agreed to stay until Ricochet was better. Andrew had awoken and fully regained his memories of the wagon robbery, which he had confessed to Mace. The Joneses had moved on to find land, as had many other families.

Katrina and the baby were doing wonderfully well; however, she had been getting less sleep because her newborn had wanted to eat almost every hour of the night. Charity had stepped in to ensure the care of both Rosemary and Ricochet. Many other things had happened too, but Rosemary was much too tired to focus on them.

Charity offered to help Rosemary back into her bed, but Rosemary refused so that she could have a few moments alone with Ricochet.

"Fine, but I'll be back to check on you in a few minutes," Charity said, acting like a mother hen. She smiled as she left the room and opened the door a crack.

Silence, apart from Ricochet's ragged breathing, enveloped the room. Rosemary left her chair to kneel on the floor next to Ricochet's cot. She felt his cheek with the back of her hand and flinched at heat of his body. He was a living furnace.

"Ric," she said in a hushed tone, "why didn't you stay away? I've brought you nothing but grief since the moment we met." She slid her hand down to his, which lay at his side. Her fingers were so small and scrawny compared to his, which amused her. She lifted his hand in hers and brought it to her cheek before kissing his palm. He'd always been so strong and able, yet now he lay in a fragile state before her. She would give much to exchange places with him.

"I meant what I said in the rapids," she confessed with her eyes lowered. "I loved you from the start, even when you knocked me into that barrel." A small laugh escaped her, and she smiled. "Even though you were a bit pushy to know my name."

She shrugged, "I suppose I gave you such a hard time because I—you were so strong and brave and I just ..." She hesitated. Her thoughts were jumbled and confused. She searched his face to find the right words, but his pained sleeping features offered no suggestions.

Swallowing hard, she opened her mouth and poured her heart and soul out to the sleeping giant of a man.

"You were right when we first met. I was afraid of you¾afraid of every man. My admirer—" She stopped short. "Victor ruined every chance I had at trusting another man, but then you showed up. You had such faith in God, and you always seemed to know just what to say and what I needed to hear. I was wrong to judge you before knowing you."

She hung her head in shame, recalling the barrel incident. She smiled at that embarrassing moment from months ago when the wagon train had started. It seemed like forever ago now. So much had happened since then.

Rosemary's cheeks were wet with tears as she moved to kiss the wagon master's forehead. She then rested her head against his, feeling the breath from his nose tickling her lips and chin. She stroked both sides of his jaw and choked on her own sobs. Every confused, frustrated, or agitated emotion suddenly fled her, until she was left with only trust and love in the man who was before her. She eased away from him and turned for the door. Her body ached and pleaded for her own bed. Tomorrow she would return to Ricochet's side.

Her hand went to the doorknob, and she had made a motion to open it when she halted. She peered over her shoulder to get one last glimpse of the wagon master's battered body. Every scratch, wound, and broken bone was because of her. The guilt was like an enormous void taking hold of her stomach. It hurt to see him in this weakened state.

*God, please don't punish Ric because of my foolish act of running away from my own problems. Heal him. Lift him up, Lord. Don't let me lose the only man I've ever loved. I can't lose anyone else.*

Rosemary inhaled sharply to suppress any loud sobs, as if her crying would wake him from this coma. Her lips parted, and she whispered, "I love you, Ricochet Chapel, and I always will."

She slowly turned to leave again. Charity would be back soon, and she wanted to be back in her own room when her friend returned. The door creaked as she opened it, and a muffled voice replied hoarsely, "I love you too." At first, she thought those words were a trick of her ears, which the door hinges had made in their awful squeaking.

She froze. Her brow furrowed as she listened for more words to catch her now-attentive ears. All was silent. Perhaps it really had been her mind playing pranks on her hopeful state. She wondered what was wrong with her. She was going loco or at least partially so.

She opened the door wider, and she heard the shifting of quilts rustling. She froze again in mid step.

"Rosemary," a croaking baritone voice beckoned to her.

Her arms fell limp at her sides, and she turned around at a snail's pace. Her breath caught in her throat at the sight, and all she wanted to do was praise the Lord for the miracle. Sitting on his cot with quilts tossed aside, Ricochet Chapel sat. His hair was tousled, and his cheeks pale, but there was no mistake in his crystal eyes of blue. He sat upright as much as his body allowed and smirked in that winning way of his.

He drew a shaky breath and wheezed, "That all the thanks I get? Tears and a kiss on the forehead?" He coughed and winced.

Rosemary pressed her back against the wall in shock. Her hand went to her mouth, and she rasped, "Ric?" She couldn't believe it was real. She wondered if he was he truly awake or this was the dream of her imagination at work. New tears streamed down her cheeks, and she didn't try to wipe them away.

The wagon master grumbled, "You know, I can't stand tears."

Without awaiting his invitation, Rosemary flung herself at him. She knelt on the corner of the cot and then threw her arms around his neck, placing kisses all over his face. "You're alive!" she exclaimed between gasps of joy and the kissing of his cheeks, nose, and forehead.

He inhaled sharply and shifted away with an expression of pure agony on his face. "Watch it, watch it," he said as he winced.

She went pink in the face and moved back, as if he were some rattlesnake about to strike. "I'm sorry!"

The wagon master chuckled, holding his side. "If this is how you thank a man for leaping into rapids after you, I'd gladly jump again." His teasing had returned, and Rosemary relished the thought of slapping that smirk off his face. However, she composed herself quickly, and she didn't do it.

"Ric," she began as her bottom lip tremble. "I can't thank you enough for what you did. And I can't tell you how sorry I am that—"

"Stop it, Rose. I don't want your apology or sympathy," he said while holding up a hand for her to stop talking. He sternly held her gaze with his own. "Everything I did was because I—" His throat constricted as if he was about to cry, but he never did. His voice rattled. "I'd do it all over again in a heartbeat. All of this was part of God's plan to bring us together. I could never wish any of it away. Not ever."

Rosemary covered her mouth with both hands and nearly doubled over with overwhelming love in her heart. Her eyes were glassy as he pulled her close. She shook her head and cried, "You're more than I deserve."

He half smiled and pulled her downward until he could reach her face. Cupping his hands around her petite face, he whispered back, "No. You're exactly what God has for me." His lips covered hers in a passionate embrace, and Rosemary melted in sheer bliss, from the top of her head to the tips of her toes.

This man, whom she had hated months ago, had taught her to love and trust again, not only in others but in God as well. She was overjoyed and overly blessed at that moment. She thanked the Lord for His loving, watchful care over her and Ricochet. She prayed that there would be many more years to come for both of them.

A gasp sounded at the door and broke Rosemary and Ricochet apart. Charity stood there with a bowl of steaming water and fresh bandages in her arms. Her mouth opened and closed like a fish out of water. Rosemary thought that the woman would drop the hot water all over herself.

Charity screamed for joy after a minute of silence. "You're awake!"

Voices chimed in from the rest of the house, and soon, every lantern was lit outside the room, and footsteps sounded. Ricochet looked at Rosemary and chuckled into her ear, "Guess the cat's outta the bag now."

She giggled as Dr. and Mrs. Webb, Mace, and Charity's father piled into the small quarters. Each glimmered with excitement and relief at Ricochet's amazing recovery. Rosemary bashfully cowered in a corner of the room as each person approached Ricochet's bedside to greet him with hugs and prayers. She stood quietly smiling. This man was hers, or at least, he soon would be.

The next few weeks passed quickly. Ricochet made an astonishing recovery from the fever and infection, although his gunshot wounds would take a while longer to heal. Rosemary had refused to leave his side during that time, and the two of them had spent nearly every second of every day together.

"Good morning, lovebirds," Dr. Webb said and grinned as he entered the room.

Ricochet straightened on the bed and greeted him with, "Mornin', Doc."

Rosemary only smiled bashfully. Normally, she would have let go of the wagon master's hand by now if others saw them together but not anymore. It was no secret that she and Ricochet Chapel had decided to officially court each other. Many had speculated that an engagement would soon be announced between the two.

Dr. Webb went through the normal routine of checking Ricochet's wounds. Then he asked Rosemary to give them some privacy so that he could do a more thorough examination. Rosemary left the two men and went outside for some fresh air.

The small town that they had settled in was quaint and lovely. The people were friendly, and they had enjoyed their arrival because many wagon trains didn't stop at their little town. Main Street was bustling with ladies visiting and talking up a storm. There was only one street in the small town, which included a saloon, general store, café, hotel, doctor's office (although there was no residing doctor for the time being), and little church building on the end.

All in all Rosemary relished being there and meeting the new faces, even if part of her still wanted to run and hide from any man that she spotted. She guessed that some of the wounds that her admirer had dealt would take longer to heal than others would.

She heard a shrill cry. "Rosie!" Rosemary turned to see the redheaded preacher's daughter scurrying down the dusty lane.

"Charity," she said and smiled.

Charity came to an abrupt halt and beamed. "Any news?"

Cocking her head to one side, Rosemary could only give her friend a confused look in response. Charity seemed exasperated and laughed, "Chapel. Did he, ya know, propose?"

Rosemary blushed red and shrugged. "Of course not. Why would you think such a thing?"

Charity covered her mouth, and her eyes went wide, "Oh no. I messed it up!"

"What?" Rosemary stepped closer and raised her brows. "Messed what up?"

"Nothing! Just forget I said anything," she said and quickly changed the subject. "Did you hear about Dr. Webb? He's planning on staying here as the presiding physician. They don't have a doctor in this town. The people practically begged him and his wife to stay. Oh, and the Joneses have already left to travel onward, find land, and stake a claim. The Garrisons have decided to stay, which I know Lily is all too happy about, seeing as how she has caught the attention of that handsome Deputy Howard Myles. But poor little Macy was heartbroken that Andrew had to leave town. The girl is just sobs all day long now."

Charity continued her rambling as the two of them walked along the boardwalk and into the general store. However, Rosemary couldn't help but think that her friend and Ricochet Chapel were up to something, and she wanted to know what that was.

# Chapter 24

"You sure you wanna do this?" Mace asked Ricochet.

The wagon master was now on his feet and dressed in a white-collared shirt and a dark vest and pants. He nodded. "I've never been more ready."

Preacher Jackson beamed from ear to ear, as he said, "She's a fine young lady, Ric. May the good Lord bless you both."

Ricochet took one last look in the mirror and adjusted his hat. He was nervous. Today would be the day. He would no longer be roaming the Oregon Trail or living at an empty shack back home. His adventurous bachelor days were coming to a close. He just prayed that the woman that he had his eyes set on would accept his proposal.

Sucking in a deep breath, he turned to face Preacher Jackson, Dr. Webb, and Mace Chronicle. "Well fellas, wish me luck."

Mace clapped him on the shoulder. "Good luck."

Dr. Webb adjusted his spectacles before opening the door for the finely dressed wagon master. "I arranged it with Miss Charity. Miss Rosemary is to arrive at the rose garden on the edge of town, just after you get there."

Ricochet swallowed hard. He felt as if he had swallowed a dozen rocks. Part of him wished he could change his mind and plan it on a different day when he had gathered more courage. His arm was still in a sling, and he limped slightly, but other than that, he was mobile and almost up to par.

He exited the small building and went to the edge of town. His heart was pounding so loud in his chest that he had to force himself to calm down by breathing in and out slowly. His mind had been set on the garden that was just a few yards outside of town. The flowers were still in bloom, even though it was nearing the middle of autumn and the cold front would soon set in. The garden's aroma was sweet on the wind. The scenery was perfect. Now he just had to wait for the perfect woman.

Minutes passed as he waited. He grew anxious and began to shift from one foot to the other in anticipation. He went over the words that he would say to her. Licking his lips, he whispered a prayer to God that all would go as planned. He removed his hat and smoothed back his hair. He waited and waited. He wondered what the ladies were doing that took so long. Charity had promised that Rosemary would be brought here at sunset, and yet here, he was waiting.

The light of the sun had just set when across the way when he saw Charity and Rosemary. He was happy. The hill of the rose garden where he stood was still hidden from their sight, but in a few minutes more, they would see him. He held his breath, placed his hat back on his head, and then stood tall. He'd been waiting for this moment for so long. This moment would change everything that he had ever known.

A loud click sounded from behind his head. He froze.

"Say one word, and you're dead, Chapel." The tone was calm and the barrel of a gun was pressed into his back.

Ricochet tilted his head to the side trying to get a glimpse of the gunman. In response to that small movement, the voice prodded him with the gun's barrel. The voice spoke again, and Ricochet swore he knew who it was.

"Git going to those trees over there," it said, and he was marched to the right. "You try anything, and I promise you won't live long enough to warn Miss Barker."

Ricochet obeyed. His mind raced with questions, but his heart ached for Rosemary. "You're him, aren't you," Ricochet said matter-of-factly.

"Quit the jabber and keep walking," the voice said, someone nudged him onward.

Ricochet did as he was told. The voice was familiar, and the wagon master knew the man's identity. He clenched his fists and trudged on.

Once they were a good ways off from the sea of flowers and roses on the hillside, Ricochet was forced to the ground and tied to a tree. His bad arm ached and throbbed behind his back, as he was tied to a tree trunk. Bark dug into his shoulder blades and tore at his hands. He peered up at his captor and said in disgust, "Isaac, stop this nonsense."

Isaac Beckett guffawed and holstered his gun. "Ya know, Ric, I looked up to you. I even tried to warn you to back off, and you refused to listen. Now, you're gonna pay for it."

"You followed her all the way out here. *You* sent those threats." Ricochet squirmed and protested against the ropes binding him. "Why?"

"Poor, poor, Chapel," Isaac scoffed and bent on one knee. He leaned close to Ricochet's face and lowered his voice to a raspy and sinister whisper. "She's mine. Just wait until I get my hands on her. Oh, she's gonna pay for everything she's done, all right. We're gonna have a mighty fun time together, her and I."

He stopped to whip out a knife from his belt. Waving it before Ricochet's face, he went on further, "First, I'm gonna have her watch you die. Then sweet Rose will follow your lead but much, *much* slower." His eyes darkened. "I'll skin her alive, Ricky-boy, one piece at a time. Doesn't that just sound fun?"

Ricochet couldn't swallow. He couldn't breathe. He attempted to say, "No," but it came out as a croak.

Isaac grabbed Ricochet's hat and tossed it aside. Then he went for a chunk of the wagon master's blond hair. He sliced it off with his knife and held it up for inspection. "Oh, yes, Ric. Luring her in will be sweeter than a slice of cake."

Ricochet struggled and pulled away from the tree as far as the ropes would allow. "Why use Victor? Why all this?" He grew angry as he talked.

Isaac shrugged. "Victor was simply a pawn in case I needed to turn the blame elsewhere. It worked like a charm, didn't it? Victor and I go way back. He was on the run from the law for several assaults and murders of young women up north. When I told him I had a woman I'd like take revenge on, he was all too happy to get in on the action.

"Course, he wanted her for himself after I set up the whole plan, so I had to get him out of the way. I led you to the rapids and had him shoot you while I tried to aim for him. It backfired." He grumbled and then continued. "That woman of yours spoiled my shot. I had planned to get to the cave and *save* her myself, but you beat me to it. Eventually, I realized that my revenge would have to wait until everything settled down a bit. And here we are."

"In other words, you were the wrangler, and he the cowpoke."

Isaac snapped, "Of course, I was! You think bigheaded Victor could manage all that by himself? That coot couldn't even read or write. He did the killing, and I simply did the planning."

Ricochet's eyes narrowed. "You were the one that set off the second shot. Victor shot Andrew."

Isaac grinned. "You ain't as bullheaded as I first pinned you to be. That kid was a nuisance. Victor let Andrew see him as we were hauling supplies from the medical wagon, which I needed so that I could drug Rose and steal her away from your watchful eye. Too bad that Victor was a bad shot, otherwise, you would still be looking for an unknown adversary somewhere in the forest."

Ricochet clenched his teeth and jerked side to side. He had to get free of the bonds. Rosemary would die if he didn't.

"Listen, Isaac," he started. "Whatever grudge you have against Rosemary, please don't go through with this madness. Take it out on me but don't hurt her. She's been through enough—"Isaac cut him off by tugging harshly on his hair.

The crazy man lifted Ricochet's head up and jerked him to the side. He replied, "If she'd been through enough, I would've let her alone a long time ago. She rejected me, and she'll pay dearly for it." With those words still lingering in the air, Isaac gagged Ricochet and whipped out his gun. "Sweet dreams, Ric." Ricochet's eyes widened, and then all went dark.

Rosemary crossed her arms. An hour had passed, and still, she waited on top the hill. She wondered why Charity had told her to wait there. She'd been standing around by herself for seemingly an eternity. She was done. Holding her head high, Rosemary unfolded her arms and stomped down the hillside.

"Charity," she called, but no answer came. She rolled her eyes and lifted her skirts as she made her way over a thick patch of flowers. "Charity Cole, this is not funny. What am I meant to be waiting around for?"

By now, the sun had sunk below the horizon and filled the stretch of hillside with shadows. The town lay only a few feet before her, yet she couldn't go any farther. The wind blew wisps of her curls along her neck and cheeks. Goosebumps rose on her skin. Something was not right. A whisper rasped on the chilly breeze, causing her to stop any further motion. She froze. The wind whispered again. "Rosemary."

"W-who's there?" she asked the supposedly empty hillside. No reply came. She didn't wait another minute. She grasped her skirts again in two pale white fists and closed the gap between her and the twinkling lights of town. She didn't stop running until she had managed to enter the doctor's office, where she and most of her companions had been staying.

The bottom half of the structure was the medical clinic while the upper half was divided into two different wings of bedrooms: the ladies and the men. Originally, she had shared a room with Lily Garrison and Charity Cole, but since the Garrisons had moved to the outskirts of town and built their own homestead, Charity and Rosemary each had a bedroom. The men's side included Minister Jackson and Isaac Beckett in one room while Mace Chronicle and Ricochet Chapel shared the other.

Rosemary locked the door behind her and then scurried up the stairs so fast that she almost fell numerous times. She slammed her bedroom door behind her and then turned the key to fasten the lock. After sliding to the floor, she put a hand over her racing heart. She was spooked, but she wasn't quite certain what had spooked her. *The admirer is gone, isn't he? So why am I so afraid?* she thought.

A knock sounded on her door, and she stifled a cry. It was Charity.

"Rosie?" Charity's muffled voice said. "Are you all right?"

Rosemary wiped away the tears on her cheeks and blinked back more of them, before she got to her feet and unlocked her door. "Charity?"

With evident concern on her face, the preacher's daughter asked, "What happened? Is everything all right?"

Rosemary sniffled and felt Charity's arms surround her in a comforting embrace. The tears came all at once, and soon, she was full-on sobbing. Her tears stained the front of her friend's dress, but she didn't care.

Charity stroked her head tenderly. "Sh," she soothed. "There now."

"He's still here, Charity. He's still lurking in the shadows," Rosemary choked. "I can't be free."

Charity held her even tighter than before. "Rosie, he's dead. He can't hurt you or Mr. Chapel anymore. The Lord saved you from that man. He's gone."

After a few moments, more Rosemary's sniffling and tears had subsided. "Thank you," she uttered.

Charity released her. "What happened on the hill?"

Rosemary shrugged and wiped away a stray tear from her chin. "Nothing. I waited, and I thought I heard something. It was only my mind playing tricks on me, I suppose."

Her friend's brow creased with confusion and concern, but in the same instance, it appeared almost sad too. "Was Mr. Chapel there? Did he speak with you?"

"What? No, I didn't see him."

The redhead blinked and huffed. "I cannot believe that. After all the trouble I went through to—" She covered her mouth after a sharp gasp.

"Went through to what?" Rosemary tilted her head to the side quizzically. When her friend didn't respond, she furrowed her brow and frowned. "Charity, what is it that you're not telling me? Why would Ric be on that hill? And why did you tell me to wait there?"

"Oh, Rosie," Charity gulped and stepped back. "I promised I wouldn't say a word."

"About what?" she pressed further.

Charity sighed and shook her head in defeat. "Mr. Chapel told me that he planned to ask you a very important question on that hill. I was only supposed to tell you to wait up there for him. I was instructed to return after a short time and chaperone you two home, but when I didn't find you up there, I came looking."

"Ask me an important question?" Rosemary thought aloud, as she lowered her eyes. She whispered hoarsely and tried not to cry, "Could he have meant to—?"

"He planned to ask you to marry him. How could you not see that?" Charity looked exasperated.

"Then why wasn't he there?" Rosemary asked.

She shrugged. "Perhaps he was afraid?"

"No. He isn't like that." Rosemary deflected the negative thought. "He must have other business he's attending to. Perhaps, I will speak to Mr. Chronicle."

"It is rather late, Rosie. It might be better to speak with him in the morning. For now, you should rest." Charity turned Rosemary around and led her to the bed. "I can go with you in the morning, if you like? I'm sure there's a simple and easy explanation for all this. Mr. Chapel might've had a relapse of his fever symptoms or something."

Rosemary grimaced at the thought but nodded. The last thing she wanted was for Ricochet to come down with another fever. She took a deep breath and smiled, as her friend left the room with a soft, "Goodnight, Rosie."

With the door closed and the dim light of a candle glowing, Rosemary found her nightgown and let down her curls. She had only undone the first two buttons of her blouse when a folded slip of paper on the bed caught her eye. A single red rose lay beside it. She slowly picked up the rose and breathed in its sweet aroma. A smile spread across her face. *Oh, Ric,* she thought. With a sudden breathlessness, she opened the letter and began to read. Her eyes drank in the words, but the blood in her veins soon ran cold. "No," she whimpered and shrank to her knees beside the bed. "Ric."

Tears stung her eyes and blurred her vision. She flung the rose across the room and then dropped the note. Her head spun until she forced her eyes closed and her lungs to breathe again. The venomous words branded her heart. All those fear-filled thoughts and deep scars began to resurface once again. *He has Ricochet,* she cried inwardly. *God, what do I do?*

She closed her eyes in an attempt to pray, think, and form a plan of action. She thought about the words again and again.

*My sweet, sweet Rose,*

*I cannot begin to express how disappointed I am in your decision to leave me behind. Did you honestly think that I would be dismissed so easily? Foolish girl! I have long awaited your punishment, and tonight, it will be carried out. My dear, I await your arrival tonight in the garden where the roses never fade, with your precious wagon master. Should you decide to tell anyone of our rendezvous or refuse my request, I will not hesitate in carving out Chapel's heart and nailing it to your doorpost. Come alone, and he will be set free.*

*Your ever-faithful Admirer*

Rising to her feet after a silent prayer to God for Ricochet's safety, Rosemary buttoned up her blouse and used a ribbon to tie back her curls at the nape of her neck. She went through her options. If she told a single soul, Ricochet would be dead before anyone could come to his aid. No, she couldn't tell anyone. She couldn't risk the chance that Ricochet would get hurt or worse. She had to go alone. She would be alone but not unarmed.

Quietly, she slipped out of her room and found that the hall was empty and dark. She didn't dare take a lit candle from her room, for fear of someone seeing the dull glow. In the darkness, she crept down the stairs and into the physician's office, where a small scalpel lay on a tray, which had recently been cleaned by Dr. Webb, after an accident involving a farmer and his young son. Her hand wrapped around the cool metal, and she stuffed it into her pocket. It wasn't much of a weapon, but it was something. A gun would be too hard to conceal, and the last time she had used one, it hadn't ended well. She would have to rely on the scalpel.

It didn't take her long to reach the garden of roses. She prayed that she could surprise the admirer long enough for Ricochet to get away. That was all she wanted and begged God for. Ricochet Chapel needed to come out of it alive.

She climbed the hill, and the night air rushed to meet her. The wind was strong and chilly. She wished she had a coat or covering, as she searched the dark greenery for any sign of the admirer or Ricochet.

Her eyes squinted as a silhouette of a man standing several feet away caught her attention. The kneeling figure at his feet was all Rosemary could think about. Her heart leapt. It was Ricochet, and he was bound, gagged, and on the ground. She neared them hesitantly.

Her eyes scanned Ricochet's body, as she stopped only ten feet away. She squinted in the darkness to see that his face had dried blood plastered all down the side of it and a large knot protruded from his hairline. His hat was gone, leaving his hair disheveled. She could faintly see a dark bruise covering his left eye.

Rosemary choked back a sob, ran, and fell before him. She caressed his cheeks, running her fingers carefully over his injured temple. "Oh, Ric! I'm so sorry."

Ricochet's hands were tied behind his back. He grimaced and wheezed, "You shouldn't have come, Rosemary."

"I couldn't let him kill you," she whispered. Tears filled her eyes.

He shook his head twice and shut his eye. It seemed to cause him pain. "No. Please run," he begged, as Rosemary drew him to her and held him tight. She stroked his head, running her fingers through his hair. "I will end this," she breathed into his ear.

Rosemary released him slightly. She didn't want to let him go completely because she feared that he would collapse at any moment. She continued to hold onto him, as she glared up into the face of the admirer, Isaac Beckett. "Isaac, why?"

His stance was cocky, arrogant, and dangerous. He was different from the Isaac Beckett she had known on the Oregon Trail. The sweet smile, the friendly eyes, and the humble spirit were gone. It was as if he had become crazy and had changed for the worse. His gaze was hard and unreadable. "I was surprised when you didn't notice me at all. You don't remember me." It was a statement and not a question.

Rosemary shook her head slowly. She wondered if she had really met him before. She didn't think so, but maybe she had. Her parents had been well known in the community back home. She and her mother would volunteer as nurses in the clinic during the hot months of the year. There had been so many faces and patients. She doubted that she could recollect any one particular face from among them but maybe she could. She blinked and then gasped sharply. "No."

Isaac smirked and nodded. "So you do remember."

"Mr. Beckett, I-I am truly sorry," she stammered. "I never meant to do you harm. I was too young, Isaac. A girl of sixteen cannot think of marriage or love. I was a foolish girl who never thought about such things. A-and once I turned nineteen, I was courting Jesse Blake. Surely, you must have understood—"

"I'm through with your excuses," he said, pulled out a revolver, and pointed it straight at her. "You rejected me! I offered you a life of love and devotion. You nursed me back to health after the war. You treated me as if I was all that mattered, and then you tossed me aside. I told you I would wait for you to turn eighteen and come calling then, but you rejected me. You laughed at me. I waited for years just for you. How could you not see how much I cared for you?"

His eyes darkened as he glared at Ricochet. "Instead, you left. You ran and found this fool. You don't even have the sense to leave this wagon master, who wants nothing more than to use you. He could never take care of you, Rose. Your poor judgement will end this man's life *tonight*, just as it did Jesse Blake's."

Rosemary's heart seized. She never laughed at Isaac. She would never do such a thing, but Isaac had asked to court her when she was sixteen. At that time, she had been too young, or at least, that's what her father had said. So Isaac had been told to wait until she turned eighteen, at the very least.

But then, Jesse, a young and handsome deputy in her hometown, had come calling. They had been attracted to one another. She and Jesse Blake hadn't been in a serious or deeply devoted relationship, yet she had found it strange that the young deputy had vanished. It never even crossed her mind that something had happened to him. All of her friends had said that Jesse Blake was a flirtatious young man who would up and leave at a moment's notice, so she hadn't given a second thought to the incident.

"What did you do to Jesse Blake?" she asked before she could stop herself.

Isaac shrugged, as if he didn't care about his wrongdoing. "He was in the way, and he had to be disposed of. The varmint had it coming."

"What did you *do*?" she reemphasized.

Isaac sighed and responded, "I caught him on his way home, the night after I set your house on fire. I dragged him into the woods and shot him. Then I weighed him down so he'd sink to the bottom of the river. He never saw it coming."

She had never dreamed that it would happen. It had happened a year ago. Isaac Beckett was a soldier who had faced a dreadfully close call with death. A bullet had struck him along the side of his skull. He had been placed under her care, alongside Dr. Winston McAlister.

Isaac's head had been covered for most of his treatment. Rosemary could faintly recall another nurse warning her of his inappropriate and mentally ill behavior toward her and many other women. He'd also begun to ask specifically for Rosemary whenever he'd been in need of assistance. He had never laid a hand on her, and he hadn't spoken rude words of indiscretion to her either. He had merely been a soldier in need of her help, and she had given it willingly.

She wondered why she had not recalled his face. She could not have. His face had been covered for almost the entire duration of his treatments. She had never really talked to him, apart from that fateful few days in the hospital. After that, he'd left without a trace. She now wished that she had taken that nurse's advice about staying away from the man. He was clearly disturbed and in need of more medical treatments. *Or maybe handcuffs and a jail cell,* she thought.

She rose to her feet and raised her chin. She couldn't show Isaac any sign of fear, not this time. "Please, Isaac, I had no idea of your devotion at the time." She had to stall him until some kind of plan formed. "I was a young and foolish girl. If only I had known of your love for me, I would certainly have given you my every attention."

Isaac lowered his gun, as if in surprise and confusion. He opened his mouth, but no sound came out for several minutes. Rosemary held her breath, she was unsure if he would take the bait that she had cast.

Isaac smiled. "I knew you would eventually see it my way, Rose. Once you saw how much I admire you and love you. I knew you would come around."

Rosemary grimaced inwardly but kept on with the facade. For Ricochet, she would risk anything. "I certainly had no idea that my admirer was you, Isaac. Forgive me for my ignorance."

He smirked and extended a hand to her. "All is forgiven, Rose. Come." His beckoning was more of a command than a romantic plea. Rosemary didn't dare disobey him. She stepped forward to take his outstretched hand. He unexpectedly—and unwontedly—kissed her knuckles with moistened lips. She shuddered inwardly but kept her expression calm and serene.

With what she hoped was an alluring smile and the shy batting of her lashes, she peered up into Isaac's lustful eyes. "Isaac," she began in a feigned breathless tone that she had never before used, "I—"

Isaac shushed her with a clammy finger to her lips. She held back a shudder. "Don't speak. Allow me first to breathe in this moment. I've waited so long for it that I fear it would be ruined with mere words."

He just stood there, staring at her for what seemed ages. At his perusal, Rosemary wanted so badly—*very badly*—to shy away and run, but she held her ground. She couldn't show fear. He would see it and know her false inclination toward him. *Let him think that he has won,* she thought.

Isaac chuckled softly and said, "You're mine at last, my dear, after all this time."

Rosemary's back stiffened when he leaned toward her. Before she could even react, a shadow sprang up from behind Isaac. She couldn't help but gasp and back away. Isaac was knocked to the ground in a still heap. Ricochet stood in Isaac's place with a large rock in his hands. He looked at her with full, worried eyes that melted her insides. "I'm not letting him touch you," he growled as his gaze lowered to Isaac.

Rosemary ran to him. "Ric!"

He dropped the rock and held her arms. He stroked her upper arms, but his gaze never once left the still form of Isaac Beckett, who lay unconscious before them. "I need to grab his gun. Stay put."

She did as she was told. She watched Ricochet hobble to him and grab the weapon. Her eyes moved across his broad and muscular form. His head had been bleeding, but the blood had long since dried up on his temple. His limp was more noticeable than it has been before.

The wagon master's injuries had been on track to healing, but that was before her admirer had gotten to him. The skin that Rosemary could see—mainly his face and arms—was layered with new bruises and scrapes. This was her fault.

Ricochet was bent over and reaching for the gun when he cried out and fell. Rosemary rushed over to him. "Ric, what's wrong?" As she reached him, a hand clasped her ankle, causing her to trip. She screamed and fell backward. Isaac was gripping her leg and pulling her to him. She lashed out, kicking and flailing her limbs. "Let me go!"

"You're mine, Rose!" he exclaimed in a tone that sent shivers down her spine.

She fought against him even as his torso covered the lower half of her body. She clawed at his arms and face. "No, Isaac, I'm not!" she cried and slapped him across the face.

Isaac produced a small but sharp knife. Blood ran down its edge and handle. Rosemary shuddered and fought the urge to look behind Isaac for Ricochet. The knife was raised toward her chest, and she reached out to block the attack, when suddenly, Isaac was pulled off her body and thrown to the side.

Ricochet now glared angrily at Isaac with the gun in his hand. His breathing was ragged, but he held the six-shooter as steady as any man could in his current state. Without looking Rosemary's direction, he said, "Get behind me."

She wasted no time in doing so. She clutched the back of Ricochet's shirt and refused to let go. Ricochet's voice was stern and harsh when he ordered Isaac to stand and stay still. "Rosemary," Ricochet said softly over his shoulder. "I need you to run and fetch Mace."

She shook her head. "But what about—"

"Rosemary, this ain't the time for a dispute. Get Mace. Don't look back and don't waste any time. I can handle things here."

Nodding and gathering her up skirts, Rosemary turned and ran for town. Her heart was pounding by the time she reached the doctor's office and ran up the stairs. She knocked lightly three times on Mace's door, but after hearing no answer, she decided to pound on it. Before she had a chance, the door swung open, and a bedraggled-but-ready-for-action Mace stood in the doorway.

His dark eyes widened upon seeing her in such an unladylike state of exhaustion. "Miss Barker, is everything all right?" he asked. His expression was like a stone.

"Ric," she said, breathed heavily, and doubled over for a breath. "The rose garden … outside of town."

Mace rushed around her without another word. He half ran and half jumped down the stairs and out the door with his gun. Rosemary could scarcely keep up with him as he sped out of town and up the hill where Ricochet was waiting. He skidded to a halt, and Rosemary had to catch herself, otherwise, she might have rammed into his back.

"Ric," Mace addressed. "What has happened?"

Rosemary allowed Ricochet to explain the ordeal to him. She remained silent as she stared at Isaac, who now knelt on the ground with his hands behind his head. His icy gaze raked over her and then Ricochet, with such coldhearted hatred that Rosemary had to turn away from him. *What brings a man this low? Lust.* she thought.

Mace shook his head and said, "All this time, he was right under our noses."

Ricochet glared at Isaac and then looked back at Mace. "We have to take him back to town and have him locked up. The sheriff will take care of him."

The two hauled Isaac to his feet. They dragged him down the hillside and into town, as dawn began to break. Rosemary followed hesitantly behind them. Her thoughts trailed away to Jesse Blake, her parents, her friends, and many more who had been hurt because of Isaac.

She shook her head. *No. Because of me,* she corrected inwardly. If she hadn't run away but had faced her fear head-on, maybe all the heartaches and lives could have been spared. But no, she had been dumb enough to run and lead Isaac to many people, whom she cared deeply for and he had hurt.

She came to a stop on the edge of town and watched Isaac being led into the Sheriff's office. He growled angrily and even fought against Ricochet and Mace, but in the end, he was taken into custody. Rosemary was relieved that it was finally over. *But what is next? Where can I go from here?* she thought. *God,* she prayed silently. *What do I do? What should I do?*

Her heart clenched at the sound of someone calling her name. She turned to see Ricochet running toward her¾or at least, he attempted to run. His bad leg caused him to limp and skip more than anything else. Seeing how bruised and battered he was, Rosemary's heart sank, and her shoulders slumped. This was all her fault. The man, whom she had been told wished to marry her, would never consider her now. Her gaze fell to her feet as she waited for him to approach.

Ricochet stopped several feet from her and said, "Isaac is going to be put on trial. We'll have to testify against him, but the sheriff has no doubt that he'll be sentenced for a harsh punishment, possibly imprisoned for life." He paused as if thinking about his next words and then said, "If worse comes to worse, he might just be looking at a hanging in his near future."

Rosemary nodded. She couldn't look him in the eye. She detested Isaac but wondered if a hanging should take place. The very thought made her shiver. She had never wished him dead, or maybe she had. A growing guilt in her stomach said that she had hoped for it. How wicked she was to ever think that.

She thought the Bible mentioned that wishing someone dead was the same as murder. That was a sin, and she knew that she would have to ask the Lord to forgive her for it. She had learned so much about forgiveness in the last few months as she had traveled the Oregon Trail. She hadn't liked it at first, but she reckoned it was in her best interest to learn these hard life lessons. Ricochet had taught her a lot about the subject of forgiveness.

She blinked as Ricochet stopped talking and stared at her. She couldn't read his expression, but she imagined that he had asked her a question. "I'm sorry," she said. "I didn't hear you."

He shook his head with an amused smile plastered to his face. "Do you ever listen to me?" The question was more rhetorical and humorous than anything.

"Why should I?" She retorted, not in the mood for his teasing. "You never have anything to say worth listening to and ..." There she went again, bashing him for toying with her. She wondered what he had ever seen in her. She seemed to only insult and push him to the edge. Maybe she had better start acting as if she cared about what he had to say. After all, she did care.

His eyes narrowed. "And what?"

Her shoulders slumped. She didn't know what to she say to mop up the mess of the retort that she had thrown at him. From the very beginning, she had been rude and hasty in judgement against him. Every comment, retort, and brash act came flooding back into her mind. She wished she could take it all back.

Ricochet Chapel deserved someone better than her¾someone like Charity Cole, who loved and served everyone and didn't wish ill to anyone, even a monster like Isaac. Yes. Charity would make a far better match for Ricochet than Rosemary ever could. Rosemary's eyes burned. She held back a choking sob.

*Lord, forgive me for my foolish and cowardly actions, my wicked thoughts and ill feelings toward others, and especially, the way I've disregarded Ricochet's tender words. I know this perfect man before me can never be mine. I don't deserve anyone who has his kind and compassionate spirit because of the way I've treated him, countless others, and especially You. God, forgive me.*

"Rosemary?" Ricochet's voice broke through her aching thoughts. "Is everything all right?"

Rosemary refused to look up at him. She wrung her hands and answered, "No, it isn't."

He took two steps closer and asked, "What's the matter, darlin'?"

It took Rosemary several moments to speak as tears began to spill down her cheeks and off her jaw. "I must be the most spiteful and hateful woman you've ever met."

"Why would you say that?" His brow creased, and he stepped even closer. She couldn't answer that question right away, and he didn't prod her for a response. He simply waited until she was ready.

Wiping away tears, she choked out a plea. "Ric, please forgive me." A sob escaped her lips, and then she was really crying. She'd never cried like this before. Crying in this way was a relief. She felt like every pent-up emotion, thought, and heartache was leaving her, as she poured out her heart to the man in front of her. She couldn't stop herself.

"I have been so unforgiving. You have been the epitome of kindness and Christian grace, and I have scorned you and pushed you away. I let my fear and anger control my spirit and actions. I regret every mean word and every hateful thought toward you. I know I don't deserve your forgiveness, but I—oh, please, Ric, forgive me for all of it." She held her head in her hands as tears slipped between her fingers.

Ricochet spoke no words for several seconds. Then Rosemary felt strong arms pull her into a tight embrace. Hands caressed her back and in between her shoulder blades. His chin rested atop her head. New tears fell down her wet cheeks.

*Is this a sign that he has forgiven me, or is it merely pity that he feels?* she thought. Either way, she didn't deserve this embrace. She sniffed against his shirt and clutched the fabric in her fists. He was so warm, gentle, and handsome that it hurt. She didn't want to let him go. She would have to. Her hands pressed against his chest, and she tried to free herself from his arms. He didn't let go. She pressed even harder. Still, he didn't let go.

"Rosemary," he whispered so softly into her ear that she shivered, "love calls us to forgive. That is what grace is for. It is unmerited favor. First John 1:9 says, 'If we confess our sins, he is faithful and just to forgive us.' If Christ can forgive, then as a child of God, I should be able to forgive." He peered down at her tear-streaked face and hooked a finger under her chin, lifting her face up to his. "The good Lord loves you, Rosemary. And so do I."

She sucked in a sharp breath and then said, "But I don't deserve—" Her words were cut off as his lips brushed hers. The kiss had happened so quickly that Rosemary thought she'd dreamt it.

Ricochet smiled. "None of us deserves it. No man or woman on this earth deserves a fraction of it. That is why it is called grace. No matter what our sins are, if we ask Him, He will forgive and love us unconditionally." He removed a strand of hair that had stuck to her sodden face. "Please don't cry," he whispered sweetly. "I forgive you. But I must ask that you forgive me too."

"Forgive *you*?" She didn't understand why he would ask that of her. In her mind, he hadn't done anything wrong.

He nodded. "For my lack of resistance when it came to your personal space and matters. It was wrong of me to get involved in your life without your permission; however, I do believe the Lord planned it all for our own good. We might not have ever ..." He trailed off as his eyes searched hers for something.

She blushed, and red splotches made their way up her neck. "I suppose that is true, but you never did anything wrong. You were the man I needed, and God helped me to realize that." Her breath hitched in her throat.

"Realize what?" He asked and then he waited as if he was expecting something.

Rosemary went silent again. Her eyes were red and puffy. She must surely be a sight, but she didn't care. Her heart felt lighter knowing that she was forgiven, both by God and Ricochet. A peace, which had long been gone in her soul, had returned. She sniffled and drew in a shuddery breath. She felt safe again. She felt renewed. She recalled what Ricochet had said. "The good Lord loves you, Rosemary. And so do I." Ricochet loved her. Heavenly bliss! He still loved her. But she wondered if she could actually admit the same thing to him.

She lifted her chin high. She *would* say it. She *had* to say it. "I love you," she blurted out at last. Once the words had left her lips, her hands flew to her mouth. Ricochet gave her a peculiar look, which she had never seen him wear before. She wondered what he was thinking. She couldn't tell.

His arms slackened around her, and he knelt down on one knee in front of her. His hands tenderly clasped and held hers. "Rosemary Barker," he started, "I promise to never dunk you in another water barrel, always swoon over your adorable temper tantrums, and most certainly love you and every curl atop your head for the rest of my days. Would you make me the happiest wagon master in the world and become my wife?"

From his back pocket, he produced a small, round object. A simple wedding band greeted Rosemary's gaze.

She gasped and shook her head once while trying not to cry again. "Ric," she began, "I couldn't—"

He stood and put a finger to her lips. "Darlin', how many times I gotta save your life in order for you to see that I love you?"

A spark of her old temper flared to life, but it was not in the same manner of aggression as it had been before. She huffed and batted his finger away from her lips in a flirtatious way. "Another dozen ought to do it, Mr. Chapel."

Ricochet smirked as a spark of flirtatious heat lit up in his own expression. "How many more admirers you got, Miss Barker?"

"Hard to say," she teased without a smile. "Are you man enough to take them all on?"

The wagon master put a hand around her waist and pulled her to him. "Oh, I believe I'm more than capable." His lips arrested hers and then he pulled back. She was left momentarily dazed and breathless. He laughed and said, "Would that be a yes, Miss Barker?"

She feigned a disappointed expression as she said in an airy tone, "Perhaps."

"How about this one?" He kissed her again more fervently than before. Rosemary could practically feel her heart leap for joy inside her. When they parted this time, she couldn't speak or even suck in a good breath for several seconds afterward. She just stared up at him.

He laughed again and offered the ring. "I suggest you give me the right answer before you faint, darlin'." Then he lowered his voice, "Or before I give in to kissing you again."

"Yes," she breathed and extended her left hand to him. "My answer is yes."

He slid the ring onto her finger and stuffed the box back into his pocket. His hands found her waist, and he lifted her into the air and spun her around several times. He set her back down and raised his fists high over his head. Shouting at the top of his lungs, he exclaimed, "Ya hear that? Rosemary and I're getting married!"

Rosemary giggled, and her face went red. If they hadn't been earlier, people were staring now and gathering around to congratulate them. They were greeted by Pastor Jackson, Charity, the Webbs, and Mace. All wished them well.

The planning of the wedding began. Ricochet and Rosemary decided on a very short engagement, as both were far too eager to wait. Within two weeks, all would gather at the small town's church. But the wedding had to wait until after the trial of Isaac Beckett, which Rosemary felt was a wise decision.

On the morning of Isaac's court session, Rosemary and Ricochet visited the sheriff's office. As they entered, Sheriff John Bailey stood up from his desk and greeted them. "Howdy, Ric." He grinned and then dipped his hat to Rosemary, saying, "Miss Barker."

"Morning, Bailey," Ricochet said, although not in his normally cheerful voice. Rosemary could see plain as day that he was displeased at having to be present where her admirer was being kept. She couldn't blame him for that. She, too, felt uneasy visiting Isaac, but the Lord had impressed the idea upon her heart until she had taken action. This was something she had to do.

"What can I do for you?" Sheriff Bailey asked.

Rosemary answered on behalf of her and Ricochet. "We would like to see Mr. Beckett before the trial begins."

The sheriff seemed uneasy because of the request. He frowned and started to shake his head. Then Ricochet spoke. "We wish to speak with him for only a few minutes."

Sheriff Bailey sighed and gave in. He led them to another door in the back of the office, which was locked. He unlocked it and opened the door for them. Inside, there was a hall with only two small cells. The one on the left held Isaac.

They entered the hall, and Rosemary couldn't seem to breathe. Her throat constricted, and she wanted to turn around and walk back the way she had come, but she didn't. She took slow steps forward while Ricochet and Sheriff Bailey spoke in hushed tones.

Isaac was sitting on an old cot in the back of the cell. His head hung low, and his eyes were downcast. Then he saw her approach the barrier between them. His eyes narrowed, but he smiled. Rosemary stiffened when he spoke, "Come to gloat?"

She shook her head. "No. I came to offer forgiveness."

He tilted his head back and guffawed. "Forgiveness! Now that's funny, Rose. Always the innocent and sympathetic little angel."

"I brought you something," she said and took out a small leather-bound book. When he gave an inquisitive look her way, she swallowed and extended the hand that held the book through the bars. She had to do this quickly, otherwise, Ricochet would see. If he were to witness her getting this close to Isaac, she would be in serious trouble, and she couldn't risk that.

Isaac stood and grabbed at her wrist instead of the gift that she held out for him. She sucked in a breath and twisted her arm. She kept her voice quiet, peeking over her shoulder to see that Ricochet was still busy talking to Sheriff Bailey. "Let go of my arm."

He held her for only a moment, and then he took the gift and stepped away. Rosemary shied away when he held up the book that she had given him. He spoke through clenched teeth, "What is *this*?" He tossed it to the ground.

She straightened and replied, "The Bible."

"Do you honestly think that I would read that foolishness? I'm no saint, Rose, and I sure don't want to be. Religion is for the weak."

She held back harsh words as her temper soared. But that was what he wanted. He wanted her temper to take flight and to stir up emotions that had already been dealt with. Taking a long breath, she said, "I didn't come to convert you but to offer you another chance at life and forgiveness."

"I don't want it," he snapped. "So keep it to yourself."

Rosemary's heart broke for him. He had no idea what he would face after the trial—death or life imprisonment—nor did he understand that his soul was destined for an eternity in a very dark place. Her flesh said that he deserved his punishment, in this life and the next, but her spirit hurt for him, knowing that he would never get another chance to experience God's love.

"Isaac, I don't believe in a religion," she said. "I believe in a relationship, one that is vital for our souls, for your soul. The Lord loves us, and He forgives—"

A hand reached for her through the bars, and she jumped back just in time. Isaac was wide-eyed and rabid as he clutched the bars between them. He let out a string of curses. "I don't want it! I'd sooner make a deal with the devil himself than to accept it! You can keep your forgiveness and preaching, Rose. If I ever see you again, I'll kill you." He was practically shouting at her, which drew Ricochet's attention immediately.

"Rosemary, are you all right?" Ricochet rushed to her side and placed a hand around her waist protectively. He glared at Isaac. "You'd best keep silent, Isaac."

"Or what?" Isaac taunted. "You'll hang me?"

Ricochet's fists clenched, and he forced Rosemary behind him, but he made no motion to grab at Isaac through the bars. Rosemary saw Ricochet's jaw twitch with irritation, yet he remained to control himself and keep his voice even toned as he said, "We were hoping it didn't have to come to that."

"Why?" Isaac snorted in disgust. "So you and your new woman can taunt me? Torture me with your religious babbling? I don't need any of it. You hear me? None of it!"

Sheriff Bailey placed a hand on Ricochet's shoulder. "I think you both should leave. It's almost time for the trial."

Ricochet nodded and escorted Rosemary out of the hall. As Rosemary snuck a glimpse back, a shiver crept up her spine at the hateful glares Isaac gave her and Ricochet. Part of her pitied the wild man that he had become. Surely, he must have lived a normal life before madness had crept in. She hoped that was the case, otherwise, the man was a very pitiful soul indeed.

The newly engaged couple left the sheriff's office. Rosemary felt a hand caress her back. Ricochet was looking down at her with a sympathetic expression. "He didn't hurt you any, did he?"

She shook her head. "No. I'm perfectly fine. I just thought that maybe, if I gave him a chance at forgiveness, he would …" Her words trailed off as Ricochet moved to stand in front of her and looked her straight in the eyes. His hands stroked her upper arms soothingly.

"I know. Not everyone is willing to accept it," he said.

She nodded and let him escort her to the town hall where the trial would take place. The trial ended up being a very short one with a harsh sentence for Isaac Beckett. Andrew Jones had testified first, and then Mace Chronicle had. Ricochet and Rosemary were the last to testify against Isaac.

The jury decided on a verdict after only a few minutes of private discussions. Isaac was found guilty and sentenced to be hung the following afternoon for the fire that had killed Rosemary's parents, the murder and drowning of Jesse Blake, the attempted murder of Ricochet, and many other crimes. The list went on and on.

The next morning, Ricochet found out from Sheriff Bailey that Isaac had taken his own life by hanging himself with a piece of his own shirt. A grave was dug, and Isaac's body was buried by that evening and without a funeral.

Rosemary insisted that the Bible she had given him be left by his grave marker. She knew the man had been a monster, a terror to her by night, and a looming shadow to her by day, but Isaac had been someone who needed the Lord just as she had needed the Lord. How different things would've been if Ricochet hadn't shown her a better path¾one of love, grace, and forgiveness. She thanked God daily for the wagon master, who had pointed the way for her. She had never been more at peace in her life.

The two weeks of stressful planning and eager longing finally brought the day that Rosemary thought would never happen.

Charity adjusted her veil and gasped in awe. "Rosie, you are going to make him swoon!"

"You think so?" Rosemary giggled. The sound struck her as odd and comical coming from herself. She wondered when she had ever giggled in such a way. She thought that she must be nervous.

She looked again in the mirror. Her reflection surprised her a great deal. She didn't even recognize the woman staring back and wearing a gown of silky white with layered ruffles and a beaded bodice, which had taken Mrs. Webb six days to finish. Pale pink and white roses, which Ricochet had insisted upon, had been woven into her curls to form a circlet on the crown of her head. Her veil was made of intricate lace, and it had been a present from Mrs. Garrison.

"I know so!" Charity laughed. "Now hold still while I fix your train."

Rosemary swallowed. Her throat felt tight and constricted. Her hands were shaking as if they would fall off. She didn't think she could take a step out of the room, much less walk down the aisle of the church. She covered her face with her hands. "I don't think I can do this, Charity."

Charity placed her fists on her hips and sighed in exasperation. "Don't be silly! Just focus on Ric. He'll be right up there waiting for you."

"But, what if—"

"Rosie," her friend said as she grabbed hold of her shoulders and looked her square in the eyes, "no more second-guessing yourself. Just go." She then pushed Rosemary out the door of the small house that was attached to the church.

Rosemary turned toward the front steps. The doors to the church were closed to hide Rosemary from Ricochet's sight until it was time for the ceremony to begin. Charity held her still to fix her veil again and to fuss and exclaim over the silly wrinkles in the gown, which Rosemary didn't think mattered.

She honestly couldn't think over the roaring of her own heartbeat in her ears. She wanted to run. She wanted to stay. She wanted to cry. She wanted to laugh. The truth was that she didn't really know what she wanted to do.

The double doors opened, and her breath caught. The aisle was clear, apart from the white runner that graced its floorboards. Everyone she knew and loved dearly was present, and there were even some that she didn't know. They all turned and smiled as she began to walk down the aisle. Charity followed her to help with the veil.

Rosemary hardly noticed anything around her when a pair of the bluest eyes captured hers. If she felt herself breathless before, she felt even more so now. She made it halfway to Ricochet and noticed an unfamiliar shine in his eyes. *Is he on the brink of tears? Surely not*, she thought.

She reached him, and he held out his hand to her. She accepted, realizing just how bad the tremors in her hand had been when Ricochet caressed her knuckles with his thumb.

He smiled down at her and then leaned close when they stood side by side. "Relax, darlin'. There aren't any water barrels nearby for you to fall in."

Rosemary refused to look at him as the corner of her lips went up. "You mean there aren't any nearby for you to *push* me in."

She heard him chuckle softly. "I'll admit that it's not exactly a traditional way of wooing a woman."

"Wooing?" She snickered. "I didn't think you even knew what such a word meant."

He smirked and almost laughed aloud for all to hear, but he stopped himself as the pastor began the ceremony. Rosemary managed to peek at Ricochet out of the corner of her eye. He was beaming from ear to ear. His hand was still holding hers, and he squeezed it briefly in his grip. Barely in a whisper, he leaned close to her ear and said, "I love you, Rosemary."

Rosemary had to blink back tears of overwhelming joy as the vows were exchanged and she and Ricochet turned to face the gathered people who were congratulating them. Together, they exited the church and entered a new life, one that would no doubt have many hardships along the way, but with them, a blooming love and peace given by the sweet Rose of Sharon, Jesus Christ, to help them in desperate times of need.

# *Afterword*

I'm thrilled to be able to share *A Rose That Never Fades* with you. The concept that fear can rule a Christian's life is very real. I've even found myself being overwhelmed with fear and anxiety. In fact, many strong Christians are overcome by feelings of being downtrodden, depressed, and fearful, due to the significant amount of stumbling blocks our enemy, the devil, places in our paths.

Because of that emotional pain, I have written this novel. Only the love of God and fellowship with other believers can uplift and encourage us to press on, just as the King James Version of the Bible says in Philippians 3:14, "I press toward the mark for the prize of the high calling of God in Christ Jesus."

God's love is deeper than any ocean. Only He can help us to overcome our fear and discouragement. I pray that this novel has encouraged you to trust in Him and to lean on Him more. Don't let your fear control you. As a wise woman (my mom) once said, "Fear is a liar." That quote is a constant reminder for me, and I hope that it will be for you.

Please be on the lookout for my next book in the Hymns of Grace series.

God bless you all,
Brieanna

Lightning Source UK Ltd.
Milton Keynes UK
UKHW010639220321
380773UK00001B/63